The Singular Adventures
of
Mr Sherlock Holmes

The Singular Adventures
of
Mr Sherlock Holmes

Alan Stockwell

ISBN 978-0-9565013-0-1

This edition published by
VESPER HAWK PUBLISHING

www.vesperhawk.com
www.mrsherlockholmes.co.uk

CONTENTS

MR SHERLOCK HOLMES
1854-1928

VERY little is known about the early life of Mr Sherlock Holmes who has recently died. It is thought he was descended from a long line of country squires. His grandmother was a sister of Vernet the French artist. His only known relative was a brother Mycroft, seven years his senior, who pre-deceased him. Sherlock Holmes cultivated his natural talents for observation and logical deduction by undertaking an erratic course of study at Oxford University and St Bartholemew's Hospital. His researches included chemistry, anatomy and botany with special reference to poisons. Early on he gained a reputation for eccentricity when in the anatomy class he belaboured the specimens with a stick to study the bruising. All his studies had the object of making himself an expert in criminal detection and in this aim he triumphantly succeeded. Setting up in business in 1878, he soon became the leading consulting detective of his generation and a pioneer of methods that have since become standard practice in police forces throughout the world.

Sherlock Holmes was an expert singlestick player and swordsman and one of the finest amateur boxers of his weight. However he preferred not to expend his energies wastefully and, considering unnecessary physical activity deprived him of food for the brain, would recline for hours on the sofa, occasionally even retiring to bed for several days to husband his thought processes. Yet, when enthused by the chase of combating crime, he would spring into action and disclose the vast reserves of strength that resided somewhat improbably in his tall spare frame.

Sherlock Holmes had a large store of *outré* knowledge gained from extensive reading and, although he had an interest in all the muses, his chief love was music, perhaps the most mathematical of all the arts. He owned a Stradivarius violin which he played excellently but when in deep thought often preferred to scrape tunelessly across his knees. His *bête noir* was ennui and he rebelled at an inactive brain, at times choosing to keep stagnation at bay by injecting himself with a seven per cent solution of cocaine. His professional career spanned some twenty-three years and in hundreds of cases he defeated the enemies of law and order in several countries. After refusing a knighthood in June 1902, Holmes retired in1903 to keep bees on the Sussex Downs where he died peacefully in his modest villa on Saturday last. This is the second time that Sherlock Holmes' death has been announced. In 1891 it was believed that he had perished in the Reichenbach Falls in mortal combat with the arch-criminal Professor Moriarty, but this proved to be a false alarm and Holmes returned from obscurity four years later to resume his career. He was a man of ascetic character and had one friend only – myself, John H Watson, MD, Late Indian Army.

Reprinted from The Daily Telegraph by kind permission of the editor.

PREFACE

OVER many years I placed before an indulgent public a series of adventures depicting the life and work of my friend Mr Sherlock Holmes. When I laid down my pen after relating the case I called *The Adventure of Shoscombe Old Place* I determined that should be the end of my effusions lest I should weary my public. I did not wish to place myself in the position of the aged actor-manager who is forever dragging his weary bones around the provinces on an endless farewell tour.

Recently, however, the announcement of the death of Sherlock Holmes has caused renewed interest in that remarkable man and the gentlemen of the public press have beaten a path to my door in their search for memoirs and anecdotes. Several publishers have urged me to write a personal biography of Sherlock Holmes but I have declined to do so. The fact is that Holmes' life was nothing more than his career. He eschewed all the comforts, emotions and yearnings of mortal man to turn himself into a calculating machine. His sole *raison d'être* was to fight crime; anything that caused him to deviate from that quest was ruthlessly eliminated from his life.

In the vaults of the bank of Cox & Co, at Charing Cross, there is my battered dispatch-box crammed with papers appertaining to the dozens of cases of my friend which I intend to preserve for the interest of posterity. The flurry of recent attention, however, has encouraged me to re-examine this extraordinary file of notes as there are many cases of great interest which I was unable to reveal to the public at the time. Sherlock Holmes served many of the crowned heads of Europe and, of course, these cases must remain secret as national securities are at stake. Others with possible libellous consequences and some concerning the honour of private persons will be destroyed. However, many years have now passed and the bulk of my notes concern a period when the present King's grandmother was on the throne of our great country and in most cases the necessity for discretion has been removed.

I have purposed, therefore, to lay before the public one last collection of cases, selected from the entire span of the extraordinary career of my friend Mr Sherlock Holmes. I have endeavoured to give some idea of the many and varied talents of this prodigious man and that has been the sole basis of my selection. The compilation of this volume has provided the utmost pleasure to me as I recall that happier time before the war to end all wars but the task has been onerous on my fragile state of health and I fear that I shall write no more.

John H Watson, MD, Late Indian Army
London and Hastings 1929

The Singular Adventure
of
THE ECCENTRIC GENTLEMAN

IN one of my previous writings I made mention of the strange case of the city gentleman who, stepping back into his house for his umbrella, was never seen again. It occurs to me that now the time is right for me to give a full explanation of this bizarre event. An event that was to become the first of several such odd happenings throughout London in that winter of 1887.

It was a typical dull, foggy London afternoon when we had a visitor at 221B Baker Street. Our caller was a typical London cab driver and he brought a typical leather suitcase with him. So far, then, the case had started unremarkably.

"Sorry to trouble you, gents," said the cabby, "but I've got a little problem and my mates at the cabmans' shelter said Mr Sherlock 'Olmes was the man to see about it."

"I am Sherlock Holmes," said my friend. "In what way may I assist you?"

"Well, sir, it's really a rather rum do and I can't give you a hexplanation for it, but I've been left with this bag at the end of it all."

"I suggest you start at the beginning, cabby, and tell us the whole story."

"Well, it was yesterday when I received a message to go to an address in Cheveley Gardens just off Park Lane. A gentleman by the name of Mr James Phillimore wanted pickin' up at twenty-three minutes past two o'clock."

"That seems a very precise time. Is it usual for your customers to demand such accuracy?" asked Holmes.

"'Ow do you mean, Mr 'Olmes?"

"I would have thought your customers would ask to be collected at, say, a quarter-past or half-past two. Twenty-three minutes past seems unusual."

"That's right, sir, it was. As you say, people usually order me to call at 'alf-past two or somethink like that."

"Please go on," encouraged Holmes.

"Well, I was there in good time, at about quarter-past, so I thought I 'ad better just 'ang on a bit as the message was so definite about twenty-three minutes past. But, in a couple of minutes, this gent appears and sez that I was early but not to worry. Then 'e 'ands me this big suitcase, this very one 'ere you see before you. Well it's quite a weight, but I 'auls it in the cab and Mr Phillimore climbs in after it. Then 'e suddenly jumps out again and sez 'Just a minute, cabby, I've forgotten my umbrella. 'Old on while I go back to the 'ouse and get it. I 'ave plenty of time, it is not 'alf-past two yet.' Then 'e pops off and I waits. Well 'e was gone ages. After about ten minutes I thinks I'd better see what's 'appened to 'im so I goes up the path and knocks on the door. The servant girl opens it and I asks if Mr Phillimore 'as found 'is umbrella yet? The girl stares at me as though I was a mad thing and shouts at me to go away. So I sez "old on my girl, stop your 'ollerin', there's no need to take on like that.' Just then this butler chap appears to see what all the noise is about. So I hexplains I'm the cabby and that I was waitin' for 'is master to find 'is umbrella then climb back into my cab. Well you could 'ave knocked me down with a feather when 'e sez 'e served a family called Fenton-Stewart and that 'e 'ad never 'eard of anybody with the name Phillimore and certainly 'e did not live there. Well I was knocked all aheap at this. Then I realises I'd probably made a mistake about the 'ouse and come up the wrong path though I'm sure it was the one Mr Phillimore 'ad gone up. So I asks about the people who live on either side and it turns out they aren't Phillimore either. So I gets the door slammed in my face and I'm left not knowin' what to do. So I 'angs on for about 'alf an 'our wonderin', then I gives up and goes back to the cabbies' shelter to tell my tale to my mates. Because I'd still got 'is bag you see. So we talks about it and my mates say the best thing is to take it to Mr Sherlock 'Olmes. So 'ere I am."

During his long narrative Holmes sat attentively then, as the cabman ended his story, asked "Have you ever seen this Mr Phillimore before?"

"No, sir."

"How can you be so sure? You must see many people in your job. While you may not remember him, you could actually have carried him before."

"Now that's true, sir. I might. But I would surely 'ave remembered 'im if 'e 'ad been dressed the same as 'e was yesterday."

"How was he dressed?" asked Holmes.

"Well 'e was dressed normally enough hexcept for one really odd thing - 'e was wearin' a yellow top 'at."

"A yellow top hat?" queried Holmes.

"Yes sir, bright yellow - like the sun."

"Perhaps he was some kind of Music Hall artiste?" I ventured to suggest.

"I couldn't say, sir. But 'e was perfectly normally dressed in other respects and behaved in a normal manner."

"Except for not coming back for his ride, nor his luggage," said Holmes musingly. "Let us open the case, it may explain everything."

But far from explaining everything, it made the whole affair even more mysterious as the case contained nothing but seven common house bricks wrapped in a great quantity of old newspapers.

"What a bloomin' frost," said our cabby friend. "No wonder the dratted thing was so 'eavy."

"I think you are perhaps the victim of some practical joke," said Holmes sympathetically. "Allow me to give you this half-sovereign for all your pains.

Leave the bag here, I'll dispose of it. Think no more about it."

"Well thank you, sir, that's very 'andsome of you seein' you're nothing to do with it like," said the cabby beaming and went off scratching his head over the whole odd affair.

"Well, Watson, what do you make of that tale?" asked Holmes.

"I can't make any sense of it. I agree with you. Some kind of practical joke I suppose, but what the trickster gained from it I couldn't guess."

"I doubt if it were an elaborate prank although that seemed to satisfy our incurious London cabby. One thing seems apparent. Mr James Phillimore was at great pains to establish the time of this affair."

"Why should that be of importance, Holmes?"

"I don't know, Watson, but that seems to be the key to the whole peculiar episode. The cabby was called for the precise time of twenty-three minutes past two and then Phillimore remarked it was not yet half-past two."

That seemed to be the end of the matter.

Some days later I was reading the paper when a paragraph about a rather odd incident took my eye and I read it out to Holmes "Listen to this, Holmes: *Diners at Simpson's in the Strand were disconcerted early yesterday evening when one of the diners complained in a loud voice about the service he was receiving. Dissatisfied diners are not unknown to the catering trade, but Mr Henry Joseph, the manager of Simpson's, said he had never previously known anyone to stand on his chair and harangue all the other diners. The man left quietly after Mr Joseph threatened to call the police.* The world seems to be full of rum people these days."

"Probably taken too much drink," said Holmes dryly.

Neither of us thought any more about it until some days later. I was passing through Trafalgar Square on my way to the National Gallery, which was holding a special exhibition on the Monarchs of England, when I beheld a man feeding the pigeons. This is something people do, in spite of being requested not to. The authorities would much rather be rid of the birds but so many sentimental people feed the wretched things that they are fighting a losing battle. So, in itself, this would not have caused much attention but the fellow was doing it in a very conspicuous manner shouting out loudly: "Come on, my beauties, here are some crumbs!" and similar expressions of encouragement. Several children with nurses or parents were a small audience for this exhibitionist. Suddenly he boomed out "Well, my dearioes, it's past five o'clock, I've been here over an hour, time I was on my way." And he immediately made off, becoming lost in the crowd, only his yellow top hat being visible until that too was swallowed up.

This was obviously Mr James Phillimore of the mysterious cabby incident. It was a pity I had not been near enough to see his face. I would have forced my way nearer if I had realised he was the man of the yellow top hat, but he was not wearing it until he suddenly donned it on electing to go. I told Holmes about the incident on my return.

"Hum, once again he made reference to the time. That seems most significant."

"But what can it all mean, Holmes? There is no harm in feeding the pigeons. If only I had realised it was Phillimore, I could have accosted the fellow."

"On what grounds? I hardly think he has done anything amiss."

"Well I could have tackled him about the cabby. After all, the poor chap was left without a fare and out of pocket on his wasted journey."

"I think there must be something more to all this than mere eccentricity. Let us make a note of the dates and times involved as they seem so important. We may, I think, assume the Simpson's Restaurant incident was the same man too. If we hear of any further examples of harmless but bizarre behaviour, we will note those also and see if we can detect a pattern."

"If you are thinking that this chap is affected by the phases of the moon, Holmes, I should warn you that so-called lunatic behaviour has been utterly discredited by modern medicine."

"I may not be up to this month's *Lancet*, as you undoubtedly are, Watson, but I rather think I have progressed from the Dark Ages." So saying, Holmes started compiling his list of dates and times.

There were further incidents over the next few weeks. These we gleaned from the newspapers, and we may have erred in the inclusion of some, as it is a fact that the oddest things do happen to the most mundane of people. For example, a butcher's boy was cycling past a cricket ground when the ball, hit for six right out of the ground, bounced in the road and wedged itself in the spokes of his front wheel, jamming it from turning and causing him to fall to the ground. We could not attribute that to Mr Phillimore! But we did find several sightings of eccentric behaviour: A man stood directing the traffic along the embankment for fully two hours before running off when police arrived. A man threatened to jump out of a fourth storey window in the City until the police persuaded him to give himself up. A customer smashed some plates in the Savoy Grill but paid handsomely for their reparation. And so on. But in none of these cases was a yellow top hat mentioned.

It seemed that the trail was going cold and Holmes had other affairs to occupy him. It was at this time that he became involved in the affair of the governess at Copper Beeches and, as always, he had his many avenues of research to pursue.

One day we had a caller who announced himself as Samuel Gossage. He was a man of about forty years and of medium height.

"You can imagine what my chums at school used to call me," chuckled Gossage. "Still you learn to live with it when you are cursed with a name like that."

"What can I do for you, Mr Gossage?" asked Holmes.

"Well, sir, I would really like your advice. Your name has been given to me as an eminent criminologist and I wonder if anything can be done in this situation. I have rather a long story to tell you."

I got up to leave.

"Perhaps you would excuse me Mr Gossage, as I have to go out now."

"Oh please, Dr Watson, if your business is not urgent I would like you to stay and hear my story also. You see it does have features of medical interest and I would so value your opinion. It is only eight o'clock and I can relate my story in less than twenty minutes. Please stay and hear it."

So I consented and Samuel Gossage started his tale.

"You must know that I am a resident of Chatham in Kent and that I live in a house situated a few streets away from my mother. I am a married man with no children and I have a brother who has a wife and family. My brother also has a house in Chatham but some two or three miles at the other end of town from me.

"My mother is a widow, my father having died several years ago. He was the master at a naval saw mill in Chatham and he left my mother with an income of some £200 a year. So she was quite comfortable and we all jogged along nicely seeing each other from time to time as families do. I made a habit of calling in at least once a week to see how the old lady was. She employed a girl to do for her and this was her only servant. She had one girl for several years and it seemed to work out all right but that girl gave notice as she was off to get married and my mother had to find somebody else.

"Well, whether the old lady was getting particular or cantankerous or what, I don't know, but none of the replacement servants seemed to want to stay and we had quite a succession of them. Anyway, to be brief, the last one was an 18 year old called Eliza Lawson. My mother was a most fastidious person - "

"You say was, Mr Gossage. Is your mother no longer alive?" interrupted Holmes.

"Oh no, Mr Holmes. She was murdered. That is why I have come to see you."

"Ah. Pray continue your most interesting narrative."

"Well, as I say, my mother was a most fastidious person and demanded high standards of her servant. Unfortunately, Lawson was far from being an ideal housemaid. In fact she was hopeless. Worse than hopeless - she was criminal. She used to sneak out of the house once Mother had gone to bed and consort with all sorts of unsavoury types down in the town. As you know, Chatham is a garrison town and is full of both soldiers and sailors coming and going. We do get quite a lot of riff-raff, if I may phrase it thus.

"This Eliza Lawson used to go and drink in some of the lowest dives in town and, not to put too fine a point on it, was notorious for going off with soldiers after the pubs had closed. It transpired that she was regularly stealing my mother's things and pawning them. Her clothes, books and jewellery kept disappearing."

"Were you not aware of the situation?" enquired Holmes.

"Not at all. I knew nothing of this until it all came out at the trial. May I proceed?"

"Pray do. Perhaps you can come to the actual murder?" asked Holmes.

"I am about to do so, Mr Holmes. On the morning of Monday 29th January, the maid was chopping firewood in the cellar prior to lighting the fires when my mother, who had by this time had enough of the girl's behaviour, went down to the cellar to give her a week's notice. There must have been a bit of an argument and Lawson struck my mother on the head with the axe she was holding. Imagine, Doctor, a 68 year old woman being felled with an axe wielded by a healthy 18 year old. The poor old lady had no chance. She fell dead instantly. The stupid girl did not know what to do, there was blood all over the place. She removed Mother's dress and stuffed it down the privy, then she dragged her upstairs and laid her on her bed. Then she saw that the bleeding had stopped so she got a bucket of water and washed Mother's face. I suppose she thought that Ma may be passed off as having died in her sleep if there was no wound showing to give her away. Then she went and changed her own dress as it was splattered with blood. As she was doing all this there was a knock at the door and she panicked. Thinking it was the police, she grabbed a knife and made a slit in her own throat and staggered to the door. It wasn't the police at all but a couple of local lads trying to earn a few pennies by shovelling snow. Well they saw the blood and ran. To me, in fact, as they knew I was only a couple of streets away.

"When I got there the stupid girl made up a cock-and-bull story about being attacked by two night-soil collectors. She claimed one had murdered Ma and the other had tried to rape her. I sent for the police, of course, and they soon sorted it all out. It was clear that the night-soil men story could not stand up as they would hardly have washed Mother's face before leaving. Neither could they have bolted the door after they left - it was all bolted when the boys knocked on it. Then the dress was found in the privy. Oh, it was all very clear that she had done it."

"So why have you come to me?" asked Holmes mildly.

"Because, Mr Holmes, in spite of all the damning evidence that was brought up at the trial, Lawson was found Not Guilty."

"Ah," said Holmes thoughtfully.

"She was certainly guilty, Mr Holmes, but she just sat there and cried and looked pathetic and melted the hearts of the men on the jury. And that was it. They totally ignored all the evidence. Let her off. Not guilty. I couldn't believe it. Nobody could. The local papers were full of it."

"Were they indeed? So what do you want me to do, Mr Gossage?" asked Holmes.

"Why, get the verdict overturned. Get justice for me."

"I'm afraid, sir, that is not possible. Surely you must know that you cannot be tried again for the same crime?"

"But it wasn't a fair trial," protested Gossage.

"Once a person has been found not guilty of murder they are free and cannot be brought to trial again. In fact the person is free to admit their guilt if they are so tactless. It is not unknown for a guilty person who has been found innocent by the courts to recklessly boast that they were, in fact, guilty all the time in the confident knowledge that nothing can be done about it."

"And is that the law?"

"It is, sir."

"Then the law should be changed. Well, Dr Watson, I am sorry to have delayed your business."

"Will you excuse me a second, Mr Gossage? I have a book somewhere that has a case which bears on your situation. Watson, pour out some whisky & sodas for us. I'll only be a minute."

Holmes went out. I thought it peculiar that he should leave by the outer door as, to my knowledge, all his books were on the shelves in the room with us or else in his bedroom where he kept a further vast library.

"I'm sorry to have delayed you, Dr Watson, but it is still short of half past and I do not mind if you wish to flee."

"Not at all, sir, here have a whisky and soda."

"You are very kind. But I think perhaps I have overstayed my time."

"Well you cannot leave until Holmes returns, so drink up."

"I really did not know that legal principle, it seems most unjust."

"Well it often seems to me that the law does not always serve justice."

"You speak truly, Dr Watson, a very profound thought I must say. Cheers!"

At that moment Holmes returned.

"So sorry to have left you, Mr Gossage. I cannot lay my hands on the book just at the moment. Ah, whisky and soda, splendid! I will think about what you have told me, Mr Gossage, and if anything occurs to me I will be in touch with you but I really do not think anything can be done at this stage. You may be able to bring a civil action for something else - theft for instance, but that was probably all part of the trial. I am not a lawyer, you see. Your best plan is to see one of the top criminal lawyers."

"Yes, perhaps that is the best thing to do. Well, thank you for your patience gentlemen. I hope I have not kept you too long, Dr Watson. It is only just gone half-past eight. You will send me your account for this consultation, Mr Holmes? My address is No 11 Ordnance Street, in Chatham."

"You will be hearing from me, Mr Gossage," said Holmes, making a note of the address before showing our visitor out.

Holmes returned, threw himself into his armchair and laughed and laughed. I thought he was having a fit. Holmes is not a man who is easily amused so I was really concerned for his welfare.

"What is it, Holmes? Are you all right?"

"Perfectly, Watson," he gasped, coming to his senses. "I rather think we have just had an encounter with Mr James Phillimore."

"Holmes, you're not serious?"

"Watson, the whole thing is hilarious but I do think that was the gentleman with the yellow top hat who goes around doing bizarre things all over London."

"But he seemed perfectly normal to me."

"He would hardly try anything too outrageous in the company of London's leading consulting detective."

"But, why? Why did he come here?"

"I think for the same reason he has done all these other peculiar antics. Although to try and fob me off with details of a fifty year old case in Chatham when probably he has never even been there, and was certainly not born when it happened, is rather pushing his luck. He is obviously not aware of my prodigious memory for criminal cases."

"So it was all a hoax?"

"He was relating the case as if it had just happened and that his family were intimately concerned. He had the salient facts but not the detail that makes it of interest and commends itself to me as worthy of note. No, I think the whole charade was merely a ploy so that he could spend half-an-hour in our company."

"But why on earth should he desire to do that? And why not merely invite us to dinner or something? I can make no sense of this at all."

"Neither can I at the moment, but it is clear that by his insisting on the correct time, and emphasising how long he has spent, it looks remarkably as though he were establishing a water tight alibi."

"An alibi for what, Holmes?"

"I don't know Watson. I am a detective not a psychic. I hope to have information to go on very soon. I have set one of the Baker Street Irregulars on his tail. I want to find out where he lives, then I intend shadowing him."

"So that's where you went when you said you were looking for a book!"

"Of course. It is essential that I find this man's base. If he's a felon, Watson, I'll have him."

I did not see much of Holmes during the next week. He seemed to be out all the time and, when we did coincide at our rooms, he was disguised in a working man's get-up that rendered him quite unrecognisable. I knew he was working on a case and thought it prudent not to question him. Then one day about a week later, there he was at breakfast looking his normal self.

"Ah, Watson, good to see you. I wonder if you have plans for this evening?"

"Nothing in particular, why?"

"I wonder if I could ask you to assist me in catching a villain?"

"You know you can count on me, Holmes. What do you want me to do?"

"It is not going to be easy and I must leave you to manage for yourself. Tonight, we will lurk outside a house near Regent's Park. A man will emerge and I want you to follow him. Keep on his tail but do not let him see you. Sooner or later this man will do some eccentric action in public, or call attention to himself in some way. He is almost sure to mention the time."

"This is our friend Phillimore, or Gossage, or whatever he calls himself, I presume?"

"Precisely. That is the trouble - he knows you by sight and so it may make a simple job that bit more difficult. When he has called attention to himself you will only have a limited time left to collar him as he usually makes off shortly afterwards."

"What exactly am I to do, Holmes?"

"You must get him arrested and taken into custody. As I do not know the circumstances, I cannot advise you, Watson, but it is most essential that this man is arrested tonight. If necessary, pick a fight with him and get both of you arrested. But, whatever you do, he must not escape being detained at least overnight in jail. Do I make myself clear?"

"Perfectly, Holmes. I will carry out your instructions to the best of my ability."

"Good man, Watson."

"And what will you be doing whilst I am risking my reputation brawling in a public place?"

"I shall be following his partner and hope to catch him red-handed. So be ready at 6 o'clock and we will go together."

At 6.30 that evening the two of us were concealed opposite a modest but respectable house near Regent's Park. We had not long to wait before the door opened and our quarry emerged. He was in evening dress.

"Damn it, Holmes, I never thought of that. If he is going to a place where evening dress is *de rigueur*, I may not be able to follow him."

"My fault, Watson, I should have anticipated that. Do the best you can. He will have to leave wherever he is going, so you could nab him when he comes out. Initiative, Watson. Quick, off you go, do not lose him."

With that whispered exhortation in my ear I left Holmes still watching the house as I followed Phillimore. He caught a cab at a rank and I was able to get the next and keep him in sight. His cab stopped outside the Lyceum Theatre and he made his way leisurely inside. This was a relief. He was obviously going to attend the play and I could gain admittance or be safe in the knowledge that I could encounter him as he emerged at the end of the entertainment. I paid off my cab and looked at the poster. I was not unfamiliar with the Lyceum Theatre as I had attended plays there myself in the past. It was the home of Mr Henry Irving and his Company and I had seen the eminent actor in *"The Bells"* and *"The Corsican Brothers"*. However, tonight he was playing in Shakespeare who is not one of my pleasures. Nevertheless, I was here on business so I approached the box office to see if I could obtain a seat. There was a place in the pit so I paid my money and looked forward to enduring Mr Irving and his delightful partner Miss Ellen Terry in *"Much Ado About Nothing"*. I thought I could dream up some method of entrapping Phillimore while the play was on.

At the first interval I mingled in the foyer. There were some comments about a person in the dress circle who was appreciating the play rather excessively. It has always been my contention that Shakespeare is obscure to the modern ear and the only persons who obtain any pleasure are students and professors who have studied the works intimately. Thus, whereas a mere mortal like me hears only gibberish, some learned professor chuckles loudly at an hilarious Elizabethan joke that means nothing to us nowadays. It seems the patron in the front row of the circle was indulging himself in that professorial manner to the discomfort of the rest of the audience.

As the play progressed this man seemed to think Shakespeare was a pantomime and his reactions were becoming more and more excessive. Needless to say, I had instantly identified the culprit as my quarry. Then I had a brainwave. I unfastened my watch from its anchor and slipped it into my side pocket. This watch was my late father's and came to me by way of my elder brother on his untimely death. It was not of great worth and much repaired but I treasured it for its sentimental value and it had an inscription on the cover that meant a lot to me.

During the final interval I left the area where the humble pittites mingled and made my way to the salon of the circle where I immediately saw Phillimore ostentatiously smoking a cigar with the rest of the patrons studiously ignoring him.

"Mr Gossage, I thought it was you. How are you?" I exclaimed heartily.

He was taken aback for a moment, then realised that here was someone who could add verisimilitude to his alibi.

"Why, it is Dr Watson. Forgive me, I did not recognise you for the moment. Are you watching the play?"

"Yes, it is very fine isn't it?"

"I am enjoying it immensely. Where are you sitting?"

"I'm downstairs in the pit. An ex-Army doctor's pension does not run to the better seats, I regret to say."

"I'm sorry to hear that. Surely your friend Mr Sherlock Holmes is a man of wealth?"

"I really do not know, Mr Gossage. That is not the sort of topic gentlemen discuss, is it?"

I was saved from having to make up more pointless conversation by the bell which signalled the commencement of the final act.

"Well do give your friend my regards, won't you, Dr Watson?"

"Certainly. Enjoy the rest of the play."

Phillimore went to take his seat in the dress circle while I went downstairs but did not re-enter the auditorium. Once the play was under way again, I went to the entrance foyer and asked to speak to the manager.

"I am the manager, how may I help you?"

"I wish to complain about one of your patrons."

"Oh dear, I know, you mean the man in the dress circle who is braying inanely. There have been several complaints but it is very difficult."

"That is not my concern. I have been robbed."

"Robbed? What, here? In the Lyceum? That is a very serious accusation, sir."

"I know, sir, I do not make it lightly. One of your patrons is no more than a common thief. I have had my pocket picked and my watch has been stolen."

"Surely there is some mistake? Perhaps you have dropped it?"

"There is no question of it. I would ask you to summon a policeman so that he can waylay the man as he comes out of the theatre at the end of the play."

"Well I do not know what to say. You have a particular suspect in mind?"

"I have. My card, sir. You may have heard of my associate, Mr Sherlock Holmes."

"Indeed, sir, I have read of Mr Holmes through your very own writings."

"Then you will know that I do not trifle where the law is concerned."

"Please step into my office."

That was my first meeting with Mr Bram Stoker who subsequently became a well-known author himself, and a very close friend. At that time, his only published work was a book concerning the duties of civil servants in Ireland.

A policeman was sent for and together we three waited for the audience to emerge. Stoker soon winkled the man out of the crowd on some pretext and he was taken into the office where the policeman challenged him to turn out all his pockets. I confess I was apprehensive lest he had been aware of my slipping the watch into his pocket as I greeted him effusively. If he had discovered it and taken it out, leaving it in the theatre, then my carefully contrived plan would have been foiled and myself rendered ridiculous.

But all was well, the watch was found and Phillimore/Gossage taken into custody. Alas, I had to leave my beloved watch with the policeman and was told to report to Bow Street police station next morning to give evidence. I felt I had done Holmes proud and went home basking in the expectation of his praise.

In the event, Holmes did not arrive home at all and I spent a restless night wondering if all had gone well with his part of the proceedings. After a solitary breakfast, I went down to Bow Street where to my surprise I found Holmes with Inspector Lestrade from Scotland Yard.

"Holmes, you are safe!" I cried.

"Ah, in perfect time, Watson. Thank you for securing our friend, the eccentric Mr Gossage."

"What is all this, Mr Holmes. Firstly you ask me to back you up apprehending a burglar last night, now you've got me to come down here and look at one that Dr Watson, of all people, has caused to be brought in. Can you explain what all this is about, Mr Holmes?" said Lestrade in mild annoyance.

"Certainly, Lestrade. The villain you caught last night is behind bars at Scotland Yard is he not?"

"You know he is, Mr Holmes, you were there too last night. He fully deserves to be behind bars seeing that we caught him red- handed."

"Exactly. Now let us have a look at the man that Watson caused to be apprehended at the Lyceum Theatre."

We all looked through the prison bars.

"I can't believe it - it's the same man!" said the amazed Lestrade.

"There is a remarkable similarity is there not? Watson, you are looking at one half of a pair of zygotic twins. The other half is at Scotland Yard."

"Astonishing, Holmes! You mean these identical twins formed a team for nefarious purposes?"

"Indeed. A very clever ploy, Watson. You see, Lestrade, the man here made a point of being far away from the scene of his twin brother's crime, and called attention to himself in some way so that he had witnesses to his whereabouts at the time of the crime. Nobody knew there were two of them. In their daily life they pretended to be one and the same man. So if, by a misfortune, the crook was suspected there was always an alibi that he was elsewhere at the time of the crime. The only way the scheme could fail was if the burglar brother was actually caught in the act. That is what I arranged with you, Lestrade. But I also arranged for his twin brother to be arrested at the same time in a distant place. So as long as you keep them well apart, Lestrade, you will secure a conviction."

"So that's why you enquired about the dates and times of various burglaries in my record sheets?" said Lestrade.

"Yes. As soon as I could see a pattern of burglaries coinciding with the record I had made of singular and curious happenings, I knew that the sole purpose was the establishment of alibis."

"And I thought you were checking on the phases of the moon!" I cried.

"Well it's up to you now, Lestrade. If this case has taught us anything in the fight against crime it is this – always be suspicious of men who wear yellow top hats!"

several of his prints which had some special merit or fond memory. Holmes was rather taken with one of Mills himself, a casual study which showed him astride a bent-wood chair, leaning on the back with his chin on the back of his hands.

"I'm glad you like that one, Mr Holmes," said Mrs Mills, "as I took that one myself. It is the only photograph I have ever taken and it is such a success. Of course my husband set up the camera and everything, so that all I had to do was to press the bulb. It is difficult to take a likeness of oneself. It captures him so naturally - much nicer than the usual stiff portrait." And off she went again until Baynes interrupted the flow.

"I'm sorry to be so pressing, Mrs Mills, but I must show Mr Holmes and Dr Watson the room where the crime took place."

"Of course, how absurd of me to rattle on like this. I'll leave you to it," said Mrs Mills. "I've some gardening to do."

I thought, that for a recently bereaved woman, Mrs Mills was rather garrulous, but my experience as a medical man has taught me that death and trauma can affect people in many different ways. Whereas some will collapse in the mind and weep for months after the death of a loved one, others will present a stoical front to those around them, their grief a private thing bottled up inside them so that they present an unfeeling visage to the world. Another thing puzzled me. "Holmes, how do you know the Mills' don't have children?" I asked.

"Surely an enthusiastic photographer would have used his own children as models many times? The only picture with any children at all is the group photograph, which obviously depicts the children at the Mills' school."

"This is the scene of the crime, gentlemen," said Baynes, opening the door to a room that was a combination of sitting room, library and salon. Immediately on entering we were confronted with the side of a massive flat-top desk and we had to squeeze past it in single file to enter the room. The room was about eighteen feet square and the door by which we entered was in the corner. The wall facing us had a central fireplace with an alcove at either side. To the right, the outside wall was dominated by a large window of the French type, the wall on the right adjacent to the doorway was occupied by bookshelves reaching from floor to ceiling. As stated, the left hand wall was mainly occupied by the desk.

Baynes and I sat down, to be out of the way of Holmes, as he prowled about on his inspections.

"When was the desk moved?" snapped Holmes.

"About a month ago according to Mrs Mills. We can verify that when the maid returns, but I would think that is correct."

"Did Mrs Mills say why it was moved?"

"Only that her husband fancied a change round of the furniture. Also, whenever he wanted to consult a book on the shelves, he had to leave his desk in the old place and cross the room, whereas, in the present position he could swivel round to look."

"But he would still have to rise from his chair and take several paces to reach the shelves," pointed out Holmes.

"Oh certainly," agreed Baynes.

"I say, how do you know the desk has been moved at all?" I asked.

"If you look to the right of the fireplace you will see marks on the carpet which indicate that a heavy piece of furniture stood there for some considerable time. The marks correspond exactly with the legs of the desk."

"Is it important?" I asked.

"It is significant. If you, Watson, were arranging the furniture in this room, would you place such a massive desk against that wall, where everybody coming into the room has to walk round it? Normally the door to a room has to open no more than 90° to allow ample ingress. In this room the door has to swing right back to the wall behind, almost a full 180°, to permit a person to squeeze by the desk. A bizarre arrangement, surely? In the alcove by the fireplace, the desk would be largely tucked away from the body of the room, the fire to the left of the sitter would give warmth, and the light from the window would be over the sitter's right shoulder. A very convenient and pleasant arrangement that obviously obtained for many years. Suddenly, a month ago, the owners decide to move everything around, ending up with the desk placed away from the warmth of the fire, inconveniently blocking the entrance way, and causing anyone sitting at it to have his back to the window effectively blocking his own light."

"I agree with everything you say, Mr Holmes. All that you have said struck me instantly on entering the room, but I cannot for the life of me see the significance, if any, of it all," said Baynes.

"No, neither can I, as yet," agreed Holmes. "I presume this is the window pane that was shattered by the gun shot?" Holmes had moved to the French windows, which comprised a dozen panes, each about a foot square. "The one with the fresh putty?"

"Yes, Mr Holmes. As you see, it has been replaced."

"Where was the glass?"

"Why, just here in front of it, on the linoleum."

"And outside were there any footprints or other indications of the assailant?"

"No. As you can see, it is paved out there with one concrete step. The weather here has been dry for some time. I could find no indication at all."

"Hum," mused Holmes as he opened the window and stepped outside. He peered round, stepped back and gazed up at the house and returned.

"This is the side of the house, is it not?"

"True."

"So Mr Mills, sitting at his desk, was not likely to have been seen by anyone passing on the road?"

"Certainly not. The murderer must have entered the garden by the gate, or climbed over the wall. As you see, a high brick wall surrounds the garden entirely, except for the entrance. One and a half acres, Mrs Mills tells me, is the area of the garden. The murderer must have crept round the corner of the house and seen the lighted window. Peering in he saw Mr Mills and then, for some reason, with his gun smashed the window and shot him."

"Then ran off to disappear into the blue yonder?"

"So it would seem."

"When you were summoned did you open the French window?"

"Of course. And it was not locked."

"It wasn't locked? Are you sure?"

"Please do not under estimate me, Mr Holmes. In my own way I am as thorough as you."

"But surely you see the significance of that fact?"

"Certainly. If the window was unlocked when the murderer was present, it means he preferred to break a window to poke his gun in rather than open the window and step in himself. Or, if it was locked at the time, somebody unlocked it after the malefactor had left and before I arrived."

"Could Mrs Mills have unlocked it?"

"I asked her and she denies all knowledge of going anywhere near it. She seems unaware that the fact could be significant."

"Could it not be simply that the murderer assumed it would be locked and did not try the catch?" I asked.

"If you wanted to shoot somebody in the back - which would you do? Creep up to get as near as possible so that you did not miss, or break a pane of glass which is, and I commend this fact to your attention, Baynes, a mere thirty inches off the ground, kneel down and push your gun through?"

"Put like that it does seem a singular way of setting about things," I agreed.

Holmes was now on his hands and knees, crawling under and around the flat-top desk, with his lens in his hand.

"Baynes, did you observe that the desk is not flush against the wall?"

"Yes, Mr Holmes, I did. I also observed that it could not have been flush against the wall in its old position either. The skirting board would prevent it in both cases."

"Quite. But did you observe that even with the skirting board accounted for, this desk in its new position could have been pushed back a further inch, possibly as much as an inch and a quarter?"

"No, I certainly did not realise that. Is that of some significance?"

"It may be, especially taken with these rather odd scratches on the wall just by the back lip of the desk top. See?"

"I confess I missed those, Mr Holmes. Surely they are no more than general wear and tear? Do you attribute some special cause for them?"

"Hard to say. Can you tell me how the body lay?"

"I can do better than that, I'll show you." So saying, Baynes got to his feet, set the chair from the desk to one side, and laid himself on the floor, carefully arranging his limbs.

"Is that the exact position?" cried Holmes.

"It is, sir, within a quarter of an inch. Mr Mills was found exactly like this."

"But you are face down with your head towards the window!"

"This is how he was," said Baynes from his recumbent position.

"Get up, man. Surely if Mills was sitting at his desk and shot in the back he would slump forward over the desk, or, if standing or rising would crumple or fall backwards?"

"That would be the expectation, but who can say? He may have wheeled round on the impact of the bullet, he may have been standing and fallen back into his chair which then toppled him out."

"Watson, would you be so good as to sit on the chair at the desk as if writing."

"Certainly, Holmes." I did as bade and pretended to be writing and both the other men were silent. I could not imagine what they were doing but I had been given my humble part to play so on I went pretending to scribble. Suddenly I heard a loud crash and, leaping to my feet, turned round to see Holmes outside the window wielding a stick which had a rather large ball head. The new window pane was shattered on the linoleum.

Mrs Mills rushed up on hearing the noise. "What on earth's going on? I've just paid good money to have that window mended and you've broken it again. Mr Holmes, I'm surprised at a grown man behaving like that in somebody else's home."

"Ah, Mrs Mills, I am pleased to note that your hearing has not deteriorated with age," said Holmes smoothly. "It is a pity that the late Mr Mills suffered from hearing problems."

"What are you talking about, young man? Mr Mills never had hearing problems. He could hear as well as you and me. Are you insinuating that my poor husband was deaf? Because he certainly wasn't. Who told you that?"

"Pray do not distress yourself, Mrs Mills, I must have been misinformed."

"You certainly have been, Mr Holmes. Mr Mills could hear sounds audible only to dogs. What about my window?"

"I shall not only pay for the damage, madam, I will arrange for the glazier myself so that you will not be put to any trouble. We shall be departing very shortly but may I ask you to leave us now as our investigation is not yet complete."

"Well I suppose you know your own business best. But how breaking windows is going to catch the murderer I don't know; and now I'm sent out of the room like a naughty child. A stranger in my own house," sniffed Mrs Mills as she left us.

"Well, Holmes, what was all that about?" I asked.

"Would you like to enlighten the good doctor, Baynes?"

"I assume you wished to prove that if Mills had been sitting at the desk, on hearing the sound of the window breaking he would have spun round, as the doctor did."

"Just so, and any bullet would have entered the body at the front or at least the side."

"Mills would have to be very hard of hearing to ignore a window breaking in the same room," I said.

"Exactly."

"Well, Mr Holmes, I did say that I was uncomfortable with this case. But my bosses say I have to leave it as there is other important work and the force at large is looking for any stranger in the district who might be involved."

"Baynes, look at this stick. Do you see those marks just below the head?"

"Little scratches? Yes, I see them."

"What do you think caused them?"

"Probably the jagged glass edges as you thrust it through the window."

"Correct."

"Well that is not very surprising."

"No. But what is surprising is the fact that most of those scratches were already on the stick before I struck the window."

"You mean the window was broken with that same stick last time?"

"That is so."

"I can't follow that, Holmes. You mean the murderer came into the room, took the stick, went out and broke the window with it, shot Mr Mills, came back in and returned the stick. That is totally preposterous," I protested.

"Of course it is preposterous, Watson. This whole case is based on a fallacy. We have been told that the window was broken by the barrel of a gun being pushed through. It is clear to me that Mills broke the window himself, using his own stick."

"Himself? Why on earth should a man break his own window, Holmes? The whole thing seems meaningless to me. The fellow moves his desk, deliberately to have his back to the window, then smashes a pane in that window. Was he insane?"

"Well done, Watson. You have hit the nail on the head, in your usual forthright manner. You have explained the matter in one brief sentence."

"Ah, you mean he was insane?"

"Not at all. Mr Mills was not only sane he was clever and intelligent. As you say, he moved his desk deliberately so that he would have his back to the window."

"But what would be the point of that, Mr Holmes?" asked Baynes who had been studiously listening to our exchange.

"So that he would be in an ideal position to be shot in the back."

"You mean he actually wanted to be shot in the back? I can't grasp this at all, Holmes," I said flabbergasted.

"You kindly demonstrated the position of the body. How was the chair placed when you arrived?" Holmes asked of Baynes.

"Why it was here, just like this, how I put it before I laid myself on the floor." Baynes placed the chair away from the desk a little way and somewhat askew.

"It was exactly like that?"

"Within half an inch."

"Does it not strike you as more likely that the chair itself would be tumbled over if a body had collapsed from it?"

"That is quite possible. Very likely, in fact. But it is equally possible that a man could fall out of a chair without upsetting it."

"True," mused Holmes. "Actually I wonder if one should say a man could fall off a chair rather than out of it?"

"That seems a bit of a semantic quibble, Mr Holmes," said Baynes with amusement.

"Not at all. I would say he fell out of a chair if it was an easy chair or perhaps a carver-type of chair with arms, but this particular chair is more like a dining chair, it lacks arms, so I would say the man fell off his chair."

"Well have it how you like. When this man fell, his stick was partly underneath him, trapped by his body."

"The stick?" cried Holmes. "You mean the stick with which I broke the window?"

"Yes."

"For God's sake man, why did you not tell me? How can I assist you if I don't have the facts? If you had called me on Monday I would have solved this case within the hour. Now I have to rely on you for second-hand clues and you deny me the very information necessary to solve the case!"

"I did not think the stick significant. I presumed he needed it to help him get around."

"Let me see that stick again."

Baynes handed the walking stick to Holmes who examined it carefully.

"This is a brand-new stick as you can see from the excellent finish of the varnish. The scratches at the head we have already noted. Look at the other end. What do you see?"

"It lacks a ferrule."

"Rather early in the stick's life to lose the ferrule. What else do you see?"

"It rather looks as though a shallow V has been sawn in the end of the tip."

"Excellent! You are now observing things. Keep at it." Holmes then wandered off, insouciantly, leaving the two of us gaping.

A couple of hours later we were on the train back to London. Holmes was visibly in a good mood.

"Come on, Holmes, I know you of old. What's amusing you? What are you holding back?"

"I have held nothing back at all, Watson. That is why I am amused. Every single clue I found in that room I pointed out to Baynes. He has all the information he needs to solve the case."

"Good Lord, Holmes, you have solved the case already?"

"Of course."

"Well who did it?"

"I see the train has increased its speed, the telegraph poles are passing at a rate of six every thirty seconds whereas formerly it was five every thirty seconds."

"Holmes," I said exasperatedly, "get to the point."

"I hope that Baynes gets to the point. I am disappointed in that man. I thought he was destined for great things but, alas, he has lost that vital spark. He has already become a plodder, he has lost his inspiration."

"We can't all match your brilliant intelligence, Holmes."

"Perhaps not, but I hope that one day I will have a worthy successor. Indeed I hope a man will arise who will far surpass my humble achievements."

"Never mind the philosophy, Holmes, just explain the facts behind the case of the flat-topped desk."

But Holmes was in one of his whimsical moods and would say no more about the case and we returned to 221B Baker Street with exasperation being my prevalent mood.

"How do you fancy some Paganini, Watson? I think a little music on the violin would round off the day nicely."

"If you are going to scrape your fiddle, I think I'll take a turn round the park and end up at my club."

"I rather thought we could go to the Albert Hall and hear Joachim do the scraping," replied Holmes.

On our return home we found a telegram had been delivered during our absence at the concert. To my surprise it was from Mrs Mills and had obviously been sent immediately after our leaving. It informed us that she was coming to visit us, indeed would catch an early morning train and come straight to Baker Street, if we would be so kind to receive her there after breakfasting.

"How very curious," said I. "I wonder what her purpose is?"

"I rather think she is afraid of what I have found out," said Holmes smugly.

As Holmes still gave me no clue as to what that was, my curiosity was in no way assuaged by this pronouncement and I was allowed to go to bed with my head full of conjecture and puzzlement. I slept very badly and throughout the night kept drifting in and out of sleep with dreams of broken windows, visions of Holmes lying dead on the floor, though it was Baynes who had played that part for us, while the stick, with the curious scratches at one end and the notch at the other, haunted me as the dagger did Macbeth.

So I was rather relieved that, after suffering a breakfast with Holmes full of bonhomie and recollections of Joachim's artistry, Mrs Mills was announced.

"You must think it peculiar, Mr Holmes, that I should follow you back home in this manner. But I do know of your reputation and I am sure that the best thing for me is to tell you everything and throw myself on your mercy."

"You need tell me two things only: what did you do with the gun? And why did your husband prefer to be a murder victim rather than a suicide? All the rest I know," replied Holmes.

"I threw the gun into the Manor pond. The Manor is the house nearest to ours, and the pond is very close to the boundary between the properties so it was very secret and convenient to merely toss the gun into the water."

"And why did your husband kill himself but try to conceal the fact by staging his suicide to look like murder?"

"The insurance, Mr Holmes. My husband took out an insurance policy to protect me financially should anything happen to him. Certain illnesses were excluded, as was any ailment from which the insured suffered before taking out the policy. These clauses would make the insurance invalid and suicide automatically renders it void."

"Ah, all is clear to me now."

"Well it certainly isn't to me!" I protested.

"Then I must explain. Mr Mills conceived this idea some weeks ago, no doubt he brooded about it for some time."

"Actually, once he had proposed the idea of suicide, we discussed many times the best way to carry it out. You see, Jack was in great pain and his condition could only deteriorate. He said it was better for us both if he could go sooner rather than later. We had many a heart-to-heart into the small hours. I would not like you to think we contemplated the scheme lightly," Mrs Mills interrupted.

"I am sure you both gave the affair the gravest consideration. However, the result of your deliberations was that Mr Mills decided he would be shot in the back by person or persons unknown. No suicide shoots himself in the back, as it is virtually impossible; it is more usual to hold the gun to the temple or place the barrel in the mouth. I see you wince; these things you must have considered. So, having decided on the shot-in-the-back death, he prepared in advance by having his desk moved to where such a thing was possible – opposite the window."

"But how did he manage to shoot himself in the back?" I asked.

"He arranged his pistol by some contrivance wedged between the back of the desk and the wall. There were distinct fresh tell-tale scratches that indicated that something had been wedged there. Then he went to the window, stepped outside, and with his newly purchased walking stick smashed in one of the panes. For some reason, probably because it was easier and less likely to cause himself hurt, he broke one quite low down near the ground. I imagine he wielded his stick rather like a golf club, as I did when I repeated the experiment. This made me suspicious immediately, as anyone firing through it would have had to lie most awkwardly on the ground over a concrete step. Surely, to shoot a seated person in the back, one would need to be at a height where kneeling was the most that was required. Mr Mills then came back inside, closing the French window but not locking it. Thus causing my second point of suspicion when I could not see why someone should shoot through a window when they could merely turn the handle and walk in."

"Of course, it seems obvious when you point it out," said I.

"So Mr Mills took his stick, in the end of which he had carefully sawn a V, and sat upon his chair. He placed the stick along the desk top until the V engaged the trigger of the pistol. Thus he only had to make a slight push on the stick and bang! The gun would go off, striking him dead."

"But I don't understand. That would mean he was shot in the chest," I protested.

"Not so, Watson. Mr Mills sat astride the chair with his back to the desk and his face to the window. A position that, I confess, I may not have hit upon as quickly as I did if you, Mrs Mills, had not pointed out your favourite photograph of Jack, posed in that same nonchalant manner."

"So I gave it away myself?" said Mrs Mills wryly.

"How fiendishly cunning!" I cried.

"So with stick under one arm, a push on the large knob with the hand of the other, the notch engages the trigger, the result – a shot in the back. He tumbled from his chair falling to the floor on top of his stick."

"No, Mr Holmes, you are wrong."

"Wrong? Are you telling me it did not happen that way?"

"When I got back home on Monday morning I was most fearful because, of course, I knew what Jack had planned to do whilst I was at my sister's. I knew that I was supposed to find him long dead – he was to do the deed on Saturday night. But what if the plan had gone wrong, what if he was merely wounded and had lain in agony for 36 hours? We had spoken of all this but anticipation does not always prepare one for the real thing."

"So what went wrong?"

"When I let myself in the house, I went straight to the room and found Jack dead all right but he was still slumped over the back of the chair. He had not fallen off it. I did not know what to do. Obviously I could not leave him like that as it would have given the whole game away. So I pushed him over. It was horrible. Just think, my best beloved for forty years whom I had fondled in the closest intimacy and it was anathema for me to touch him."

"I see. So you pushed the body over but replaced the chair upright?"

"Yes, I did not know what to do – whether to leave the chair overturned or what. So I put it on its feet and hoped it would look as though Jack had toppled from it."

"Well that accounts for the odd positioning that so baffled Inspector Baynes," I said.

"So you then ran to get help, pretending that you had just arrived home, when you had in fact got rid of the weapon, toppled the body and done who knows what else? Made a cup of tea, perhaps?" said Holmes sarcastically.

"You must think I am a very unfeeling woman, Mr Holmes. But the reason that we embarked on this hazardous enterprise was because we loved each other so passionately. Jack was willing to do all those underhand deeds so that I could live without him, in reasonable comfort. Do not think I did not oppose him many, many times when he propounded his scheme to me. He made me swear to go along with it and I did, because I loved him so much."

"But your position is very serious, madam. You are an accessory before and after the fact. You have connived at a scheme to defraud the insurance company, thus obtaining money by deception. You have assisted in a suicide. Your position is very grave."

"I realise that, Mr Holmes. I always knew I would have it on my conscience, even if the plot succeeded. And for a time I thought it would succeed. Inspector Baynes is not as astute as you and, I am sure, would have remained baffled, but he sent for you, and you saw immediately through the whole fabric of lies."

"Inspector Baynes is a very capable detective and he will arrive at the truth eventually. I have not explained my deductions to him but I have pointed out the clues that revealed the truth to me. I showed him the marks on the stick, the sawed V on the stick, I called his attention to the extreme lowness of the window, I showed him the marks on the wall at the back of the desk, I pointed out the gap between desk and wall. He had discovered many things for himself in his investigations, however, he made one fundamental mistake, one mistake only, but that rendered the rest of his case inexplicable. He believed that some person had broken the window and fired a shot through it. Having established that as a fact in his mind, the other clues had to be distorted to fit the theory, or discarded as having no bearing. He could not understand the position of the body or the significance of the marks on the wall or the new stick. Hence he found the whole case odd."

"Whereas the only thing making everything else seem odd was his own misinterpretation of one single fact," said I.

"That is so, Watson."

"What are you going to do, Mr Holmes?"

"I am not going to let you play havoc with my moral conscience, Mrs Mills. If I were employed by the insurance company then you would be in jail now. But I have no allegiance to them. If I had been engaged by a principal, then my duty would be to him. But nobody has employed me, madam. My friend, Inspector Baynes, merely asked my advice and I gave it. He was there when you spoke about the difficulty of taking one's own picture and called attention to your late husband's proclivity for sitting on chairs back to front. I shall do nothing more. You will be dismissed from my mind."

"Thank you Mr Holmes."

"But be warned. You will not get away with this. Inspector Baynes may be slow but he is thorough. I have no doubt, no doubt at all, that when he has re-examined all the clues I called to his attention he will gain the truth at last."

"That is the chance I have always taken. I still thank you, Mr Holmes, for not interfering. Otherwise I would have had no chance at all." The sad, frightened woman left the room.

"That was nobly done, Holmes," I stated.

"Please, Watson, I am not at all sure that I have done the right thing. I am a citizen of this country and, more than most, dedicated to the rule of law and order. Should I be allowing criminals to go free?"

"There is a thing called compassion, Holmes."

"Do not weigh me down with false emotions, Watson. I cannot function as a machine must, if I am to consider emotions."

As it happened the law did catch up on Mrs Mills. She had had some six months of freedom when an unwise remark to her maid led that good soul to go to the police. Inspector Baynes, hearing of this, re-opened his file and soon hit upon the truth, just as Holmes had expounded months before. However, justice was cheated in the end as, knowing that she was about to be arrested, Mrs Mills drowned herself in that same convenient pond that concealed the gun.

"Have you seen this report in the paper, Holmes?" I asked. "I wonder what the theology is of two suicides meeting in heaven? Rather like Romeo and Juliet, I suppose, although Jack and Florence Mills doesn't have the same theatrical cadence to it."

"What are you talking about, Watson?"

"You remember Mr and Mrs Mills and the flat-top desk case in Shalford?"

"I have never been to Shalford," said Holmes firmly.

The Singular Adventure
of
THE SULKY PONY

I RETURNED home to find my friend Mr Sherlock Holmes crouched over his microscope in much the same position as I had left him several hours previously.

"Good Lord, Holmes, you look as though you'd never moved all the time I've been out."

He sighed and pushed away from the table. "A waste of time, Watson. Either my theory is wrong or my sample is flawed. I will have to commence the whole thing from the start tomorrow. I'm sorry you didn't get your game of billiards, I hope your friend Thurston wasn't ill? But a tour of the pictures in the National Gallery will be more beneficial to the soul."

I stared in amazement; I was still hanging up my coat and in one sentence Holmes had deduced my activities over the afternoon.

"In the olden days you would have been burned as a witch," I said. "How on earth can you know I went to the National Gallery instead of the club?"

"Oh, Watson, you know my methods. I have the advantage of knowing that your weekly Wednesday afternoon visit to your club is as fixed as the pole star and the purpose is to play billiards with Thurston. I know you do not play with anyone else. You invariably return with chalk dust between your finger and thumb but I see none on this occasion. It may have been rubbed or washed off, but when I see a catalogue from the National Gallery peeping out of your overcoat pocket I deduce that a visit there was a substitute for the club. You have often remarked that Thurston is a philistine, so he is hardly likely to have accompanied you. Therefore, it seems likely that Thurston was indisposed rather than the table was unavailable."

"You never cease to amaze me, Holmes! You are right in every particular. There was a message awaiting me at the club from Thurston saying he has the 'flu so I didn't linger there and on the spur of the moment decided to have a look at the newly acquired Raphael that is on exhibition."

"Pah, mere party tricks," he said grumpily. "What I need is some criminal activity to get my teeth into. Nothing happens in London these days. Where are all the criminals? My brain is getting rusty."

"Well I should think that, thanks to you, many of them have ceased their activities, and a good job too. Surely that is enough justification for your efforts?"

"But I'm stagnating, Watson, chemical experiments are no substitute for the thrill of the chase. I'm bored, I need stimulus. I need a master criminal to pit my wits against."

I felt fearful at those words because when Holmes had needed stimulus in the past he had turned to taking drugs, and I flatter myself that I have had some success in weaning him off this noxious habit. So I in turn, law abiding citizen that I am, longed for some dastardly crime to take place so that my friend could be galvanized into activity. But little did either of us know that the very next day would bring the stimulus that Holmes craved.

We were at lunch when we had a visit from a tall austere man dressed in black coat and striped trousers. Though clearly agitated, his demeanour, cultivated over many years, kept his turmoil under control and he spoke calmly.

"I'm sorry to intrude upon you at your meal, Mr Holmes, but my master, Lord Egerton, has commanded me to ask you to accompany me back to Hamden Hall where a heinous crime took place earlier this morning."

"Whom have I the honour of addressing?" asked Holmes.

"I am Phillips, Lord Egerton's butler. My lord fears that you have many calls upon your time and as a token of his earnestness commands me to give you this cheque to recompense you for the inconvenience of dropping your immediate plans. A cheque for a similar amount awaits you at Hamden Hall. These are merely *ex gratia* payments to ensure your attendance, your fees and expenses etc will be met in the usual manner."

Holmes, who can be quite prickly when treated as a hired servant, took the cheque and glanced at it.

"Lord Egerton is very generous. I am exceedingly busy at the moment but I am not a rich man, so I think I can spare today to look into his lordship's business. Permit my colleague Dr Watson and myself five or six minutes to prepare ourselves then we will accompany you."

"That will be most satisfactory. I have a cab outside that will take us to Charing Cross station. Hamden Hall is situated near Ashford in Kent. I will explain about the theft in the train," said Phillips.

In no time at all we found ourselves in a first class carriage bowling along through the Kent countryside. It was springtime and the fruit trees were in blossom and England had never looked so lovely. I spoke my thoughts out loud.

"It's a sham, Watson. Behind all that rustic beauty lies more wickedness than you ever find in the stews of London," said Holmes grumpily. "But let us hear Mr Phillips tell us about the business in hand."

"Well, sir, you must know that Lord Egerton is shortly to host an international conference at Hamden Hall. It is an event of great importance and ambassadors and ministers from several European countries are to attend. It is not to overstate the importance of the conference to say that the future peace of Europe depends on its outcome. I do not fully understand these things, I am merely a butler. However, the entire control of the Hall and the domestic running of the conference is under my command. Extra staff has had to be engaged, rarely-used rooms have had to be opened, many additional provisions have had to be ordered. I cannot begin to tell you the amount of preparation that has been done and, now on the eve of the conference, the work that has still to be put in hand.

"We are catering for forty delegates – all gentlemen of the first rank, and each is bringing accompanying secretaries and staff. In many cases the gentlemen will be accompanied by their wives who in turn will have maids and so on."

"How long is this conference to be?" asked Holmes.

"It will be for three days, starting on Sunday."

"So in three days time."

"Yes, Mr Holmes, and preparations were going wonderfully well. I pride myself that my household management is second to none and I have organised the delivery of comestibles so that we have a constant supply over the period. We have butchers and bakers calling daily and kitchen staff working twenty-four hours. It is really quite a feat, believe me."

"I can imagine. But what dastardly deed has thrown the spanner into your well oiled works, Mr Phillips?" asked Holmes

"Lord Egerton desired to display his family silver at the conference. He thought it advisable to indicate to some of the foreign delegates, who perhaps do not know him sufficiently, that he is a man of substance and an influential personage in this country. Also he wished to display a beautifully worked gold rose bowl that had been presented to him five years ago at a similar conference in Zurich. The bowl, which eminent critics have said is the finest piece of workmanship in gold since Benvenuto Cellini, is, apart from its value, a kind of symbol of the Movement that underlies this conference."

"What is there to prevent your master's wishes being carried out?"

"The bowl, some silver plate and several pieces of family jewellery were stolen this morning."

"But surely they were protected in some way?" I protested.

"My lord had made arrangements with a firm of locksmiths in London to construct a special display cabinet. They brought it down last week to be fitted in the designated place. The various items of jewellery – including a tiara which once belonged to Catherine the Great of Russia – and plate are normally not all gathered at the Hall. Some pieces are kept there but others at Lord Egerton's London residence, a few at his shooting lodge in Scotland and the most valuable of all in bank vaults. They were all collected together after the arrival of the display cabinet and installed therein. The head of the firm, Mr Chubb himself, came to supervise all the arrangements. The pieces were put in place yesterday. The doors of the cabinet, which are of plate glass, are made to be locked and there is an ingenious alarm system which sounds bells if any of the pieces is lifted from the base of the cabinet."

"So how was this system defeated?" asked Holmes.

"Unfortunately, the system was not completely finished. Mr Chubb had to return to London late last night to bring some additional apparatus."

"And the valuables were left on open display in the unlocked cabinet?"

"Alas, I am afraid so. But no one of the household would touch them. Even on open display, they would be quite safe for ever if it relied solely on my staff," protested Phillips.

"Pray continue," said Holmes dryly.

"As I have said, there is much preparation taking place at the Hall. Decorators are painting, extra equipment is arriving, foodstuffs are being delivered. In the grounds additional gardeners are employed, livery staff are preparing for an influx of extra coaches and horses. You cannot imagine the turmoil. Of course there are many extraneous people on the premises. I am sure they are all honest tradesmen with honest staff. But this morning a person was seen to enter the hall with a hessian sack."

"Did no one challenge him?" I asked.

"There are people everywhere, coming and going, Dr Watson. This man was seen at various times by several people, but they thought nothing of him, as they have become used to seeing many strangers about all the time. A man with red hair carrying a sack going into the kitchen door could be delivering rabbits or something of that sort. He was seen in the hallway. He was also seen coming round the corner of the stables where he had parked a curious cart."

"What sort of cart?" asked Holmes.

"Well from the way it has been described by various people, and several persons saw it as I shall relate, it seems it was merely a pair of wheels with a small seat on the axle, as it were, and a pair of shafts connecting it to the single pony."

"I can visualise what you mean. Pray go on."

"Well, the man with his sack got on the cart and whipped the pony off. A couple of the stable lads remarked on the strange contraption but did not realise that the man should not have been there."

"Where was the cabinet located?"

"In the hallway at the base of the grand staircase."

"And was all the plate taken?"

"By no means. Of the plate, the gold rose bowl and some small silver pieces are gone, but mainly the tiara and jewellery in the form of necklaces and ear-rings are missing. Fortunately some of the most exquisite pieces were in Lady Egerton's dressing room as she is to wear them at various times over the period of the conference."

"So when were the pieces missed?"

"Almost immediately. I, myself, was passing through the hall and saw the doors swinging open. As I went to close them I saw at once that the display had been rifled."

"What action did you take?"

"I immediately commanded several footmen to position themselves at the doors and instructed them not to permit anybody to leave the house. I sent a boy over to the stables to tell the head groom to set men guarding the gate. I, myself, reported to Lord Egerton who ordered someone to go for the police. It was at that point that Ponsford, the head groom, came up and said it was too late as the man with red hair had been seen galloping off down the drive."

"So the police have been called?"

"Yes, Mr Holmes. But I left before they arrived as shortly afterwards Lord Egerton decided that this was a job for Mr Sherlock Holmes and despatched me to fetch you without delay."

On our arrival at Ashford we found Lord Egerton's coach waiting for us at the station and we were conveyed with speed towards the scene of the crime.

"We may arrive to find that the culprit has been apprehended by the Ashford police and all is well," said Holmes, as the carriage turned in through the mighty pillared gates of Hamden Hall and proceeded up the magnificent straight drive way.

However, the culprit had not been apprehended and all was far from well.

"Welcome, Mr Holmes, I am right glad to see you." The greeting from Lord Egerton was generous and effusive. "This nasty business has put a shade over the preparations for my international conference. I am sure Phillips has explained the position to you?"

"Very clearly, my lord. I understand you have called the local police?"

"Yes, their man is in the library as we speak. I'll take you to him."

We were shown into the library and, after introductions and pleasantries, Lord Egerton and Phillips the butler went about their pressing affairs with the assurance that they would attend on Holmes the instant he required them. We were left with Inspector Rudd from the local force; a dour-looking fellow who did not inspire confidence but turned out to be remarkably efficient.

"I'm glad to see you, Mr Holmes. I know of your reputation, of course. This is a rum business."

"Oh, in what way?"

"Well it seems the thief vanished into thin air."

"Please explain. I know about the circumstances of the theft and the fellow escaping on a pair of wheels."

"Yes, it seems to me the people in charge here were abominably careless. But no more of that. The thief made his escape, as you say, on this two wheeled carriage affair. He went down the drive, which is about half a mile long, to the lodge gates."

"A trifle longer, I fancy," said Holmes.

"Be that as it may, that's the way the fellow left. Now, when you get to the lane, you have a choice of turning left to the village of Hamden or right towards the main London-Dover road. The thief turned right."

"How do you know that?"

"The moment he left the gates coincided with the arrival of Grants Provision Merchants vehicle. In fact the driver had to reign in abruptly to prevent an accident. This chap careered wildly, then shot off down the lane towards the main road. Now, the lane from the lodge gates to the main highway passes chiefly through woodland. There is no turning between the gates and the main road. I must also tell you that on the drive, returning to the Hall after her morning ride, was Miss Hortense, daughter of Lord Egerton, and the thief galloped past her. Miss Hortense reached the stables to find the head groom, Ponsford, with a couple of lads mounted up already and about to give chase, so she joined them."

"A spirited lady," said Holmes.

"Of course the thief had a start, but only a short one. This quartet of horsemen and woman soon met the Grants Provision wagon and thus gained the knowledge that the thief was making for the Dover road. They went off in hot pursuit and coming towards them on the lane was a farmer's cart piled high with hay. They reigned in and the driver said that he had just been passed by the two-wheeler going like the wind, so off they went again and passed nothing else, or caught up with anything, until they reached the London-Dover highway."

"At which point the thief could have gone either way."

"Exactly. But now, Mr Holmes, we come to the interesting part. By a great stroke of good fortune for us, there are repairs taking place at the very junction of the lane and the highway and a night watchman is on duty. He was still at his place."

"So he could tell which way the thief went!" I cried.

"Unfortunately not, sir. He says that he saw no sign of any pony and cart at all, either coming or going along the lane."

"Aha!" said Holmes, rubbing his hands. "The case begins to assume some aspects of interest."

"When the watchman told the pursuers this, they were obliged to retrace their steps and, assuming that the felon had left the lane somewhere within the woods, carefully watched on the way back. There was no sign of him. He had vanished into thin air.

"I have spoken to the Grants Provisions driver, the lodge gate keeper, and the night watchman and confirmed all the particulars I was told. I have examined the lane and whilst there would be room between some of the trees for a pony to pass, it would be impossible for a wheeled cart, not only because of lack of width, but also the nature of the ground. In any case, I saw no tracks of either wheels or horse at the side of the road. If the man had left the lane mounted on the pony he would have had to abandon the cart. There were no signs of such a thing."

"Well, Inspector Rudd, I think you have explained the position very thoroughly. I am sure you will understand if I now conduct my own investigations."

"I would expect you to, Mr Holmes. Now, do you need me to accompany you?"

"I prefer not," said Holmes.

"In that case I will write my report here in the library and then return to Ashford police station. If I have gone on your return you can find me there, should you wish."

"Thank you, you have been most helpful. There is one point I would like to clarify. Did you, yourself, speak to the farmer with the hay cart?"

"No, Mr Holmes, I did not. He had gone on his way long before I arrived."

"No matter."

We left the Inspector and Holmes began his investigation by examining the cabinet. Of course it was now completely empty, the remaining pieces having been placed in safekeeping elsewhere. Holmes thoroughly examined all around with his lens and, as was his wont, examined the floor on his hands and knees. With a grunt he then set off towards the door where the malefactor had made his exit. In short, Holmes traced the entire journey on foot examining everything as he went.

A chat with Ponsford the head groom confirmed all that the Inspector had told us, and so we pressed on down the drive to the lane. As the inspector had stated, it was quite enclosed on either side by dense woodland. It was a fairly narrow lane, but every now and then there was a widening and I should imagine that these areas were relied upon for large farm carts passing one another.

"There does not seem to be any place where a cart, no matter how modest, could pull off the road," I remarked.

"Not without leaving a trace, certainly," agreed Holmes.

Slowly we made our way along the lane. It had been dry for weeks and although there were tracks in the dusty road, it was impossible to say what carts had made them as this lane was the main thoroughfare to the village of Hamden from the London-Dover road. Soon we reached the junction with that main road and immediately saw the works in hand. A few enquiries revealed that the man who had been on watch had returned. Instantly I felt one could take his word as he was a very alert man. I had thought to myself that he had probably slumbered and missed the pony and trap meanwhile, but now I was sure this was not so.

"I understand you were here on watch all night?" asked Holmes.

"That's right, sir. As I told Lord Egerton's groom and Inspector Rudd."

"Now this theft took place fairly early in the morning, soon after the working day had started. The groom and his men chased the pony and trap along this lane."

"They say so. The three of them arrived here, together with a lady on horseback. They were the first people to come along that lane this morning. I will swear to that in a court of law, sir," protested the honest fellow.

"Thank you, I do not for a minute doubt your word. I just need to be clear about it. You did not see a pony and trap?"

"No, sir, I did not."

"Neither did you see a pony and rider?"

"No, sir, I did not."

"You were on duty all the time?"

"I was."

"Please think carefully. Did you desert your post for an instant? Perhaps to relieve yourself?"

"No, sir, I can swear that since the hour of dawn I was on that bench. There was very little traffic, even on the main road, at that time and certainly none on the lane."

"Thank you, you have been most helpful."

So we retraced our steps to the Hall where Phillips had organised some refreshment for us. Inspector Rudd had returned to Ashford. Holmes, with foul fumes emerging from his noxious pipe, brooded. Knowing that my presence was superfluous while Holmes cogitated upon his problem, I went roaming around the magnificent pile that was Hamden Hall.

In the short time we had been there, Lord Egerton and Phillips had devised a scheme of badges so that nobody was admitted to the Hall unbeknownst. All deliveries were left at the door and the staff of the Hall had the additional task of carrying everything indoors. Entrances were limited to a minimum of certain doors and a sentry placed on each. These precautions were to have been implemented once the conference started, but it was now realised that they should have been in place several days in advance.

I returned to find Holmes as I had left him.

"Well, Watson, this is a pretty case. It is not often that we have several witnesses to a crime and still there seems no solution."

"A pony and trap cannot disappear into thin air," I said.

"Of course not," replied Holmes.

"It must have left the side of the lane somewhere, we just haven't found the place."

"Watson, I know it did not leave the lane. I have examined both sides."

"Then it must have gone along the lane one way or the other," said I.

Holmes stared, then leapt to his feet.

"Good old Watson! As usual you put your finger on exactly the right point. How blind I've been. You are the whetstone of my mind! Come on, we must commandeer one of Ponsford's dog-carts and visit the night watchman again."

At the stables we readily obtained a cart with a youth to drive us. Holmes took the opportunity to question Ponsford.

"When you stopped the hay cart to question the driver, was the man known to you?"

"Not known, no. I have seen him around, he's a carrier from over Frosinghurst way. That's the village beyond Hamden."

"A carrier you say?" pounced Holmes. "Not a farmer?"

"Oh no, not a farmer. He's a general carrier, does a trade in transporting things to and from the town, extra vehicles at harvest, meets trains at the station, all that sort of thing. I think he's called Milligan or Mulligan. Something like that."

"Why would he have a huge haystack on his cart this morning?"

"Probably somebody had bought a load of hay and had no means of transporting it so engaged this fellow to do it. That's the kind of way he gets his living."

"Thank you, Ponsford, you've been very helpful, now may we take your cart?"

In no time at all we reached the main London-Dover road and Holmes was pleased to find the watchman still at the roadworks.

"I'm sorry to trouble you again, but I have another question to ask you."

"Ask away, sir. I'm always pleased to assist the law," replied the stout fellow.

"Can you tell me at what time the hay cart passed you?"

"I don't rightly understand you, sir."

"You know the farmer's cart piled high with hay? It came along the road and turned into the lane. How long was that before the party from the Hall came galloping up?" asked Holmes.

"I don't know what you mean, sir," said the fellow in bewilderment. "I saw no cart with hay. This is the first I've heard of it. I was asked about a pony and trap."

"You mean you never saw a hay cart at all?" cried Holmes.

"No, sir. I told you, the first traffic on that lane were the people on horses. I had been here all night and that was the first movement I'd seen. There was some traffic on the main road, but nothing had turned into the lane before they came up."

"Why did you not tell me or Inspector Rudd this before?"

"How could I? Nobody asked about a hay cart," protested the poor fellow. "I said the party of riders from the hall were the first people I'd seen."

"Quite right. Of course. Thank you, my good man. Here, spend this for me."

Holmes gave the watchman a coin and in high glee commanded our driver to return slowly along the lane. Suddenly he called the youth to halt and sprang from the cart. We were at a part where the road widened and Holmes whipped out his lens and prowled about. I remained in the cart and was amused by the expression on our driver's face as he watched Holmes' apparently meaningless antics.

"It's quite all right, boy," I assured him. "Mr Holmes knows what he is doing. He has not taken leave of his senses." I heard a cry "Look, Watson, hay on the hedgerow!"

I looked where Holmes indicated and indeed there were strands of hay caught on the twigs of the hedge. But, as far as I am aware, the countryside is full of hedgerows with hay embedded therein. At last Holmes climbed back aboard flushed with triumph.

"Drive on!" he commanded. "Watson, I am losing my grip. I can not expect to find the truth if I do not ask the right questions. We all assumed that this mysterious cart of hay must have come from the highway and never queried the assumption. We now know that it did not – the watchman could have told us that but he was never asked. I shall never forgive myself. It is clear as day what happened – the hay cart came from the village direction, passed the entrance gates to the Hall and on reaching this wide part in the lane, turned round, to face the way it had just come. The signs are all there, the hay in the hedge where the load scraped along, the tracks at the extreme side of the road. There are several cigarette ends where the driver obviously waited. I should have seen all these things, Watson!"

"But what has the hay cart to do with the theft? I thought we were looking for a pony and trap?"

"The hay cart is the key to the whole affair."

On our return to the Hall, a message from Inspector Rudd awaited Holmes. It read: *The two wheeled cart used by the red-haired thief would appear to be the type used for harness-racing, a sport popular in the country of Ireland. In the United States of America this type of carriage is called a sulky because only one person may ride upon it and could thus be deemed anti-social. I have officers out attempting to trace such a vehicle. Perhaps you will communicate with me at Ashford police station if you make any progress in your investigations. Rudd.*

"Inspector Rudd seems to be alert. However, I think I am ahead of him. We must now go over to Frosinghurst and call upon this Milligan person."

It was early evening by the time we reached Frosinghurst but dusk had not yet fallen. It was salutary to realise that in the country one could not merely hail passing cabs to get about. Everything was much slower and if we had not had Lord Egerton's household to call upon I do not know how readily we could have passed from village to village. The carrier's premises were pointed out to us and we entered a yard which had two or three carts, some spare wheels propped against a wall and an assortment of boxes and barrels. I do not recall visiting a carrier's premises before but I had a distinct impression that this was not a particularly well-run example. Holmes nodded at a huge pile of straw against the side of the house.

"Can I help you, gentlemen?" said a voice with an Irish accent. We turned and looming up behind us was a great beast of a fellow with yellow broken teeth and a scowling visage.

"Ah, Mr Milligan, I presume?" said Holmes in a cheery voice.

"Mulligan. The name's Mick Mulligan," said the beast sourly.

"So sorry, I was told Milligan. Well the fact is, Mr Mulligan, I am looking for a carrier," said Holmes. "I have taken a cottage for the summer and I have some furniture I wish to bring down from London. I can get it on the train, of course, but it will need conveying from the station to the cottage."

"Which cottage is that?" asked Mulligan.

"It is not in this village, it is in Hamden," replied Holmes smoothly.

"Oh yes? Well I know Hamden and I don't know of any cottages to let."

"I assure you I have just agreed the let with Lord Egerton's Estate Manager."

"Oh, one of his," said Mulligan contemptuously. "Why not use a Hamden carrier? There's two there I knows of."

"Really? I did not realise that. I was given your name so came especially to see you about it. You would be interested in the work?"

"Oh, aye, I can do that. I go to Maidstone every Tuesday and Ashford every Friday – that's market day in each town. If you haven't a lot of stuff I could collect it from the train one of those days or if you want a different day I could come specially – that'd cost you a bit more, for a special journey."

"That would be quite all right. I think I would need a special journey. I have a lot of furniture. Would you have a large enough cart? Is this your entire fleet?"

"That's my biggest there. That'd take anything. I've had entire sale rooms piled up on that. You wouldn't want bigger than that."

"No, no, that should be ample. And how about men? Are you alone, you would need assistance in loading."

"Don't you fret about that, sir. My son can come with me and I have other labour I can call upon if required."

Mulligan's hostility gradually dwindled as he smelt money and he became almost civil as he and Holmes made arrangements to transport the entire non-existent contents of a non-existent cottage. Holmes was so convincing I was beginning to picture myself leaning upon a rustic gate in the twilight with a straw in my mouth.

We took our leave with Holmes promising to send the details of the date and time of train when he had made his plans back in Town.

"Watson, as it is Friday tomorrow, I fancy an overnight stay in this village. What do you say? I wonder if the village inn can offer suitable accommodation?"

So saying, we enquired, and having engaged rooms at the inn, despatched Lord Egerton's dog-cart away, requesting that he would return for us at 10am the next day. We had a simple but ample repast, followed by a pint of home-brewed ale in the bar and some pleasant conversation with the local inhabitants before retiring for an early night. Holmes was in convivial mood and promised me that all would be resolved on the morrow and that we would return to London before the day was out.

When I descended to breakfast the next morning the landlord greeted me with the news that my friend had risen some time earlier and had gone out to admire the dawn chorus. I distrusted Holmes' excuse as he is not a great lover of nature, but I knew he would have good reason for being up and about so early, so I contented myself with doing justice to the landlord's ham and eggs. I was just finishing when Holmes appeared, drenched through.

"Good heavens, Holmes, what has happened?"

"Pray order a fresh pot of coffee, Watson, and I will get myself changed. I will then acquaint you with my adventures," he said with a laugh and strolled off to find mine host.

He returned shortly wearing some borrowed garments, for we had brought a minimum of baggage and such as we had was still at Hamden Hall. I poured the coffee and waited for my friend's explanation.

"I really will have to go back to detectives' school, Watson. I have conducted this case abominably. As you know, today is Friday, market day in Ashford. Mulligan goes to market and I suspected he would leave early so I was lurking concealed to see his departure. Sure enough, shortly after first light, he left his yard with a younger red-headed man beside him, presumably his son and almost certainly the thief we seek. I gave them time to get well clear and sufficient time to ensure that they would not return through forgetting something. I then crept into the yard and did some ferreting around. There were several outbuildings, all locked but in such poor repair that I could see through cracks and chinks. In one I saw a sulky."

"Proof enough, surely!" I cried.

"Not in itself, but my case was gathering. I then saw in the back of the yard, a wooden frame, a little like a sow's farrowing pen in shape but much taller and wider. There were distinct traces of hay clinging to it."

"I do not see the significance," said I.

"I believe that framework was mounted on the cart and covered with hay."

"To what purpose?"

"I think the pony and rider were concealed there."

"How artful!" I gasped.

"I believe the cart was waiting with a ramp already in place. The son galloped up, unharnessed the pony, placed the sulky on its side in the framework and led the pony inside and concealed himself with it. Mulligan then lifted the ramp and arranged the straw over the entrance. They then set off back home."

"Diabolically ingenious," I breathed.

"Never underestimate the Irish." said Holmes drily, "I was peering through a split in a plank wall when I was deluged with a bucket of filthy water. I turned to face an Irish harridan who shrieked at me some incomprehensible gibberish of which I made out the words *you snooping, skulking spalpeen* before she started belabouring me with a yard-brush."

"Good heavens, Holmes."

"Yes, the great detective was driven out. And serve me right, Watson. What a bungling fool not to ascertain if the premises were occupied. I should have given thought that Mulligan was likely to have a wife. I deserved all I got," Holmes said ruefully.

"What will you do now? Surely Mrs Mulligan will raise the alarm?"

"I have done all that is required. I concealed myself and saw Mrs Mulligan approach a fellow who was nearby sharpening stakes. He immediately disappeared and reappeared on a decrepit horse and trotted off, no doubt going to Ashford market to warn Mulligan. The parish constable here, in whom I confided, has already set off to report to Inspector Rudd. On our transport arriving at 10 o'clock we will, ourselves, arrange a posse with Lord Egerton and I have no doubt that with these efforts the miscreants will be caught. Do pour another cup of coffee, Doctor."

The Mulligans, father and son, were duly apprehended as planned and Holmes' reputation was unsullied. Mr Chubb had returned to complete the security system on his cabinet and the treasures were once again placed on display, ready to impress the delegates at Lord Egerton's international conference. On the train returning to London Holmes laughed out loud.

"Lord Egerton has been exceedingly generous in his remuneration. It is fortunate he does not realise at how many points I almost bungled his case. Watson, if at some future date I appear to show overweening confidence in my powers, just whisper to me the words *Mrs Mulligan.*"

The Singular Adventure
of
THE DISAPPEARING BUBBLES

"How do you fancy a trip to the seaside, Watson?" asked my friend Mr Sherlock Holmes one summer day. I was somewhat surprised to hear this suggestion as Holmes was very much a man of the city and disliked leaving it unnecessarily.

"That is not like you, Holmes," I answered.

"It may not be necessary but, as I am expecting a client who is the Chairman of the Town Council in Ullacombe which appears to be a seaside resort in Devon, I fear I may have to travel to the West Country."

"Well I would certainly be pleased to accompany you if that event should come to pass. London has been particularly stifling this summer."

At that moment our expected visitor was announced.

"What brings you all this way from your seaside dwelling, Mr Trevillion?" asked Holmes pleasantly.

"Oh, Mr Holmes, there are grave crimes taking place in our pleasant corner of the country."

"Indeed?"

"We have had a rather nasty murder."

"Perhaps you will relate the facts?"

"There is really little to tell. Last week the body of a young woman was found underneath the pier. Well, we like to call it a pier but really it is little more than a jetty. Ullacombe is a very small family resort but we have a lovely sandy bay with donkey rides, the pier, and a bandstand where concerts are given two or three times a week."

"Who was the unfortunate woman?"

"Well we don't really know. She wasn't a local person."

"A holiday maker you mean?"

"We don't know; nobody has stepped forward to identify her. We think perhaps she may be a seasonal worker. In summer we have an influx of workers in the area at the hotels, restaurants and so on."

"No doubt you have notified the local police and they are efficiently dealing with the matter. Why have you come to me?"

"Well, Mr Holmes, if that had been the full story, I would not have dreamed of troubling you; but a further rather peculiar incident has occurred and the local police do not know if it is connected with the woman's murder or not. They are nonplussed by the event and inclined to dismiss the affair as trivial. I, myself, am sure there is a connection. Why, otherwise, should our Punch & Judy man vanish."

"You do not make yourself clear, sir. Please explain the connection between the murder and the Punch & Judy man."

"I am sorry, Mr Holmes. I must calm down and explain. The girl was murdered last week."

"You did not say in what manner, Mr Trevillion"

"Oh, the police say she was battered to death, with a rock from the shore."

"How terrible," I murmured.

"Then the very next day, in the middle of his performance, the Punch & Judy man disappeared."

"How do you mean disappeared?"

"He vanished."

"Vanished?"

"In the middle of his performance, he just vanished."

"I am sorry, sir, I must ask you to explain in further detail. I do not seem to have grasped the point of your statement."

"I will explain. Every day in the summer season we have a Punch & Judy show on the beach. It is presented by Uncle Bubbles. He sets up his booth on the sand, facing the promenade, with his back to the sea. He performs at 11am and 3pm each day. He is very popular. The children love Mr Punch. Uncle Bubbles always attracts a good crowd. The children sit on the sand and the grownups stand round, some on the beach and some watching from the promenade."

"I understand the explanation. Now what is this about a disappearance?"

"Well, Uncle Bubbles was half way through his show when it suddenly stopped."

"Stopped?"

"Yes. The dolls were withdrawn and the show stopped."

"What happened then?"

"The children started shouting for Mr Punch to come back, but when nothing happened one or two of the bolder men rushed round the back to see if perhaps Uncle Bubbles had fainted or something like that."

"And what did they find."

"Nothing."

"Nothing?"

"No, there was no Uncle Bubbles in the booth."

"How extraordinary!" I burst out in surprise.

"Did nobody see him come out?" queried Holmes.

"No. There were people watching all the time. The local bobby reckons a hundred people were present that afternoon. He could not possibly have left the booth unseen."

Holmes rubbed his hands together with a kind of glee. "What happened then?"

"Lillian – that's Uncle Bubbles' wife, she goes round with the hat for him –"

"Goes round with a hat?"

"Yes, collecting pennies from the crowd. That's how the show is paid for."

"I see – do go on."

"Well, Lillian was just standing there repeating 'He's gone, just vanished' over and over."

Holmes pondered a moment then asked "Why do you think this extraordinary incident is connected to the death of the woman on the previous day?"

"Well I don't really know. We have had Uncle Bubbles every summer for eight years and there has never been trouble of any kind but then we have a horrible murder and the very next day Uncle Bubbles disappears in this odd fashion. There must be some connection."

"You say your local police do not necessarily think so?"

"No, they do not know what to make of the disappearance of Uncle Bubbles but say it is no crime to vanish."

"But surely he could be a murder suspect!" cried I. "They must take cognisance of this incident."

"Exactly my sentiments, Dr Watson. I have expressed myself very forcibly on the matter. It is because of that I have come to appeal to you, Mr Holmes. There is nobody in our part of the world who could deal with a matter like this."

"When crimes are beyond the local constabulary it is the custom for detectives to be sent from a larger force, even London, if necessary."

"We only have a local bobby in Ullacombe, but this matter is being dealt with by detectives from Exeter."

"I see. Well I must confess your story intrigues me."

"Do you think you could come in person and investigate? You see we are a small family resort and if the news of the murder becomes widespread it could well prevent families coming for their holidays. The news has hardly had time to circulate but already there have been some cancellations. If the story gets out that our Punch & Judy man is responsible for this heinous crime nobody will bring their children to us ever again."

"You, yourself, suspect that Uncle Bubbles is responsible and has fled?"

"Well I do not like to think that. I have known the man eight years and he always seemed a harmless sort of fellow to me, but I confess it does rather point that way."

"Can you arrange rooms for us both at Ullacombe? We will set off in the morning."

"Oh, Mr Holmes, I cannot tell you how grateful I am. Of course, you shall be most comfortable at the Imperial Hotel – it is the best in town."

"Then please engage rooms and say we will be there in time for dinner."

Ullacombe proved to be a quaint old fashioned place that seemed popular with small families who had small children. It was quite genteel and the thought of a murder of a young woman would be abhorrent and unbelievable to anybody who knew the area. We were comfortably placed in the Imperial, a slightly dowdy but friendly hotel catering for families. I noted that the children we came across in the hotel were all exceptionally polite and well behaved.

The morning of the day following our arrival brought an early visit by Mr Trevillion and a policeman in uniform.

"This is Constable Stirling, our local man on the beat."

"Good morning, gentlemen, Stirling by name and, I like to think, sterling by nature."

"Good morning to you, constable. I shall have much to ask you about," said Holmes in his friendliest manner.

"You ask away, sir. It is a great honour you do us by coming all this way from London to probe into our criminal affairs," replied the stout guardian of the law.

After bidding farewell to Mr Trevillion we walked abroad in the company of Constable Stirling who took us to the scene of the crime. In truth it was a gross exaggeration to call the flimsy wooden jetty a pier but I suppose the Town Council try to make as much as possible of their limited amenities.

"Just here, sir, by this stanchion. The girl was found face downwards with the back of her head stove in."

"By a rock, I believe?" asked Holmes.

"That's right. The rock was lying alongside her, covered in blood. The sight fair made me feel sick."

"Were you the first to find her?"

"Oh no, sir. Not at all. She was found by a chap coming down to do some early morning fishing. He raced back up to the café where the owner had just arrived to take his deliveries. It was he who came round to my house and roused me. By the time I got here there were quite a few people about."

"What did you do?" asked Holmes.

"I asked Barmwell the café man if he had any canvas. He came back with both canvas and boards and we made a sort of tent over the body. I then asked the fisherman, who was a chap I knew, to stand guard while I went to telephone my head office. Men came within the hour and, shortly after, the body was taken away and I was told to keep guarding the place until detectives came out from Exeter. I was there all day and well into the evening before they had finished."

"I see. I understand nobody has identified the woman?"

"No, but that's not surprising, is it? Even if somebody knew her they would not own up to it, would they?" answered the bobby.

"I do not understand you, why do you say that?"

"Well, she was but a prostitute. Nobody respectable would identify her."

"I see. Your Town Chairman said she was likely to be a seasonal hotel worker."

"He wouldn't like to think that his pretty little town harboured the likes of prostitutes. But she was one of those all right. You did not have to be a policeman to know that."

"Are you telling me that prostitutes are commonplace in this town?" asked Holmes.

"Oh no, sir. But they do exist. Well hidden, but they exist. You see, these respectable families come down here for the summer but after a week or so papa gets bored and starts asking around to find out if there is any grown up fun to be had. There is a certain amount of gambling and whoring takes place in the neighbourhood. Not here in the town centre, but round and about there are places."

"And you turn a blind eye to it?" asked Holmes.

"Certainly not, sir. I do not. I am ever vigilant, but they are very close these villains who carry out that business and they are very fly. Very fly indeed. They know how to keep within the law. I have been on their tail several times but they are always one step ahead. The places where they meet are always changing. But I'll catch them one day."

"I wish you luck," said Holmes. "Now please show me exactly where the Punch & Judy booth was situated."

We were taken over to a place on the beach which was now busy with little ones and their fond parents playing in the sand. The spot the constable indicated was about forty feet from the sea wall that supported the promenade.

"Uncle Bubbles always built up here. That way people could watch from the prom as well as the beach."

"I see. And what is the booth like?" asked Holmes.

"Oh, you know, tall, striped canvas on a wooden frame."

"How big are the dimensions?"

"Oh, I couldn't say. About a yard each way and about seven feet tall. Something like that. Actually you can see it at the council offices over the road. It was taken there after Uncle Bubbles disappeared. It's still there all built up, dollies and all."

"Then let us go and have a look."

The booth was typical of such puppet theatres. Just large enough for one man to stand in and work the puppets above his head. The way to enter the booth was via a long slit making a flap of the canvas at the rear. The policeman pulled the flap and held it clear so that we could all peer inside. The stage was a small wooden ledge in front of a large square opening which was edged with an elaborately carved and painted frame. Inside the booth the puppets were hanging upside down from hooks screwed into the wooden cross-pieces that supported the upright poles. Each puppet had a little ring at the bottom of its dress. Holmes took up Mr Punch and one other doll and put them on his hands and held them above his head in the approved fashion.

"They are quite a weight, Watson."

"Yes, sir," spoke up the bobby. "It is not an easy job showing the puppets. The heads are all carved from wood. Mr Punch usually goes on the right hand and is on stage most of the time. Uncle Bubbles brings the others on and off using his left hand. He gets into them as they hang there. Plunges his hand in – like a glove."

"You seem well versed in the business, constable," said Holmes.

"Yes, sir. I've watched the show many a time as I've passed on my round. And I know Percy pretty well after all these years."

"Percy being Uncle Bubbles?"

"That's right, sir. Percy Preston."

"Then you must also know Mrs Preston?"

"Oh yes, I know Lil. A grand bottler she is."

"Bottler?"

"Yes. That's what they call the chap who goes round with the hat."

"Then why is he called a bottler and not a hatter?"

"Ah well, according to Percy, in the olden days they used to collect the pennies in a bottle. That way the Punch man could hear if the bottler tried to shake some pennies out for his own benefit. Once in the bottle the coins were supposed to stay there until after the show when the Punch man could tip the pennies out and divvy up the loot. Percy used to say the best bottler was a one-armed man because he couldn't get the money out without your knowing. 'Course Lil being his wife, there's no bother about sharing the collection so she uses a hat; thinks it's more friendly."

"There is a hat on top of the booth," said Holmes. "Is that the one Mrs Preston uses for the collection?"

"That's the one. She always puts it up there out of the way," answered Stirling.

"Well we must certainly interview Mrs Preston, but I would like to try to find somebody who can tell us exactly what they saw while watching the show. Do you know of anybody we could approach?"

"I certainly do, sir. I myself saw it all."

"You did?" cried Holmes. "Then please describe everything in particular detail."

"Let us step back to the promenade, gentlemen, and I will explain from the exact vantage point," replied the stout fellow.

So we retraced our steps to the promenade. Stirling halted alongside a bench where three formidable-looking matrons were chatting. They glanced up as we stood alongside them but then resumed their gossiping.

"I was standing exactly here. Now, see where that little tot is counting pebbles? Well, as near as I can tell the booth was set up down there."

"The stage was facing this way and the back with the entrance slit was facing the sea?" clarified Holmes.

"That's right, sir, exactly that."

"Please continue."

"When I arrived here Uncle Bubbles was in front of the booth performing conjuring tricks. He usually does that for ten minutes or so to attract a crowd. Lil gets the little ones to sit on the sand in front and she tries to get the adults to come closer. I don't know why it is but the adults always want to hang back and watch from a distance. The Council don't like too much of the beach taken up with a scattered crowd. Lil does her best but it is a problem. She reckons they want to see the show while avoiding putting pennies in her hat."

"So there is some clear area around the booth?"

"Oh yes, of course it's all clear behind except for Percy's bits and pieces."

"What are they?"

"Oh, nothing much. His box that he carries the puppets in and a pair of wheels that he clamps to the booth so that he can move it without dismantling. There is less space at the sides because as the show goes on people tend to gather there."

"So there is no gap or space between the booth and the edge of the crowd?"

"Oh yes, there's always two or three yards; people won't be able see if they are too sideways on."

"I understand, pray continue."

"Well, after conjuring, Uncle Bubbles went behind the booth and the show started. All went as normal until the part where Mr Punch throws the baby out of the window –"

"Good heavens! What can you mean?" expostulated Holmes. It was obvious to me that Holmes had never seen a Punch & Judy show.

"Mr Punch is given the baby to mind and he hits it with his stick then throws it out into the audience."

"The baby is a tiny doll in swaddling clothes," I explained to Holmes.

"Ah."

"Well Uncle Bubbles takes Mr Punch down out of view and comes out round to the front where one of the children hands him the baby. Uncle Bubbles then lobs it back inside the booth and goes back in himself. Mr Punch comes back with the baby and then throws it out again. The boys and girls have got the idea now and toss the baby back. This happens three or four times."

"That seems rather tedious," remarked Holmes.

"Oh they love it, the little ones. Percy says he could go on doing that all day and they would never tire."

"How extraordinary," murmured Holmes.

"Well after a bit of that business, Mr Punch went down and didn't return. The show just stopped. The children started shouting for Mr Punch but he didn't come back up. It became apparent that something was amiss and two chaps dashed round behind the booth. I thought I had better investigate so made my way to those steps there and descended to the beach. When I got round the back of the booth Lil was there, just saying over and over 'He's not here. He's gone.' There was quite a group of people so I dispersed them.

Gradually the excitement faded and the people dwindled away to do other things."

"Thank you for your summation. I have a very clear picture of the proceedings."

"But where did he go, Mr Holmes? Percy couldn't just disappear into thin air."

"Of course not, he must have slipped away unobserved."

"He could not possibly have done that, Mr Holmes. All eyes were focussed on the booth. We would all have seen him emerge."

"When we have eliminated the impossible, whatever remains, no matter how highly improbable, must be the truth."

"So we must search for the highly improbable!" cried Stirling.

"Once we have eliminated the impossible," said Holmes blandly. "I would like to see Mrs Preston now. Do you know where she lives?"

"16 Finkle Street. You go up the High Street and it's the third turn on the right. There's a cobblers' shop on the corner. But I don't think she's there. I think she has returned to London."

"To London?"

"Yes, the Prestons live there. He only comes down in the summer to work on the beach here. The rest of the year I think he goes round the grand houses doing children's parties and such. Mrs Mowatt is the owner of the house in Finkle Street; she lets out a room to the Prestons every summer."

"I see. Well thank you once more for your help, Stirling. How can I find you if I have future need?"

"My house is just behind the Council Office. Ask anybody for the policeman's house. They will direct you."

"Thank you. Come, Watson."

We found Mrs Mowatt's house very easily and Holmes knocked at the door. It was some time before it opened unto us, preceded by much twitching of the window curtains and the drawing of bolts. When it did open it revealed but a small chink of the landlady's face as there was a heavy chain across restraining the door from opening more than a crevice.

"What do you want?" demanded the woman.

"Mrs Mowatt?" asked Holmes in his most dulcet tones.

"Yes," snapped the visage.

"We are looking for Mrs Preston –"

Before Holmes could say another word the harridan screeched "I told the other two. She's not here. She's gone back home to Manchester."

"We were enquiring about the puppets and booth," said Holmes.

"They've gone. Everything's gone. She's taken them all with her to Manchester and she won't be coming back. You'll have to look for her in Manchester." And with that she slammed the door in our faces. I stared at Holmes in dismay.

"Should I ask if the good lady can accommodate us for the night?" said Holmes whimsically.

"Good Lord, what a dragon!" I said with feeling.

"Come, Watson. We can find out nothing further here."

"Nothing further? We haven't found out anything at all," I protested.

"On the contrary. We have found out two important things."

"Really? What things are those?"

"We have found out that, prior to ourselves, another two men have been enquiring."

"Is that significant?"

"I think that is most significant when you recall that the first people to react to Uncle Bubbles' disappearance were two men who ran round to the back of the booth."

"Ah yes. I recall the constable saying that."

"And the second thing is that Mrs Preston is almost surely not in Manchester."

"Why do you say that?"

"Because in the few words Mrs Mowatt had to say she was very insistent to tell us that Mrs Preston had gone home to Manchester. She told us that three times. According to Constable Stirling the Preston's home is normally in London. We also know that she wasn't telling the truth about the puppet show as we have just been examining it. As the show obviously has not gone to Manchester I think it most unlikely that the owner has."

We returned to the promenade and Holmes expressed a wish to speak to the café proprietor so we entered and ordered coffees and scones.

"Mr Barnwell?" The man nodded assent. "We have been retained by Mr Trevillion your Town Clerk to make enquiries about the murder of that unfortunate female. I understand you helped Constable Stirling to cover the body with canvas?"

"That's correct, sir, I did. She was not a fit sight for Christians to behold."

"Did you know the woman?"

"Certainly not! I'm surprised you should think that, sir."

"I apologise; I just wondered if you had seen her before, when she was alive, perhaps on a previous day?"

"Well, yes, I had seen her from time to time, hanging about the pier. She seemed to suddenly appear about three weeks ago and I did see her now and then late at night. Never during the day. You see, sir, some nights I have to stay late to clean out the kitchen and dining room because of opening so early for the morning fishermen. I have seen one or two women hanging about there. I just presumed they were up to no good. You know, sir, women of the streets."

"I understand. So you say there were other women besides the one unfortunately killed?"

"Well I can't really say. I took no notice of them. They were just figures in the dark, you see. There was the one done to death, the small one and a taller one. I don't know how many more. As I say, I took no notice."

"Thank you for your assistance," said Holmes politely. "Your scones are very satisfying, Mr Barmwell. Keep the change."

"Why, thank you, sir," replied the proprietor taking the proffered coin.

"Not much help, there, Holmes," I remarked.

"No, the people of this town are singularly unforthcoming. I suggest we go our own ways now, Watson. I want to see Stirling again and you, if you would be so kind, while you enjoy the sun and amenities of this pleasure resort, might see if you can quiz any other eye witnesses to the disappearance of Uncle Bubbles. We will meet up at dinner at the hotel."

The afternoon of that day was one of the most pleasant that I have ever spent. I strolled along the promenade and treated myself to an ice cream. I then followed a winding path that took me away from the little bay and led to a beautiful cliff top vista. Sitting down, I leaned against a rock and dozed off in the warm sunshine. On waking I retraced my steps to the promenade and had a spot of late lunch in a delightful little café. I then ventured to walk down to the edge of the sea to paddle my toes in the water. While walking back across the sands I came upon a mama with two little children who were wailing because their sand castle kept collapsing. I paused.

"I am an architect and structural engineer. If you do not think me presumptuous I believe I can discern the flaw in your construction," I said in avuncular tones. The two little mites gawped at me.

"I am sure my children would value your expertise, sir," their pretty young mother replied. I then explained that the sand was too dry and they must take their little tin buckets to the waters' edge and fill them with water. "Come, I will go with you," said I. So we trooped to the sea, filled the buckets and returned. We then spent a jolly hour making a very fine sand castle.

"I'm very grateful to you, sir, for entertaining my little ones. Are you really a structural engineer?"

"No, I confess I told an untruth; I am a doctor – but doctors cannot be expected to know about sand castles can they?"

She laughed heartily. "Well I am obliged to you, Dr –?"

"Watson," I supplied, "Dr John Watson, and very glad to be of service."

"My children are feeling disappointed. At this time of day it is usually possible to watch the conjuror doing Punch & Judy but it seems he is no longer appearing."

"No. Last Wednesday he suddenly left and has not been seen since."

"A most peculiar affair. We were all there watching. One minute we were laughing at Mr Punch's antics, the next minute they stopped and the operator had vanished."

"So I have heard. I think he must have slipped away unseen for some reason."

"Oh no, Dr Watson, everybody would have seen him. It is impossible for a man in a clown suit, ginger wig and red nose to make himself unobtrusive."

"I suppose so. Can you recall what happened when it was realised that Uncle Bubbles had disappeared?"

"I think the first people to realise were two men who rushed round the back of the little theatre. Then they ran up to the promenade. I presume they went to summon the police as a policeman appeared very soon and dealt with the situation."

"What did the two men look like?"

"Well, to be honest, Dr Watson, they were rather rough looking men – not untidy, they were neatly dressed – but they looked as though they may have been labourers. Not at all the sort of men one expects to see in Ullacombe, and certainly not watching a Punch & Judy show."

The children were beginning to whine and become tiresome so mama declared they would leave the beach in search of tea. I tipped my panama, bade them all good afternoon and went on my way. The idea of tea seemed a good idea so I repaired to the lounge of the Grand Hotel where a string quartet was scraping away accompanied by the sound of tinkling cups and saucers. I was just leaving when a pleasant looking fellow stepped alongside me.

"I saw you in there; it did not look as though torturing catgut is your kind of entertainment."

"It's a jolly enough adjunct to a cup of tea," I replied.

"If you want something a bit more lively, there's a party on tonight."

"Really?"

"Yes. Gentlemen only. In the upstairs rooms of the Crown."

"The Crown?"

"Yes, it's a pub at the back of town. Keep going up the High Street as far as you can then turn right when the road bends left. Everybody knows it."

"And who's giving this party?" I asked.

"Oh, they have them twice a week in the summer. There's a small admission charge."

"I see."

"But don't tell the missus." The man winked and nudged my arm. "There are a few sporty gals there and two or three card schools. You'll enjoy it. Here, take this card – show that at the door and you'll get in for half price."

"Thank you, I might just do that."

"See you there then. Any time after ten o'clock," said my new friend wandering off.

This was obviously one of the dens of vice that Constable Stirling had told us about. I looked forward to telling Holmes about my day. It had been rather fruitful. I had had confirmation about the disappearance of Uncle Bubbles, and I must say the presence of the two men seemed very significant, especially when I recalled that Mrs Mowatt had screeched at us about two men. It seemed to me they must have been the same two. Now I had gained knowledge of where this clandestine gentlemen-only party was to take place. I looked forward to hearing

Holmes' praises for my efforts. However I was to be disappointed as, on arrival at the hotel to dress for dinner, the reception clerk had a message for me saying Holmes was detained and would not be dining with me.

By 11 o'clock Holmes had still not returned so I set forth on my own to investigate this mysterious gentlemen's party. On arriving at the entrance I was somewhat taken aback to have two guineas demanded of me, but on my showing the card given to me this was, as promised, reduced to one guinea. I entered a large room which at first sight seemed sumptuously furnished but on closer inspection the furnishings were tawdry rather than elegant. A couple of card schools were under way and there was a billiard table at one end of the room. A bar occupied the other end. I was immediately accosted by a pair of young women and before I knew what was happening I had bought a bottle of champagne at a ludicrous price.

I will not weary the reader with the *minutiae* of the evening. I observed that occasionally one of the men would disappear through a door in the corner accompanied by one of the women. If I write the phrase 'wine, women and song' – with a mixture of upper class men and low born women – I think that will suffice. I was getting fed up and debating with myself whether there was any point in staying longer when a portly chap struck up a conversation with me.

"Hello, old sport," he said. "I haven't seen you here before. Is it your first time?"

"Yes, I have only recently come to stay in the town," I replied.

"It's usually a bit jollier than this. Dull lot of fellows tonight, only seem interested in gambling."

"Not as lively as usual then?"

"Well it varies with the company of course, but this is very quiet. You should be here when Percy's in – he's a real scream."

"Oh?"

"Yes, I've never known such a man for jokes. Don't know where he gets them all from."

"It's a pity he's not here tonight then. Perhaps he will still come along?"

"Oh no, he's left town. Did you not hear? He mysteriously disappeared in the middle of his Punch and Judy show. The whole town's talking about it."

"Oh, that Percy."

"Yes. Not the sort of chap one would normally mix with is he? But he is quite an asset to this club with his card tricks and jokes."

"Club?"

"Well, it's not a club, of course, but we regulars like to think of it as one."

"Are you on holiday?"

"Me? No. I live here. I am a man of leisure. Daddy left me a tin mine and I sold it at a good profit."

"So Percy Preston is a regular here?"

"Old Percy is here most nights. I think the management pay him a few shillings to liven up the scene."

"They say he's done a runner because he murdered that poor woman under the jetty last week."

"Pier, sport. That jetty is a pier."

"Pier then. Was the woman from this club?"

"Oh no. I think it's common knowledge that she was a tart from Bristol trying to ply her game here. Nothing to do with our Percy. He's only a hired entertainer."

"But why was she killed?"

The man lowered his voice. "I shouldn't say too much about that here, sport. I suspect that the men running this place didn't want any competition – no matter how humble."

"But that's terrible!" I cried.

"Shush, keep your voice down. The fellows that did that girl in might well be lurking about in here."

"I do not think this is the sort of place where I would like to linger."

"Stay! Have a nightcap before you go. I say, this is one of Percy's jokes – two tarts on holiday from London were paddling in the sea and one says to the other "Ere, Sal, your feet 'aint 'arf mucky' and Sal says 'Well I couldn't come last year.' That's rich isn't it! Ha! Ha! Ha!"

"I'm off now. Good night, sport," I said sarcastically, and left.

As I made my way down the dark side alley that led to the main thoroughfare two men stepped out and blocked my way.

"We'd like a word with you, Mr Sherlock Holmes," said the older of the pair.

"I am not Sherlock Holmes," I replied.

"Don't give us that. We know all about you. Coming down here from London to snoop into affairs that don't concern you."

"I assure you my name is not Sherlock Holmes," I protested.

"I don't care what your name is. Just listen – and listen good. Get out of this town first thing in the morning and don't come back. And here's something to take back to London with you!" The villain raised his hand and I discerned in the gloom the shape of some sort of cudgel. The smaller and younger of the pair got behind me and tried to pinion my arms. When being attacked by footpads the natural inclination is to recoil but over my years of accompanying Holmes on his missions I had picked up a trick or two and I suddenly dropped forward into the fellow's nether regions and grappled him around in a rugby tackle. I am not sure but I think the cudgel blow landed on his confederate. However, powerfully built as I am, I was in a hopeless position against two villains with clubs. The three of us were in a tangled *mêlée* in the dark alley when I heard a welcome voice "There they are, constable, quick, bring your lamp!"

On hearing this, my assailants immediately ceased their blows and fled into the night.

"Are you all right, Watson?" My rescuer was Sherlock Holmes.

"Holmes, am I glad to see you!" I exclaimed in relief, struggling to my feet.

"Take it easy, old chap. Are you badly hurt?"

"No, no. They had only just started their work when you two interrupted."

"I am on my own, Watson, but I thought it expedient to pretend otherwise. I am sure together we would have been more than a match for them but I fear they would not have stuck to the Queensbury Rules."

"But what are you doing here, Holmes?"

"I have not long returned from Exeter where I have been consulting with the detectives who are active on this case. When I saw your note saying where you had gone, I immediately followed."

"I got a lead, Holmes. I was investigating a sink of iniquity."

"Yes, old fellow, I know. Do not try to talk now. Let us get you back to the hotel. It may not seem so to you, but this little incident is the best thing that could have happened. Come, lean on me."

When I went down to breakfast the following morning I was pleased to see Holmes heartily tucking into his kedgeree.

"Good morning, Watson. How are you?"

"A trifle sore about the ribs, and a swollen lip but very little else."

"I'm sorry I was not able to join you for dinner last evening. I did not get back until midnight. I trust you spent a pleasant day?"

"A pleasant afternoon and a very interesting evening. I was following clues on your behalf."

"Excellent. And what have you found out for me?"

"Well the poor girl who was so foully murdered was most likely a prostitute from Bristol and was killed by bully boys from a gang who control all the crime in this area." I paused, awaiting Holmes praise.

"Price and McCoy. Price is a retired third rate pugilist. McCoy is simply a thug."

"You know their names?" I gasped.

"Yes, Watson. They are the men who attacked you last night.

"How do you know all this?"

"By the simple means of conferring with the detectives who are on the case. The law in Ullacombe as represented by Constable Stirling is useless but the men from Exeter are most efficient and needed little help from me. They know all the local villains and suspicions fell on Price and McCoy immediately. Unfortunately the law requires proof and time and time again these villains get away with things because people are too afraid to testify against them. To make matters worse, in a place like Ullacombe, whose entire income is derived from visitors, everybody has a vested interest in not rocking the boat. Now Price and McCoy made the mistake of attacking you, the police can round them up under the charge of grievous bodily harm, and you can identify them."

"Yes, I will certainly recognise them again. But what about Uncle Bubbles? I suppose they told you where he is too?"

"Alas no, and I am bound to say that, infuriating as it may be to the audience, it is not a criminal act to vanish halfway through the performance."

"But there must be a connection between the girl's death and Uncle Bubbles' disappearance?"

"I am sure there is."

"Well what connection could there be?"

"You will recall that all the eyewitnesses of the events at the Punch & Judy show mention two men running round the back of the booth? I think those men were Price and McCoy. Further, I am of the opinion that these men were known to Bubbles, that he knew they were there and were after him, and somehow he took the opportunity to flee."

"Why should these bully boys be after Bubbles?" I asked.

"It is possible that he was a witness to the murder. He probably saw it happen quite by chance, then fled. But Price and McCoy recognised him and thus needed to shut him up before he gave them away. However, I cannot understand why Bubbles should not inform the police if that were the case."

"I cannot answer that, Holmes, but I can tell you that Percy Preston is a regular attraction at these men-only parties. He does card ticks and tells jokes to the customers."

"Excellent, Watson, you have done well. It is clear that there is a strong connection between the murder and the defection."

I confess I glowed with an inner pride at my friend's words. So often I have tried to be useful to him but he is usually one step ahead of me. While I was still basking in his praise we had a visitor. It was Mr Trevillion who approached bearing a sheet of paper.

"I am sorry to interrupt your breakfast, gentlemen, but this morning our town clerk received this letter and naturally I have brought it straight round to you." Mr Trevillion held out the paper to Holmes who, after reading it, passed it to me. This is what I read: *To Mr Rawley, Town Clerk, Town Hall, Ullacombe, Devon. Dear Mr Rawley, I am very sorry that personal matters made it necessary for me to leave Ullacombe without any notice. I regret that personal matters also prevent me from coming back. I have found a replacement to work the show if you will kindly engage him on the same terms as me. He is called Professor Hobson and is a very well known punch man in London and does a very good show. He does not dress up or do the conjuring. I am sending him down and if you want him to stay he will work my show at the usual times. If you do not want him then he will pack up my equippage and bring it away back to London. I am sorry if I have caused any trouble to your visiters. I hope my long association with Ullacombe will excuse me. Your obedient servant, Percy Preston (Uncle Bubbles).*

"Well I am very pleased to learn that Mr Preston is safe," said Mr Trevillion as I handed back the letter. "I regret that you have been summoned for a wild goose chase, Mr Holmes, although the police have not yet found the murderer. My mind is eased somewhat. It is unlikely to be Mr Preston. He would hardly send a note like this if he were implicated in the murder."

"Very unlikely, of course, certainly," replied Holmes in a distant manner. "That is a rather odd sentence in Preston's letter. He tells us that Professor Hobson does not dress up or do conjuring tricks. What do you suppose that means?"

"Well," said Trevillion, "I presume he means that the new man does not – er, dress up, or – er, do conjuring tricks –" he tailed off lamely.

"But he does not say Professor Hobson does not juggle or do acrobatic postures either. The implication being that although Hobson does a Punch & Judy show like Bubbles he does not, however, do conjuring tricks like Bubbles nor dress like Bubbles."

"Yes, I presume that is exactly what he means," affirmed Mr Trevillion.

"In what way did Bubbles 'dress up'?" asked Holmes.

"In a clown's outfit," replied Trevillion.

"With a ginger wig and a red nose," I added.

Holmes stared at me. "You were aware of this fact, Watson?"

"Why yes. People who described his disappearance made a point of saying that one could not miss a man dressed so outrageously."

Holmes groaned audibly and smote his forehead. "Is it possible you have a photograph of Uncle Bubbles in his costume, Mr Trevillion?"

"I am sure Rawley will have one. I will have one sent over."

"No, I will call in at your office. I must return to London."

"But, I do not understand! We do not know why our entertainer fled, how he disappeared, who murdered the stranger under the pier, or anything," protested Trevillion.

"I am quite clear on the answers to all those questions, Mr Tevillion, but to complete my investigations I must return to London. Before we leave I wish to have another word with Constable Stirling."

Finding Stirling ambling along the promenade, Holmes showed him the newly acquired photograph which was printed on an advertising leaflet that Preston obviously used to send to prospective customers.

"I would like to ask one or two questions, constable," said Holmes.

"Fire away, sir."

"This clown costume of Bubbles. Is it all in one piece?"

"Yes, it's a sort of coverall garment made from a very light material. Cotton I suppose, I'm not really up on that sort of thing."

"And he wears that over his normal clothing?"

"Yes, he says it makes him stand out, draws attention to himself as he parades along the beach banging his drum to attract custom to his show."

"And the wig?"

"That's made from ginger wool. It just pulls on like a hat."

"And the nose?"

"I think that is made from a red rubber ball. Something of that nature. It is held on by means of a piece of elastic round the head."

"So it would only be a matter of seconds to doff the nose and wig?"

"Oh yes. He takes them off when he goes into the booth."

"And the cotton suit?"

"He usually keeps that on but it only takes a minute to step in or out of it. He has two or three of those. Lil is always washing them."

"Thank you, constable. There is one more thing. When you were watching the show at the time of the disappearance you said that Bubbles came out in the middle of the show to retrieve the baby that Punch had thrown into the audience?"

"That's right, Mr Holmes."

"Does he usually do that?"

The constable paused and then said "No, he's never done that before. I never gave that a thought. No, Lil is usually standing at the side of the children and she throws it back in before she starts going round with the hat."

"But on this occasion, Lil was not in view?"

"No, no. I didn't see her. She was already round at the back of the booth when I went round. She was just standing there saying over and over 'He's gone, he's not here, he's gone'."

"Thank you constable, you have been most helpful. Keep up the good work. Carry on."

"Why, thank you, sir," beamed the honest fellow as he continued on his way.

"Come, Watson, we must pack and catch the next possible train from this exceedingly dozy town."

As we were waiting on the deserted platform for the train, Holmes asked me to look into the refreshment room to see if it were busy. "There is nobody at all in there," I reported back.

"I have never seen such a quiet station," he said.

"We are on a branch line," I pointed out. "We have to change at Taunton. I suppose we will stop at every little halt on the way." The train arrived and we settled into a first class carriage.

As I had predicted, the train was slow, stopping at every station on the way to our exchange point. At one pretty little halt Holmes said "Look out of window, Watson. Why have we stopped here? Is there anyone there?"

"Nobody getting on or off," I confirmed.

"Is there anybody on the platform at all?"

"Not a soul in sight."

Holmes groaned. "I will be glad to get back to the bustle of the city. I cannot stand this soporific atmosphere."

We boarded an express at Taunton and were soon bowling along merrily. Holmes' mood lightened, "Well, Watson, it is not often a case is solved so easily."

"I am still puzzled as to how Preston got away from Price and McCoy."

"The whole affair is absurdly simple, Watson. It only appeared mysterious because not one person I interviewed pointed out the most obvious thing. You, yourself, Watson, knew that Uncle Bubbles dressed as a clown but did not tell me. If I had known that fact at the start I would have realised immediately how the escape was effected."

"But I don't see the difference that made!" I expostulated. "Surely it would be much harder for a man to pass unnoticed dressed as a buffoon"

"As for that, Watson, Ullacombe has a buffoon dressed as a policeman."

We sat on a silence for a few minutes while I cogitated. "Of course! Now I see the point of those questions you asked Stirling. Bubbles could get out of his outfit in a minute. He always takes his nose and wig off when he goes in the booth anyway. He started his show then, at some point, stripped off his costume and slipped out." Holmes did not speak. "Ah, that wouldn't work. Price and McCoy would have been round the back before Bubbles could get any distance. No, no, I can't get at it, Holmes."

"People believe what they do not see and do not believe what they do see."

"How do mean, Holmes?"

"I asked you to look in the refreshment room at the station and you said it was empty."

"So it was."

"Not so. There was a lady attendant behind the counter at the tea urn."

"I was not counting her; I thought you meant passengers."

"At that benighted halt you said, and I quote your exact words, 'Not a soul in sight'."

"Well that's true. It was deserted."

"There was a porter arranging luggage on a trolley."

"Was there? I didn't notice him," I confessed.

"That proves my point, Watson; because your eye is accustomed to seeing a porter on a railway station platform your brain omits to register the fact."

"I still don't see what all this has to do with Bubbles though."

Holmes gave a weary sigh. "Bubbles was in front of his booth doing conjuring tricks. Obviously he noticed Price and McCoy take up position at the edge of the crowd. He knew why they were there. They were out to get him and stifle him in some way to prevent their exposure. Once in the booth he got out of his costume before starting his show. He told his wife Lil to put the things on. As she is a lady of above average height, the costume fitted her excellently and no discrepancy was apparent. At the point where Punch throws the baby out into the audience he dropped the puppet down and slipped out of the rear of the booth at exactly the same time as Lil, dressed in his costume, went out to retrieve the baby doll and toss it back over the stage. Lil then went back into the booth and put up Mr Punch and threw the doll out again, repeatedly, as the children threw it back in. Lil could not continue any longer because she did not know how to work the show or do the voices. The voice of Mr Punch is created by a singular piece of apparatus called a swazzle. This item is made from a silver coin and a strip of some vibrating material and is placed in the mouth. It is a specialised technique to articulate with this placed behind the teeth. When it is the turn of the other characters to speak, the operator flicks the swazzle into his cheek so he can assume a different voice by normal means. Then back in place goes the swazzle as Punch speaks again. Lil could not do any of that, neither could she hold up the heavy puppets for very long, hence the show fizzled to a halt. It was a minute or two before anybody realised that something was amiss and went to investigate; Price and McCoy being the first. That was sufficient time for Lil to divest herself of all the costume trappings."

"Amazing, Holmes! So all the time Preston had slipped out in full view while everybody was busy watching Mrs Preston – thinking it was Bubbles himself."

"Precisely. The bully boys were at the edge of the crowd at one side so Preston went the other way, behind the crowd, up to the promenade. I should think as soon as he got there he legged it as fast as he could go. People do not realise what they are really looking at. They only see what they expect to see. After eight summers of seeing a conjuring clown they would not expect to see somebody else, especially a woman, in his costume. They see the costume and assume it is he. Similarly they do not expect to see the man who is the clown without his costume, so do not notice him when he appears the same as everybody else. Just as you, Watson, did not see the porter on the platform."

"You say Lil Preston is a tall woman. You have never met her. How can you know that?" I queried.

"I think you will agree that only a lady of above average height would be able to reach to place her hat of pennies on top of the booth."

The day following our return to Baker Street, Holmes asked me to accompany him to an address in Brixton.

"Is this a new case, Holmes?"

"On the contrary, I hope it will be the culmination of the present affair of the disappearing Bubbles."

"How did you obtain this address?"

"It was furnished by Mr Rawley the Town Clerk who has corresponded annually with Mr Preston for several years."

We found the address to be a small artisan's cottage in a broken-down row of similar dwellings. Holmes knocked on the door. There was no reply.

"Looks as though the place is empty," I remarked.

"I think not, Watson. See that smear of mud on the step? It is very fresh and has obviously been picked up from that patch on the pavement. Someone has recently entered."

Further knocking produced no better result than previously.

"We've drawn a blank, Holmes."

"I think not," replied Holmes, producing a piece of paper and a pencil. He printed some words on the paper and pushed it through the letterbox in the door.

"What now, Holmes?" I asked.

"I do not think we will have long to wait."

Suddenly we heard a low noise behind the door and shortly afterwards the door swung open permitting a woman's face to peer cautiously out.

"Mrs Lillian Preston, I presume?" asked Holmes, raising his hat.

"Yes. Who are you? Are you from Mr Anstruther? Are you the police?" The woman spoke in obvious fear and apprehension.

"No, madam, I am Sherlock Holmes and this is my colleague Dr Watson. We have been retained by Mr Trevillion of Ullacombe to investigate the death of a visitor. May we come in?"

"I suppose so," said the woman doubtfully, standing aside permitting us to enter.

Mrs Preston was a tall thin woman with a care-worn face and ill fitting clothing. The room we found ourselves in was tiny but obviously the main room in the house. I could discern a scullery through a door in the corner and I suspected there was but one bedroom above us. There were two chairs drawn up to the fireplace and Mrs Preston offered them to us. Holmes turned them away from the fire and requested that Mrs Preston took one as he settled himself in the other. I was left to lean myself against the table that was pushed in a corner.

"I would really like to have a word with your husband, Mrs Preston. Is he here?"

"No, I don't know where he is."

"Do you mind if I smoke?" asked Holmes drawing out his pipe. The woman shrugged assent. "Dr Watson has cigarettes. Are you going to offer one to Mrs Preston, Watson?" I took out my cigarette case and proffered it but Mrs Preston declined saying she did not smoke. "Did you understand the meaning of the words I wrote on the paper?" continued Holmes.

"It says Price and McCoy are in jail. I hope it is true. I let you in because I thought it was true."

"They have been arrested for attacking Dr Watson in an alleyway in Ullacombe. They are remanded in custody and, when they come to trial very shortly, Dr Watson will have to identify them. The police also suspect that these two men are responsible for the murder of a young lady called Rachel Bristow."

"Young lady! Pah! She was nothing but a slut, a common prostitute!"

"So I believe, but that does not permit men to slaughter her at whim," replied Holmes.

"She was no good. She tempted poor honest men into wickedness!"

"I think she tempted your husband to consort with her."

"She did! The wicked woman led him astray! She came between me and my man! I won't have that!" cried the woman in anguish.

"I think you had better call your husband in, Mrs Preston. I know he is here. You do not smoke but there is a recently stubbed out cigarette in the hearth and the smoke from cheap cigarettes is particularly pungent on entering a room."

"I have heard everything!" cried a man appearing at the scullery door. "I do not know who you are but you seem to know all!"

"Uncle Bubbles, I presume?" said Holmes, rising from the chair.

"You say you have come from Mr Trevillion?"

"He is employing me in this affair."

"Mr Trevillion is a good man. He has given me employment every summer for eight years. It was wrong of me to run out on him but what could I do? They were after me. My life was in danger."

"Price and McCoy are in custody for the lesser crime of grievous bodily harm but, more importantly, they are also under suspicion of murder. Your life is not in danger at the present time. You had been carrying on an *affaire* with Rachel Bristow, a prostitute newly arrived in Ullacombe."

"Rachel wasn't a prostitute. She wasn't like that. She was a performer. She was a singer and dancer. I met her here in London at Shoreditch Music Hall. In the winter months I sometimes get engagements on the halls as a conjuror. We were on the bill together one week at Shoreditch. The two of us hit it off and – well, I know I'm a married man – but these things happen. I kept seeing her until it was time to leave for Ullacombe, as Lil and I do every year. I thought it would all die out once we were apart but we couldn't not see each other, Mr Holmes. We were truly in love. Rachel turned up in Ullacombe and I saw her regularly, whenever I could get away."

"I believe most evenings you were engaged doing card tricks?" asked Holmes.

"I was. I worked for the Anstruthers – they are the big crime bosses down there. Price and McCoy are their front men, do all their dirty work."

"I say," I interjected, "would one of these Anstruthers be a portly chap who had been left a tin mine or something by his father?"

"That's James Anstruther, the younger of the two brothers – calls everybody 'sport'."

"Pray continue, Mr Preston," said Holmes.

"Well the Anstruthers got it into their heads that Rachel was a prostitute from Bristol – I think they had misheard her name somewhere. Anyway, they decided to set Price and McCoy on to her. Warn her off. One night while she was waiting for me under that jetty thing they call a pier they turned up and gave her a beating. I was kept at the club doing card tricks for the customers. I realise now they did it deliberately because when Price and McCoy returned they talked in loud voices about how we wouldn't be troubled by foreigners from Bristol any more and that sort of talk. I did not realise what had happened until the following morning when Rachel's body was found. It seems that they had overdone the frighteners and killed the poor girl." Preston started to weep. "She did no harm. She was only there to see me. She wasn't any competition to their women."

"So, having boasted about their deed in front of you, they knew you could betray them."

"That's it. People in that area would turn a blind eye to a bit of roughing up, they do so all the time. That's how the Anstruthers get away with it. But killing somebody is a bit strong, even for them. I don't know what went wrong but Price and McCoy must have overdone things and ending up killing the poor creature."

"Realising they had now become murderers they knew their own lives were in danger if you gave them away?"

"Yes. As you can imagine I was terrified. After all, men who have killed once have nothing to lose by killing again. I was frightened that they would come for me to shut me up. I didn't know what to do. I wanted to flee immediately but when I got to the station I saw McCoy lurking there so turned back before he saw me. I had my show to do that afternoon so I went on with that but just before I started the Punch & Judy I saw Price and McCoy come up to stand at the back of crowd. I didn't know what to do."

"So you persuaded Lil to dress up in your costume and create a diversion by throwing the baby doll back and forth while you slipped out unnoticed and fled up on to the promenade."

"That's right, sir, I did. A bit of my conjuror's training came in handy there. It's called misdirection in the trade. As soon as I was off the beach I ran like the wind and got a motor taxi and left town. The driver took me to Exeter where I got the main line train back here to London."

"Why did you not go to the police once you were back? You were out of their clutches. If you had reported the matter to the police Price and McCoy would have been arrested and you could have safely given evidence."

"I was scared they would find me. After all, you have tracked me down."

"Then what will you do now? Price and McCoy are in custody charged with GBH. Dr Watson here will testify against them. Surely you will now come forward and accuse them of murder?"

"Of course he will, Mr Holmes!" cried out Lil Preston. "You'll nail 'em, won't you, Percy?"

"Well, I don't know, it may not be so easy. I heard them say they had done it but I didn't actually see them. They could deny they said anything."

"But hadn't they boasted in front of other people, not just you?" asked Holmes.

"Yes, but most of them are in the Anstruthers' employ. The few visitors that were present will not come forward – it would embarrass their families," replied Percy Preston.

"Then it looks as though Price and McCoy will get away with it if you do not testify against them," Holmes pointed out drily.

At the Devon Assizes I gave evidence of the attack upon me by Price and McCoy and they were sent down for twelve months with hard labour. However, their trial for the murder of Rachel Bristow collapsed as the principal witness Percy Preston refused to testify.

"Why do you think that was, Holmes?" I asked when I read the report in the *North Devon Times* that had been sent to us by Mr Trevillion.

Holmes puffed on his pipe. "I rather think it is because Uncle Bubbles is an honest man and he knows that Price and McCoy, while undeniably causing injury to Miss Bristow, did not, in fact, kill her."

"Not kill her? What can you mean Holmes?" I asked in amazement.

"Alas, I am unable to prove it, Watson, but I think another lady – a rather tall lady – was out near the pier that night. In affairs of the heart *cherchez la femme!*"

The Singular Adventure
of
THE BLUE SILK UNDERWEAR

IT was during my first year of marriage that this bizarre case came to the attention of my friend Mr Sherlock Holmes. I had seen very little of him during that early period of setting up home and developing my practice, and it was my wife Mary who said to me one day that I ought to call and see my erstwhile friend before he accused me of neglect.

So early one evening, my rounds being finished, I decided to call on my dear friend and renew acquaintance with my old bachelor quarters at 221B Baker Street. I found Holmes in a peevish mood.

"There are no crimes worthy of my attention, Watson. Where are all the master criminals these days?"

I ventured to suggest that it was likely that, through his own previous efforts, the criminal fraternity was diminishing, and a jolly good thing too. He was not placated.

"I must keep my faculties honed, Watson. The crimes that are perpetrated nowadays even Lestrade can solve unaided."

I was gratified to see that my friend's opinion of Scotland Yard detectives had not improved. I tried to jolly him out of his black mood as it has always been my fear that he will indulge himself in his beastly drugs when in one of his melancholy bouts. I started to tell him about Mary and our life together and how I was building up my modest practice but I fear he took little notice. He was never very interested in affairs that did not directly concern him.

"You're prattling, Watson," he said.

I confess that this statement rather hurt me.

"In that case I think I had better be off. I have much to do that is of great concern to me and I can use my time more fruitfully than sitting here being either ignored or insulted."

Sherlock Holmes gave a great laugh.

"Capital, Watson! You do well to chide me. I am disagreeable company tonight. Why do we not arrange to go St James's Hall one evening and listen to some sublime music?"

I was just assenting that this would be a suitable idea when we were both aware of voices at the street door. One voice was clearly Mrs Hudson's, the other a younger woman's voice. It seemed that Mrs Hudson was trying to prevent the other woman from coming in. She obviously thought that my presence was more important to Sherlock Holmes than any prospective client and was trying to prevent a premature end being put to my visit.

Holmes sprang to his feet, wrenched open the door and called out to Mrs Hudson to admit the person immediately. A young woman entered, indeed little older than a girl. She was smartly and expensively dressed and was quite agitated, although she made great efforts to conceal this.

"I have come to see Mr Sherlock Holmes," she said serenely.

"I am he," replied Holmes, "and this is my friend Dr Watson. Anything you have to say to me may be freely said in front of him. He has my full, entire and complete confidence and is privy to the deepest depths of my soul."

I think this extravagant statement was made to me, rather than to our visitor, in an effort to heal the wound caused by his previous pettishness. Whatever the reason, it made me feel very proud to hear him say it.

"I would like you to find a missing person, Mr Holmes. I have money, I am able to meet your fees. I have heard that you can achieve the impossible. This is a photograph of the person."

Our young visitor offered a *carte de visite*. Holmes held up his hand in protest, smiling indulgently.

"Not so fast I pray you. Other than the fact you are named Sally, have recently been abroad and have come to me unbeknownst to your maid or parents, I know nothing about you."

Our visitor stared.

"How do you know these things?"

"It is my business to know," replied Holmes somewhat smugly. "If you wish to conceal your name I suggest you do not have it stitched in embroidery on your handkerchief and, even more, do not twist it so agitatedly between your hands."

"You are right, of course, Mr Holmes. I have been told you are never wrong and that is why I have come to you in my distress."

"Please start by telling me your name and where you live."

"My name is Sally Devereux. I was christened Sarah but I have never been called that and hope I never shall be. I live with my father at a house called Whitegates not far from Godalming. We have only been there a month, until then I was at school in Switzerland and my father worked out in India. My mother died when I was very small."

"And it is your father whom you say is missing?"

"I did not say it was my father I wished you to find. How did you know?"

"It is my business to know, Miss Devereux. So you and your father are the sole occupants of this house?"

"No, there is an Indian man. My father calls him Singh. I don't know if that is his surname or – well it won't be a Christian name will it?"

"And is this Mr Singh a servant to your father?"

"It sounds odd to say this, Mr Holmes, but I don't really know as at some times he is like a valet and others a boon companion. Often he dines with us and, actually, I think he would eat with us every day, but his own tact is such that he realises my father and I may wish to be alone together after many years apart. Other than occasional visits, I have not seen my father very often, as he has been based in India ever since I can remember."

"What was his occupation out there?"

"I don't really know, Mr Holmes, something in the civil service I believe, but he told me he had finished with all that and was now retired and that we would live together companionably from now on like a normal family. He said he had one last business call to make in London and proposed that we should go up and make a day of it. Have a treat and look round the shops, he said, visit an art gallery and perhaps go to the theatre. I was very excited at the thought and was really looking forward to it. We spoke about it a lot and my father jokingly said it would be a good opportunity for me to wear a pair of knickers he had brought for me all the way from India. They are of blue silk which is unusual for me; all my other knickers are white. These are blue with white lace trimming. I really thought it was not sensible to wear such beautiful knickers to travel in and walk about town, but he was very insistent. He said to wear them but to carry an extra pair in case I needed to change whilst in Town. I thought it an odd suggestion but he was most insistent."

"Just a moment," interrupted Holmes. "What are knickers?"

"Ladies' underwear, Holmes," I murmured to him.

I have never seen Holmes disconcerted about anything, but this moment was the nearest.

"I thought it your business to know these things, Mr Holmes?" said Sally Devereux. Holmes gaped. In all his dealings with the mass of humanity he seldom came across the modern pert young miss. "In the event our trip was most disappointing. The man my father specifically wanted to see was not there and we trailed aimlessly about for a couple of hours then returned home. Daddy did not seem to have the heart to do anything properly."

"Perhaps you had better now come to the purpose of your visit. You say he has disappeared?"

"Yes. He left me this note."

Miss Devereux handed Holmes a note which he read in a second then passed to me. It said: *Dearest Sally, I have had to go away on business. I will be back soon. Love, Daddy.*

"And when was this note left?" asked Holmes.

"Tuesday the 28th."

"That is merely four days ago. I think you are worrying needlessly. Your father says he will be back and I am sure he will be."

"But he says he will be back soon. I think that means back later the same day."

"My dear young lady. You do not need a detective. You merely need patience."

"You are wrong Mr Holmes. I know my father and I fear something has happened to him."

Holmes was obviously getting bored with the conversation. As he disappeared for days on end without telling other people, he really did not see any reason to be concerned when other men did likewise.

"I suggest you return home and wait a little longer."

"I can't stay any longer in that house with just that awful man for company."

I thought I would interject here as my practised medical eye showed me that the girl was getting distraught.

"You are alone in the house with this Mr Singh?"

"Yes, Dr Watson."

"Are there no servants? No cook?" I asked.

"No, we had a woman who came in every day but left after she had prepared dinner. Now she has stopped coming in because my father had not paid her wages before he left."

"So you are fending for yourself?"

"Yes. We have some foodstuffs in, and there is a shop in the village that delivers, so I can manage."

"And what does Mr Singh say about all this?"

"He says to wait."

"Sensible chap," interjected Holmes dryly.

"Does he speak English?" I asked.

"Not very much. Although I think he understands more than he speaks. My father speaks to him in the Indian tongue."

"There is no such thing as the Indian tongue. Many languages are spoken in that vast country – Bengali, Gujarati, Punjabi, Hindi, Urdu, Marathi, Oriya and so on. I have made an extensive study," said Holmes complacently.

"I do not wish to give the impression that Mr Singh is a bad man. I do not like him but he is never anything other than correct in his manner towards me. It is that I fear he is always going to be with us and I do not know quite who he is or why my father needs him."

"It seems to me, young lady, that you are making a fuss about nothing. Your father has gone off on business for a few days and you, as a prim English miss, think anybody with a dark skin is a source of evil," said Holmes sternly.

"Holmes!" I cried. "This is unworthy of you."

"It's all right, Dr Watson. I can see now that my petty worries are nothing to a great man. I am sorry to have wasted your time, Mr Holmes." She gathered herself together and got up to leave. "I will probably return to find Mr Singh rummaging through my things again."

"What do you mean?" I asked.

"Yesterday I went out for my usual walk and when I returned I found Mr Singh in my room. He had some of my underwear in his hand. He hastily thrust it back in the drawer and pushed past me, muttering unintelligibly."

"This underwear being the blue silk knickers your father had given you and insisted you wear to London," said Holmes dryly.

"The man is obviously perverted!" I cried. "You cannot possibly go back there until your father returns."

Suddenly all composure deserted our guest and she started to cry.

"I want my Daddy!" she wailed.

Bringing my best bedside manner to bear, I took her in my arms and comforted her. At the same time I did some rapid thinking. Holmes was obviously out of sympathy with his visitor's distress.

"Ye gods, that the world's greatest detective should be concerned with a child's underwear!" he exclaimed and strode off into his bedroom.

"There, there, Sally," I soothed. "Now I know exactly what to do. I will take you home with me to meet Mrs Watson. She is a very dear kind soul. She will look after you and let you stay with her for a few days. I will speak to Mr Holmes when he has calmed down and I am sure he will make enquiries as to your father's whereabouts. He is a little distraught at the moment, he is not quite himself. Don't you worry. We will find your Daddy and all will be well. I, myself, will go down to Godalming at the first opportunity, speak to Mr Singh and leave word where you are for when your father returns."

This speech delivered in my calm reassuring voice seemed to do the trick. She perked up and agreed to accompany me home. As we left she called out to the closed bedroom door "Good night, Mr Holmes!"

There was no reply.

As I had thought, Mary took Sally to her bosom and mothered her wonderfully. This left me free to concentrate on carrying out my promises, so the next day, after my round of calls, I returned to my friend Sherlock Holmes.

"Well, Holmes, have you thought any further about that little matter of yesterday?"

"There is nothing to think about, Watson. As I told you last night, no crime has been committed. Heads of households leave their families every day. It is lamentable and much to be deplored but it is not criminal."

"So you do not intend to do anything to alleviate this child's distress?"

"I am a consulting detective, Watson, not a nursemaid."

"Well I shall do as I promised and go down to Godalming to see this Singh fellow. Also it will be necessary to leave word for Mr Devereux concerning the whereabouts of his daughter."

"Do as you please, Watson, you are a free agent."

So with that statement ringing in my ears, I set off to catch a train to Godalming. I will not bore the reader with the many vicissitudes I had to undergo before reaching my destination, but on arriving at Whitegates I found it to be an old, dark, austere looking building in grounds of about five acres as far as I could judge in the twilight. As no lights showed in the house, I thought the best approach would be to knock boldly on the front door, and accordingly I did so, but was disappointed in that there was no reply. I walked round the house and peered in at the ground floor windows. The interior did not seem particular comfortable and I imagined that the whole place had been rented furnished from a landlord who thought any old medley of junk comprised furniture. Some of the windows were filthy and I had to wipe a space to peer through. But nowhere did I see any signs of life, no fires burning in a cheerful hearth, no newspaper recently laid aside, nothing.

Yet I had the feeling that there was someone about. I felt I was under observation all the time. Perhaps this Singh devil was there watching everything I did while concealing himself. So I returned to the front door, tolled the bell and knocked with all my might. If I was being observed I made sure whoever saw me knew I was not being furtive about my presence.

At last I realised that my mission was fruitless. But at least I could leave my letter for Mr Devereux, Sally's father, should he return unexpectedly. So, in the absence of a letter box, I slid the envelope under the front door and came away.

On reaching London once more, even though he had expressed such coldness about my scheme, I thought I had better tell Mr Sherlock Holmes about my mission so, late as it was, called on him before going home.

"Well done, Watson," he said.

I looked to see if there was any look of irony in his face but I saw none.

On reaching home I recounted my adventures to Mary and Sally; she was much reassured that there was information left as to where she could be reached. After Sally had gone to bed I asked Mary how she was and my dear wife said that Sally was a darling and that she kept her occupied by setting household chores like shelling peas and so on, so that she did not have time to brood.

The next day passed in the same way and I busied myself in my work. I did not see Sherlock Holmes as he was obviously totally uninterested in my affairs. However, the day after, I was reading my usual morning paper when I suffered the most appalling shock. There was a brief item about the murder of an Indian gentleman at a country house near Godalming. It could not possibly be any other than Whitegates, a coincidence was out of the question.

I hurried over to 221B Baker Street. Holmes was not there. I waited around a little not knowing what to do. Mrs Hudson did not know of his whereabouts, but then she never did, so I left a note for Holmes, together with the newspaper, where he would see it on his return. In my agitation I deliberated whether to go down to Godalming but saw the folly of this. I realised that I could do nothing and that I must see Holmes. Surely he would now realise that something evil was afoot.

Three times I went back hoping to find him in but it was not until seven o'clock in the evening that I succeeded. I had been there about twenty minutes when in he came looking exhausted.

"Well met, Watson. Pour me a drink, there's a good fellow."

"I have been waiting all day for you. Have you seen the newspaper?"

"I've seen much more than that, Watson. I've seen the corpse of Mr Singh. I've examined the scene of the crime. I have been in the company of Inspector

Hubble of the local constabulary for most of the day."

The relief this news gave me was immense. I pressed him to tell me more but he insisted on finishing his drink which he sipped singularly slowly.

"You were right to chide me over this matter, Watson – I think the lack of activity had dulled my brain. I suddenly sat bolt upright in bed last night as I realised the significance of Miss Sally's underwear. Clearly, the two men, Devereux and Singh, were charged with delivering that piece of clothing to a certain person in London. Devereux attempted to do so and failed as the recipient was absent. Then the next day Devereux disappeared, for some reason unknown, so Singh had to ensure that he had not taken the underwear with him."

"So that's why Sally found him going through her drawers!" I cried.

"Very well put, Watson. I belatedly realised that here was something worthy of my attention after all, and at first light went down to Godalming where I found a police investigation in progress. There is something criminal happening at your Miss Sally's house. As yet I do not know if the absence of her father is connected. It seems that Mr Singh was alone in the house and an intruder got in through the window and attacked him with a knife."

"Are there any clues as to the murderer?"

"Inspector Hubble found lots of clues. He found many footprints of a heavily built man all round the walls of the house. Obviously this man had been peering in through the windows. He had left fingerprints all over the place, wiping panes of glass and so on. The man had been seen arriving in a train at Godalming station. He had hired a carriage to be taken to the village nearest the house. A place called Woodend. There he had dismissed the carriage and made his way on foot."

"Holmes, I did all these things!" I cried.

"Exactly Watson. Not only did you go blundering around like a rogue elephant, you even put a note through the door with your name and address on."

"Oh, my God!" I said desperately. "So Singh was inside lying dead all the time I was trying to gain access?"

"Quite possibly," said Holmes dryly.

"What am I going to do, Holmes?"

"Have you thought about escaping to the Continent on the boat train? You might just make Victoria if you set off now."

"But, Holmes, surely you don't think I was the murderer?"

"Well, Watson, you were very irate about Mr Singh. You said he was perverted and you were going down to deal with him. Who knows what a man may do when confronted?"

"But you know what my intentions were, Holmes. I told you when I returned that I could not get a reply."

"Certainly that is what you told me, but your letter to Mr Devereux was somewhat indiscreet. If I recall correctly, you said that his daughter was in your care because you feared he was harbouring a person with a warped personality –

I think that was the expression you used – and she should not be left alone with him. Something on those lines."

I was in despair. Of course I should not have committed any such thought to paper. What a fool I had been. I had been trying to be a good Samaritan and instead I had become the prime suspect in a murder investigation. What was I to do? If Holmes had seen the letter then obviously Hubble had found it. The police could be at my home at that very moment.

"What am I going to do, Holmes?" I again pleaded miserably.

"My dear fellow, I suggest you take back your letter and consign it to the flames of my fire. Do give it a poke while you're about it. This room is quite chill."

I was amazed as Holmes handed me the envelope I had slid under the door of Whitegates.

"Indeed you are fortunate that Inspector Hubble's investigative methods are not quite as thorough as mine. You slid your letter, not only under the door, but also under the ill-fitting linoleum where it would no doubt have reposed for months. Certainly Sally's father would not have found it."

"Holmes, I cannot tell you how relieved I am."

"Burn it, Watson. I can also set your mind at ease about your many footprints and fingerprints. Inspector Hubble came to the conclusion that they were made by a wandering tramp who thought he might try his luck while passing. You see, there was sufficient other evidence of a window being forced – it was still flapping open when I arrived – and several footprints of a naked foot on top of the ones you had left. Together with other clues that I won't bore you with, Hubble came to the conclusion that Singh had been murdered by a fellow countryman. The type of knife used, the rather ritualistic stab wounds, etc. all pointed to some kind of sect. The murderer had made no effort to conceal his presence. The fact that all these footprints were on top of yours prove that Singh was alive at the time of your visit."

"And what did you deduce?"

"Oh, I quite agreed with all his conclusions. He is a sound man – I also found a further seven additional clues that confirmed his thesis. However, whether he ever finds the culprit I very much doubt."

"Surely there are not so many Indians around that the murderer can get away?"

"I have something else that may interest you, Watson. Here!"

He tossed a paper bag to me and I withdrew a cloth garment. I saw white calico, blue silk and white lace.

"Good heavens, Holmes. Are these the drawers that Sally told us of?"

"Not quite, Watson. The reality is even more bizarre. Investigations were still underway when I got to the house but Singh's body had been taken away to the mortuary, which I visited later. There they had stripped him of his clothes and I was able to examine them. This is a cambric shirt and it would appear that the legs have been cut off Miss Sally's underwear and crudely sewn around the sleeves of the shirt."

"Extraordinary!"

"Hubble obviously thought the garment was merely an Indian fashion as Singh's other clothes were such as is worn in that country. I, myself, whilst noting that blue silk and lace sit awkwardly on a man's shirt, would perhaps not have realised the significance, had we not been told the curious episode of Miss Sally's underwear."

"But what is the significance, Holmes? I confess I can make nothing of the affair at all."

"Surely the whole solution to this mystery – the murder and the disappearance of Devereux – depends on this garment. It is a mistake to theorise before having all the facts but it would seem to indicate that Singh was of the opinion that Devereux would not return and therefore the underwear would be safer in his keeping. Obviously he could not wear them himself, so attempted to conceal them as shirt sleeves. I am tired, Watson, I have had a long day. I shall repair to my bed and in the morning I shall consider the mystery of this garment. As you have been so good as to interest yourself in this case from the outset, could I prevail upon you to call around here tomorrow after you have dined? I should have the solution by then. Good night, Watson, you are a good, kind fellow."

And with those words I was dismissed.

As requested I called on Holmes the following evening to find him smoking his pipe and the room filthy with fug; doubtless he had spent a strenuous day wrestling with his problem.

"Come in, Watson," he said genially. "Have you heard of any of those gentlemen before?"

He nodded to the table. On it were the lace cuffs from the drawers – now laid out as two flat strips, a great number of pieces of paper with scribbles, which I identified as part of the lace pattern traced in sections, and a paper with the following names: Henry Bustard, Alfred Dunn, Gordon McMaster, George Spooner, James Rook, Arthur Kingsley.

"No, I can't say they mean anything to me, Holmes, although Gordon McMaster rings a faint bell. Who are they?"

"No idea, Watson, but together they are enough to kill a man. I found that the lace on the leggings of the underwear was not merely a delightful conceit to please the wearer. The purpose of the lace was to carry a secret message. In the pattern was a hidden cypher. As you will see, it has taken me some time to crack the code. But I've done it. You will observe the lace pattern is no pattern at all. In fact there is very little repetition. Just at here and here, and here and here. It was quite simple once I had found that certain elements of the design stood for letters. That daisy-like shape is an O. As you can see, we have seven of them including two grouped in pairs. The fancy cross is a letter N – six of those including a pair. And so on – I'm sure you see the process."

"You are amazing, Holmes!" I cried in admiration.

"Unfortunately, Watson, we do not know the significance of the names. I rather think we need Devereux now to explain all."

"But perhaps he is unaware of the cypher. He may be the unwitting bearer, don't you think?"

"That is the obvious inference. Otherwise I am intrigued why a person of average intelligence should not be able to remember six simple names without setting them down in this cryptic form."

"What are you going to do now, Holmes?"

"I am awaiting a reply from Mycroft. I have sent the names to him."

Mycroft was Holmes' brother. He worked in a very secret position for the government. I had met him before in connection with Holmes' cases. His capacity for deduction and logical thought surpassed even my good friend's abilities and the position he held in the government utilised these capabilities to the uttermost. He was a sort of general post betwixt all departments, he was the only man in the government who knew everything. His brain was able to collate diverse information from each different department and tie it together to make sense.

"I've just realised why I know the name Gordon McMaster. It was the name of a fellow doctor when I was out in Afghanistan. I don't suppose it will be the same."

"The name is not an uncommon one. What happened to your erstwhile colleague, do you know?" asked Holmes.

"I believe he transferred to India to take up a position with the government."

Holmes eyes sparkled.

"Let us not jump to conclusions, Watson. But I am sure India is at the root of this affair."

At that moment one of Holmes' urchins arrived. He had a team of street arabs who carried out various errands for him. He called them the Baker Street Irregulars.

"You 'ave to come at once, Mr 'Olmes. That's wot the gent said. I've got a cab for you. Tell 'im to come at once was the message."

"Stout fellow! Here, that's for you. Come Watson!"

Tossing a shilling to the urchin, Holmes bounded out of the room leaving me to hurry in his wake.

We found Mr Mycroft Holmes in the visitor's lounge of the Diogenes Club. This queer club was for misanthropic men and it was forbidden to talk to other members except in this one room put aside for the purpose. Mycroft Holmes was to be found at the Diogenes Club whenever he was not in his government office.

"Dr Watson, how nice to see you again. It must be all of two years since we last met. And you, Sherlock, are you well?" Mycroft Holmes always seemed affable enough to me and I could never understand why he wished to contain himself in such austere unsociability as was offered by the Diogenes Club. "Did you find Lady Cheltenham's diamond necklace all right? It was, of course, still in her dressing room?"

"Yes, that could be deduced from the press reports. There was a secret cupboard behind the panelling."

"And of course it was the maid?"

"Yes, she was under the thumb of the butler."

"Ah. Well now – this list of names you have sent me. Where did you get it, Sherlock?"

"I decoded it. The names were in cypher form in a piece of lace."

"A piece of lace? How ingenious. Where did you find the piece of lace?"

"The lace was used to trim the – er, undergarments of a young lady."

"How extraordinary."

"Do you know a man called Devereux?"

"He is a recently retired civil servant, newly returned to this country," said Mycroft Holmes.

"From India," said Sherlock Holmes.

"Exactly. He was prevailed upon to bring the names of a group of subversives who were plotting the overthrow of the British Government in India. It is incredible to believe, I know, but there are some British citizens who wish to undermine their own country. In India there is a movement to stir up another Mutiny. The purpose is to drive the British out, and there are some Britons who are actually conniving with these anarchists. Those six men have all got responsible positions in the British Government out there. So you see why we must root them out. Devereux did not know that he was carrying vital information. It was essential the names should be concealed in some way but – ladies underwear? Really! What is the secret service coming to? He was accompanied by an Indian called Singh."

"Who is now dead. You know he is dead?" asked Holmes.

"Yes, I know all about that, except I was not aware that you were involved. Singh was an excellent man but had very limited English. It was necessary that he should lie low for a long while, so it was thought expedient to get him out of the country altogether. As cover he travelled to England disguised as Devereux's manservant."

"Where is Devereux now?" I asked, thinking of his daughter.

"We don't know. He reported, as arranged, on the 12th to the Indian Office but the Secretary had been called away. Although Devereux did not know the importance of his mission, he was instructed to give his charge to nobody else but the Secretary himself, so he was unable to fulfil his duty. The Secretary has returned but Devereux is missing. Now it does not matter because you have found the names, Sherlock, and they have been relayed to the appropriate channels."

"Pardon me, sir!" I burst out heatedly. "You cannot just forget about Devereux because he is no longer needed. He may be ill, injured, dead even. He has a young daughter who is anxiously waiting news of him."

Sherlock Holmes explained how we both had become involved in this case, how I had gone to Godalming and how he had investigated the death of Singh.

"I can put your mind at ease about that, Sherlock. The murderer has been found and, er – punished. Devereux has no fear from that quarter."

"You mean one of your agents has done away with their spy, just as their man did for yours," sneered Sherlock Holmes.

"Something like that," agreed Mycroft Holmes complacently.

"It's a dirty business you are involved in, Mycroft. At least my criminals are honest open blackguards!"

"If Devereux is alive, which I am sure he is, Dr Watson, I will make arrangements to find him. He is in no danger, I assure you, and he may return home as soon as he likes. Have no fear, leave it with me."

With those reassurances we left the Diogenes Club and returned to Baker Street.

"So, Watson, you see what murky depths your gallantry drags you into."

I was well-used to my friend's heavy-handed chaffing and I did not mind now I was sure all would turn out right for Miss Sally.

Two days later at my home, a knock at the door announced the presence of a stranger. I was alone in the house as Mary and Sally had gone out shopping and it was the maid's afternoon off.

"Dr Watson?"

"Yes?"

"I have come in reply to your advertisement."

"My advertisement?"

"About the underwear from India."

"You are Devereux?" I asked, recalling the photograph Sally had shown Holmes.

He confirmed that he was, then held out a morning paper where he had ringed this advertisement in the personal column:

If the gentleman recently returned from India has mislaid his daughter's blue silk underwear, he can reclaim both underwear and daughter from Dr J Watson at No 8 Norfolk Square, Paddington.

"I am sorry I looked so blank. You see, I did not know about the advertisement," I said and laughed as I detected the unmistakeable hand of my friend, my very dear friend, Mr Sherlock Holmes. It was so typical of him not to rely on his brother to get a message to Devereux.

We had quite a yarn as I recounted our recent adventures while awaiting the return of the ladies. Then the door opened and Mary and Sally came in. The expression on Sally's face was a picture I shall treasure for the rest of my life.

"Daddy!" she cried throwing her arms round her parent. It did my heart good to witness the fond reunion of father and daughter and we were all very merry. However I felt constrained to enquire if they would be so kind as to call on Holmes with me on their way home, to which Devereux readily assented.

Once there, Holmes said he was unclear on one point.

"I cannot understand why a fond parent should leave his only child alone in a house with a strange man, knowing him to be involved in some very dirty espionage," said Holmes.

"For God's sake, Mr Holmes, surely you do not think I willingly stayed away? The position was – I had just retired as a government official in Delhi. I was not involved in espionage work – I was a mere civil servant. It was because I was returning to England that I was asked if I would bring a certain article that had to be delivered to the Secretary for India in person. Of course when I saw the article in question I knew there was more to it than meets the eye but I had no knowledge of what it concerned. They were clever about that. If I had been captured and tortured I could have said nothing." Devereux spoke bitterly. "On the day appointed I went with Sally to hand over my article, thankful to be rid of it, but the Secretary wasn't there. He had been suddenly called away to attend an emergency conference in Paris. So we returned home. But in the night I got to thinking. I decided I would go over to Paris the next day, confront the Secretary and tell him to either be at his desk or authorise some other man to take the wretched underwear; otherwise I would just leave them with the doorman. I was so fed up with the whole thing. I got the boat over to Calais but before I could catch the Paris train I was knocked down by a runaway horse and cart."

"Oh, Daddy!" cried Sally in distress.

"Yes, my love. I was taken to hospital with concussion and bruises but no broken bones – although the blow on my head did my brain no good and I couldn't remember what I was doing there or anything. Then the doctors and nurses were all French, of course, and didn't have much of our lingo between them so I was in a bit of a stew for a day or two. Eventually my memory recovered and I knew I had to get back."

"When you returned you found your colleague, Mr Singh, had been murdered and your daughter fled," added Holmes.

"That's right, Mr Holmes. Although Singh was hardly a colleague as I'd never met him before we travelled back together. I gather it was expedient for him to leave India for his own safety and he was to accompany me in the guise of a manservant until my parcel was delivered, when he was to return to India with any reply. I had no idea where Sally was. I dare not go to the police as I read in the papers that I was suspected of killing Singh."

"Surely not!" I protested.

"Inspector Hubble did give out that information at one point, to allay fears that a mad Indian was roaming the Godalming area ready to stab all and sundry," said Holmes.

"I knew that Singh could have said nothing so I feared that the assassin would be after me next – he was not to know we were both ignorant of the whole affair. So I laid low. But I made enquiries all over for you, my love," said the father fondly turning to his daughter.

"Fortunately she was safe with my wife," said I reassuringly.

"My gratitude knows no bounds, Dr Watson."

"To tell you the truth, Mr Devereux, it will seem very quiet at home without her. We shall miss her. It was rather like having a daughter ourselves."

"And living with Mrs Watson was like having a mother," said Sally.

"Well from now on I shall be both father and mother to you, my dear. We will look around for some pleasant cottage in an area where there are lots of young people and we will be jolly and companionable."

"And as Mr Singh destroyed your *knickers*, I suggest you prevail upon your father to take you shopping for a replacement," said Holmes indulgently.

The Singular Adventure
of
THE SPORTING GENT

THE man who had come to consult my friend Mr Sherlock Holmes seemed a breezy fellow, not yet forty, well dressed but with a touch or two of the flashy about his garb.

"Take a seat, Mr Humphrey Porritt, this is my colleague Dr Watson, he is privy to all my affairs. What have you come to tell us?" asked Holmes benignly.

"I have come to tell you that I am the most stupid, cretinous and brainless person who ever walked on God's earth," said our caller with a wry smile and a shrug of his shoulders.

"Perhaps I may be the judge of that when you have told me your story," said Holmes.

"Oh, there is no doubt of it. I have given away my entire life savings, freely and voluntary, to a perfect stranger."

"I do not think such charity is a sign of stupidity. Somewhat cavalier perhaps, but –" said Holmes.

"Oh I didn't do it for charity," interrupted Porritt. "I did it to try and make more money."

"Ah!" said Holmes and waited.

"I will tell you all from the beginning but I must say I do not see how you or anyone else can help me. I come in desperation as I have heard that you can do amazing things, though I doubt you can reclaim my £3000 from the Lord knows where."

"Again I think I will be a better judge of whether I can help you if you explain your business coherently," said Holmes sternly.

"Indeed. Well it's this way. I am a bit of a sporting gent. I do not mean I play any, but I take a great interest in all sports – horse racing, football, rugger, athletics, boxing, cricket, whatever. I also like to have a financial interest in a variety of them."

"You mean you are a betting man and you do not confine your activities solely to the turf?" interrupted Holmes.

"You read me exactly, sir. Now don't get the wrong idea, I'm not a heavy gambler and I don't gamble on the turn of a card or anything like that, it's just that I think spice is added to a sporting event if I have a little flutter on the outcome. I am not a wealthy man by any means, but I am not married and have no family, so there is no danger of my dragging my nearest and dearest into degradation through my habits."

"Do you have an occupation, a private income, or do you subsist on your gambling?" asked Holmes.

"I have several part-time occupations – I am a proof reader for one publisher; I am a reader for another, I read unsolicited manuscripts and recommend whether they are worth pursuing; I write for two or three sporting papers and I am the theatre critic for the *Globe*. I am also a stringer for several provincial newspapers and send pieces to them from time to time – gossip about London society and so on."

"You must have a remarkably busy life."

"It is very varied and I am always out and about."

"Perhaps you will come to the point of your story?"

"About a year ago I received a note through the post. Unfortunately I threw it away as I did not think it of importance but I remember exactly what it said. It read: *Oxford will win the boat race. Put your money on it. Nemo.*"

"That's all it said?"

"Yes. Just that, no address or anything."

"And presumably you had no idea who sent it or who this Nemo person was?"

"No idea. But in my various activities I meet many people and, to be honest, people often send me bits of information, tittle-tattle mostly, thinking I might be able to use it and thus pay them a few coppers for the info."

"But this wasn't like that?" asked Holmes.

"Not at all. This was obviously from somebody who knew I was a betting man."

"Why do you say that?"

"Because a few weeks later I received another note. That said: *Jem Smith will win the big fight. Put your money on it. Nemo.*"

I could see the interest leap into Holmes' eyes and he leaned forward.

"Before you proceed – did you put money on Oxford to win the boat race?"

"No, I backed Cambridge as I fancied it was about their turn, but Oxford won yet again."

"And this fight? Did you bet on Jem Smith?"

"I did."

"And did he win?"

The depths of Holmes' ignorance never ceased to amaze me. The fight between Smith and Pritchard for the heavyweight championship had exercised the public prints for weeks. The jubilation when Jem Smith felled Pritchard in the second round had not been seen in London since Her Majesty's Golden Jubilee and here was Holmes, the most astute detective in the country, totally ignorant about it.

"Yes, he won and I had placed ten guineas on him to do so."

"You were tempted to back him because this Nemo person had tipped him and his previous tip about the Boat Race had been correct?"

"That is so, Mr Holmes. After all, when the two men are equally matched it is only fancy that makes you decide on your favourite."

"Please continue."

"Well a few more weeks went by and, sure enough, a third tip arrived. Just the same. I kept that one. Here it is."

Porritt passed over an envelope that Sherlock Holmes perused carefully with his lens, he then studied the contents, handed it back and said "Typed on a Remington machine. Very new, probably bought especially for the purpose of sending these cryptic messages. Posted in central London. Business stationery, manila envelope. It tells us nothing, which is the intention."

"How do you know the typewriting machine was newly bought?" I felt urged to interrupt.

"Come, Watson, look at the clarity of the type and the blackness of the ink."

"But surely that only indicates a new ribbon has been used?" I protested.

"Any machine that has been used soon develops characteristics unique to that machine. One of the keys perhaps develops a weak tension in its spring and the letter on that key is thus always stamped slightly fainter. Letters become misaligned or slightly askew through use. Deposits build up on the letters, especially on the *e* and the *a* and, even with a new ribbon, these letters get the spaces filled in with ink, and so on. I have written a monograph identifying the differences between all the current models of typewriting machines listing over fifty points where differences occur both initially and with use. However, in this instance the message is the matter: *The Old Etonians will win. Put your money on it. Nemo.* I assume this is another sporting event?"

"The annual cricket match between the Old Harrovians and the Old Etonians."

"Surely a match like that doesn't attract the bookies?" I cried.

"Not all bets are with book-makers. There are many sporting gents like myself who will bet against each other. I've known some men, who have nothing else to gamble on, bet which fly will leave a window first. To be sure, Doctor, you can get somebody to take a bet on practically anything."

"So did you place a bet on the Old Etonians?" asked Holmes.

"Indeed I did. I put the money I had won on Jem Smith plus another ten on to it and again this Nemo person was right and I was quids in again."

Holmes rubbed his hands in glee.

"Have you the next note?"

"Yes, this one concerns the final of the Wimbledon Lawn Tennis Championship."

Holmes took the paper, glanced briefly at it and read aloud: *"Baddeley for the Championship. Put your money on it.* And?"

"I put a hundred guineas on Wilf Baddeley and as you will know after a close fought game he won in the final set."

"I am fascinated by your story. What happened next?"

"I had a visitor. One day there was a knock at my door and I opened it to admit a man who said his name was Nemo."

"Excellent!" cried Holmes. "Can you describe him?"

"Well, he was above average height, well built, clean shaven with a ruddy face and pendulous cheeks. He had a serene air of benevolence about him. The impression he gave me was that he might be a clerical man although he wasn't wearing a dog-collar or anything, but his entire manner of speech and bearing reminded me of a clergyman. Not that I am acquainted with many of those."

"Did you look at his ears?"

"His ears? Not especially, I presume he had two, one on each side of his head and I think I would have noticed if he hadn't. Are his ears important?"

"The left could be vital. But please to proceed."

"He asked very politely if I had received his letters, which I affirmed, then he asked if I had acted upon them and I said that after the first one I had indeed placed a bet according to all his suggestions. He then, still very politely, suggested that through his good offices I had increased my wealth by whatever modest amount I could afford and thus was, in a small way, somewhat in his debt. However, he went on to say that as his letters were unsolicited, he did not expect payment for them in any way."

"So what suggestion did this kind beneficent gentlemen then make?" asked Holmes with a hint of sarcasm.

"He said he knew the winner of the FA Cup Final."

"I note that none of these sporting events were horse races. One might think the Derby and Grand National would be of interest to Nemo. Neither were there any athletic events, bicycle races and so on."

"Perhaps he would have got round to those in due course. Anyway he was prepared to tell me the winner of the FA Cup Final but he would be infinitely obliged if I would give him 10% of my winnings. Well, this seemed a reasonable suggestion to me, the man had given me four winners free of charge, and if this was to be a fifth winner, then I could well afford to pass on 10% of my winnings."

"Did you ask him what the conditions were if you lost the bet?" asked Holmes.

"Of course; he would not entertain the possibility of losing the bet. He actually said 'I know the winner, you cannot lose' but I pressed him and he replied that if I lost, then, of course, he would not expect any payment whatsoever. He merely requested 10% of my winnings, and whether I placed a stake of £5000, £500 or £50 he only required 10%. What is more, he pointed out that he could not compel me to give him anything, but he trusted a gentleman like myself would deal justly with him."

"I cannot see the catch in all this," I remarked. "He seems to be a very astute tipster and could make much more than he has been doing."

"Oh, Watson," said Holmes, shaking his head, "too much of your army pension is wasted on galloping horses as it is. I assume Mr Porritt is now about to reveal the catch, as you call it."

"Well I was a bit taken aback by the sums mentioned. As I told you, I am a fairly small wager man. Prior to all this, the biggest single bet I had ever placed was £100; generally I bet in tens, twenty-fives, that sort of thing. I tried to convey to Nemo that my stakes were not usually very high and he, again very politely, said that the stake was entirely my affair and that I would be foolish to gamble more than I could afford. Naturally for his part, he hoped that I would place a larger amount rather than a smaller, as his 10% would also be larger, but I was to feel under no duress whatsoever."

"So did he give you the tip?" asked Holmes.

"Yes, he said the winner would be Aston Villa."

"Why –" cried I.

"Patience, Watson, let us hear the end of the story."

"He said Villa for the cup and I believed him, although I did point out they were the underdogs. In fact West Bromwich Albion, the favourites, were 5 to 4 on and Villa were 3 to 1. Nemo then looked slightly alarmed and said that, whilst Villa had been at 3 to 1, the odds had shortened to 2 to 1 which, of course, indicated that further money was being placed on Aston Villa. He asked me where I usually placed my bets and I replied that I had several men I could go to but they would all quote the latest odds. He then said that he knew a book-maker who was actually a gentlemen who dealt in financial matters, the stock market and so on, and he was often a bit behind in quoting the latest odds because he was not really of the book-making fraternity, it being merely a hobby with him. Nemo thought it likely that I could still get 3 to 1 with him if I moved quickly."

"Have you spotted the catch yet, Watson?" asked Holmes sarcastically. "So, Mr Porritt, you agreed to place your wager with this financial gentlemen who was a little behind the times?"

"Yes. Looking back, I must have been incredibly naive but it all seemed so straightforward at the time. Nemo appeared so genuine."

"Of course; pray continue."

"Nemo then asked how much I would wager, as this financial gentlemen only dealt with considerable amounts. I said I could place a couple of thousands –"

"Great heavens!" I cried.

"You did not wish to seem cheap, did you, Mr Porritt? You were dealing with people used to high finance and you did not wish to appear a small gambler who was out of his league."

"Well, yes, that's about the size of it, I suppose," said Porritt, somewhat shamefaced.

"And did Nemo then suggest that it would be better if you could raise the wager a little higher as he was not sure the financier would deign to take such a trivial amount as two thousand pounds?" said Holmes.

"Not in so many words, but I suppose that was the effect. I knew I could raise two thou by cashing in some shares I held, together with an insurance policy and other stuff I could rake up, but, quite frankly, that was my absolute limit and I was beggaring myself to reach that."

"So you settled for two thousand?" asked Holmes.

"Well, no. I agreed to wager three thousand," admitted Porritt.

"Oh, Mr Porritt, you are becoming mired ever deeper as you speak, I shudder to hear what you will tell us next."

"I went to my club and borrowed £500 from each of two chums there." Holmes remained silent. "I agreed to meet Nemo and we took a cab to a house in Golders Green. It was a very imposing residence in its own grounds. Nemo pressed the bell and the door was opened by a gentleman of Hebraic aspect who Nemo introduced as Mr Goldstein. He ushered me into a room somewhat like a library with a large desk. Nemo said he would wait for me in the hallway as the business did not concern him. He did not even know the actual money I wagered, we had said three thou but I could have been betting five and then only give him 10% of three. So he was really trusting me."

"I am sure that was the effect he wished to create. Go on," commanded Holmes.

"Mr Goldstein accepted my drafts."

"How did you hand the money over?"

"I had three cheques, my own for two thousand and two more of £500 each from my friends."

"How were they made out?"

"To cash."

"I must warn you, Mr Porritt, my patience is wearing very thin at your folly. Did your friends come in on the bet?"

"Oh no, I just borrowed the money temporarily, I did not say why, but I promised to repay them within four days."

Holmes groaned. I felt sorry for Porritt. When he had arrived he had been quite chirpy and tried to shrug his misfortune off with a laugh, but as he told his story he could now hear his own mouth relating how foolish he had been. Obviously he had not told his tale to anyone and it was only when he heard his words spoken out loud he became aware that the whole tale was a flimsy tissue of trickery from beginning to end. Porritt pressed on.

"As Goldstein was writing out my receipt, the telephone rang and he begged to be excused while he answered it. Of course I could only hear Goldstein speak, but the way he looked at me as he was conversing made me fear that something was untoward with my wager. After he had hung up the telephone on its cradle he said that he had just been speaking to a colleague who informed him that the odds on Aston Villa were now 2 to 1. However, he said that he was halfway through writing my slip and he had already taken my bet and had actually written 3 to 1 on the slip so that as he was a gentleman he would abide by it."

Holmes threw his head back and laughed, clapping his hands.

"Excellent! We are dealing with a pair of rogues with infinite finesse! Carry on."

"Well there's little more to tell. Goldstein said that he kept office hours, though this house was his home, and that as it was now two o'clock on Friday afternoon he would be closing at 4.30 to re-open on Monday morning at 10am. I was welcome to come on Monday at any time between that hour and 4.30 to collect my winnings. I was ushered out and Nemo was waiting in the hall. We shared the cab back to the West End and Nemo asked diffidently if it would be convenient for me to meet him at noon on Monday at Goldstein's house so that I could pass the 10% on to him from my winnings. I agreed to that and we parted company."

"Did you go to the match?"

"I did, Saturday afternoon I was in the crowd and suddenly I went numb. It may be hard for you gentlemen to realise, but everything I have related seemed so natural and logical as it was happening, and it was only when I saw the pitch that I realised I had £3000 dependent on whether a little leather ball passed more often between one pair of poles rather than the other. I think I went into a kind of coma. The crowd was cheering all around me and I was totally unaware what was happening. All I could think was that I could lose my life savings and owe a thousand pounds. I did not even know if a goal was scored, much less which side had scored it. At last it was all over and the crowds surged out of the ground with much noise and banter. I was obliged to ask a fellow who had won. He must have thought me barmy! Aston Villa had won by one goal to nil. My money was safe! Not only safe – I had won nine thousand pounds! My coma turned to euphoria. I spent Saturday night in a dream, I went to bars, I ate at the Savoy, I went to a music hall, I don't know what I didn't do. I got home very late but couldn't sleep. I had done it! I had won nine thousand pounds because of one single goal. You can imagine how restlessly I spent Sunday. On Sunday night I could not sleep again for excitement."

"And on Monday, promptly at noon, you went to Mr Goldstein's house expecting to meet Nemo."

"Yes."

"And Nemo wasn't there."

"No."

"And neither was Mr Goldstein."

"No. The door was answered by a manservant. I asked for Mr Goldstein and he said nobody of that name resided at the house. I insisted that I had visited only three days previously. Eventually he fetched his master who clearly thought I was raving mad. He said his name was Bulstrode and that he and his wife, together with the entire household, who I gather was the manservant and a couple of maids, had been on holiday to Buxton from the previous Saturday to the Saturday just gone. He said: 'My wife and I have been to Buxton in Derbyshire for the whole week. The house was locked up for the whole week. There was nobody here at all. We have been to Buxton to take the waters. It is a spa. Good day to you, sir,' and I was more or less forcibly ejected."

The bouncy man who had entered our rooms a bare half hour ago crumpled before my eyes and to my astonishment started to quietly weep. I went to the drinks cabinet and poured him a brandy and made him drink it. Holmes looked at the forlorn figure.

"Get a grip of yourself, man! Don't give way to this girlish weeping!"

"I don't know what to do. I don't know what to do. I can't repay my friends, I daren't go near my club. I'm ruined," Porritt groaned pitifully, head in hands.

"Holmes," I said, "have a little compassion for a fellow creature, the man is ill, he has had a tremendous shock."

"Listen to me, Porritt, you have nobody else but yourself to blame. Do you hear? At any stage in your miserable story you could have said *no*, but you didn't, you said *yes* every time, because you wanted more. You were not content with winning once, twice, thrice, you wanted to go on winning, you wanted to be richer and richer. I have to tell you I despise you."

"Holmes," I protested, "this is not like you."

"I despise you, Porritt, but I will help you. I very much doubt if I can retrieve your money. I doubt that very much; please be clear on that point. I can, I think, find the men and have them arrested by the police. But listen. You will then have to go to court and the whole story will become public. The newspapers will play riot with your name, you will be a laughing stock throughout London. Do you want that? Answer me!"

"No, no," snivelled the miserable fellow, "that would do more harm than good."

"Right," snapped Holmes, "I will take on your case. I promise nothing. You deserve nothing. Come back here on Friday evening at seven. Do you hear? I will tell you all I have been able to find out, but for God's sake do not presume I can get your money back. You may go as soon as you are well again."

With that, Holmes strode into his bedroom slamming the door behind him. Within two minutes I heard the sound of a violin, while I tried to comfort the unhappy Porritt. Eventually he pulled himself together and I saw him downstairs into a cab.

I saw little of Holmes during the next few days apart from the odd glimpse of him in some rather unusual clothes. He came and went at irregular hours and it was not until Friday that he was at home. In the late afternoon I returned to find him seated, affably smoking his pipe and received a pleasant "Good afternoon" from him.

"You will recall that you asked the unfortunate Mr Humphrey Porritt to call at 7 o'clock this evening," I said.

"I recall that fact very well indeed as I have spent the time since his woebegone departure entirely on his affairs," said Holmes complacently.

"Have you had any success?" I asked.

"Perhaps you will permit me to await his arrival then I do not have to tell my tale twice," he said in that maddening way he has when he knows I am bursting with curiosity. So I had to be content until the arrival of Porritt at 7 o'clock.

Promptly at that hour Porritt came and sat under Holmes's gaze looking chastened.

"Well, Mr Porritt," said Holmes breezily, "I have bent my best endeavours to your behalf. The confidence tricksters comprise a gang of two, the man calling himself Nemo is the mastermind. He is Henry Peters of Adelaide in Australia, known as Holy Peters and specialises in impersonating clergymen. When you described him to me I came to the conclusion it was he, our paths have crossed previously. If you had seen his left ear there would have been no doubt, as the lobe is torn and ragged, but the description sufficed. The man Goldstein I did not know previously and I rather think it is a recent pairing of the two. Perhaps specifically for this swindle. That is really all I can tell you. You could go to the police and I have no doubt your evidence will put them behind bars."

"But you said that would not benefit me personally."

"That's true. One could argue that it is a sacrifice one should make to prevent further innocent people being gulled. Your own conscience will tell you. However, that is entirely your affair, but I must warn you that I cannot support you in the matter as I have put myself against the law in this."

"Holmes!" I cried.

"Tush, Watson, you and I both on several occasions. We have broken into houses before now, what is housebreaking but a crime?"

"So that's that, Mr Holmes. I am ruined."

"It would appear so. I regret I cannot ask you to stay to dinner, Mr Porritt, but our excellent fowl will not suffice for three people. It is there on the table under the cover. It is quite choice. Do have a look at it as you leave."

"I am sure it is, Mr Holmes," said the bewildered Porritt.

"Do lift the cover and admire the bird beneath," urged Holmes. "It is smaller than we would wish but welcome all the same."

Porritt lifted the lid with some reluctance, then gasped as he saw several bundles of bank-notes.

"I said I doubted if I could return your money. You will find I have not been able to do so. However, there is a total of twelve hundred pounds. You will be able to return the two amounts of £500 to your friends. I insist that I must remove £100 as my fee for my efforts on your behalf." Holmes stretched out his hand and lifted one of the bundles and placed it in his pocket. "You have £100 left to help you get on your feet again. Not a great deal out of two thousand but some men have to live all year on such a sum. I hope you will soon be able to resume your career in proof reading and editing. A moralistic person would no doubt make you promise never to gamble again. I am a detective and have seen all human frailties. I do not ask that. Again it is something between you and your own conscience. Watson, would you pop the money into that paper bag I have left conveniently to hand? Mr Porritt, I do urge you to take a cab from the rank outside and travel straight to your club where no doubt your friends await you. It would not do to carry such a large amount of cash through the streets. There are so many criminals about. Good evening."

"Well, Holmes," I said after showing our visitor out, "are you going to tell me any more than you told the unfortunate Porritt?"

"I apologise for the rather melodramatic *dénouement*, Watson, you know it is a weakness of mine."

"I suppose, judging from what you said and the way I caught you dressed yesterday, you have been in disguise consorting with criminals?"

"Well put, Watson. Firstly, I went to the house of Goldstein in the guise of an engineer from the telephone company. I said a fault on the line had been reported and I had come to check the telephone. The manservant there said they did not possess a telephonic instrument. I apologised, grumbled about head office and came away."

"And what was the purpose of that?"

"I wished to be sure that my theory was correct. I suspected that the telephone on Goldstein's desk had a wire running no further than into the hall. At a pre-planned moment Nemo, who remained, you will recall, in the hall, merely touched the wire to a battery causing the bell to ring. The conversation that Goldstein held was a mere farce."

"But how did they get into the house in the first place?"

"That was very simple. They found out, probably from servants' gossip in the neighbourhood, that the family was going away for the week, Saturday to Saturday. They merely forced an entrance in a back window. Then half an hour before Porritt was due, Goldstein installed the phone on the desk and sat with his receipt book at the ready. As soon as Porritt left, so did Goldstein with his telephone."

"But wouldn't it be obvious the window had been forced when the household returned?" I protested.

"Probably not, or perhaps Goldstein repaired any visible damage. In any case, even if it was found, the owner would think an attempt at burglary had failed and the household would thank their blessings that nothing was taken."

"Very cool," said I. "But how did you locate the money?"

"As I knew whom I was looking for, and knew all the details of the swindle, I was able to masquerade as a crook myself. I asked around among sporting gents and petty criminals, the two societies have a lot in common and there is considerable overlap in the memberships. I located Holy Peters and his accomplice and spun them a tale that my boss had the finger on poor Humphrey Porritt over a gambling debt and he didn't take kindly to them muscling in. The average petty criminal is not frightened of the police but he is very much afraid of crossing another criminal, especially one in a bigger way of business. So, dropping a few names like Colonel Moran and others known to me, I made poor old Peters see sense. I intended asking for a thousand pounds to let the matter rest. I did not see why Porritt should not suffer for his folly, and determined merely to get the money to repay his chums at his club. But I did not see why I should be out of pocket so added £100 for my fee. Then I thought I had been a bit hard on the innocent so demanded £1200. Thus I put myself completely beyond the law's protection and no better than the miscreants themselves."

"But surely a little harm is permitted to do a great good?" I protested.

"Have you been reading Shakespeare, Watson?"

"The thing I don't understand is how Nemo, Peters, was able to be right every time as regards the winner? Surely he could have placed bets himself and cleaned up without all this farrago?"

"You are still leaving your door open to confidence tricksters, Watson," Holmes laughed. "Of course he did not know which side would win. That is impossible, and during my enquiries I found confirmation of my suspicions when I turned up several more sporting gents who had had notes from Nemo. It seemed strange to me that all the bets proposed were for a winner from only two sides. No races with several entrants. That seemed very significant. This is how it worked: Peters draws up a list of, say, forty names. To twenty he sends a letter saying Cambridge will win the boat race, he sends the other twenty a letter saying Oxford will win the boat race."

"So twenty are bound to win!" I exclaimed.

"Exactly. The twenty losers are discarded. The winning twenty are split into two sets of ten and at the next big fight half are given one boxer, half the other. So once again the losers are abandoned. So ten men have been given the winner on two separate occasions. The ten are split into two fives, cricket this time, Harrow versus Eton, losers dropped, so now five men have been given three winners. Split the five into three and two, the tennis final arrives, and as it happens, the set of two are given the winner. So out of the original forty, two men have been given the winner on four separate occasions. So, understandably, they believe that they are on to a good thing. Peters decided to halt there and try to extort money from the final two. I managed to trace the other man and he had not fallen for it. However, friend Porritt did, hook line and sinker."

"Devilishly ingenious," I breathed.

"Cheap too. All Peters had to do was send a few letters through the penny post. As we saw, Porritt placed his money with his usual book-makers."

"Until the last wager."

"That was particularly clever. Book-makers do not like paying out, as you know, so his regular men would not be too keen to take a large bet from him anyway, as he had had so many recent winners. They would also be very wary of a punter who normally bets a hundred putting up three thousand pounds. No doubt he knew they would refuse it. Then when his greedy little ears heard he could get better odds through the mysterious Mr Goldstein he leapt at it. Who would prefer to win £6000 when they could win £9000?"

"So the whole scheme was set up and carried out so Peters and his accomplice could steal the stake money?"

"The whole ploy was a softening-up process so that at each stage their victim became more and more pliable. By the end he was putty in their hands."

"I feel a bit sorry for Porritt though, Holmes. Admittedly he was rather naive but the trick was very cunning."

"It was cunning and will be again. But Porritt was not merely naive. He was gullible, of course, but much worse than that, he was greedy. A confidence trickster can only flourish when his victim is avaricious. When the world rids itself of greedy people then, perhaps, we will see an end to the confidence trickster. But I don't think you or I will live to see it, do you, Watson?"

The Singular Adventure
of
THE BRIDE OF THE MOON

MY purpose in laying before the reader this collection of cases from the career of my friend Mr Sherlock Holmes is to give an indication of the staggering talent and intellectual ability of this prodigious man. To that end I have selected cases which give the general reader some insight into the varied facets of my friend's personality. Often Holmes has chided me on my selection, complaining that I have written up cases which were to him superficial and of little merit whilst neglecting others which were of a deeper intellectual challenge.

I fear my reader would soon get bored if I were to narrate in detail the many cases which depended on Holmes merely waiting, day after day, for something to happen as a result of his carefully planted schemes. Neither would the reader be charmed if I set out the beginning of an intriguing and bizarre adventure, only to confess that Holmes had got nowhere and that no more was to be said. For it must be realised that in Holmes' long and distinguished career he had many cases which were mundane and routine, and also many which he failed to solve for one reason or another.

This does not detract from his abilities as a consulting detective in any way, for without a doubt, he was the pre-eminent criminologist of his day. Often his finest attempts were thwarted by people intimately connected with the case withholding knowledge from the great man.

The case I am about to relate was such an example. Knowledge was withheld but, in spite of that, Holmes solved part of the mystery. That he did not bring it to a satisfactory conclusion cannot be laid at his door. But, as will be seen, we did find out in the end what had happened to the missing dancer, so I am able with a clear conscience to relate Holmes' part in the adventure without depriving my readers of a satisfactory conclusion

It was a spring morning in the year 1895 when we had a visitor whose name would have meant instant identification to half of London.

"I am John Nevil Maskelyne of *Maskelyne's Mysteries.*"

"Good morning to you, Mr John Nevil Maskelyne, I am Sherlock Holmes and this is my colleague Dr Watson."

It was clear to me that Holmes was completely unfamiliar with the name of the man who had been, for so many years, an indispensable part of the London popular entertainment scene. Holmes never ceased to surprise me with his breadth of knowledge and equally so with his profound ignorance of certain subjects. I have related how, early in our acquaintanceship, I had to explain to him the workings of the solar system of which he knew nothing. Now, I endeavoured to hint, without offence, at our visitor's place in the scheme of life.

"It is a pleasure to meet you, Mr Maskelyne, I have very fond memories of visiting your theatre and delighting in the wonderful conjuring you present there."

"Why, thank you, Doctor, most kind. We are in our 22nd year of operation and I am pleased to say the public is as loyal as ever," replied Maskelyne enthusiastically.

"What can I do for you, sir? It would seem that, being a magician, you could conjure up your own results without consulting a mere detective," said Holmes with a touch of asperity.

"Ah, Mr Holmes, this is the most bizarre case you can ever have had presented to you. I, the master magician, have caused a girl to disappear and I cannot bring her back!"

"Come, Mr Maskelyne, you are not in your theatre now, would you like to expound to a simple detective, in elementary terms, what your problem is?"

"But that is the problem, Mr Holmes. Let me explain. You see, my theatre is run like a happy family. I am the head, the father if you like, and around me I have a small group of workers who are as family to me. Most have been with me many years. So we all know each other, and, apart from the petty squabbles you find in all families, we all get along famously. That is what I cannot understand. I cannot conceive of a reason why one of my family should disappear, much less how it was done."

"You talk around the subject, sir, please come to the core of the matter."

"Certainly. My current show ends with a wonderful illusion that I call *The Bride of the Moon*. In this scene, my assistant Miss Emily Donkin, known professionally as Princess Zelda, enters a rocket ship – actually it is merely a box but it is decorated to resemble a rocket ship. The whole concept is modelled on Mr Jules Verne's story about a rocket travelling to the moon. Do you know it?"

"I regret I have little time for reading fiction, Mr Maskelyne."

"Ah well. It is the thirtieth anniversary of the first publication of *Voyage from the Earth to the Moon* and the English publisher has brought out a new edition to commemorate the fact. We have made a special arrangement between us to our mutual benefit."

"Is this relevant?" asked Holmes.

"I digress, I apologise. Well, in the illusion, Emily steps into the rocket ship which is lifted from the stage on a cable. Whilst in the air I ask her if she is comfortable and she calls out that she is. Then her hand appears waving a scarf that I have previously borrowed from the audience."

"Do you really need to tell me all this, Mr Maskelyne?" asked Holmes.

"But yes! It is essential that the audience believes that Princess Zelda is still in the rocket ship. Then I clap my hands and the rocket ship – that is the box – falls open and the sides clatter to the stage leaving a mere empty frame. Princess Zelda has gone to be the Bride of the Moon."

"Well you have saved me a visit to your delightful entertainment by describing it so succinctly," said Holmes with a trace of sarcasm.

"That is what the audience sees. That is what happens every night, with matinées on Wednesdays and Saturdays at 3. But last Thursday evening it was different."

"In what way?"

"Well, after the gasp from the audience, the curtains close and I step in front of them to receive the applause. While I am doing this, behind the curtain, the full company is assembling for the final *tableau* which is the Wedding of the Bride of the Moon. As I exit, the curtains part, and there in the middle of the *tableau* should be Princess Zelda on the right hand of the Man in the Moon. But she wasn't there. And she has not been seen since." Maskelyne stopped dramatically and stared at Holmes. "That is why I have come to you. Almost a week ago, Miss Emily Donkin vanished from the stage of my theatre and has never been heard of since."

Holmes was at last interested in the magician's tale and began to ask questions in his inimitable manner.

"Very intriguing, sir. Perhaps you will be so kind as to explain what actually happens at a normal performance after the lady vanishes."

"Certainly, although I hope you will come down to the theatre and examine my stage and facilities, for, although I created the illusion, I have no idea how Emily could disappear in actual fact."

"I will come. I will come now and perhaps the affair will be clearer when explained *in situ*."

We immediately went down to the famous Egyptian Hall where *Maskelyne's Mysteries* had its home, and as it was a Wednesday it meant we could watch the matinée performance which was continuing as usual with a substitute dancer for the absent Miss Donkin in the role of Princess Zelda.

In the interval of the performance, which to me was a jolly amusing and baffling show, I asked Holmes what he thought of it all.

"I cannot imagine why all these people wish to waste their time here. Surely they do not believe the man is performing miracles?" said Holmes.

"Of course not. They are puzzled with the tricks and do not know how they are done."

"I can't see why not. There is nothing remotely puzzling in any of it."

"But surely, Holmes – what about that trick where Maskelyne borrowed the man's pocket watch then smashed it all up with a hammer. That was amusing, wasn't it, to see the chap's consternation?"

"But it was obvious that a substitution had taken place. No gentleman would ask to borrow a watch then destroy it in the public gaze. He must have changed the package to another one got up in a similar manner."

"Well of course he did, we all know that. But the real one was found in that set of boxes all nestling one inside the other. How did it get right in the middle of all those, eh? They were in view the whole time and Maskelyne never went near them. He told us that and I noticed the fact particularly."

"Of course he went near them. He went to get them even as he said he'd never been near them. He opened them. He was not only near them, he put the watch inside the smallest box himself before our eyes."

"Well I never saw him."

"Of course, you didn't. Neither did the rest of the audience. But I did. I have seen everything as it really is. You watch but you do not observe. You see what the conjuror wants you to see, but I see what is really happening. It is the same in real life. People will not tell the truth because they do not know it. They state what they believe, not what really happens. I have trained my mind to see things as they are."

At that moment the bell went to summon us back into the auditorium for the second part of the entertainment. I reflected on what little pleasure Holmes must get out of life when he could not surrender himself up to a harmless diversion like a conjuring show.

When the show reached the climax, which was the *Bride of the Moon* illusion, Holmes sat up, alert to take notice of every single thing. As described to us earlier, the rocket ship was no more than a quaintly painted box just large enough to contain the form of Princess Zelda. The top of the box was pointed like a pyramid to convey the idea of a rocket. Attached to the point was a ring with a stout cable. The dancer entered the box via a door at the front and, as soon as it was closed, the box was hauled up above the stage where it remained suspended about eight feet above the floor.

"Are you comfortable, Princess Zelda?" called Maskelyne.

"Yes! I look forward to a safe passage to the Moon!"

"Will you not wave farewell to your subjects?" asked Maskelyne.

"Farewell!" As the voice spoke, a hand appeared and waved a silk scarf that Maskelyne had borrowed from a member of the audience. The hand was drawn back into the box and Maskelyne suddenly called "Then speed on your way, Princess Zelda!" and clapped his hands. All the side panels of the box fell to the floor with a clatter leaving a mere skeletal frame suspended. There was hearty applause as the curtains closed and the master magician stepped forward to bow to his public.

Then the curtains opened and there was a *tableau* with Princess Zelda on the arm of the Man in the Moon with sundry weird moon creatures posed around them. Maskelyne stepped towards them and Princess Zelda held out the silk scarf which Maskelyne took and, walking to the front of the stage, handed back to the lady in the front row who had earlier loaned it. The magician stepped back into the *tableau* and bowed low as the curtains closed for the last time.

"Stunning, Holmes!" I cried.

"Really, Watson, a child could see through all that flummery. When we go to examine the workings, I will expect to find a trap-door in the surface of the stage which will lead to a space or tunnel to where the Princess can descend."

"Impossible, Holmes. She was up in the air. We heard her."

"We heard a female voice. It was the first time Princess Zelda had uttered a word. How do we know what her voice sounded like? I should imagine that some other female of the company called out from behind the scenery somewhere."

"Oh. But we saw her wave to us."

"Probably an artificial mechanical hand worked by clockwork."

"Oh. But – ah yes, what about the silk scarf? That belonged to a lady in the audience. The Princess still had it at the final scene! Explain that."

"I will give it thought, Watson, but we are here on a more serious mission."

At that moment the manager of the theatre approached us.

"Good afternoon, gentlemen, I am Morton, the manager of the theatre. I understand that Mr Maskelyne wishes you to visit him backstage. If you will follow me?"

Mr Morton conducted us through a door at the side of the stage. This led to a minute area, no larger than six feet square, where the three of us stood whilst the manager knocked on another door facing us.

"Sorry about this, gentlemen, but I cannot open the door from this side. Owing to the nature of the entertainment, it is essential that no-one can wander in and discover the secrets of Mr Maskelyne. Visitors are not normally admitted. Mr Maskeylne, personally, has to sign a permit to allow anybody in through either the stage door or the pass door."

"Which is the stage door?" asked Holmes.

"That's the entry for the artistes; it is down a narrow alley at the side of the theatre. The performers are only permitted to enter and leave the theatre by that means. It is forbidden for them to come front of house. That's what we call the auditorium. It is a rule that the artistes remain backstage. So they must always use the stage door, which is guarded by Charlie, the stage door keeper. He will not allow anybody not connected with the show to enter without a signed permit. The Queen herself couldn't get by him without a permit."

"And this here is the pass door?"

"That's right, sir. It is the only connection between front of house and backstage. All theatres have to have them because of fire regulations and so on, but Mr Maskelyne keeps his side locked so that curious patrons cannot wander in. It is only used during the performance by myself if I need to visit backstage. Of course, it is open during rehearsals, and at the end of the show invited visitors, such as yourselves, may use it. Ah, here comes somebody."

The door was opened by a small wizened man who said suspiciously "Yes?", then seeing the face of Mr Morton, "Oh it's you, sir," opened the iron door wide allowing us to step through.

"Mr Sherlock Holmes and Dr Watson. I think Mr Maskelyne is expecting them."

"Ah yes, yes. Thank you. Please to come this way, gentlemen. Mr Maskelyne will be with you in a moment."

"I'll leave you in Wilkins' capable hands, if I may. He is in charge of everything at this side of the pass door as I am responsible for everything on the audience side."

We were at the side of the stage. With the door behind us, we looked left on to the stage itself. On our right was a wooden rail with some stone steps leading downwards. Straight ahead was a narrow corridor formed by the wall of the building on our right and by the stage scenery on our left. I was rather cast down to see that what appeared to be wonderful scintillating scenery was really very tawdry when viewed near to and the back of it was nothing more than flimsy wooden frames. The splendour of the Court of the Man in the Moon was nothing but painted canvas.

Maskelyne appeared, clad in an old robe thrown over his stage clothing.

"Welcome, gentlemen. Now this is Wilkins, my stage manager. He works the entire show. All the staff are under his jurisdiction. Mr Holmes is here to tell us what has happened to Emily."

"I assume that the lady escapes through a trap-door in the stage before the rocket ship box is hauled into the air?" said Holmes.

"Ah, I can see your reputation is not inflated, Mr Holmes. That is correct."

"Guvnor?"

"Oh, have no fear, Wilkins, we can have no secrets from Mr Holmes. We must all be frank. Our petty little tricks and flap-doodles do not matter when there is a crime to be solved."

"A crime, guvnor?" gasped Wilkins.

"Well perhaps not a crime. But we don't know, do we? We do not know where Emily has gone. We do not know if she has gone of her own free will or if she has been abducted by malefactors."

"What happens after she goes down the trap-door?" asked Holmes.

"Ask Evans to come, will you, Wilkins. Come down these steps, gentlemen, they lead under the stage." Maskelyne took up a lantern and led the way down the stone steps.

"Watch your heads, it is quite low."

It was indeed low. Perhaps only a matter of five feet from the hard concrete floor to the underside of the wooden stage. The stage planks were supported on stout joists about one foot apart but in several places there was a greater space where a trap-door was situated.

"You see, there are six trap-doors in all. The one here is the one used for the illusion."

"Are the others not used?"

"Not in the present show. You see, we introduce new illusions from time to time and, if we need a trap-door in another place, we simply cut one as required. These six have been cut over a period of thirty years. The other five are screwed closed at present."

"I see. So what exactly happens in the *Bride of the Moon* illusion?"

"Ah, here comes Wilkins with Evans. He will show you exactly. Evans, I would like you to show these gentlemen exactly what part you play in the Moon Bride illusion."

"Well, sirs, I wait here until I hear that the box is in place."

"How do you hear that?" asked Holmes.

"I place the box on the stage and bang with my heel when it is in position." said Wilkins.

"I see," said Holmes, "please continue."

"Well when I hear the signal, I undo the two bolts that hold the trap closed fast. The trap-door is now only held closed by the wooden pole. I then lift the base of the pole from the floor, and at an angle move the base to one side, thus allowing the trap-door to slowly fall open. As you can see, the pole is hinged to the trap-door."

"On the stage the illusion proceeds. The Princess goes into the box and the door is closed. Once in the box she lifts the floor of the box upwards – that too is a trap-door. This enables the girl to drop right through the stage safely into the arms of Evans here," said Maskelyne.

"Once the trap-door is open, I stand like this, ready to catch her. It is more like steadying her. It's all done in a moment. She drops, I catch her, set her on her pins, she dashes off up the stairs, I push the pole to close the trap-door. I then shoot the bolts. Then I dash up the stairs and round to the far side of the stage ready to pull the curtains."

"That all seems perfectly clear. What I do not understand is – at which point did the girl disappear?" asked Holmes.

"Now you come to it, Mr Holmes. The girl dashes up the steps – the only way out from under the stage. At the top of those steps she must turn left and go upstage –"

"Upstage?" interrupted Holmes.

"Towards the back of the stage. It is called upstage at the back and downstage at the front. The stage has a rake or slope to assist with sight-lines."

"I see. So this dancer goes towards the back of the stage."

"Yes, in that direction, but in the wings."

"The wings?" asked Holmes.

"The side of the stage is called the wings. You will understand that the top of the steps are in the wings and the only ways the girl could proceed would be back on to the stage, which is impossible as she is supposed to be still in the box, or behind the scenery towards the back of the stage. Which is what she does, because just at the top of the steps is a dresser who assists her into her bridal costume."

"Dresser? Please explain," asked Holmes.

"Emily comes up the steps in the costume which she wears in the first part. She then has to hastily change into the Bride of the Moon costume before hurrying into position in the *tableau*. To help her to do this there is a lady attendant called a dresser who assists her changing. It is all done very rapidly without a time for pausing. Evans, after closing the trap, comes up after her and follows the same path – there is no other place to go. He actually passes Emily while she is changing, to make his way to his next task which is opening the curtains."

This explanation was very clear and it showed how rapidly every person in the team must work to ensure the success of the illusion. While these procedures were carried out below the stage, in the wings Wilkins was instructing the raising of the box and Maskelyne was onstage holding forth.

"So what went wrong on Thursday night?" asked Holmes.

"Everything went well until the point when Evans passed the dresser – Mrs Wilkins."

"My wife," explained Wilkins.

"She is our head wardrobe lady – maintains the costumes, and generally oversees anything to do with laundering and mending, as well as dressing during the performance. When Evans came past her, Mrs Wilkins asked 'Where's Emily?' She was not there."

"I couldn't stop as I had to go and pull the curtains, so I don't know what happened," said Evans.

"Mrs Wilkins called down the steps for Emily – well she couldn't call, people would hear – rather, hissed for her. But there was no sign of her. She had vanished. The show had to go on and Evans opened the curtains on the *tableau* to reveal a wedding without the bride. As soon as the curtains closed again, I rushed down the steps to look for Emily. I assumed she had come to grief under the stage – as you can see it is possible to fall over or perhaps knock yourself out on one of the joists if you do not keep your head down. Although Emily is a small person she would still have to lower her head."

"So what did you find?"

"Nothing, Mr Holmes, nothing at all. It was completely empty all under here."

"Can I speak to Mrs Wilkins?" asked Holmes.

"I'll fetch her," said her husband.

"Shall we go up again?" asked Maskelyne.

"Please leave me the lamp, I will come up shortly to join you," said Holmes.

So we left Holmes prowling about under the stage and the rest of us went up the stairs to stand in the wings until Mrs Wilkins joined us. Holmes was not long as it was clear there was nothing to observe that we had not seen readily.

"Ah, Mrs Wilkins, could you be so kind as to show me exactly where you stand when awaiting to assist Miss Emily to change her costume?"

"Why yes, I stand here, like this, my arms out like that with the bridal costume at the ready. She steps into it and I pull it up around her and close the fastenings at the back," said Mrs Wilkins demonstrating her actions in mime form.

"She puts this on over her existing costume?" asked Holmes.

"Oh yes, there is no time for any other way. As it is, I usually end up running upstage after her, still trying to do the fastenings. I'm sure Mr Maskelyne knows that sometimes the Bride of the Moon is standing there onstage with her dress all open at the back."

"So on Thursday you were waiting, and Emily did not come up the steps?"

"She did not, sir. I called to her but she did not appear."

"But you said, Evans, that she left ahead of you," stated Holmes.

"I caught her and she dashed off in the usual way. That's all I know. I was on her heels the same as usual. And when I got to Nell, that is, Mrs Wilkins, she said 'Where's Emily?' I had to dash, so just said 'I dunno' and hurried on."

"Most singular." Holmes looked about him and said "I wonder if I may have a peer about on my own? Dr Watson will tell you that I like to examine the ground carefully with my lens. I do not expect to find much, Mr Maskelyne, because you have waited a week before calling me in to investigate. If I had been summoned the night it happened, I have no doubt clues would have been left that would reveal all. But you have repeated this course of action each night, with a matinée on Saturday and today, so I hardly think there will be much of a trace of the particular events of Thursday night."

We all went our several ways. It seems that the custom of theatre folk is to go out for something to eat between the matinée and the evening performance. For those without sufficient time to get home and back, it is the thing to either frequent an eating house or, if of the poorer sort, buy food and bring it back to eat in the theatre. But almost all prefer to leave the premises for some sort of break. Only the stage door keeper regularly maintains his post.

Mr Maskelyne invited me to join him for a glass in his private dressing-room whilst we waited for Holmes to conclude his thorough examinations.

"I fear this is quite a teaser for your colleague, Doctor," said Maskelyne.

"I have no doubts he will find an explanation," said I loftily.

"But to vanish without a trace from under the stage. It is quite impossible! The only way out is the staircase and that was guarded by Mrs Wilkins, who sees everything! I can not see how it was done and I am a professional magician."

"Perhaps when Holmes has discovered the answer you will have a new trick to add to your show," said I jovially.

"That's a thought, eh?" agreed Maskelyne.

It was not long before Holmes joined us, looking thoughtful.

"Well, my dear fellow, have you solved it?" asked Maskelyne.

"Tell me, Maskelyne, why should anybody disappear when in ten minutes time they would be going home anyway?"

"I do not follow you."

"Normally Emily would finish in the *tableau*, presumably change from being Princess Zelda back to Emily Donkin in her every day clothes, and go home."

"Well yes, she would. The first thing I did was to send to her lodgings to see if she had turned up there. But she hadn't – still hasn't. I've sent several times to her lodgings but she hasn't been back there."

"Let us suppose that for some reason she did not want to work for you here at the theatre any more."

"But she loved her work. Loved it!"

"Why should she not just leave in the normal way though?"

"Perhaps she was compelled to leave. Kidnapped," I suggested.

"It certainly seems odd that she should leave the theatre at that most crucial time – half way through an illusion," mused Holmes.

"Completely ruined the *finale*," said Maskelyne.

"But we don't know that she left the theatre, Holmes," said I.

"Good old Watson, as usual, you have put your thumb on the nub of the problem."

"But she must have done," protested Maskelyne, "or she would have been found. There is nowhere to hide. Besides she never passed Mrs Wilkins."

"So you seriously think she vanished into thin air, do you, my dear sir?"

"Well no, of course not, I of all people know that there must be a rational explanation, but I'm damned if I can get at it," blustered Maskelyne.

"I have no doubt the explanation is as simple as your tricks, but there is some missing piece of information. Not how she vanished but why."

Holmes asked to interview the stage door keeper who turned out to be a taciturn old codger.

"Nobody gets past me without a signed pass from Mr Maskelyne himself, and not many of them are given out."

"Can you remember last Thursday –" began Holmes.

"'Course I can, the night Emily Donkin disappeared."

"Exactly. Now did Miss Donkin have any visitors that night?" asked Holmes smoothly.

"Visitors? Certainly not! No visitors are allowed without a pass and even then they have to be out and away again by the half."

"The half?"

"That's a signal to the entire theatre," said Maskelyne. "Half an hour before the performance starts all visitors must leave the backstage area and all personnel connected with the show should be in the theatre."

"So there were no visitors for Miss Donkin for you to eject?" said Holmes.

"Likes of her ain't allowed visitors," growled the curmudgeon.

"I do not encourage my staff or the lesser performers to have visitors backstage at all, Mr Holmes. In this type of entertainment secrecy is of paramount importance. I am liberal with my free tickets for my employees and that seems to satisfy all," said Maskelyne.

"Thank you, Charlie, you have been most helpful," said Holmes benignly to the stage door keeper, thus antagonising him as unhelpfulness was a trait he obviously cultivated.

Back in the master magician's dressing-room, Holmes broached the feasibility of watching the show from backstage.

"I would like to see what happens tonight in the *Bride of the Moon* illusion. Could I lurk in the wings near the top of the stairs and could Dr Watson crouch in a corner under the stage?" This was the first time I had heard of this proposal.

"Um, it should be possible. I tell you what – could you take up your positions in the interval and stay in them until the end of the show? I really cannot have strangers moving about while the show is on."

"That should be perfect, Mr Maskelyne, perfect. When I have seen it all I think we will have a solution."

Holmes and I dined at Simpson's in the Strand whilst waiting for the appointed time of our watching.

"What do you make of all this, Holmes?" I asked. "It seems quite inexplicable. It is totally impossible that Emily Donkin can have disappeared like that."

"I think we will find, as usual, that when we have eliminated the impossible, whatever remains, however improbable, will be the truth."

"You think there is a rational explanation then?"

"Of course. Everything is rational. It only appears bizarre or singular if there is an element missing from the facts as presented. In this instance there is a missing element. We have been given an assorted bundle of facts but we have not been told of one vital thing, of that I am sure. Furthermore, I am convinced that the explanation is not only rational but extremely simple."

"I do not know how you can assume that."

"Look at the people concerned, Watson. We are not dealing here with highly intellectual brains of a criminal bent. This is not a Professor Moriarty at work. We are not even dealing with low cunning. We are talking about a young girl of perhaps twenty years who earns her living as a dancer in a conjuring show. Now I do not wish to malign the lady, but would you expect her to be a product of Girton Ladies College?"

"I take your point."

"Finish your claret and we will return to the scene of the mysterious disappearance."

We arrived at the Egyptian Hall in time for the interval. The brusque door keeper Charlie begrudgingly allowed us in as he had been instructed and Maskelyne greeted us warmly.

"A splendid house tonight. The show is going particularly well. Now let us place you ready for the second half." The magician led us to the wings where Holmes elected to stand with his back leaning against the iron pass door, to be well out of everybody's way, and I was shown down to the under stage area. Wilkins had produced a small box from somewhere and proffered it to me to use as a stool to sit on. This was a great comfort as, owing to the restricted headroom, I would have had to crouch. It was agreed that I would place myself in the corner nearest the bottom of the steps, but out of the way of Evans and the new Princess Zelda who, of course, had their rapid journeys to make.

It was very dark under the stage as there was no illumination at all. There was a faint shaft of light from the stage above that shone weakly down the steps, and as my eyes became accustomed to the gloom I could make out the stout pole that wedged the trap-door closed. I could hear the progress of the performance fairly clearly and, remembering the show from the afternoon, could imagine what was happening a mere five feet above my head.

As the time for the *Bride of the Moon* illusion drew near I felt a tingle of excitement as I now knew what really happened in that extraordinary spectacle. I was aware of a light coming down the steps and Evans appeared carrying a lantern. He made his way to the trap-door, put the lantern on the floor and unshot the two bolts. He then stood waiting and in a minute or so both he and I heard a smart double rap as the stage manager Wilkins gave the signal from above. Evans then slid the pole and allowed the trap-door to fall open. He then took up position and very soon I saw the body of a girl drop into his arms. She immediately dashed in a crouching posture to the steps, then up them and away.

Evans quickly replaced the pole, closing the trap, shot the bolts, picked up his lantern and he too went in a similar manner. He had never even glanced in my direction. In fact I do not know whether he had been told I would be there. I waited a couple of minutes then decided it would now be safe to arise, myself, as I could hear the show had reached the disclosure of the *tableau*.

After the gloom of the under-stage cellar, the wings seemed quite light but, of course, nothing like the brightness of the stage itself, where the curtains were closing for the last time on the finale spectacle. Holmes was nowhere to be seen. There was nobody at all in the wings until the cast trooped off upstage to go to their dressing rooms. Then Holmes came through the pass door and Maskelyne approached from the stage.

"Well, Mr Holmes, have you solved our mystery?" he cried.

"Do you consider your family speak the truth, Mr Maskelyne?" asked Holmes.

"I should hope so. They have no reason not to. Whom do you accuse of lying?" asked the magician.

"I rather think Mrs Wilkins has not told me, or you, the truth."

"I'll summon her immediately." Maskelyne hurried off.

"What have you found, Holmes?"

"I have found that I cannot rely on people volunteering information if I do not ask the right questions, Watson. Ah, here comes the good lady."

Maskelyne returned with Wilkins the stage manager, and his wife.

"Now, Nell, you must tell Mr Holmes all you know and answer his questions truthfully," said Maskelyne sternly.

"But I have, sir, I've said the truth," protested the wardrobe lady.

"Mr Holmes says that you did not tell him the truth last time."

"I swear I did, sir," gasped Mrs Wilkins.

"Now I watched you tonight, Mrs Wilkins, and after you helped the young lady into her wedding dress, you bustled after her up to the back where I saw you helping another member of the cast – a man – into some strange costume with lots of arms – *papiér maché*, perhaps?"

"Well, yes, I always do that. That's Mr Hansard, one of the principal actors, he cannot manage without help because of the way the costume is made." The named actor was dressed in the guise of some fantastical moon creature and I remembered him posed at the side of the finale *tableau*.

"You always do that, you say?"

"Why yes. What is this, Mr Maskelyne? What am I accused of?" said the bewildered woman.

"On Thursday last week, when Emily Donkin did not appear to don her wedding dress, did you go help the man with his costume?"

"Well, yes."

"Thank you, Mrs Wilkins. You may go."

As the still bewildered woman left us, Maskelyne sighed "Alas, now it is all too apparent, Mr Holmes. Emily paused below the stage until Mrs Wilkins had to leave her post to attend to her next chore. She then came up unobserved because we were all busy getting on to the stage for the *tableau*."

"Exactly."

"But we would have seen her in the wings. We would have all come offstage. I, myself, came straight round from the other side, Evans came across the stage, we were all here at this spot within seconds of the curtains closing. There was nobody here!" declared the stage manager Wilkins.

"No, Emily was not here. She had gone through that door," said Holmes pointing.

"But that's the pass door!" protested Wilkins. "No artiste is ever allowed to open that! Why, even when the show is not on, the performers cannot go through it."

Maskelyne smiled. "You see how disciplined a company we are, Mr Holmes, because our rules say we are not permitted to go through the pass door, we have assumed that we are physically incapable of doing so. We have been very foolish."

"I have been remiss for not asking exact enough questions. I think all is now clear. Miss Emily lurked under the stage instead of coming straight up. Evans did not see her and did not have time to return to search. Mrs Wilkins did not have time to wait any longer as she had to assist Mr Hansard. When the coast was clear for Emily, only a matter of two minutes, she slipped up the steps and through the pass door."

"But she would be in costume, the audience would see her as she entered the auditorium," protested Wilkins.

"Of course. So she waited in the space between the two doors. The very space where Dr Watson and I were kept waiting this afternoon. I have no doubt that she had some kind of wrap or coat ready either under the stage or between the doors. She would delay until the show had finished, then join the audience as they shuffled out through the exit doors."

"Well this all seems very clear now you have explained it, Mr Holmes.

Except for one thing – why?" queried Maskelyne.

"That is the next step in my investigation. I must ask your most excellent stage door keeper a further question."

Maskelyne took Holmes and myself back to interview the curmudgeonly Charlie again.

"Now, Charlie," said Holmes easily, "you know earlier today you told me that last Thursday evening Miss Emily Donkin had not had any guests or visitors?"

"That's right. She didn't," said Charlie.

"I forgot to ask you if anybody had enquired for her at the stage door. Perhaps to ask the time the curtain fell or something like that?"

"A couple of young fellows did ask when she was likely to come out," agreed Charlie.

"Ah," said Holmes, "and what did you tell them?"

"I said the show didn't end until ten past ten and they'd have to wait outside with the rest."

"The rest?" asked Holmes.

"There's usually half a dozen folk hanging about. That's why I'm here. To stop them getting in."

Maskelyne spoke up "There are sometimes admirers who seek my autograph or to press small gifts upon me, and other members of the company often have people to meet them."

"That Maisie has a chap, either her fiancy or husband – he's here every night to walk her home, so he's one who's always outside," volunteered Charlie.

"And these two men enquiring for Emily – had you seen them before?"

"No, never."

"And have you seen them since?" asked Holmes.

"Yes."

"When?"

"They came again on Friday."

"And what did you tell them?"

"That she hadn't come to the theatre."

"And did they come again after that?"

"Yes."

"When?"

"They called again on Monday."

"And you told them that Emily had not been in?"

"I did. I said not to come bothering me again as she had not been seen since Thursday. They've not been back."

We returned to Baker Street with Holmes brooding in silence. I attempted a little levity. "I think drawing teeth would be easier than getting answers from that stage door keeper. But you reached the solution."

"I missed the obvious, Watson. If the girl chose to disappear ten minutes before her normal home time it should have been clear to me that she wished to avoid meeting somebody who was waiting at her usual exit. Her only option was to go out another way. Her only alternative was the forbidden pass door. We must now find out who these men are and why they are so abhorrent to Miss Donkin."

The next day Holmes and I went in search of Emily Donkin's lodgings in Brixton. The landlady was at first inclined to be disagreeable.

"That young woman's had more visitors since she went missing than when she was here," said she.

"Then we are not the first to enquire about her?" asked Holmes.

"I should say not. Anyway I don't see why I should talk to you. She ups and offs owing me a week's rent, now she's been gone another week. I'm going to let her room. I can't afford to lose money like that."

"Of course you can't," said Holmes smoothly. "That is why we are here. Perhaps if you will invite us in, I can pay you the outstanding amount."

At this the landlady changed her attitude and ushered us in.

"Now how much is owing?" said Holmes benignly.

"Well it's five and sixpence a week and there's two weeks due."

"If I give you a sovereign, that will clear matters?" said Holmes handing over the coin.

"Oh, thank you, sir."

"You say several people have been enquiring after Emily Donkin?"

"Well, the same ones have kept coming. There was a man from the theatre, he came two or three times, and then there was a couple of young fellers who came nearly every day 'til I told them not to bother me any more."

"Do you know who they were?"

"No, sir."

"I wonder if I could look at her room?"

"Oh, I don't know about that," said the landlady doubtfully.

"I expect you will want to clear it in readiness for a new tenant." So we mounted the stairs to the rather basic room formerly occupied by the missing dancer. "I wonder if I could prevail upon you to make us both a cup of tea? Dr Watson, here, will assist you, I'm sure."

"Oh are you a doctor, sir? Of course I'll make you a cup of tea."

"Occupy her, Watson, while I look round," whispered Holmes.

So it was my task to entertain the landlady over the vilest cup of tea I have ever drunk while listening to a comprehensive list of all the poor woman's ailments. It was not long, thankfully, before Holmes returned.

"I wonder if I could ask you to make a bundle of Miss Donkin's things and have them sent to this address." Holmes handed over a paper slip. "Also, if anybody comes asking after her, please refer them to the same address."

On the way back to Baker Street in the cab Holmes pulled out a photograph. It showed a group of men and girls obviously at some merry party.

The girls were sitting on the men's knees and they all appeared very familiar with one another.

"A somewhat *louche* looking party," I said.

"The one there is Emily Donkin. At last we know what she looks like."

"Quite a good-looking girl too," I commented. Then I noticed the man she was with. "I say, Holmes, isn't that the Honourable Edwin Carstairs?"

"Is it?"

"I'm sure it is. He is always being mentioned in the newspapers. He's a well-known man about town. The sort of fellow who brings the aristocracy into disrepute with his shallow and selfish ways."

"Then I think we will pay him a visit."

Later that day, following on a wire Holmes had sent, we arrived at the elegant bachelor chambers in Albany occupied by the Hon Edwin Carstairs. His manservant let us in whilst he went to see if his master was at home. As I looked around me I was forced to compare and contrast this apartment with the primitive accommodation we had visited earlier in the day. The Hon Edwin entered.

"I received your wire, Mr Holmes, and it is not convenient to see you, but as you are here, I can give you two minutes. What is your business?"

Holmes produced the photograph and said "I have come about this young lady with whom you appear to be somewhat familiar."

"Ah, you do come straight to the point. Well you have backed the wrong horse here. I do not care tuppence who knows my business, I have no secrets, you cannot blackmail me. Publish and be damned, say I!"

"You mistake my purpose, sir. Emily Donkin has disappeared and I am retained by her employer to find her. I am following all the clues I can."

"Oh, you are one of those detective fellows, I see. Well I am of no help to you. Who the hell is Emily Donkin?"

"That is the name of the lady who is sitting on your knee in the photograph," said Holmes icily.

"Oh, right. Hardly a lady, some theatre trollop. Well, I've no idea who she is, much less where. That picture is a year old. It was taken at Stiffy Longmore's birthday. That chap there is Stiffy, I think the fat man at the end is something in the City, I don't know the other one."

"What about the girls?"

"They are just girls. Chorus girls, I suppose, I don't know. Perhaps I should tell you gentlemen a little about my life. There are many late night drinking and supper clubs throughout London. I go to one nearly every night of the week when I'm in Town. I am a bachelor, I have an inordinate amount of money and I spend it prodigally. I wine and dine and play with girls every night. I've no idea who they are. If I am still sober enough when I come home, I will bring one back here with me and we will be intimate on the silken sheets of my four poster bed. That is what I do. I also go to Henley for the Regatta, Cowes for the yachting, Ascot for the racing and go shooting in Scotland. I am welcome in the finest houses in the land because of my birth and breeding. Sensible parents keep their daughters away from me. That is the sort of man I am. I do not care tuppence for any woman, much less showgirls. I don't even know if I see the same girl twice. So I regret I can be of no help to you. Good day gentlemen."

With that amazing speech he left the room and his manservant showed us out.

"What a cad!" I cried when we were outside.

"Come, let us call at the Egyptian Hall," said Holmes.

Once there we braved the stage door man's wrath and Holmes gave him a sum of money and a slip of paper bearing our address. His instructions, like those to the landlady, were to direct any enquiries to Baker Street.

And there it appeared that the trail turned cold. The landlady sent Emily Donkin's effects to us but there was nothing to give a clue. A couple of weeks went by, then one day two young men asked for me and were shown in.

"Dr Watson? We were told we could find Emily here?" said one.

"I'm afraid not," said I. "But this is my friend Mr Sherlock Holmes. He is a detective and is investigating Miss Donkin's sudden disappearance."

"I left your name at the Egyptian Hall theatre, Watson. Who are you, sir?" asked Holmes.

"I'm Emily's brother, Billy, and this is Sam, her intended."

"We are affianced. We should have been married now if she hadn't disappeared," said the other young man.

The two men were not much more than youths, both of them being in their very early twenties. They did not strike me as artisans and I guessed that they were clerks in some lowly capacity.

"I presume you are the two men who have been persistently enquiring at both your sister's lodgings and the Egyptian Hall?"

"We are worried out of our minds, Mr Holmes. We can't think where she can have gone. We keep asking at all the places we can possibly think of," burst out Billy Donkin.

"I share your concern, Billy. Now listen, Dr Watson will confirm this I am sure, sometimes young women who are about to get married, suddenly, at the very last minute, become scared and want to call the whole thing off."

"That is quite a common thing, actually. More often than you may suppose," I agreed.

"Do you think it may be simply that? She is apprehensive and has gone into hiding?" continued Holmes.

"No, sir!" cried Sam, "We truly love each other and I cannot think she would back out like that!"

"No. If she felt like that she would have said. She's not the sort of girl who wouldn't tell a chap the truth. She is quite straight. She would not be scared to say she had changed her mind," said her brother.

"Then," said Holmes, "I fear that this matter is very serious. You must tell me all you know, no matter how trivial. Tell me what you know of her friends and her haunts."

The two young men were with us for some time and we learned practically the whole history of the Donkin family, how they lived, their neighbourhood, their friends and acquaintances, but nothing that seemed to convey a clue as to why this rather common-place young woman should have disappeared in such odd circumstances.

After the youths had gone, I suggested to Holmes that there was no great mystery, simply that the girl had sought pastures new as many a young person did. Perhaps she had run off to marry a soldier?

"I do not think so, Watson. Surely even the most ardent lover would wait to slip away at a more discreet moment, not at a time when all eyes are on her? The whole crux of the matter hinges on the fact that Emily wished to avoid her fiancé and brother and has done so ever since. I think for some reason she is in hiding and I must find her or this case will never be solved."

The case never was solved by Holmes. For weeks he peered and probed the recesses of London. He adopted several disguises to worm his way into the confidence of lowly people but everywhere he drew a blank. Other cases came along which took his attention and still he would not forget Emily Donkin, returning to the matter time and time again.

Billy Donkin called two or three times but soon realised that, although Holmes was doing all he could, the results were fruitless. His friend Sam had given up all hope and tended to think, as I did, that she had thrown him over and fled with another man.

Then one day, some four months later, we had a visit from Billy Donkin.

"Emily's been found, Mr Holmes."

"Where?" I asked before Holmes could speak.

"In the Thames."

A girl's body, great with child, had been pulled out of the river. Billy had read of it in a newspaper and, with dread suspicion, had made his way to the morgue.

"It was her all right, Mr Holmes. They said she had not been in the water more than a couple of days. I reckon she had got knocked up by some fellow and was lying low all the time we were searching, God knows where."

"Did they say how much the child was developed?" I asked.

"Oh yes, nearly due to give birth they reckoned."

"Poor woman," I said. "Have you told your pal Sam?"

"Yes. He was devastated. He swore blind he had never laid a finger on her. I believe him – he's an honest sort of bloke. Though it wouldn't have mattered, would it, she was going to marry him anyway – the kid would have been born in wedlock right enough. No, some other fellow had taken advantage of her."

"I'm so sorry, Billy," I said.

"Yes, well. That's life, ain't it?" he replied, trying to brave the world. He went to the door and, just before it closed behind him, he paused and said "And ain't life rotten."

Holmes had not said a word.

The Singular Adventure
of
THE HOLY ROOD

IN setting forth these narratives of my friend Sherlock Holmes I have concentrated on those cases which provide sufficient interest to the general reader as well as the *aficianado* of crime. There are many cases in my records which have a specialised interest but which would prove unsatisfactory to relate because of some inherent flaw in the story. The reader would not thank me for whetting his appetite with a most fascinating case, only to be let down when I confess that Holmes had failed to solve it.

The adventure of the Holy Rood could have been one of those unsatisfactory examples but for the mere happenstance that several years later the true ending of the tale was revealed.

The reader may have received the impression that my entire life revolved around the activities of my friend Sherlock Holmes and I had no existence other than as his *confidant*. I realise I have caused this version of myself by casting Dr Watson as the mere observer or reporter, rather than as an individual with a life of his own, with interests entirely apart from Holmes' activities. Thus it may surprise my readers to learn that one June day I took myself off to stay with an old college chum of mine who had taken up residence in the great county of Yorkshire. He had a small but charming manor house in the Vale of York which had descended to him from his father's brother. Robert Dawson was a bachelor and having sufficient, but not ample, means, jogged along quite cosily with the assistance of a matronly lady who acted as cook and housekeeper, and a gardener-handyman who coped with his enclosed garden and manual household chores. We had been great chums at medical college, but he had failed to take his finals as he had inherited his modest competence at roughly the same time and decided that he would prefer to pursue his many interests rather than tend to the sick and maimed.

We had kept in touch over the years and sometimes met up on his occasional visits to London but I had never visited him before, in spite of his entreaties repeated from time to time. So, finally, I gave way and made the long journey up to Yorkshire with the intention of staying until the end of June. Bob put me at my ease immediately and we both stepped back into that familiar and comfortable relationship we had enjoyed all those years ago. My friend had several local interests, sat on various committees, had regular visits to pay in the area and so on, so we soon got into the way of spending some time together and at others going our own ways. If he had to go into York, for instance, he would warn me during the previous day, thus I could accompany him and whilst he was at his regular meeting, discussing farming prices or whatever, I was free to explore that fine old city.

So my stay would have been exceedingly pleasant except for one thing: the weather. It must have been the dullest, coldest, rainiest June in living memory. Because of the casual nature in which Bob's household was run, I was at liberty to please myself as to when I came and went but, truth to tell, I spent more time browsing in his library than I would have liked.

Shortly after my arrival he gave a small dinner party to introduce me to his closest friends. There were some six guests only, plus the two of us, and whilst they were very pleasant and affable people who pressed me to call on them, I need only trouble the reader with the mention of one – The Rev Alistair Cooper who was the incumbent of the village church. This clergyman was a special friend of Bob's as he too was a bachelor with wide ranging tastes and interests, although he was mainly interested in antiquarian and historical themes, whereas Bob's chief interests were crops, animals and natural phenomena. They met at least once a week to play chess or backgammon and dropped in and out of each other's home as though they were both permanent residents of each.

Bob, whilst not being a rich man, had sufficient means; the Rev Alistair, however, was a poor man dependent entirely on his stipend which seemed to me to be little above penury. But he appeared to manage perfectly well in his decrepit vicarage looking after himself, doing his own cooking and household chores. Should he require the collar on his shirt turning or a new cushion making for his easy chair, various good ladies of the parish would come to his assistance. Between his pastoral duties he roamed around the countryside poking and digging about for historical remains.

The Rev Alistair may be thought eccentric as he cared little for his appearance, wearing the strangest assortment of clothing, and he was no respecter of conventional hours. Although he did maintain accurate times for the commencement of his services, in his own time he would frequently sally forth to explore an ancient burial mound just as sensible folk were sitting down to dinner.

I saw quite a bit of the Rev Alistair as he often dropped by the house and, should Bob be absent, he would chat to me for a while before going on his way. His habitual garments for fossil hunting were a shapeless navy blue smock affair, some stout corduroy trousers and a wide-brimmed battered hat which, apparently, was made of felt in winter, being replaced by a straw version during the summer months.

I had been at Holyrood House (for such was the name of Bob's residence) for some seven or eight days when Bob announced that on the 21st were to be held The Midsummer Revels. On enquiry, I was told that, whereas in most of the land May 1st was the day for revelling and maypole dancing, in this village, for some reason that even the Rev Alistair could not discover, there was a tradition of celebration on Mid-Summer's Day. Over the years this tradition had become the most important feature of the local calendar and for miles around people came annually to join in The Revels of Little Fordham.

"What it will be like this year with such foul weather, I can't imagine," moaned Bob. "It is usually a nice day for The Revels but it doesn't look like it this year. I'm sorry it has been such poor weather for you, old boy."

I hastened to reassure my host that I did not lay the vagaries of the local weather at his door and that I was happy to take my chance from day to day with whatever the good Lord sent us. Preparations for the Revels proceeded apace and meetings were held to decide if some alternative arrangements should be made in case of inclement weather. Bob, of course, in his position as quasi-lord of the Manor, was much involved and I would receive exasperated exclamations as he would return from a meeting, drenched through, pull off his coat and boots and fling himself into a chair with "Stupid dolts want to hire a marquee from York!" or "The fools think that a Punch & Judy show in the church will be an adequate substitute!"

As it happened, the 21st dawned dry and bright and as the sun rose it gained in power until by midday it was as hot a day as we expect in the height of summer. It was especially extraordinary as even on the days previously, which had provided no rain, it had been excessively gloomy and chill. Bob was delighted and kept saying "Now you will see Little Fordham in its true colours!"

The weather held steady all day so that the dancing and the races and the tug-of-war all took place as scheduled and everybody was especially gay as right until the last minute they had feared disaster on Revels day. The beer tent did a roaring trade as suddenly throats were parched and the Punch & Judy man was able to perform as he had done for the last dozen years, under the shade of a spreading oak tree and not in the chill of the church nave.

All the village turned out for the celebrations, the old folk sat in the sun and yarned of Revels stretching back a hundred years, and the young people regarded the event as licence to behave more forwardly with each other than would have normally been considered seemly. After all, as the Rev Alistair pointed out, maypole dancing and so on began as ancient fertility rites to propitiate gods who could, if so inclined, damn the coming year with a lack of fecundity in beast, mankind, and crop.

"Where is Alistair? I haven't seen him about," I asked my host during the afternoon.

"He's not here. It seems he has to attend some sort of ecclesiastical convocation."

"Oh, what a shame. I suppose the weather is the same at York," I said.

"Oh, he's not at York. Had to go to Canterbury. Some big thing for the clerics, you know. He's not missed the Revels before, in all the time he's been here."

"And is that long?" I asked.

"About fifteen years. He is a southerner by birth in spite of his Scottish name. To be honest, I don't think The Revels are much in his line. He's a sober-sided fellow at heart and though he usually puts on a good show of enjoying himself, I think he would rather be grubbing through the parish records."

"This sun is exceeding hot. Can I get you another beer?" I asked and we made a bee-line for the beer tent once again.

At the end of the afternoon Bob, by virtue of his standing in the village, was called upon to present the prizes for the various races. That being concluded, we felt that we had enjoyed the Revels sufficiently and made our way back to the house. Later on there was to be a dance and after dark who knows what the youngsters would get up to, but we left the revellers and returned to Holyrood House.

Neither of us had drunk to excess but we had drunk more than we were accustomed to in the afternoon, and so were very relaxed with the sunshine and good fellowship. We ambled back in desultory fashion wondering what repast Mrs Crummit, his housekeeper, had left us, for, like the rest of the village, she was given a holiday from noon of the 21st June. In spite of my straw hat I felt I had taken too much sun on my nose although Bob waggishly implied it was the beer that had made my nose red! And in this fashion we walked up to the house and round to the side door. The front door faced the formal entrance drive and that led away from the village so the side way was used far more than the main entrance.

Turning the corner of the house we were walking across the flagstoned terrace which is such a feature of the south elevation when it happened – I tripped, stumbled and fell. I am quite a heavily built man and I went down like a felled ox. To my dismay I heard and felt a distinct snap and the excruciating pain that followed left me in no doubt that I had broken my ankle.

Bob, the dear fellow, hauled me upright and taking all of my weight upon himself aided me into the house where I crumpled myself on to the sofa. As I am a doctor I was able to ensure that Bob did the correct things in such an emergency and he made me comfortable while he went out to harness up a cart.

I will not bore the reader with details of my journey to the nearest cottage hospital, or the setting of the bones with plaster of Paris and our subsequent return. Suffice it to say that it was almost ten o'clock before we were back home and able to do justice to Mrs Crummit's cold collation.

The next day's weather was a return to its former state and the sole topic of conversation in the village was how lucky we had been with the weather for The Revels. My activities were now somewhat cramped and I feared Bob would find having a semi-invalid on his hands a very different thing from having an active guest. Therefore, I determined that I would spend another couple of days to get used to hobbling about on crutches, then I would return to London once I felt confident enough to clamber on and off trains.

Bob, the dear fellow, assured me that I was no trouble and that I could stay as long as I liked but my mind was made up. I wrote to Holmes about my unfortunate accident and of my determination to curtail my stay and return home. Imagine my surprise, therefore, when, as we were sitting in the parlour after supper two days later, the bell jangled at the front door.

"Who the devil's that, at this time?" grumbled Bob. "Obviously a stranger, someone from the village would come to the side door."

Before he could complain further, Mrs Crummit entered and said that a friend of Dr Watson's had arrived and may he come in. Assent readily given, who should stride in but Holmes himself.

"What are you doing here?" I gaped.

"Well, Watson, I reckoned you could do with a bit of support, both moral and practical. I couldn't let you undertake such a long journey on your own when you're knocked up like this. Now I've endured the journey here from King's Cross myself, I realise how sensible I was to think of it."

I was very touched. Here I was with two stout friends who both wished to comfort me in my adversity. Having introduced them to each other, Bob got Mrs Crummit to whistle up a bit more supper for Holmes who had eaten very erratically and sparsely throughout the day and we sat around cosily having a nightcap. It was decided between us that Holmes would stay that night and the next, we would both relax during the day then we would leave together on the morrow following.

As luck would have it, the next day was inclement in the morning so Holmes and I sat in the library mulling over Bob's collection of tomes while he went about his normal business. There was a rather splendid volume devoted to Holyrood House itself, with engravings of the various elevations. There was an excellent picture of the south side with the stone terrace where I had so recently had my accident. The artist had delineated every separate flagstone in the terrace, with the balustrade and steps beyond.

"So this is the scene of the crime, eh, Watson?" remarked Holmes jovially.

"Crime?" I repeated blankly.

"Your accident. Did you not say you took your tumble here, on this terrace?"

"Oh yes, that's right."

"X marks the spot," he remarked in the same humorous vein.

"I don't follow you, old man," said I.

"Here, look. One of the flagstones is marked with a tiny cross. Small but clear." Holmes produced the lens which was always a permanent feature of his pocket.

"I say, so it is, how very odd. It would be about there that I went a purler."

"I can't make out if this little cross is part of the engraving or if someone has added it later in ink. I can easily ascertain which by dampening but I would not care to blemish the picture."

"Well the weather looks as though it may clear up shortly. We'll go out and examine the terrace. I haven't actually looked at it since I fell, and I don't think Bob has."

"Why would anyone want to mark a particular stone on the ground?"

"On maps it usually depicts buried treasure," I cried with excitement.

"Just so, but in those cases the cross is generally an ordinary common diagonal cross, such as anybody makes who cannot write his name. This, as you see, is clearly an upright cross – the symbol of Christ."

"Here comes Bob, we will ask him," I said as Bob appeared.

"I say, fellows, how about a spot of lunch?" asked Bob.

"Excellent idea," replied Holmes, "but, whilst you are here, perhaps you could throw a bit of light on this picture."

"Oh that's the south elevation as it was in 1780. Still pretty much like that now."

"We are intrigued to observe the terrace so accurately drawn. What is this cross here?"

"Cross? Let's see. Damn me, I've never noticed that before. Oh it's probably one of those compass things they draw to show north."

"I don't think so. Surely when those are included they are prominent, with a large N, if not the other cardinal points. This is so tiny you have never noticed it previously. Apart from which, if this is the south elevation, it is facing the wrong direction."

"Mmm. You're right, Holmes. I can't think what the purpose is."

"We think it might mark buried treasure," I said excitedly.

"That would be a jolly thing," said Bob.

"But why an upright cross?" persisted Holmes.

Bob gasped and sat down with a suddenness. "My God!" he said. "The Holy Rood."

"What do you mean?" I asked.

"It can't be. Come on, we must look outside. Come on, Holmes, you take one of John's arms, I'll take the other then we can all go out together."

So the three of us went outside on to the terrace. There was no doubt as to where I had fallen. Amongst all the stones that were as flat and level as could be expected, having laid a great age, was one that protruded a full inch at one edge. It did not need the world's greatest detective to see, instantly, that this single flagstone had been recently lifted and negligently replaced.

"So that's why you stumbled, John. And I thought it was the drink. I humbly apologise."

Holmes was on his knees, lens in hand as he crawled around the periphery of the stone.

"Can we find a spade and raise the stone?" asked Holmes.

"I'll get one," said Bob and briskly hurried off.

"What does it mean, Holmes?"

"I cannot say as yet. But, when we raise this stone, do not be surprised to see freshly dug earth beneath."

"But what did Bob mean about the Holy Rood? That's the name of his house."

Soon Bob was back with a spade and set to, prising up the stone. As Holmes had conjectured, underneath the soil had been recently disturbed.

"Shall I dig, do you think? Perhaps something has been buried?" said Bob.

"You can see, but I rather think something that was there has been dug up. You will observe there is no excess of soil. When compacted soil is disturbed it appears to enlarge in volume and not all the soil will go back in place, unless pounded heavily. If anything of size had been buried, then that would have displaced even more soil."

"Eureka," said Bob cryptically.

"Exactly," replied Holmes. "In this case not only is there no excess earth but there is space between soil and stone which would indicate that a certain volume has been removed, leaving a void for the soil to fall into."

"Come into the library again, if you have finished, Holmes," said Bob.

So we struggled back inside, my handicap being a frustration to my able friends.

"I fear that a possession belonging to me, no, not to me, one belonging to this house, no, more than that – one that belongs to the whole Christian world – has been stolen. A priceless relic of our Lord." Bob, visibly shaken, sat down. He was not a man for sitting; he was the kind of man who strode about, stamped, marched, when emotional, not a man who slumped and crumpled.

"Explain, man, what do you mean?" cried Holmes.

"This house, as you know, is called Holyrood House. There is a reason for that name."

"I assumed it was named after the royal palace in Edinburgh," said I.

Bob shook his head. "The Holy Rood is a piece of the cross on which Our Saviour was crucified. Sir Stephen de Blois, who held this manor at the time of the crusades, captured the holy relic while fighting in the Holy Land and brought it back here to England. He built a new house especially to hold his relic. That was, of course, prior to this present house and the terrace was not laid until centuries after de Blois' time. I don't know the full history by any means. You'll have to ask Alistair for the details, he is the village historian. But it has always been a local legend. You know the sort of thing – a secret tunnel from here to the church – a ridiculous distance for anybody to build – Robin Hood shooting his arrow and being buried where it landed – about twenty miles away! Legends, but absolute nonsense."

"But what is the legend of the Holy Rood?" I asked.

"Well, simply what I have said. That it was brought here by the crusaders in the – what would it be? 13th century? The Lord of the Manor built a grand new building to house it. Then, in the time of Henry VIII and the dissolution of the monasteries and all that terror, the Holy Rood was hidden away so that it could not be destroyed as so many religious treasures were at that time. The house was a rallying point for Roman Catholics here in Yorkshire, so was slighted on orders of the crown."

"Slighted?"

"Pulled down, more or less demolished. The house you are now standing in dates from the time of Queen Anne. But the rumours persisted that the Holy Rood was still here, safely concealed. It would seem that, at the time of building the house, the relic was hidden under the new terrace."

"And it has remained there unbeknownst to anyone for all those years," said I in awe.

"It must have been known to someone, hence the cryptic cross marked in your book and the fact that somebody has been searching and possibly found it," said Holmes dryly.

"We'll have to go and see Alistair. He's the man to tell us all the details."

"I would very much like to see him again, to bid him farewell, as we leave early tomorrow, but I fear I am not practised enough to cover the distance to the vicarage on crutches," I had to feebly confess.

"Not to worry. I know the very thing. I've got a wheel-barrow. You sit in that and Holmes and I will wheel you down."

"Capital idea!" boomed Holmes. So, with much merriment and fooling, it was organised so that I could be rolled along in a garden wheel-barrow, much to Holmes' amusement.

"I wonder if any person convenient has some photographic equipment to hand," he mused ostentatiously.

Thus, with my friends taking turns every few yards to propel me, we arrived at the vicarage gate from where we could see the Rev Alistair hanging out his washing. He looked round.

"Hello, Bob, you've caught me putting my washing out. With this weather I've been in and out like a rowing blue trying to get it dry. Hello, what have we here? Dr Watson in a wheel-barrow?"

"Forgive my not rising to greet you, Alistair, but my leg is broken at the ankle and standing on it causes great pain," I explained.

"You poor chap, how very unfortunate. Is this your physician?" asked Alistair, indicating Holmes.

"Ah, no. May I introduce my very good friend from London, Mr Sherlock Holmes. He has come to escort me home. Tomorrow. Holmes, this is the Rev Alistair Cooper, vicar of this parish and no mean chess player."

"Pleased to meet you, Mr Holmes, albeit in such unfortunate circumstances, but how good of you to travel all this way to collect your friend."

"Shall we talk here at the gate or are you going to ask us in?" said Bob.

"Do step in. Can we assist Dr Watson out of the wheel-barrow?" The three of them made a concerted swoop, pulled me out of the barrow and carried me bodily into the house.

"You missed an unusual thing at the Revels, Alistair," said Bob. "Adam was defeated in the weight lifting competition."

"So I heard. He will be down in the dumps," said the vicar.

"Adam is the local blacksmith, Holmes, and has won the weight lifting for the past nine years. A farm-hand from Upper Fordham defeated him this year," explained Bob.

"Every dog has his day, so they say," replied Holmes affably.

"And how was your Convocation of Bishops?" asked Bob of Rev Alistair.

"You make a rather boring assembly sound much grander than it is. We lesser mortals have to merely sit and listen while our superiors tell us what we should do."

"Alistair had to attend a religious conference on the day of the Revels, so missed the fun," Bob explained to Holmes.

"Indeed? Was that at York?"

"Canterbury, actually."

"What was the weather like there? I understand it was hot and sunny here, for the Revels?" asked Holmes.

"Oh, I think it was much the same in Canterbury, but we were immured indoors, so did not receive the benefit of the sunshine anyway."

"Well, I fear you may have missed the summer for this year, Alistair, as that one day was the only time we've seen the sun," Bob added.

"We really have come to ask you about the story of the Holy Rood," said I, thinking all this chat about the weather had gone on long enough.

"Yes, my friends here were asking me about the legend and I couldn't remember it all in great detail so said you were the chap to ask," said Bob.

"Oh well, it is quite simple, but most interesting. The Holy Rood is supposed to be a piece of the True Cross on which Our Saviour was crucified. The lord of the manor here, in the 13th century, was one Stephen de Blois and he went on a crusade with King Edward I in 1270. As you know, from the time of William the Conqueror, various European kings went on crusades to try to free the Holy Land from the control of the Moslems.

"This was probably the last proper crusade from England and it lasted about four years but really achieved nothing and Edward I returned empty handed, as it were. But Stephen de Blois brought back a Holy Relic – a piece of the True Cross he had captured in battle in Jerusalem. In those pious times relics of saints were very important and pilgrims made lengthy journeys all over the country to visit Holy Shrines and, it has to be said, made the repositories of the relics very wealthy in the process.

"Stephen de Blois built a grand chapel to house the Holy Rood and it was a place of pilgrimage for many years. A piece of the Saviour's cross was more important to the pilgrim than the toe bone of a minor saint so Stephen's chapel became very well endowed. One would hesitate to say that Stephen personally benefited from the pious offerings but the fact remains he built a magnificent new house thereafter."

"But not the house that is there at present?" I asked.

"Oh no. We have to now come forward to Tudor times when, in the reign of King Henry VIII, Thomas Cromwell dissolved the monasteries to enrich the king. At that time, as you will know, Henry VIII broke away from the established church and as a result the religious houses collapsed. Here, in our own little village, the Chapel was plundered and the house thrown down," continued the vicar.

"But what happened to the Holy Rood?" I asked.

"What indeed? It is said that the lord of the manor at that time hid the relic before fleeing for his life. It availed him naught as he was caught and hacked to death on the spot for defying the king. For centuries the rumour was that the Holy Rood was still somewhere in the village, but nobody knew where. The thing is, even if the relic were to be discovered, we have no means of knowing if it is a piece of the True Cross or if it is merely any old piece of wood brought back from the Holy Land."

"You mean that Stephen de Blois was offering a counterfeit to the British people?" I asked.

"We don't know. He would have thought the relic was genuine and it may actually have been what it purported to be."

"But just think, man, if that should be the case and it were to be rediscovered! It would be priceless!" gasped Bob.

"Yes, well, we will never know, will we? Your house was built in the reign of Queen Anne, many years later. There is no trace of the former house or chapel remaining. I hope that explains the legend to you, gentlemen? If you have any questions?"

"The thing is, Alistair, the reason why –" Bob was interrupted by Holmes suddenly saying "Yes, I have a question! I would like to know why my old college friend Samuel Gethin is calling himself Alistair Cooper and posing as an Anglian clergyman!"

We all gaped at Holmes.

"What can you mean, sir?" asked the astonished vicar.

"Come off it, Gethin. I don't know what reason you have for assuming a pseudonym, but you know as well as I do that you are my old sparring partner Samuel Gethin," cried Holmes.

"Have you taken leave of your senses, sir?" said the bewildered vicar.

"Don't tell me you have forgotten me – Sherlock Holmes? Why, we won the double oars together! I defeated you in the singlestick final."

"I have never seen you before in my life, sir. You are greatly mistaken!"

"I do not think so. My friend, Watson, will tell you I never mistake my man. Why, what about all those drinking binges when I had to carry you back to our rooms? And that time we went to London for the weekend and ended up at Limehouse." Holmes turned to us. "We were well and truly in our cups and found a place that did sailors' tattoos. We decided to have the operation done to ourselves. At the last minute I jibbed, but Gethin here had a most fetching lion tattooed on his shoulder. You must remember."

"Sir, I think you are quite mad. Dr Watson, I am sorry for this, but I must ask you to remove your friend from my house," said the harassed vicar.

"I think you have perhaps committed some sin, or crime even, that compels you to hide in this country backwater and change your identity. If so, I am sorry I have revealed your disguise, but please do not say I am mistaken," said Holmes sternly.

"You are mistaken. Completely! I do not know of anything that you speak. I have never rowed a boat in my life!" cried Alistair in desperation.

"But you were Oxford's finest rowing blue in our day!" protested Holmes.

"There you are, you see!" cried Alistair. "You are wrong! I am a Cambridge man! What do you think, Bob, is the man insane?"

"Well I don't know what to say. I mean, Holmes does seem very confident that he knows you."

"For Heaven's sake, man! Don't tell me you give him credence? You have known me for years – my closest friend. Oh, I give up! Please leave my house!"

"I don't wish to upset you Gethin, old man, pray don't get worked up," said Holmes mildly.

"I think, perhaps, you must be mistaken, Holmes," I ventured.

"Actually this can be easily settled, I think," said Bob suddenly. "You say your friend Samuel Gethin had a lion tattooed on his shoulder?"

"That is certainly so," said Holmes.

"Well I haven't!" said Alistair. "I damn well haven't!"

It was indicative of the pitch of anger to which the vicar had reached in that he resorted to swearing and simultaneously wrenched the shirt from his body. "Can you see a lion? Can you see a tattoo? Can you see any attempts to erase a tattoo? Will you believe your own eyes?"

I have never seen Holmes look so chastened. The embarrassment when he spoke was palpable.

"My dear sir, how can I apologise to you? I must appear an utter fool. The resemblance was so striking. Watson, I am sorry, I have insulted your new friend by my unwarranted insistence and so brought you into disrepute; and you, Mr Dawson, who so kindly welcomed me to your house as a friend of Watson. I cannot find words to express my abject apologies," said the humbled Holmes.

"I think perhaps we must leave now and get your luggage ready for the trap to take you to the train," said Bob stiffly.

We awkwardly took our leave of the vicar. I returned to my recumbent posture in the wheel-barrow and Holmes pushed me on his own, all the way back to the house, as Bob strode out angrily ahead.

Holmes and I were seated in a first-class carriage on the London bound train. I reflected on the last few hours and wondered how a respectable doctor could find himself being pushed in a wheel-barrow by a man whose behaviour was, if not actually insane, certainly bizarre. Bob had behaved very stiffly and correctly once we got back to his house and had ordered the trap to take us to the station. As a result of our precipitate exit we were at York some two hours before the train was due and, because of my incapacity, were unable to do anything but sit in the waiting room with some impatience. I am bound to say that Holmes was most solicitous concerning my welfare and took a great deal of trouble to ease my journey. He bought a quantity of newspapers and magazines and organised the transportation of the baggage.

As the train rattled along Holmes sat contentedly reading and puffing at his briar in great good humour. I could stand the man's complacency no longer "So what was all that about?"

"All what, Watson, old chap?" he replied as though to a child.

"Don't play the innocent with me, Holmes. I know you too well. If you indulge in such singular behaviour as to accuse a perfect stranger of being your old college chum then you have good reason. So why did you do it?"

"How would you get an English clergyman to remove his shirt in public, Watson?" replied Holmes.

"Is that the reason we all had to endure that display of extraordinary ill manners?" I gasped.

"I did contemplate spilling something on to him, or even setting light to his shirt in some way, but your friend Mr Dawson was about to blurt out the circumstances of your fall, so I was obliged to act quickly."

"But why on earth did you wish the man to take off his shirt?"

"I wished to ascertain if his arms were sun-burned."

"I am afraid I do not follow you. Perhaps you would explain to a simple physician who is unable to heal himself."

"You tripped over the paving stone that had been disturbed by whoever had been searching for the Holy Rood. As soon as Dawson said his friend the vicar was the man who knew all about it, it seemed to me more than possible that he was the man who had, in fact, done the digging."

"Impossible, Holmes, he was in Canterbury, hundreds of miles away on that day."

"Was he? How do we know? He said he was at a convocation of clergymen – I think if you enquire you will find that there was no such event on that day. Even if there had been, the vicar was not present at it. You may recall I enquired about the weather there and he claimed to have been indoors. I need not remind you, Watson, that for almost your entire stay in Yorkshire the weather has been foul. The one day when the sun shone like high summer was the day of the Revels. You, yourself, said you had caught the sun on your nose in spite of wearing your panama."

"That's true, it was suddenly seasonably hot, just as it had been unseasonably cold."

"When we approached the vicarage, your friend Alistair was hanging out his wet clothing to dry. Did you observe that one of the garments was a kind of artist's smock with sleeves cut off by the elbow? There was also a pair of coarse trousers."

"Yes, I have seen him wearing them. Those are the clothes he wears when digging for fossils and so on. Oh I see –"

"Exactly. If he had been wearing the smock on the day of the Revels then the chances are that the sun would have burnt his forearms."

"And they were red –I noticed that when he removed his shirt but thought nothing of it."

"Because of the peculiarity of the weather we know that burnt arms could only have happened on that one day during the recent week. The day when the vicar claimed to be indoors many miles away. I am afraid that I think your friend is lying."

"It certainly seems so. I can't believe it though, Holmes; a vicar of the church in England deceiving his closest friend. He obviously chose to explore when he knew Bob was absent at the Revels."

"It all seems to indicate that."

"But did he find the Holy Rood?"

"Now that I cannot deduce. I am inclined to think he pulled something out of the hole as the earth under the flagstone was, if anything, somewhat lacking, rather than the excess one normally gets when merely refilling with the loose soil that had been previously compacted."

"But why did you not explain all this to Bob? As it is, he thinks you are of unstable mind and character and, by my association with you, his friendship towards me has considerably cooled if not totally soured," I protested.

"I do not know the rights and wrongs of this matter, Watson, but those two gentlemen are the dearest of friends. It is not my place to set one against the other over a business that is no concern of mine."

"You prefer to be thought a nincompoop, rather than endanger their friendship?"

"They have to live in harmony with one another. I will not see either of them again. Why should I disturb their complacency with wild thoughts of distrust?"

"I will write to Bob and explain the reason for your irrational behaviour."

"You will do no such thing, Watson. Let sleeping dogs lie. I do not mind my reputation being sullied in Little Fordham, so neither should you. Peace, Watson. Our task is to get you safely and painlessly home. That is why I came – all else is irrelevant."

That would be the end of the story as my association with Robert Dawson was never resumed. However, it would be tedious of me to have laid the story before the public with no more final outcome than the above paragraph. Quite by chance, I am able to bring a more satisfactory conclusion to the attention of my readers.

In due course my leg healed and, as such things are, forgotten with the passage of time. My life proceeded and many years and adventures with Sherlock Holmes passed by. Then one day I was reading a magazine when I chanced upon an article by The Rev Alistair Cooper. It was in a series in which amateur archaeologists related their discoveries to others of like mind. Alistair set out the story of the Holy Rood much as he had related it to Holmes and myself all those years ago. He then went on to disclose how, in his friend's library, he had found an engraving with a holy cross marking a flagstone and he had deduced that was the resting place of the Holy Rood.

"*It was with great excitement that I prised up the flagstone I had so carefully found. Underneath, the earth was compacted but soon, with the aid of my ice-pick and small shovel, I started scooping the earth out. My excitement can be imagined when I struck a solid object which was eventually revealed as a small casket. It was about one foot each way and some six inches deep and mainly made of lead. I hastily replaced the earth and stone and hurried away to examine my find in private. To my great joy it opened readily and inside was a small prayer book and several objects: a coin bearing the head of Queen Anne; a twist of sheep's wool and a hank of finished spun and dyed wool; a small bottle of what seemed to be beer or ale; some glass spheres which I took to be stoppers or children's marbles; some seeds; a horse-shoe; some wooden butter-pats and a silver ring.*

"*Inside the cover of the prayer book was inscribed:* Holy Rood House built in the year AD 1710 in the eighth year of our beloved monarch Queen Anne. These articles of common usage placed by me, Theodore Perrin, master mason, to commemorate the laying of the final stone by The Most Reverend the Lord Archbishop of York. The 20th day of October 1710. God Save the Queen.

"*As the place where I found this treasure was on the premises of my friend Robert Dawson Esquire and the contents appertained to the very origin of his house, I purposed to present them to him on the occasion of his birthday which was a few days hence. I duly did so at a grand party held at Holyrood House and these same treasures, with their case, can be seen to the present time by all who call at the Church of St Michael and All Angels in the village of Little Fordham in the County of Yorkshire, where Mr Dawson very graciously placed them.*"

The Singular Adventure
of
THE OPPRESSED TRAGEDIAN

I HAVE related in a former chronicle how I met Mr Bram Stoker, the manager of the Lyceum Theatre. It was as a result of our subsequent friendship that his employer, the eminent actor Sir Henry Irving, sought the assistance of Mr Sherlock Holmes. It was in 1894 when the greatest actor the world has ever known, and probably will ever see, graced 221B Baker Street with his presence. At that time he was still plain Mr Henry Irving, as it was the year prior to his receiving the accolade from Her Majesty.

I had seen the tragedian on stage several times but I had never met him face to face before. Apart from a rather mannered way of pronunciation, and a habit of lapsing into the occasional exaggerated pose, he was rather disappointingly ordinary. Holmes had never previously seen Irving as he rarely went to the theatre.

"It is very good of you to receive me, Mr Holmes."

"We are very pleased to welcome you, sir. Watson, here, is an *habitué*, of your theatre and we have whiled away many a tedious hour as he has related the extraordinary effects you have achieved upon the Lyceum stage."

"I am pleased to meet you, Dr Watson. It is really because of you that I am here. Stoker, my manager, said that your friend Mr Sherlock Holmes was the very man to help me and possibly relieve my distress."

"I will do all in my power to assist. Pray proceed with the details of your trouble."

"Mr Holmes, I am being blackmailed and the terrible thing is that I have been in this scoundrel's clutches for upwards of three years."

"My dear Irving!" I cried. "Who is this villain?"

"Alas, that I do not know. He calls himself plain Tom Smith, a pseudonym that could hide anyone," said Irving despairingly.

"Pray proceed. How did it start and what hold has this Tom Smith got over you?" Holmes asked crisply.

"First of all you must know that I am a married man with two sons. I have been estranged from my wife for many years. Since my sons were babies, in fact. They are now fine strapping fellows – both are actors. Possibly you have heard of H.B. Irving, he is now 24 and making satisfactory headway in the profession.

My younger son Laurence is not really as successful as yet. He is a more introspective character – much given to reading gloomy Russian novelists and rather depressing poets."

"This is very interesting, Irving, but is it relevant to the case of blackmail?" asked Holmes.

"Yes it is, in the initial stage. You see, when Laurence left the 'varsity he wanted to go on the stage. I had opposed it earlier and had compelled him to study for a degree, hoping he would settle on a more suitable career. After coming down he was still determined to become an actor and as he was now his own man I could not stop him. All I could do was to apply economic pressure by cutting off any allowance I had been giving him. Well to be a young actor is to be penniless. That I know, Mr Holmes, as I was in such a position for many, many years. So he resorted to theft. Much as it pains me to say so, my son stole something from one of my dearest friends and colleagues. He stole a bundle of letters from Miss Ellen Terry. It seems Laurence had heard of a dealer who specialises in the trading of eminent persons' autographs and letters. Apparently there are collectors who acquire the signatures of politicians, authors and the like, and these have a monetary value. Well Miss Terry keeps up a voluminous correspondence with many important people in many walks of life. So Laurence, knowing this, stole a bundle of letters from her to sell to this dealer."

"Who uses them for the purposes of blackmail."

"No, Mr Holmes, I am assured that the dealer is an honest man and trades fairly. I think the material he handles is quite harmless. It seems people will pay good money for a note to a tradesman, if written by an eminent hand. I do not think he is the blackmailer. Well, amongst the stolen bundle were some letters I had written to Miss Terry many years ago." Irving paused in some discomfort. "I am sure what I am about to reveal will go no further than this room and that you are both gentlemen of honour."

"If you have any doubts, sir, do not reveal your secrets to us."

"I'm sorry, Mr Holmes, of course I must tell you everything. How can you assist me otherwise? A number of years ago Miss Terry and I were lovers. It has all been over some time but, whilst we had our *affaire*, indiscreet letters were written. It appears letters of mine were amongst the ones stolen. As you know, I have grown into a figure of some public repute. I can confide in you, gentlemen, that it is almost certain that Her Majesty will honour me with a knighthood in the next list. I shall be the first actor ever to be so honoured. It is a mark of esteem that the theatrical profession has at last gained respectability."

"Chiefly through your own good efforts, Irving," I interjected.

"Thank you for saying that, Dr Watson. It has been my earnest endeavour, throughout my life, to elevate the status of the theatre. So you see, Mr Holmes, I cannot afford, at this of all times, to have anything besmirching my character, even from some years ago."

"How did your letters fall into the hands of this Tom Smith?" asked Holmes.

"Laurence took them to the dealer and sold them as a job lot. He said he never looked at them and did not even know who the letters were from, or anything. It seems the dealer gave him some paltry sum and that was that. I assume the dealer then sold them on, as individual items, to these collectors and mine fell into the hands of some unscrupulous rogue who saw how he could make capital out of them. Of course, Laurence was filled with remorse immediately afterwards and, whilst on tour in Ireland, attempted to kill himself."

"How terrible!" I cried.

"We heard that there had been some sort of accident with a gun. I was, as usual, appearing before my public, so could not leave at once for Ireland, but his mother went immediately and dealt with it all most efficiently. Laurence was only slightly wounded and confessed all that I have told you to his mother. It was possible to issue a statement that it had been an accident whilst he was cleaning his gun. I am afraid Laurence is one of those men whose every plan seems to go awry. He could not even shoot himself efficiently. When I visited him a couple of days later, he repeated to me the whole story. I am afraid I ranted and raved at his folly but I am his father and, of course, forgave him. I realised keeping him in penury was not a sensible way to discourage him from acting. So, since then, I have discreetly assisted him. Over the lengthy years I have acquired a network of colleagues all over the country and, from time to time, when Laurence needs a job, I can contact one of these friends and ask them to offer him something appropriate to his station. So he gets supporting roles offered from various provincial managements and he thinks it is on his own merits. Sometimes I have to subsidise the manager, secretly, but it is better for the boy's ego that way."

"So we now know how Tom Smith got your letters. How did the demand for money start?"

"I received a letter at the theatre informing me this man had my letters and that he was sure I would not like the contents to be known. He said, if I paid him £20 a week, he would suppress them."

"That is unusual, I think. Normally blackmailers ask for a large sum in exchange for selling the incriminating documents back to you."

"I really would not know, Mr Holmes. This, thank God, is my only experience of blackmail."

"So what happened then?"

"I did as asked. I sent £20 every week, in cash, to the address given."

"But you did not come face to face with your tormentor?"

"No. I did as I was bid for a year. Then the sum increased. I was to pay £30 a week. So I did not send the money but demanded to meet the man. He replied with a day and time when I should call."

"And where was this appointment to be?"

"At the address where I sent the money."

"How curious. Go on, please."

"So I went as arranged and found it was a common rooming house. The woman in charge, the landlady I suppose, showed me the room which this Tom Smith occupied and I knocked. A voice answered and I had to do all my conversing through the door. It was ridiculous. There I was, trying to convince this villain that I refused to pay any more money but having to keep my voice down so that I would not be overheard by passers-by. It was all most unsatisfactory."

"So what was the outcome?"

"I went away, and started sending £30 a week."

"And how long before Mr Smith raised his weekly stipend again?" asked Holmes dryly.

"Each year it went up ten pounds. £40 this last year. Now the villain demands £50."

"You are a fool, Irving."

"Really, Holmes!" I protested.

"He's right, Dr Watson. I am a fool."

"You should have come to me as soon as all this started. Then, I may have been able to help you. Now, I doubt if I can do anything."

"So Stoker raised my hopes only to have you dash them," said Irving sadly.

"You see, you should call the blackmailer's bluff right at the start. 'Publish and be damned!' as the noble Duke once famously said. Often the blackmailer will then cave in, as he can switch his attentions to some more pliable person. But once give way, he has nothing to lose. If, later, you refuse to pay, his income is going to be cut short, so in spite, he reveals all the poor victim has been trying to hide. Quite often a victim dies still in thrall to the villain. Then the blackmailer announces to the world what the poor devil has spent his life paying to conceal. There is no option. If you have done some deed of which you are ashamed then you must be prepared to stand up and admit it to the world. There is no other sure way to defeat a blackmailer."

"I know you are right, Mr Holmes. But I am afraid I am neither worldly-wise nor a person of strong character. I make my living by counterfeiting passions. I am no better than the next man in dealing with them in real life. I am certainly not ashamed of my *liaison* with Miss Terry, but I am cursed, as most public figures, with the necessity of keeping up appearances. My career, my reputation, my honour, are all at stake, not to mention those of Miss Terry."

"Well, let us see what we can do at this late stage. I cannot work miracles. I do not wish to build up false hopes. I think the best thing I can do is treat with this man on your behalf. Tell me the address to which you send your payments."

"I have written it on this paper." Irving pushed over a slip of paper.

"Continue sending your weekly contributions. Do nothing to alert Tom Smith into realising anything is other than usual. I will do a little discreet investigating. I will communicate with you at the Lyceum Theatre if I have anything to report. But I repeat – do not build up your hopes."

The eminent tragedian dejectedly left our humble dwelling.

"What a sad case, Holmes."

"Blackmail always is. Who of us is so pure in word and deed that, in the past, there does not lurk something of which we are ashamed. And there is always a section of the community which rejoices or makes capital out of our shame. What a depraved species is mankind."

Holmes was absent for much of the next few days. The few glimpses I had of him were in the guise of a street loafer as he came and went at odd hours. It so happened that one evening I took myself to the Lyceum where Irving was playing Becket in the play by Tennyson. This was his latest success and a very fine performance he gave. It was difficult to equate the man on stage with the rather crumbling figure who had sat in our old chair. Although I was becoming more intimate with Stoker, I did not presume on our acquaintanceship and always queued for my place. Indeed, sometimes I did not see him at all, as his duties took him hither and thither in the building. At other times, on entering or leaving the theatre, I was favoured with a brief word as Stoker stood in the foyer greeting or saying farewell to his patrons. On one occasion he saw me prior to the start of the performance and bade me sit in a more expensive seat that was vacant, instead of the modest place I had purchased.

Some days later Holmes was back in his usual position and said casually "I've asked Irving round."

"Have you made progress in his case?" I asked eagerly.

"Calm yourself, Watson. I regret I have made no progress apart from finding out where his tormentor lives and what he looks like."

"But he gave you the address himself," I said in protest.

"A mere accommodation address, Watson. I found by extensive and boring lying-in-wait that the rooming house does not, in fact, contain anybody called Tom Smith, or any person using that pseudonym. It works like this: Irving sends his money to this address. The landlady, a slatternly woman who looks as though she would sell her grandmother for tuppence, keeps it until collected by a man. This fellow, of medium height, with a handsome face and a rakish air, then takes the envelope and travels to a rather respectable address in Wharfedale Street, West Brompton, where he descends from the carriage with a swagger and disappears through a majestic oak door."

"Did you find out who he is?"

"Not yet. I need to speak to Irving." And, like the great actor he was, Irving made his entrance right on cue.

"You have news for me, Mr Holmes?" he asked eagerly.

"I warned you not to expect anything, my dear Irving. I have made progress in my investigation but nothing, alas, that helps you. As I suspected, the address you visited is a mere sham. The villain lives elsewhere. I propose bearding him in his den. I think the best I will be able to do is treat with him. Of course, if admitted, I shall take the opportunity to examine the place, but I think all I will be permitted to do is bargain. So – I need to know what price you are prepared to pay for the return of the letters."

"Oh Mr Holmes, if you had asked that question five years ago, I could have said twenty thousand pounds and laid the sum on your table in sovereigns. Alas, since that time, I have had one calamity after another. In an endeavour to save money, Stoker and I agreed to cut down on our insurances – we have, of course, a legal obligation to adequately insure the theatre – but we ceased payments on our scenic stores in Walthamstow. You probably heard about the fire there, two years ago. Forty entire Lyceum productions were destroyed. Last year, the production of Shakespeare's *Coriolanus* was a failure. It lost £12,000. My forthcoming production of *King Arthur* will cost £8000 to mount."

"But *Becket* is a great success, isn't it?" I broke in eagerly.

"Indeed yes, but the running costs are such that we need to play to 90% of capacity to recoup the money. We are playing to an average of 75% only. People think it is making a fortune for me but it is losing money all the time I keep it on."

"Then why do you play it?" asked Holmes.

"Mr Holmes, I was not put on this earth to make money. My purpose is to put the finest productions I can conceive on the stage. I am dedicated to giving the world's greatest authors the best possible interpretation of their genius. If I was a sensible man, I would tour the country with one production – *The Bells*, and I would make a handsome profit every week and have no troubles in finding new plays, commissioning music, scenic designs, casting and rehearsing players and so on. But I am not a sensible man – as you said on my last visit – I am a fool."

"So I am not able to offer any sum on money on your behalf?"

"If you can obtain those letters, Mr Holmes, then I will find the money, whatever it is. I shall play *The Bells* every single night if necessary."

"I will see what I can achieve. I presume you would not wish me to come to the theatre, but that you would rather visit here, to receive my report?"

"It would be more convenient if I came here, I think."

"Very well, I will send you a message when I have been to Wharfedale Street."

Irving stared in amazement. "Wharfedale Street? Why should you go there?"

"Because your tormentor lives there," replied Holmes.

"At which number?" asked Irving hoarsely.

"Number 14."

"That is my house," said Irving.

"Your house?" said Holmes taken aback. "I do not understand."

"That house was leased to me when I married in 1869. Both my sons were born there and my wife Florence still lives there. I still pay the rent for it. My wife and I parted in 1871. I have not set foot in the place since. I, myself, occupy a pair of bachelor rooms in Grafton Street."

"Do you know a man about 35 years of age, perhaps a trifle younger, with black wavy hair, a dashing moustache, handsome features and a swaggering gait?"

"That is Florence's steward – his name is Alec Mountjoy. He is supposed to be her servant but, between you and me, I rather think he is her lover. Although I have had no communication with my wife for 23 years, certain so-called friends seem to think they must keep me informed of my wife's daily doings. So he is the villain!"

"This puts quite a different complexion on the case," said Holmes. "I may be able to assist you a little more than I thought. You say that you have had no dealings with your wife for 23 years? Your sons?"

"I have paid for my wife's maintenance and my sons' upbringing as a Christian man and dutiful father and husband should. My own lawyers have been the intermediary with Florence's lawyers. I did not see my sons for many years. I missed all their childhood and saw very little of them as youths. It is only now they have reached man's estate and are removed from the pernicious influence of their mother, that we are as intimate as we should have been these past two decades."

"My dear fellow, I had no idea," I murmured sympathetically.

"No one does, Doctor, no one does, except, perhaps, dear Nell – Miss Terry. Florence hates me, you see. I invite her to my first nights and she sits there in the stage box exuding malevolence. I am never at my best on the first night of a new play."

"But why invite her, man?" I asked.

"The first time it was bravado. I never thought she would accept the invitation. But she has more guile than I, and sat there preening, for all the world to see. After that I was obliged to keep doing it for the sake of appearances. Her absence would have caused tongues to wag."

"But why not a divorce?" I could not but ask.

"She will not divorce me, even though she hates both Miss Terry and myself. I have no grounds for divorcing her. Any scandal of divorce after all these years would undo me. I left her on the greatest night of my life – 25th November 1871 – the first night of *The Bells*. Up to that night I was a respected leading man, a reliable actor with a penchant for comedy roles and grotesques. That night, in one leap, I became the head of my profession. On the way home in the carriage my wife turned to me and said 'Are you going to go on making a fool of yourself all your life?' I stopped the carriage and got out. I have never seen or spoken to her since." Irving slowly rose to his feet. "I will await your summons, Mr Holmes."

After Irving had left, we both sat in silence a while, then Holmes spoke, "To think how little a wife should comprehend her husband."

"For all our progress in medical knowledge, we still know nothing of the human soul."

A few days later Holmes was rummaging about in his box of visiting cards. He had a collection of cards which had been given to him, and also some that he had had specially printed. With this range of cards he was able to assume various identities if he chose to introduce himself *incognito.*

"Ah, this one I think," he murmured and laid it on the table as he disappeared into his bedroom.

He emerged twenty minutes later, transformed. Never inclining to the masher in his dress, he was now clad even more primly and sombrely than usual. He had done something to his features and hair that had aged him, and the general appearance was of a family solicitor who was advanced in years.

"My card, sir," he said, in a voice unlike his own, as he proffered his card. It read *Algernon Runcible; Runcible, Runcible and Peabody; Solicitors* with an address in the city.

"I have an appointment with Tom Smith," Holmes said in his normal voice.

It was late afternoon when Holmes returned to our rooms. He threw himself down on the sofa. He looked as depressed as I had ever seen the man.

"Did your interview not go well, Holmes?" I asked.

"Watson, I am a man with a scientific mind. As you have had cause to remark more than once, I am a calculating machine devoid of all emotion. I have trained myself to be like that, for the benefit of my work. But, sometimes, even I am touched by the inhumanity of the human soul. I would not willingly endure this afternoon's experience again. What is the time? The Lyceum has a matinée today and I sent a message to Irving asking him to come round when his play was over. I must get changed and remove this disguise."

A short while later Irving arrived.

"You sent for me, Mr Holmes?" said the eminent actor as though he were a mere lackey.

"I have some news for you, my dear fellow," said Holmes with a show of heartiness. "I have solved your problem. You may put it out of your mind. Simply forget all about it and do not send any more money. There will be no repercussions of any sort."

"You are amazing, Mr Holmes. How can I ever repay you?"

"Easily, my dear Irving, you will receive my account in a few days. My charges are standard and relatively modest."

"But how? What did you do to that villain Mountjoy? I cannot believe you settled the affair so readily," said the amazed actor.

"Tush, my dear fellow, do not ask me to reveal the secrets of my trade. I do not ask how, in your estimable play, you turn pale at the sound of the bells and freeze the blood of your audience. But rest assured, all is well. I was mistaken about the address being in Wharfedale Street. It seems that Alec Mountjoy, apart from attending upon your wife, also did errands for a bed-ridden gentleman at another address near-by. He was merely an innocent messenger. This bed-ridden person of exceedingly low morals is well-known to the police. He is not expected to live very much longer and I have persuaded him, by dint of knowledge known to me and Scotland Yard, that his rapidly declining months would be best served by ceasing all intercourse with the outside world."

"Mr Holmes, I can never thank you enough. You, and of course you, Dr Watson, will always be welcome at the Lyceum as my guests. I will send you both an invitation for my opening nights. But apart from that, you are welcome any evening."

"You are most generous, Mr Irving, as I know what an honour it is to be invited to your opening nights," said Holmes. "Now as I have put you to the inconvenience of travelling over here to Baker Street, when you have another performance to undertake at 8 this evening, I must let you get away for a bite to eat. But I thought you would prefer to hear my news at the first opportunity."

"Indeed, and I am most humbly grateful. I see I should have come to you long ago, then, perhaps, my recent years would have been less burdened. Good evening, Mr Holmes, Dr Watson." The good fellow left looking ten years younger than when he had first arrived some days ago.

I looked at Holmes and was about to challenge him concerning the preposterously glib story he had told Irving, but he avoided my gaze.

"After dinner, Watson, after dinner."

Holmes arrived at 14 Wharfedale Street and knocked. The door was answered by a maid to whom he gave in his card and asked if he could see Mrs Irving. He was shown into an elegant room and asked to wait. Shortly Alec Mountjoy entered.

"Can I be of assistance to you, Mr Runcible? I am Mrs Irving's steward, I deal with all her business affairs."

"That's very good of you, sir," said Holmes, in his lawyer's tones, "but I have been instructed to address my remarks to the lady herself. They are concerning the relationships between her husband and herself."

"I gathered they would be. But you are not Irving's usual man?"

"That is so. Mr Irving has grown dissatisfied with his previous representatives and has entrusted my firm with his legal affairs."

"Well, as I say, you can discuss your business with me, as I am fully conversant with Mrs Irving's wishes."

"I am sure you are, Mr er – ?"

"Mountjoy."

"Mr Mountjoy. But you see, legally, Mrs Irving is the principal involved in this, and, whilst she may choose you to deal with it, I must insist that I relate my business to her in person."

Holmes was saved from further prevarication by the entrance of Mrs Florence Irving. A woman of haughty bearing and handsome features, soured by self-inflicted unhappiness.

"What is it, Alec? Who is this gentleman?" She glanced at Holmes' card, which Mountjoy handed to her. "So, Irving's changed his lawyer, has he? Ross could get nowhere with me, so in desperation he has gone elsewhere."

"Florence – " Whatever Mountjoy was going to say remained unsaid, as Mrs Irving cut him off.

"All right, Alec, you can go. I'll deal with Mr Runcible." Mountjoy left the room, his handsome features glowering.

"Now Mr Runcible, let me tell you firmly and clearly, that I will not in any circumstances divorce Irving. If he wants to cavort with that harlot Ellen Terry, that's up to him, but I will not give him the freedom to do so. That is all I have to say."

"Well you have certainly made your position clear, madam."

Florence Irving rose. "Exactly; so there is no further point in prolonging your visit."

"Please sit down, Mrs Irving, and tell me about Tom Smith." Florence Irving sat down rather more gracelessly than she had arisen.

"What do you mean? Who is Tom Smith?" she gasped.

"I was rather hoping you would tell me," said Holmes mildly.

"What is this, Mr Runcible? Please say what you have to say."

"Very well. You, Mrs Irving, have been demanding money from your husband. Not content with the generous allowances and provisions he has made for you these last twenty-odd years, since 1891 you have been demanding money by blackmail."

"I don't know what you are talking about. I suggest you leave my house before you say something that you will be sorry for."

"Stay. Your son stole some letters from Miss Ellen Terry. He intended to sell them all to a dealer in autographic material, but somehow you obtained them. Or perhaps you merely abstracted the ones from your husband to Miss Terry, and your son completed his intention by selling the rest."

"I suppose Irving told you all this nonsense?"

"If it is nonsense, why have you been sending Mr Mountjoy to a squalid address in the East End every week, to collect payment in cash?"

"If you do not leave immediately I shall call a policeman."

"Oh, Mrs Irving, that would be most unwise. I suggest you give me the letters in question and, before your eyes, I shall burn them, there, in the fire, then leave you in peace; and you can leave your husband in peace also."

Florence Irving suddenly threw her head back and laughed a mirthless laugh. "At first I thought you knew all. But now it is clear you know nothing."

"I know you have been blackmailing your own husband, a man admired by all the world, a man of integrity and dignity."

"A mere pomping player!" The future Lady Irving spat out the words. "When I married him he was nothing! Nothing! A poor mountebank who preferred to carouse with his drunken companions until late into the night, instead of living a respectable life. A hollow man who thinks the adulation of a lot of empty-headed applauding fools is sufficient recompense. A man who would choose to spend 24 hours in his theatre playing at being other people, rather than come home and be a proper husband and father."

"These flaws that you see are not sufficient reason to hound a man and bleed him to death with menaces for money."

"Mr Runcible, I have heard you out. As I have nothing more to say, I suggest you leave."

"I have no intention of leaving until I get those letters."

"There are no letters!" cried Mrs Irving triumphantly. At that moment Mountjoy burst in.

"Silence, Flo, you'll ruin all!"

"Ah, Mr Mountjoy," said Holmes, "I'm rather glad you were eavesdropping. I think you should now be party to our conversation, as you are Mrs Irving's accomplice in this shameful charade."

"What is that to do with you, Runcible?"

"There is more acting going on in this house than ever took place on the Lyceum stage. Mrs Irving pretends to be a wronged, deserted wife and is really a blackmailer called Tom Smith; Mr Alec Mountjoy is supposed to be a loyal steward but is, in fact, an impoverished lover living on his mistress' bounty; and I pretend to be a humble family solicitor and am really the private detective Sherlock Holmes."

The revelation was sufficient to bring Mountjoy to his senses.

"So you are Sherlock Holmes? The game's up, Flo."

"I suggest that neither of you would want your unpleasant little swindle to be advertised to the world, no more than Mr Irving would. Why are there no letters?"

"There never were any letters, clever Mr Sherlock Holmes!" sneered Mrs Irving vindictively. "That stupid man Irving let his imagination get the better of his commonsense."

"What are you going to do, Mr Holmes? About us?" asked Mountjoy.

"You have committed a very serious offence, for which you would both get ten years if it came to court."

"You have no proof!" blazed Mrs Irving.

"Shut up, Flo!" snapped Mountjoy. "I know your reputation, Mr Holmes. You must realise that, if you take us to court, the whole thing will balloon into a colossal scandal that will damage Irving for life."

"Perhaps that is a price worth paying to see justice done," said Holmes dryly.

"I think your client would be better served if you forgot all about this. We will cause no trouble."

"Do you think you are in a position to bargain, Mountjoy?" asked Holmes sternly. "Perhaps you would be so good as to relate the full story and I will decide what action to take."

"Don't tell him anything, Alec!"

"Flo, the game's up. It's all over. Don't you realise? Just shut up and I'll do the talking. I don't want to go to jail even if you are so spiteful that you would ruin yourself to get even with Irving."

"I think Mr Mountjoy speaks sense, Mrs Irving," said Holmes.

"I came to this house as steward to Mrs Irving. I did not intend to come under her thrall, but I did and that's that, and I don't regret that part of it one bit. I was talking to Flo's son Laurence one day, about people who deal with old letters and so on for money. I had no ulterior motive, I swear to you, Mr Holmes. It was just an everyday conversation. Anyway Laurence must have brooded on this idea as a way of raising money. He was always short of cash."

"He always had money when I looked after him. He wanted for nothing!"

"Yes, Flo. Well, when he left home to be an actor he was an adult and his father was not legally responsible for his welfare any longer. In fact, he did give him a small stipend that was sufficient to keep him from penury, but it was galling to a young fellow, who aspired to eminence in the same line as his father, to be kept down, as he saw it. His father did not want either of his sons to follow him on the stage."

"The selfish sod knew they were better actors, that's why!"

"Florence! Hold your peace! Anyway, Laurence must have thought this was a good idea to raise a bit of the old readies, and so stole some letters from Ellen Terry. That was easy, as Miss Terry had known him all his life and was like a moth –, like an aunt to him. He had the run of her house in Town and visited her at her country home in Kent. He took the letters and asked me to sell them for him. I refused, but told him the name and address of the dealer. I also told his mother what he had done. I had to do that as Laurence tried to commit suicide shortly afterwards, when he was acting in Ireland. That was when the whole story came out."

"That bastard Irving drove his own son to suicide by keeping him short of money!"

"Mrs Irving, please do not interrupt," said Holmes gently.

"That would have been that, as Laurence fortunately botched the job in his usual inept manner, and the letters were sold anonymously, presumably being treasured by collectors at this very moment. There were no letters from Irving. If Ellen Terry ever had letters of Irving, she either destroyed them or kept them elsewhere. Of course Laurence told his father what he had done and it was concealed from Ellen Terry – to this day she knows nothing about it. But Florence saw a way of extorting money from Irving by pretending that some of the letters were incriminating to him."

"I knew about him and that harlot Ellen Terry. She may fool the world with her airs and graces, but she's a whore with her bastard kids, and I know she and Irving have been at it like rabbits for years."

"You do your case no good by using foul language and maligning respected persons, Mrs Irving," said Holmes sternly.

"Respected persons! The whore of Babylon!"

"Well, Mr Holmes, Florence wrote to Irving in the name of Tom Smith, claiming to have these letters and demanding a regular payment to suppress them. She was clever, I think, by being modest in her demands. Irving fell for it. If she had asked for more he may have enquired further. But his own guilt and imagination did the job for us, as obviously he had at some time written compromising letters. I admit I was party to it. Flo dreamt up the idea and I suggested the means of carrying out. I don't say I am innocent of it. I wrote the letters at Florence's dictation, as Irving, of course, would have recognised her hand. So there you have it, Mr Holmes."

"If you had not been greedy and kept your demands modest you may have got away with it for life but, like all blackmailers, you can never be satisfied, so you increased the money. What you probably do not know is that as you increased your demands, Henry Irving's income was falling. He has never taken more than £60 a week in salary all his life. All profits he puts back into running his theatre."

"What will you do now, Mr Holmes?" asked Mountjoy anxiously.

"You are right, Mountjoy, no good will be served by bringing this shoddy business to court. Your miserable body will not be tested by the rigours of prison. You are safe to remain here as Mrs Irving's tame poodle. As for you, madam, I can say in all my experience, I have never met such an evil woman. If we cannot expect loyalty, decency and honesty from our womenfolk, civilisation will descend into barbarity. Good day."

That is what really happened that day at Wharfedale Street. As the world now knows, Irving was knighted in 1895 and died in 1905. The most respected actor of our times was honoured by burial in Westminster Abbey. Lady Irving lived a very secluded life and died unmourned in Folkestone. Laurence Irving, unfortunate to the last, was drowned at sea returning from an acting tour of the Americas. I visited Miss Ellen Terry in her retirement at her beautiful country home at Smallhythe in Kent, to gently ask about the theft of her letters. She had no recollection of the incident at all. Now she, too, is dead, I am able to lay the facts of this story before the public.

The Singular Adventure
of
THE DEAD TREE

"IT is no doubt a very trivial thing about which I have come to consult you but it is most mysterious. Perhaps I am presumptuous to trouble you with the matter. But I cannot go to the police about a dead tree. They would laugh me out of the office."

"You have Dr Watson's habit of presuming I know what you are talking about. Please be so good as to inform me of the reason for your visit."

My friend, Mr Sherlock Holmes, pulled at his pipe and stared expectantly at our visitor. He was a bluff honest-looking fellow in his mid-forties. A prosperous man but one with no obvious pretensions.

"I'm sorry, Mr Holmes, you are right to chide me. But this thing has got me rattled, I don't mind telling you. I have every faith in my brothers and would not dream of questioning their honesty, but the tree is undoubtedly dead."

"My dear sir, you start your story in the middle. Please do not be deceived by my reputation for deducing information from the tiniest clues. I repeat – I do not know what you are talking about," said Holmes with some asperity.

"I do apologise. First I should tell you who I am – my name is Norton Haffenden and I am the eldest of three brothers. After me is Jerome then Rupert, the youngest. My father was the Augustus Haffenden of whom you may have heard."

"The Hero of the Afghan War," I interjected.

"Indeed, he was known by that nomenclature after his gallant defence of the garrison at Kandahar."

"A truly great general," I ventured.

"He was, but strange to say, his heart was not in soldiering. He expressly forbade any of his sons to follow in that career. As a result of his persuasion, I am afraid that we three are rather dull fellows. I am a banker with Childs & Porteus, Jerome is a broker, and Rupert is a tea merchant. All honourable professions, in which we have succeeded admirably, but somewhat dull compared to topping fuzzy-wuzzies way out east."

"I do not wish to hurry you along to the detriment of your tale, Mr Haffenden, but we still do not seem to have arrived at the purpose of your visit," reminded Holmes.

"I am coming to that, Mr Holmes, but it is essential that you know about my family. I assure you that it is necessary for me to inform you that I am a widower with three children, my brother Jerome has a wife Lucy and six children, and Rupert is unmarried. We all share the same house – Haffenden Hall near Chislehurst. As I am a widower, my sister-in-law has become a substitute mother to my children and it is in everyone's interests that we exist as this family unit. Rupert, being unmarried, has also declined to leave the ancestral home but he maintains a bachelor apartment in Town as well."

"I have a clear picture of your family, Mr Haffenden, please proceed," said Holmes dryly.

"Our mother died, when we were all quite small, giving birth to what would have been our sister, but the child died with the mother. Our father, the general, never really recovered from the loss."

"I would have thought slaughtering *fuzzy-wuzzies* would have inured him to death somewhat. Do carry on," said Holmes suavely.

"Our father was a no nonsense sort of chap and he took it upon himself to rear us in a God-fearing righteous way. He was determined that we would not suffer from the want of a mother, so he, himself, saw to our up-bringing when young and kept a close watch on us after we went away to school and university. Yes, we are all well-educated even though engaged in prosaic occupations. My father was nothing if not practical and he made sure that we three learned the ways to support ourselves."

"You mentioned a tree?"

"Yes. I now come to the tree. On the birth of every one of us my father planted a tree. A conifer in each case. As you may know this type of tree grows very high and stretches skywards tall and straight. These trees were to be our exemplar. We were to grow as tall and straight as the tree planted for us. Thus, before the Hall is a row of three trees, each some sixty feet tall."

"An amusing conceit," said Holmes.

"It was more than that, Mr Holmes. Those trees came to rule our lives. As we grew older and the trees grew taller, there was great rivalry between us to be as tall and strong as the trees. At first, my tree was the tallest as, naturally, it had a head start, my being the oldest by three years. But, just as men grow at different rates, so the trees caught up with each other and now they are all of a similar height. Indeed, Rupert's is slightly taller, just as he, himself, has turned out the tallest of the three of us. We lived for those trees, Mr Holmes. Each school holiday we couldn't wait to get back home to see how they had grown."

I ventured to comment that such an apparently harmless idea could become obsessive if there should be rivalry between the boys.

"Certainly, Doctor, you are correct, it was obsessive and Father encouraged it. He said as long as our tree grew tall and straight he knew that we had been good boys. If ever a tree failed in some way then that was a sign that there was something reproachful in our character. You can imagine that we kept on the straight and narrow after that! The general lived to be 75 and made a will dividing his property equally between his three sons. He did not believe in primogeniture – all his sons were to be equal."

"Quite right too," I agreed, being a younger son myself.

"But he made a proviso which stated if anything happened to one of the trees, it would be a sign one of his sons had transgressed in some way, and that son's share would be taken from him and divided between the other two."

"An eccentric and bizarre idea certainly, but not unlawful. Why have you come to me about it?" asked Holmes.

"Because, Mr Holmes, six months ago my father died and, shortly afterwards, so did one of the trees."

"Ah!" Holmes leaned back in satisfaction. "You suspect that the tree did not die from natural causes, as I presume your father the old general did."

"Well it does seem a trifle odd that, after forty years of healthy growth, one tree should succumb within weeks of my father's death."

"But surely, even if your tree has died now, it is after your father's death and not subject to the clause in his will?" I tentatively suggested.

"It is not my tree that has died. It is Jerome's," said Mr Norton Haffenden.

"Tell me frankly, Mr Haffenden, do you seriously think that your brother's tree has been deliberately poisoned to make his entitlement under the will null and void?" asked Holmes.

"Well it does look a bit that way, though for the life in me I cannot imagine who would want to do such a thing, or why. Jerome's money would then be divided between Rupert and myself. I know that I haven't poisoned the tree and neither can I believe for a moment that Rupert would stoop to do so."

"But surely, if the two of you are the only one's to benefit, the suspicion is bound to fall on you both and on nobody else?" Holmes protested.

"That is the position, certainly. But we are all very close and if, by any chance, one of us lost his inheritance, in whatever manner, the other two would share theirs' with him. I would insist on it and I know Rupert would too, as would Jerome if he were in a position to inherit and one of his brothers were not."

"So the decease of this tree is purely academic?" asked Holmes.

"As far as the will is concerned, yes. The lawyers are dealing with the proving of the will at this moment and there will be no necessity to alter the proposed triple sharing. But we have all led totally blameless lives and a tree should only die if the owner had done something wicked. Well, not necessarily evil, just something of which Father disapproved."

"Superstitious nonsense!" snapped Holmes.

"I suppose it must seem like that to you gentlemen but, when your whole life has been dominated by the story of the trees, it is hard to dismiss it as mere fancy."

"Let us suppose the tree has been deliberately poisoned in some way, as you suspect. To what purpose and by whom?"

"That is the precise reason I thought it worthwhile to consult you. I have read of your interest in the singular and bizarre so thought this problem might be to your taste."

"Surely the first thing is to determine whether the tree has been poisoned or died of natural causes," I cried.

"Thank you, Watson. As usual, you home in on the nub of the matter. Very well, Mr Norton Haffenden, I will investigate your dead tree for no other reason than to extend my education. I am very well versed in the causes of death in man but my knowledge of arboriculture is limited. Pray give me your address and I will call to inspect your brother's tree."

Thus it was that, two days after this conversation, we found ourselves on the train to Chislehurst in the company of Mr Aloysius Crabtree of Kew Botanical Gardens. At the station we were met by a carriage and whisked at top speed to Haffenden Hall where we were introduced by Mr Norton Haffenden to his brother Jerome and Jerome's wife Lucy, who acted as the lady of the house, as well as his youngest brother Rupert, the tea importer.

All three men were of a respectable sober appearance and of such a dull character that I, for one, could not imagine any of them doing harm to an innocent tree, even by default. Holmes and Mr Crabtree went out to examine the trio of trees. It was rather chill and my time in Afghanistan has taught me to endure the heat rather than the cold so I remained indoors with the family by the fireside. Mrs Lucy Haffenden summoned tea and we all sat companionably talking about nothing important. I glanced from time to time through the magnificent bay window that gave a splendid view of the grounds.

Holmes, as was his wont, crawled on all fours with his glass, examining the ground around the trees and the base of the trunks, whilst Crabtree prodded about with a little spade or trowel.

It was a mere twenty minutes later when the two men re-entered the house.

"Well, gentlemen, my colleague informs me that your trees are of the genus *larix decidua*, commonly called the European larch, which has a growth rate of some two to three feet a year and he confidently attests that the middle tree has been poisoned. The method is a series of copper nails which have been hammered into the trunk of the tree about twelve inches from the ground. My colleague Mr Crabtree tells me this is a little-known but well-established method of killing a tree slowly and stealthily. The nails are hammered in as far as possible and the bark grows over the heads. The copper spreads its poison slowly through the sap. The significant word is slowly. It is a very gradual process. Mr Crabtree confidently asserts that the nails must have been *in situ* for a period of over eighteen months – possibly two years – for the tree to succumb at this time."

"So Father's death has no relevance?" said Jerome Haffenden.

"No sir, pure coincidence. The tree would have died about this time, give or take a month or two. Your father could have died at any time before or, indeed, could well have been alive still."

"But who could have done this deed?" asked Rupert Haffenden.

"Rather you should ask: who could have done this deed two years ago," said Crabtree sagely.

"Perhaps you could think back to a period two years ago when one of you may have caused an affront, albeit unknowingly, to a person who might seek this peculiar form of revenge," I suggested.

"Doctor, we are all men of the utmost rectitude and probity. We are pillars of our community, we do not go about causing affronts," said Norton Haffenden rather pompously.

"Perhaps we should concentrate on the possibility of somebody seeking a form of revenge on Mr Jerome, as it is his tree that has suffered, and not the others," said Holmes.

"Well I think I speak for us all, Mr Holmes, and you too Mr Crabtree, when I say that the best thing is to consider the matter closed. Whoever has done this deed is beyond discovery at this remote time and it makes not a scrap of difference to the will. Even if the damned lawyers stick to the letter of the law, Rupert and I shall ensure that you receive your fair share, Jerome. I dare say Rupert will agree with me," said Mr Norton.

"Oh undoubtedly, without question," agreed Rupert Haffenden.

It was perfectly clear that there was no animosity between the three brothers and that their thinking coincided on all matters. Obviously they lived lives of harmony, content in the happy habit of mutual agreement.

"You are quite right, Mr Holmes," said Norton Haffenden, "when you say it is all childish superstition. We are grown men and for too long have lived under the dominance of our military father. They are only trees. Let us consider the matter closed. I am sorry to have dragged you gentlemen all this way on so slight an errand. Mr Holmes, pray let me have your account without delay for settlement."

After returning to Town and before parting with Mr Aloysius Crabtree, Holmes asked "What is your fee for today's work, Mr Crabtree?"

"Oh, I don't really know, Mr Holmes. It was such a trivial affair. It hardly taxed the brain. Put me down for two guineas."

"Nonsense, man. I insist you take these ten guineas. You must charge, not merely for your time and trouble today, but for the years of knowledge and expertise you have accumulated. You have been of inestimable value. Take the ten guineas, I beg you, I will allow for it in my account. I think the three Brothers Smug can well afford it."

"A bit of a rum affair, Holmes," I commented, after we had parted with the horticultural expert and made our way back to Baker Street.

"Pshaw, hardly worth the while of a Lestrade, much less Sherlock Holmes!"

"Oh of course not, but what an odd thing for anyone to do – hammer nails into trees."

"Watson, as a medical man, you should know that there is nothing in the whole world that does not seem perfectly normal to some people, no matter how odd and bizarre it appears to the rest of humanity."

Some days later we were surprised to receive a visit from Mrs Lucy Haffenden, the wife of Mr Jerome Haffenden.

"I am sorry to trouble you, Mr Holmes, perhaps you will not remember me?"

"Of course we remember you, dear lady," said Holmes jovially. "How are things at Haffenden Hall? You must be aware that your brother-in-law has settled my account very promptly, so the affair is now closed."

"Yes, I do know that. But I am still bothered by it. You see, my husband has been most unsettled ever since your visit. When I tax him about it he tries to shrug it off as of no moment, but then he says it is damnable to know that someone, somewhere, dislikes him for an unaccountable reason. He is such a good man, Mr Holmes, that he finds it disagreeable to have an enemy."

"None of us likes to have enemies, Mrs Haffenden. I, myself, have many because of my profession, but I venture to suggest that even the best of us has made some sort of enemy, albeit unwittingly. Probably the Archbishop of Canterbury is disliked by some of his clergy because he preferred one bishop against another."

"I would like to engage your services, Mr Holmes."

"To do what, exactly, madam?" replied Holmes.

"Surely it is obvious, Mr Holmes? Someone dislikes my husband so much that they wanted to deprive him of his birthright. I have been brooding on this. It is a most terrible thing for my husband to realise he has enemies when all his life he has made a point of being at one with his fellow man. I do not like the idea of an enemy. My husband is too good a man to have this shadow over him. I want you to find out who has done this deed."

"I understand your feelings, madam, but I do not see how I can help. Your husband is the only man able to determine whom such a person might be."

"But that's the utter impossibility of it all! I cannot think of anyone who would want to ruin my husband in such a way."

"Is it possible that he has inadvertently crossed someone in his business? Perhaps somebody has lost money through his advice, or something of that nature. It is not impossible," I suggested, to try to assuage the lady's distress.

"But what will your husband say if I take up the case? And your brother-in-law? I should have to visit your home again."

"My husband can only be relieved if the malefactor is found, surely? As for Norton, he has no more authority than Jerome. We are all equal at the Hall. I must know who was responsible for maiming that tree and why. I owe it to my husband's peace of mind," said Mrs Haffenden with spirit.

"Well, madam, I will do what I can, but you and your husband may have greater peace of mind by not knowing."

"I think certainty is always preferable to doubt, don't you, Mr Holmes?"

"Very well, I will bend my greatest efforts on your behalf but I have no great confidence in finding out what you seek to know."

With that qualified assurance from Holmes, Mrs Lucy Haffenden left us.

"Well, Holmes, I still say this is a rum business."

"It is singular indeed. But is it criminal? Is it even important?"

"It would surely be criminal if it prevented someone inheriting," said I.

"But it hasn't, Watson."

"No, but that must surely have been the intention. I wonder how much of this tree story spread beyond the immediate family? They seem such a close circle I would not have thought much could go on that was common knowledge to anybody outside it."

"Once again, my dear fellow, you hit the nail on the head. This is obviously a family affair – some skeleton in the closet. As in all families, a united front is presented and ranks are closed against outsiders."

"So you do think there is something in the affair?"

"Oh most certainly. As soon as our friend, Mr Crabtree, exposed the method of poisoning the tree, Mr Norton Haffenden could not wait to usher us off his estate, suddenly pretending that it was a matter of trivial importance. Even you, Watson, with your idealistic view of mankind, must have observed the change from a man who seeks the truth to a man who wishes to conceal it."

"But if there is some skulduggery going on surely you are the man to uncover it."

"If any man can, certainly it is I, Watson. But even I cannot penetrate a secret in a united family. I am under no illusions – I do not think any of my skills are of use here."

But we had no time to discuss the matter further as we had another visitor.

"I am sorry to intrude without an appointment, gentlemen, you will not know me –"

"But I do – you are Mr Arthur Horncastle, butler to the brothers of Haffenden Hall."

"That is correct, Mr Holmes. I did not think you had noticed me when you visited the Hall."

"It is my business to notice."

"Quite. I believe Mrs Jerome Haffenden has been to see you?"

"I preserve my clients' confidentiality."

"I would not expect a man of probity to do other. But I know she has been here and no doubt engaged your services."

"I repeat, my clients' dealings with myself are confidential."

"I would not like you to waste your time and talents on a wild goose chase, Mr Holmes. It is not possible to ascertain the truth about the dead tree."

"Mr Holmes can invariably ascertain the truth," I said somewhat loftily.

"In this particular instance I suggest that there is nothing to find," the butler replied smoothly.

"The tree was alive and is now dead. I ascertained the truth that it had been poisoned by copper nails. Somebody purposefully did that deed. It is possible to find out who did it and I shall do so if requested."

"I repeat, Mr Holmes, there is nothing to find."

"I think perhaps you, yourself, are responsible for destroying the tree," said Holmes unperturbed.

"Certainly not! How dare you suggest that?" said the butler angrily.

"Why should you warn me off? Why trail Mrs Haffenden from Chislehurst to here? Perhaps you come on your master's instructions?"

"I know nothing. I merely wished to save you the trouble of wasting your efforts. All right, I see that you are too intelligent to be fobbed off. I must confess the truth. I am sent by Mr Jerome Haffenden. His wife is not herself. She has periods of distress. She is subject to fits of mild insanity – nothing major, you understand – but she often harbours delusions and is under constant medical care. Mr Jerome has asked me to take especial care of her when the fit is upon her. She does not know what she says or does when in the throes of the malady. Then, in a few days, she is well again and knows nothing of it or what she has done during it."

"Oh, Mr Horniman, how good of you to explain! I would not, of course, dream of taking advantage of a deluded woman. You must return at once in case some mischance falls on the poor lady whilst in transit home."

"So you will not be carrying out any further investigations?" asked the butler.

"Oh, I certainly could not take instructions from a poor deluded woman, rest assured."

The butler gave a slight bow and silently glided away.

"Well that explains much, Holmes."

"It certainly does, Watson."

"Obviously the three brothers are doing their best to keep the lady's malady secret. As you said – a very close family."

"This affair becomes more intriguing by the hour. I will not rest now until I get to the bottom of it."

"But you assured the butler that you would drop your interest in the case."

"I said I would not take instruction from a deluded woman. Mrs Haffenden is as sane as you or me."

It was some two weeks before I saw Holmes again. It appeared that he had not been sleeping at our rooms, there was evidence that he had called in from time to time but his visits did not coincide with my being at home. So I could only assume that he was on a case. One afternoon at about four o'clock he appeared, dressed in the manner of a working man, and threw himself down on the sofa.

"Do you know the price of a pint of porter, Watson?"

"I can't say I do offhand, why?"

"Or the weight of a keg of beer?"

"What is this, Holmes? Why do you ask?"

"Because I have spent the last two weeks adding to my frugal knowledge of the licensed victualler trade. I now know everything appertaining to the job of cellar man and pot-boy"

"You have been working in a public house?"

"A village inn, Watson. At Chislehurst."

"Ah, I see. The Haffenden affair."

"Exactly. The local inn is the one place to find out the truth. Amongst all the local gossip there is always a grain of truth. I have been attempting to sort the wheat from the chaff."

"And you have solved the case?"

"Not quite. There is a missing piece that I think only Horniman, the butler, can supply, but I know enough to make him supply it. Would you care to accompany me to Chislehurst tomorrow afternoon when I hope to reveal the *dénouement* to this odd affair?"

"I should be disappointed not to be included."

The following afternoon we appeared at Haffenden Hall once again. Holmes had requested the presence of the brothers at 5pm and they had left their respective businesses to be present. Mrs Lucy Haffenden was also of the party.

"What is this all about, Mr Holmes?" asked Mr Norton Haffenden. "I understood our business together was concluded some time ago."

"Your sister-in-law, Mrs Lucy Haffenden, has now retained my services and it is in answer to her request that I conclude my investigation."

"Is this true, Lucy? Have you instructed this detective to pry into our family affairs?" asked Mr Norton Haffenden heatedly.

"I thought you had agreed to stop your investigations, Holmes. Horniman assured me that it was so," stated Mr Jerome Haffenden.

"Conclude? Then you have arrived at the truth, Mr Holmes?" asked Mrs Haffenden, ignoring her husband and brother-in-law.

"I have indeed. I know all. This family has behaved in a most shameful manner."

"That is not true, Mr Holmes. I do not know what you claim to have discovered, but no member of this family has done anything of which to be ashamed," said Norton Haffenden.

"Perhaps you would ask your butler to join us?" asked Holmes.

"Horniman? What on earth for? What has a servant to do with this?" blustered Mr Jerome Haffenden.

"Pray ask him to join us," repeated Holmes.

"Oh, very well," grumbled Mr Norton and rang the bell. The butler himself answered the summons immediately.

"Now what I am about to reveal cannot be a surprise to anybody in this room except for my friend, Dr Watson, and perhaps to Mrs Haffenden. I am not clear how much she knows of these proceedings."

"My wife knows nothing, and I suggest she be allowed to leave the room at once," said Mr Jerome Haffenden.

"Your good lady is my client, sir. All my efforts have been on her behalf."

"Nevertheless, I think I know what is best for my wife and family, and insist that she leaves the room before you make any further statement. Please be advised, my dear. I will relay to you anything of interest that Mr Holmes has to say."

"I have engaged Mr Holmes and am meeting his fees from my own private purse. Surely I am entitled to hear his report. Certainly I shall stay to hear what he has to say," replied Mrs Haffenden. "Pray proceed Mr Holmes."

"You have all been wilfully and shamefully concealing information from me, but I have learned all without your assistance. You have a small staff here – your butler, his wife who is the cook, a governess, a nurse, a manservant, two maidservants and a boot boy. The outside staff does not concern us. Two years ago you had a maidservant called Maisie Dewhurst."

"That is correct, Mr Holmes, and I am proud to say that Miss Dewhurst consented to be my wife and is now Mrs Horniman and, as you say, the cook in this establishment," interjected the butler smoothly.

"I have said I know all. I also know that the incumbent cook was dismissed to make a place for your new wife."

"I trust that is not the shameful behaviour of which you accuse this family, sir. Our old cook left to take up a position elsewhere," said Mr Norton.

"I believe she obtained a position at Colwyn Bay, in Wales," added Horniman.

"So I understand," said Holmes, "with a parting gift of a hundred pounds."

"We are generous to our employees," said Mr Norton.

"I believe you have a small child, Mr Horniman?" asked Holmes.

"That is so," said Horniman with a smile. "Our union has been blessed with little Susan who is our pride and joy."

"About two years old, is she, Mr Horniman?" asked Holmes.

"A little under, Mr Holmes," replied the smiling butler.

"Look here, Holmes, I hope all this is not coming round to the business of Rupert and the maidservant. Because, if it is, we all know about it and there is nothing to be ashamed of. The whole family behaved impeccably and my wife is fully conversant with my father's actions in the matter," said Mr Jerome.

"Indeed that is the horse I ride. I know you are all aware of the facts; that is what I have said all along," said Holmes.

"Mr Holmes, I must point out that we are a very united family and we are all aware of the transgression of any member of it. In the instance that you seem to have discovered, I repeat my husband's statement – the entire family behaved impeccably, as did the staff. I cannot see that any of that business has anything to do with anyone outside this family. I asked you to investigate the death of the tree and to find the person who poisoned it."

"That is precisely what I have found out, madam."

"Then please reveal your brilliant deduction," said Mr Rupert.

"If you will bear with me a little longer, I would like Dr Watson to hear the full story as all of you seem to know it. Much to the old general's disgust, one of his son's seduced your maidservant Maisie Dewhurst and got her with child. The general, being a compassionate man, did not throw the wretched girl out as many employers have done in the past and no doubt will do in the future. No, your father prevailed upon his faithful servant Horniman to make an honest woman of her. Your butler married her and pretended to be the father of the child."

"I would do anything for the general, he was a wonderful man. I am like a true father to Susan. I could not do more for her than if she were my own," burst out Horniman.

"But why did Mr Rupert not marry her, he is a single man," I asked.

"Really, Doctor, do you think that a Haffenden would stoop to wed a mere servant girl? My brother-in-law has refused marriage with daughters of peers of the realm," said Mrs Lucy Haffenden loftily.

"Look here, Holmes, this is probably very sporty to you, washing our family's dirty linen for the gratification of your friend, but we, here, see nothing amiss in this. We are all men of rectitude and probity," said Mr Jerome.

"If this is all your deduction comprises then perhaps you would leave? It is, after all, strictly a private family matter," said Mr Norton. "My sister was unwise to encourage you to delve into our family affairs."

"It would not seem an example of rectitude and probity to get a servant with child then wash your hands of the poor creature," said Holmes sternly.

"Tush, man, there's nothing in that. We all know about that. There is nothing to shame us there. You have discovered how our father dealt with it. The girl is handsomely provided for with a stable position, home and husband. Indeed, she has bettered herself more than she deserves. Our father sorted everything out very satisfactorily," said Mr Jerome.

"Yes, he made it all right for all of you, didn't he? As usual. But he had his own peculiar way of disapproval. He put nails in the tree so that it would die. Perish, just as his vision of a blameless son had perished," said Holmes.

"Father killed the tree?" gasped Mr Rupert.

"He did. Personally, with his own hands. His heart was broken by the callous attitude shown to Maisie. If his own son could not tell right from wrong after his staunch upbringing then he despaired. I doubt that even Horniman knew that, did you?" asked Holmes.

"No, Mr Holmes, I did not know, but I am not surprised. The general was a noble man of high principles. None of his sons is a patch on him and I say that to their faces. They are feeble men of no character. The three of them put together would not equal the general. As you know, I have tried my best to protect them but I doubt if they are worth it. I have kept my peace as I gave the general my word, but do you suppose my wife enjoys her enforced marriage? We servants can easily be sacrificed to uphold the good name of the family."

"But, Mr Holmes, I think, after all, I find you at fault," said Mrs Lucy Haffenden with a smile that was almost a smirk. "You say the general poisoned the tree himself, but surely of all people he would know which tree belonged to which son. The action of all too human frailty, that you apparently find so terrible, was committed by Mr Rupert Haffenden, yet the tree that has died is the one belonging to my husband, Mr Jerome Haffenden. I think your conclusion is a little awry."

"I am not wrong, madam. I will not submit my bill to you. Bad news is ill enough to bear without having to pay for the privilege. It must be very comforting to live in such a close united family. Good day."

The Singular Adventure
of
THE RAMBLING DETECTIVE

MY friend Mr Sherlock Holmes had passed a very arduous winter. He had travelled extensively throughout Europe in connection with the disappearance of secret government plans and he had survived no fewer than three bungled attempts on his life. His arch enemy Professor Moriarty had escaped the net which Holmes had so painstakingly woven. In short, the man was completely exhausted. I had often urged him to take a break from his customary taxing labours but he had always scoffed at my concern. It was a measure of his complete breakdown that, when I proposed he should spend some time in the country during the spring, he made no protest at all but fell readily into my proposal.

Thus it was that we were idly rambling about the countryside in Norfolk. I thought some not too strenuous walking in flat countryside may be gently restorative. We lodged simply at country inns and strolled, rather than hiked, about the vicinity before moving on to yet another village hostelry. Holmes had developed an interest in church architecture and whenever he spotted one of the typical round flint towers off we would go to examine the attached church.

We were in the village of Wroxley St Margaret and, after a simple but filling breakfast, we walked over to look at the church. Whilst in there we were surprised by the rector.

"Are you two gentlemen visitors? I am not familiar with your faces."

I explained we were Londoners on a walking holiday and that my friend had a passion for churches.

"Indeed, then you may be interested in our modest treasures here. We are very proud of our charter. See, here on this wall. The charter was given to the village by Queen Elizabeth, who passed through here on her way from Ipswich to Norwich. It entitles us to hold a weekly market and officially gives us the status of a town. It is hard to believe, I know, when you see the tiny sleepy village today, but in Elizabethan times we were a bustling centre for the exchange of cloths – worsted, kersey and so on."

Holmes took out his glass and examined the ancient charter.

"Are you staying in the village?" asked the rector.

"Yes, we are putting up at the Dog & Gun," I replied.

"Ah, well if you look at the wall in the snug you will see a large photograph. It was taken by myself some twenty years ago, not long after I came here. I am rather proud of it – photography is a hobby of mine. The reason I mention it is that the subject is the Charter Fair held that year. Some enterprising villagers got up a pageant to mark the Tercentenary of the bestowing of the Charter. It was a very big affair, people came from miles around and the entire village, or I should say town, dressed up as if in days of yore."

I began to think that the good fellow may become tiresome to Holmes with his prattling, so I tried to make an excuse. "Holmes, would you care to look at the outside?"

"You go on ahead, Watson, I know you prefer the sunshine to medieval history. I'll poke about in here with the guidance of the Reverend –?"

"I am the Reverend Augustus Stoop, incumbent of this parish. And I trust I am not in error when I jump to the conclusion that you are the famous detective Sherlock Holmes and his companion Dr Watson?"

"See, Watson," said Holmes wryly, "your records of my cases have penetrated even the wilds of Norfolk."

"I am honoured to meet you, gentlemen. I have followed all your adventures avidly."

I was rather annoyed at this as I feared that it may cause Holmes to be discontented. "We are travelling incognito, sir. Mr Holmes has been advised to take a restful holiday."

"Please be assured I will not reveal your true identities. I am very honoured to meet you. May I shake your hands? Honoured indeed. But have no fear, your secret is safe with me, I shall not allude to it again. Please wander where you will. If you would like me to show you round I should be delighted, if you prefer to find your own way, I shall efface myself."

Holmes listened with great good humour to this speech and then said "For my part, I should like to see all you have of antiquarian interest, if you would be so good as to show me, though I fancy Watson would prefer to poke about the gravestones in the sun, eh, Watson?"

Holmes thus enabled me to escape with good grace to outside, whilst the two of them started delving into a medieval palimpsest. It was a lovely day and soon I had spread myself comfortably against a wall and dozed off to the sounds of bees and birds.

I was woken by a muttering voice. Not far from me was a rough-looking fellow crouched by a grave; a recent burial judging by the heap of wilting flowers covering the mound. He was not aware of my presence and although he was quite alone he still kept up the muttering until I realised he was saying the same thing over and over. Gradually I made out the words "Where did you put it you old bastard, where did you put it?" repeated like a litany. Eventually, tiring of his muttering, he made off.

I went into the church to find Holmes and the rector putting away the manuscripts that had so interested them. I told the rector about the man I had seen.

"I think I may have just seen your village idiot," I said laughing.

"I don't think we have one, Dr Watson," replied the Rev Stoop.

"A rough-looking fellow, muttering over that recent grave."

"Oh, that would be Jake Mellon, the local ne'er-do-well. We buried his father just a few days ago. Frank Mellon was the head gardener up at the Hall for many years. A very popular and well respected parishioner. He was turned seventy and still in harness when he passed away. He was a widower, his wife died in childbirth and he was left to bring up six children. Two died while children and, of the four remaining, one went off to be a soldier and was never heard of again, the two girls got married to local men, and Jake – well, he was always a bit sly, and he rubs along doing a bit of poaching, a bit of casual work and a lot of scrounging. But, I must not detain you any longer, you will be wanting your lunch. The landlord of the Dog & Gun puts on quite a spread. Do not worry – I will not tell anybody who you are. Good day." The Rev Stoop raised his panama hat and walked away.

On our way back to the Inn we passed the village green which obviously also acted as the cricket field. There was a patch near the boundary where the turf had been all dug over and small piles of earth were scattered about.

"It looks as though they have a problem with moles, Holmes," I said, but he merely grunted, absorbed in his own thoughts. The holiday was working wonderfully well. He had never been a robust figure, but Holmes had lost that drawn emaciated look that had so worried me in the depths of the recent harsh winter. Now it was almost summer and even Holmes, who was never comfortable away from the Great Wen, was beginning to bloom with the season.

As the rector had said, the landlord laid on a noble lunch for us and when he at last brought the cheese board I remarked about the moles on the outfield.

"That digging wasn't moles, sir. That was done in the night by some villain."

"Surely not! Who would wish to destroy the cricket field?"

"Well I couldn't say, sir, but we have an important match on Saturday against Little Fenham. I wouldn't be surprised if some lout from over there hasn't done it."

"To what purpose?" asked Holmes mildly.

"I couldn't say, sir," replied mine host.

"Any fault with the outfield would affect both teams equally, surely?"

"I suppose so. But somebody's done it and it weren't no animal, begging your pardon, sir." As the landlord shuffled off, Holmes raised an eyebrow, shrugged and tucked into the cheese.

We spent the afternoon looking at *tumuli* some four or five miles from the village and went a little astray on our return journey, so we were both pleasantly tired on our return and after dinner retired to bed early. We had decided that on the following day we would set off early towards Norwich, which was now only some twenty miles away. We reckoned on perhaps one more overnight halt if necessary. If we made good progress then we would go all the way. Holmes wanted to reach Norwich without delay as our holiday had to finish on the Saturday and it was now Tuesday night.

I slept very soundly on the whole but was disturbed by some shouting and the noise of people moving about. I opened a bleary eye and, although it was light, my hunter told me it was but 5.30, so I turned over and was asleep again without really waking. At breakfast I asked Holmes if he had been disturbed, but his room was at the back of the house and he had heard nothing.

We were examining our Ordnance Survey map to ascertain the best route to take when the landlord came in looking flustered.

"I'm very sorry to disturb you at breakfast, gentlemen, but I have here both the squire and the rector who insist that I bring them to you. I am hardly in a position to refuse their request but I do not wish to cause offence to you gentlemen."

"We have met your rector, landlord, and I am sure he would not intrude if it were not of some importance. Show the gentlemen in," said Holmes.

Much relieved, the landlord went out of the room and within seconds the Rev Stoop entered with a burly man sporting a fine moustache and side whiskers.

"I do apologise, Mr Holmes, Dr Watson, for intruding upon you. When I promised you yesterday that I would leave you unmolested I truly intended that it should be so, but something very dreadful has happened in the night and I feel sure that you will forgive me for breaking my undertaking. This is Squire Brotherton, he is a justice of the peace and the chief personage of our community."

"I am honoured to make your acquaintance, Mr Holmes. Please do not be angry with Mr Stoop for informing me of your presence. It is most fortunate for us that you are here."

"What has happened? Mr Holmes is here on a relaxing holiday. He cannot oblige in any professional capacity," I protested.

"Calm yourself, Watson. I am not to be molly-coddled. What is the matter, gentlemen? Pray explain."

"A murder has been committed in the night," said the JP baldly.

"A foul and heinous crime has been committed in my parish. A parish that has hitherto been entirely free from any kind of wrong-doing, much less murder."

"Silence, Stoop! The facts, Mr Holmes, are, that at some time in the night Miss Wheatley, an aged spinster, left her cottage with only a shawl over her night attire, went on to the village green and was stabbed to death by a person unknown with a gardening fork."

"How horrible!" I cried.

"Where is the body now?" asked Holmes.

"I had it carried back into her cottage. It is the little thatched one next to this inn."

"It would have been better to summon me as soon as it was found so I may have examined the scene of the crime with the body *in situ*, as it had occurred."

"Indeed, Mr Holmes. But the body was found at first light by Jonas Webb, a farm labourer, making his way to work. He roused the inn and it seemed to be the correct thing to convey Miss Wheatley's body back inside her own cottage."

"So that was the noise that disturbed me," I said.

"A message was sent to me and I came post-haste down from the Hall and met up with the rector who gave me the glad tidings that Mr Sherlock Holmes, the world famous detective, was actually here right on the spot. Of course, I have sent to Norwich for the police but I am sure you will concede that it would be foolish to neglect the fact that we have the country's leading detective here to hand."

"Very well, I will come and examine the scene of the crime. Watson, perhaps you would enter the cottage and examine the body of the unfortunate Miss Wheatley."

I did as bade. Miss Wheatley had been aged about seventy and the location of her cottage would indicate that she had been disturbed in the night by some noise and had drawn on her shawl and sallied forth to investigate. Her cottage was opposite the patch of village green that had been turned over, and when I looked at it again it was in an even greater mess. The disturbed area had been greatly enlarged and earth was strewn randomly all over the place. Holmes was on his knees, closely examining every inch of the disturbed earth with his lens.

Inside the cottage Miss Wheatley had been laid on a couch and covered with a sheet from the bed. The sheet was stained with much blood and, when I lifted the corner to look, it was very evident why. The entire upper part of the abdomen was red with blood which had flowed freely from a number of stab wounds. As the squire had said, a garden fork was obviously responsible as the wounds were in lines of four where the tines had penetrated the frail old lady's body. I dropped the sheet and went outside. I am a medical man and have served in the Afghan Wars but I was sick at the sight of this callous and brutal murder.

Holmes was still at the scene of the crime so I re-entered the inn where the rector sat dolefully alone. The squire was outside, ordering a group of men to place a rope cordon around the plot where Holmes was working, and trying to compel everybody to go about their usual business but in vain.

The rector looked up at me and said "In all the time I have been here there has only been one crime previous to this. That was a burglary. A fine haul for somebody, mind you. The squire was robbed the very day we had the Charter Fair. You will remember I told you about the Fair. The photograph I took that day is through there in the snug. While the squire was making merry down here on the village green, some villain entered his house and stole a great many valuables. Silver candlesticks, jewellery, that sort of thing. I wondered what sort of parish I had come to, but since then – twenty years of perfect peace – not even a stolen chicken. Now this. It seems odd that both these crimes occurred when strangers entered the village. There were lots of strangers about on the day of the Charter Fair, now there are the two of you from London."

"I trust you are not accusing Mr Holmes and myself of murdering your parishioner," I said rather hotly.

The Rev Stoop realised what he had said. Of course the poor man was overwrought. "No, no, how foolish of me to say that. I don't know what I'm saying. I do apologise, Doctor. Of course we are fortunate that you and Mr Holmes are here to assist us in our distress. Please forget what I said. I am talking nonsense."

Eventually Holmes came in accompanied by the squire. He had also seen the poor woman's body.

"Well, Mr Holmes, what can you tell us?" asked the squire.

"I think you are going to be disappointed with the great London detective," said Holmes wryly. "I can add little to that which you told me. Somebody has been digging up the turf of your village green-cum-cricket field in the dead of night. Miss Wheatley hears a noise whilst in her bed. She puts on her slippers and shawl and comes out to see what is happening. The man, yes, I can confirm there was only one person and that it was a man, being surprised, uses the fork with which he has been turning the soil to strike at the poor woman. He stabs her three times causing twelve separate wounds any one of which would have been fatal as I am sure Dr Watson will agree. The man, realising too late what he has done, abandons his mysterious digging and flees at speed in the direction of the oak tree beside the cricket pavilion. There his traces disappear. If the murderer is a local man I am sure he will have fled and thus announce his guilt. If he has chosen to stay and brazen it out we can find him by examining his boots and fork. I have observed several perfect prints and can identify them instantly. If, however, he has destroyed his boots and fork, then we have no other evidence with which to confront him. That is all I can tell you. I am afraid in this instance the famous detective can tell you little more than your parish constable could."

"Then I think we had better search the village and see if any man is absent and find out if he has just cause to be so. At the same time we will search for the gardening fork."

So saying, the squire swept out followed by every other person in the place leaving Holmes and myself alone.

"Let us go into the snug, Watson," said Holmes leading the way. "This affair has rather played havoc with our intentions. We can hardly leave now, before the police arrive from Norwich."

"Of course not. Perhaps if the officers of law and order come in a carriage, we could cadge a ride back with them and so catch up on our itinerary?"

"Capital idea, Watson!" Holmes was silent for a while then asked "What do you make of all this business, Watson?"

"Well it seems to me exactly as you expounded it."

"But why would anybody be digging up the playing field at dead of night?"

"I presumed he was looking for buried treasure of some kind, or possibly secretly retrieving some object that he had buried previously."

"But that doesn't make sense, Watson. All around are fields and gardens where a man could bury some treasure secretly and then discreetly retrieve it later. Why in a public area covered in grass? Right opposite the inn, in full gaze of everybody?"

"I cannot imagine. As you say, there are many places more suitable for the purpose."

"Of course it need not have been as we see it now. It may not have been a cricket field, not even grass, when the treasure was buried. Perhaps it was long ago before the inn was built? The treasure could have been hidden centuries ago."

"Do you know that this is only the second crime ever committed in this parish in the last twenty years?"

"How do you know that?"

"The rector said so."

"I do not believe that. It may be the only crime he or anybody else has heard about but the country is full of evil. There is more wickedness going on behind these verdant hedgerows than in the direst stews of London."

"Well, according to the rector, the only previous crime of note took place twenty years ago on Charter Fair day when the Hall was robbed by a stranger to the village. The rector, himself, took that photograph there on the wall. It was a sort of Elizabethan pageant."

"And did they catch the thief?"

"No, to this day neither haul nor thief was ever found."

Holmes sat with his head back and gazed lazily at the photograph; suddenly he sprang to his feet with an oath.

"Blast you, Watson!"

"Holmes!"

"You and your restoratives – you have almost destroyed my perceptive faculties! This relaxing holiday you have forced me into has relaxed my brain so much that I cannot think logically. The picture, man, – take it down and bring it outside!"

Holmes rushed out of the inn on to the village green. He strode to the centre then turned to regard the inn.

"Bring the picture, Watson!"

I hurried to where he stood and held out the picture. The photo was taken from where we were standing and showed the facade of the Dog & Gun. In front of it, on a high stage or platform, was a bunch of local worthies all dressed up in Tudor costumes.

"See these trees on the photograph? They are the ones there, now somewhat bigger."

"Certainly, the same ones with an extra twenty years of growth."

"So the stage erected for that pageant would be about from there, to – about there. Can you find four sticks, Watson, and we can put them where the corners of the stage would have been."

I hunted round and soon found four suitable sticks and pushed them into the ground under Holmes' direction.

"The murderer, whoever he is, was somewhat out in his calculations."

"I do not follow you, Holmes, what is this about?"

"I have at last seen what I should have realised at first. Whoever buried what you are pleased to call the treasure, did so while concealed from the world. You now tell me of a robbery committed on the very day that this platform stood there. The thief buried his booty under the platform. Imagine, Watson, he could actually have been under there at the very moment that this photograph was taken. Whilst the players were enacting their pageant, the thief was concealed underneath the draped platform. That is the difference between the time the booty was buried and now, when somebody is trying to find it. A large platform hid the man burying the treasure, the man digging it up has to rely on the hours of darkness."

I gazed at the photograph and imagined how easy it would be for someone to dig underneath it in complete concealment. At that moment the squire returned.

"Well, Mr Holmes, we have had some slight success. We found the fork, it was thrown over that hedge there, where it landed in the cornfield." The squire indicated. "It was covered in blood."

"Where is it now?" asked Holmes.

"Still there. I've left a man on guard. I thought you would want to examine it *in situ* and I should imagine the police will prefer we do not touch it."

"Quite right. I will await your local official and examine it with him. Meanwhile, I wonder if you would be so good as to order half a dozen men to gently turn over that rectangle of ground I have marked out."

"What is this? Destroy even more of our cricket field?"

"I think you will find it worth the effort."

Some men were put to work and under Holmes' guidance they carefully uncovered the area, turning over the sods. Soon one of them let out a cry "There's something here, sir!" Holmes, the squire, the rector and myself, together with all the men, stood round while the fellow gently probed about, finally pulling out some old tattered sacking.

"It's a sack that has rotted away," said Holmes crisply. "If you feel around you will undoubtedly find the contents."

In short order many items were brought to light. Tarnished and filthy as they were through many years of burial, the squire had no difficulty in recognising his property.

"It is all the plate stolen from the Hall years ago!" he gasped. "Mr Holmes, this is a miracle. We ask you to investigate a murder and you find stolen property from a previous age."

"A miracle indeed," said the rector. "It is barely a sennight since I was told that the valuables were gone for ever and would never be found."

"What are you talking about, Stoop? Explain yourself," barked the squire.

"Well, I have been in a most difficult position these last few days and to tell you the truth I did not really know how I should act. I have, in fact, made arrangements to see the bishop next week as I sought his guidance as to what I should do. I rather think this alters things. You see, by virtue of my cloth, I cannot reveal things told to me in confession."

"'Strewth man, you're not a papist are you?" cried the squire.

"No, no, of course not, but the principle is the same."

"Perhaps you had better come into the inn and tell us what you know," said Holmes kindly, and the four of us went inside.

"You see, your head gardener Frank Mellon asked for me on the day he died. He said he had a confession to make. On the day of the Charter Fair all those years ago, he had found a fellow in the grounds with a sack. He knew the man but did not say who it was. He followed the thief, hoping to wrest the sack from him and return the valuables. But he was too late, the things were missed and the alarm raised. However, he got the sack from the man, who fled cursing."

"But why did he not return the loot immediately?" asked the squire.

"I don't know, but he said that he had to work with great haste as he was afraid that, if he was found with the stolen property, it would be thought he had stolen it."

"Nonsense, nobody would have thought that of Frank Mellon. Honest as the day is long, old Frank."

"Well that is what he said. So he concealed the booty and had never been near it since. He would not tell me where it was hidden and said it was gone for ever. He wanted to ease his conscience before he met his maker and that is the story he told. I did not know whether I should reveal this to you, Squire, or what I should do, so I resolved to ask my bishop how I should act. But now it has been found by this amazing gentleman, I think perhaps I need not see the bishop after all."

"A damned curious business. So we don't know who the thief was and we don't know who the murderer is. I have got my plate and jewels back but we are still ignorant of either culprit."

"At this remote period of time it is unlikely that the thief will come to light unless he chooses to confess, and he may well be dead, but we may find the murderer yet," said Holmes.

"I think I know who the thief and the murderer is!" I cried. "Surely it is none other than Frank Mellon's son, Jake. I told you, Rector, that I overheard him muttering in the churchyard yesterday morning."

"Damn me, you could be right!" said the squire, "We have not found him yet, he could have bolted."

"When we were looking round the church I overheard Jake at his father's grave saying 'Where did you put it, you old bastard?' He must have meant the treasure, sorry, the booty."

"You told us of the man; you did not tell us what he said," Holmes said tartly.

"Jake's father must have taken the sack from him, buried it and refused to disclose to his son where he had hidden it," I said.

"That would explain why he was reluctant to tell who the thief was. He would not want to shop his own son, even if he was a disgrace to the family," said Holmes. "Jake must have wheedled something out of his father on his death-bed so had an idea where to dig. Unfortunately he guessed the location of the stage inaccurately. He need only have moved a few yards to the left. If Miss Wheatley had not interrupted him he would probably have gone on to find it eventually, but time was not on his side. He was getting desperate because the villagers would not ignore interference with their cricket field for ever. I should think he feared the possibility of a night guard being mounted. Desperation drives men to extreme actions."

"Well, Mr Holmes, I think you have it all there. We are very fortunate that you were here to solve not only our current crime but also one from years ago. Your reputation understates your extraordinary powers. I must confess I was rather disappointed earlier when you could tell us little more than the obvious, but you have surpassed anything I could have hoped for."

On the train from Norwich to London I ventured to suggest that it was unlikely that Jake Mellon would ever be found. He had lived rough and on his wits all his life and that sort of fellow could disappear for ever.

"I agree, Watson. Yet another aspect of the affair worries me too. I have often said it is futile to build up a theory on insufficient facts. I am rather concerned that you, of all people, were in possession of all the facts in this case and neither solved it yourself nor gave the facts to me so that I could solve it."

"Holmes that is unworthy of you! You were there for a relaxing holiday, not to pit your wits against a double crime."

"Your relaxing holiday was very nearly the death of my reputation! You had got my brain into such a state of idleness that I could not see the obvious. No more relaxing holidays for me, Watson. I must re-hone my intellect, there is much work to be done in the city. I cannot afford to relax my vigilance for a second."

The Singular Adventure
of
THE ABANDONED BICYCLE

"WHAT nonsense!" I exclaimed. "Listen to this, Holmes. An article here claims that educating people encourages them to commit crimes. It is well known that ignorance breeds crime."

"That is a theory certainly, Watson. If you lay down absolute morals like the ten commandments, then the ignorant man knows where he is. Thou shalt not kill, thou shalt not steal and so on."

"Well what's wrong with that? Don't tell me you disagree with the commandments of God?"

"If you educate a man he may find that these commandments are not absolute. He may wish to challenge them."

"You cannot argue against 'Thou shalt not kill' – not even you, Holmes."

"I suggest that when you were faced with a jezail-wielding Ghazi aiming at your heart, during the recent campaign in which you were wounded defending your Queen and country, you would not have thought twice about shooting him at point blank range."

"That's different, Holmes, that's war."

"And I also venture to suggest that, if you were an honourable man but completely destitute, then it would not impugn your honour to steal a loaf of bread to feed your starving wife and children."

"Stealing is morally wrong, Holmes, whatever excuse you give for it. Wrong is wrong."

"I merely point out that if you educate a man he may start to see the world in a different light. That different light may lead him to commit a felony, as he does not regard it as a crime. Ergo, education breeds crime."

"So you agree with the writer of this article, do you?" I growled.

"I cannot say, I have not read it. But I will do so when you have finished with the paper."

"Well this chap says it is through educating the lower classes that we have this spate of thefts from noble houses."

"Spate of thefts?"

"There have been four major thefts from grand houses, all on the outskirts of London, and only one showed any evidence of a break-in."

"What about the other three?"

"Valuables just disappeared, no sign of any damage, no forced entry, nothing. Obviously inside jobs, employees stealing from their masters, or so the author of this report suggests."

"Have any of these servants been accused?"

"Well this is the problem. In the absence of any evidence entire staffs are under suspicion. In three of the houses the atmosphere is most uncomfortable, as servant suspects servant and the household does not know whom it can trust. In the fourth house the entire staff has been dismissed, which has caused much bad feeling and it is proving difficult to find good replacements."

"A curious state of affairs, Watson. You say one of the houses did have signs of a forced entry?"

"Yes, Lord Winstanley's residence, Mosscote Manor. The study window had been forced and it is presumed the thief came and went by that entrance."

"Is Scotland Yard on the case?"

"Yes, your old friend Lestrade is in charge, but he admits that he has nothing he can go on as, apart from the valuables being absent, the houses are just as normal."

"Hum. I wonder." Holmes puffed at his acrid pipe and mused to himself.

"What do you wonder, Holmes?"

"Perhaps the items were not stolen. Perhaps the householders themselves have removed them in order to claim insurance money for them. What do you think of that theory?"

"Preposterous, Holmes!" I was outraged. "Do you seriously think that the first families in England would stoop to such infamous practices. I am surprised you should even think the thought, much less utter it!"

"Quite right, Watson. You do well to chide me. I have often said to you that it is fruitless to theorise without sufficient facts. Still, it is naught to me. I have not been consulted on the matter."

But only a few days later Holmes was consulted. We were at breakfast when we had a visit from a man who, for all his attempts at concealment, was rather perturbed.

"Mr Holmes. I am sorry to intrude upon you at this early hour, but I am sent to entreat you to return with me immediately. I have a first class train ticket for you and my master has sent this cheque to defray the inconvenience. But he begs you to come immediately, before the snow melts."

"Pray calm yourself. On reading the noble name on this cheque, and perceiving the munificent sum stated thereon, I shall certainly return with you. May I bring my colleague Dr Watson with me? Are you game, Watson?"

Holmes held out the cheque to show me that it was drawn on Coutts Bank and that the sum of one thousand pounds was to be transferred from the account of Lord Mersham to Mr Sherlock Holmes.

On the train further details of the case were furnished to us by Mr

Bellingham, who was the butler to Lord Mersham. It seemed that the noble lord had awoken early that morning and had looked out of the window to see that there had been a fall of snow in the night. He also saw, a little way down the drive, what appeared to be a bicycle on it's side. Lord Mersham had then roused his butler and together they had gone out to investigate.

"My lord was most circumspect, Mr Holmes, he realised that the freshly laid snow would aid our investigations, so we kept right at the side of the driveway, completely distant from the marks already on the drive. It could be seen from footmarks that one man had left the house by a back door, walked over to an outhouse where some bicycles are kept, chosen one, pushed it round the side of the house to the front and continued pushing it down the drive. There the footsteps disappeared and the bike was left."

"You say the footprints completely ceased?"

"Totally vanished. The snow all around the bicycle showed considerable trampling, then no signs of further footsteps."

"Could it not be that the man retraced his steps by walking backwards, stepping in exactly the same places?" I suggested eagerly.

"Why, I never thought of that!" exclaimed Bellingham.

"I did. Several years ago, when a ghillie was found shot dead on a hunting party," grunted Holmes. "But, apart from the curiosity of the bicycle, why would Lord Mersham be concerned?"

"Because the bust of Athene has vanished."

Bellingham went on to explain that only the previous week Lord Mersham had given a party to invite his closest friends to view his newly acquired piece, a masterwork by Canova, the eminent Italian sculptor. Lord Mersham had had his library completely remodelled to embrace an antechamber, which had been especially constructed to display the bust on a marble pedestal.

"You say Lord Mersham threw a party to show off his new acquisition? How many attended and do you have a guest list?"

"It was a select gathering. No more than thirty guests all told. But surely you do not suggest that my lord's friends would stoop to steal from him? My lord's friends are personages from the highest strata of society."

"That was not my suggestion. If I am to investigate thoroughly, I must ask questions that may seem offensive. They are not. All my questions are designed to elicit the truth. At present I do not know if such a list of guests will aid me or not. I merely request that you furnish me with such information, if it is in your power to do so."

"Certainly, I am able to do that as soon as we reach Mersham Hall, as I have details of all the preparations in my household accounts, but I will have to place your request before my lord."

Bellingham organised a pony and trap at the station and in a short time we were at the gates of Mersham Hall, where a fellow was lounging against one of the mighty stone gate posts. He sprang up when Bellingham alighted.

"Ah, Thomas, these are the gentlemen from London who have come to investigate the theft. You have not allowed anyone past?"

"No, Mr Bellingham. The only person who wanted to enter was the carrier from Warrenhurst. He had a crate to deliver. I told him to throw it off here. That's it there."

"Good man. You see, Mr Holmes, my lord did not want the snow disturbing, so Thomas was posted to prevent any entrance. Those footsteps you see there, right at the side, are mine and those of Thomas. Otherwise nobody has stepped upon the driveway."

"Then we shall add our prints to the same track. Lead the way Mr Bellingham, Watson and I will follow you like the Red Indians of the United States of America."

So we marched in single file up the driveway to the hall. The drive, very straight and regular, was about half a mile long, some twenty feet in width of hard surface, with a yard of longish tufty grass at either side. Beyond the narrow grass verge both sides were exactly alike, having a deep ditch with a high dense hedge, very neatly and squarely cut, and it would have been impossible for anyone to penetrate the hedge without hacking a great opening in it with some sharp instrument.

We reached the place where the bicycle was still lying on its side in the middle of the drive.

"Might I examine all this whilst you take Watson inside to meet your master? I will follow shortly."

"Should you not meet my lord first?"

"The sun is up, man, the snow will not last for ever. Time is of the essence."

Bellingham saw the logic in this. After all, the purpose of his errand was to get Holmes to the scene before the snow either melted, or was covered by a further fall. So while Holmes crawled about with his lens in the snow outside, I met the noble lord and warmed myself with his fire and his genial personality.

"I must tell you, Dr Watson, that I am a great admirer of Mr Holmes and it is through your work recording his brilliant talents that I knew to consult him. I thought he would not want lots of feet trampling about the place so I have kept all the staff indoors, except for Thomas guarding the gate. I think I've done the right thing, don't you?"

"Indubitably."

"A rum business altogether, Doctor. You see I can't fathom why the chap should walk with the bike. Why not ride it?"

"Perhaps there were two of them? One riding, one walking."

"I say, I never thought of that. You must have picked up the way of it from your friend Holmes."

"Well I suppose a bit of his skill has rubbed off on to me after all these years."

"Another brandy? It's damnably cold out there."

As we were agreeably chatting, Holmes entered and introduced himself. He thawed out a little by the roaring fire, then went off with Lord Mersham to examine the library where the statue had stood. I remained by the fire.

When Holmes had finished his examination we were invited to lunch with the noble lord and his lady. They were a most charming couple, the very essence of all that is finest in the aristocracy of our great country.

"These burglaries are becoming almost commonplace, Mr Holmes," said Lady Mersham. "We must be the fourth or fifth in a row. Do you suppose they are carried out by the same gang?"

"My dear, we do not even know if there was a gang. All we know is the Athene has gone, with the peculiarities of a track of footprints that ends nowhere and a bicycle that has been removed from its shed and dropped in the driveway. Unless, Mr Holmes, you have found further evidence?"

"Nothing that adds to that, my lord."

"I hate to suspect one of the staff but, if nobody has broken in, how else do you account for the loss?" asked Lady Mersham.

"I suppose it is possible that the door was left open. The thief used the little scullery door at the back of the house."

"Bellingham swears most vehemently that he locked it as usual last night."

"I am sure he did, my lady," said Holmes.

"You are very calm, Mr Holmes," said Lady Mersham.

"Mr Holmes has not lost an expensive work of art," replied Lord Mersham wryly.

"I think Scotland Yard should be doing something. Look at poor Lucy Washington. She has had to dismiss her entire staff because she cannot trust any of them any more. It is too bad, especially after she held that wonderful Christmas Ball. Do you know, Mr Holmes, Lady Washington entertained two hundred guests at her ball. It was the talk of the town; you could not be considered anybody if you were not there. And afterwards she was so pleased with all the additional work that her staff had undertaken she rewarded them with bonuses and extra holidays. She was thrilled with her people, absolutely thrilled, then she is repaid by this awful theft and cannot trust anybody. Thousands of pounds worth of gemstones simply gone – vanished! Of course, Lucy always had dubious taste and some of the items were a little overwhelming, but, nevertheless, of great value. Scotland Yard really should be doing more to protect us."

"I am sure they are doing their best, my dear," said her husband.

"On my return to town I will go and see Inspector Lestrade who is in charge of these cases. I think he may have information that will assist me," said Holmes.

Holmes, who had seemed rather distant throughout lunch, had now perked up and after a few more minutes we made our leave. As there was no further point in preserving the virgin snow, Lord Mersham ordered one of his coaches to take us to the station.

"When you get to the gate perhaps you will be good enough to tell Thomas he can return to the house."

After passing the site of the bicycle mystery I suddenly noticed something and called on the driver to stop.

"Did you see that, Holmes?" I indicated an area of flattened snow some distance away from where the bicycle had lain. It was roughly square shaped, about eight feet across

"I saw everything, Watson," replied Holmes with touch of asperity.

"Then what did you make of that flattened square?"

"What do you make of it, Watson?"

"Well it looks as though the fellow has tried to cover his traces. It looks as though he had the edge of a plank and used it to scrape and tamp down the snow. In a similar manner as one levels the ground to construct a lawn or whatever. Like when you lay concrete, you know."

"I have never laid concrete, Watson, but I take your meaning. Where is this plank?"

"He threw it over the hedge," I suggested.

"Then where did he go?"

"Into the ditch?"

"It won't do Watson. There are no footprints leading to the square, or leading from it. Apart from the fact that there is an absence of scuffling, that area is very similar to the first one and gives us the same problem. A greater one in fact, as there are no footprints going to or from it. He did not go into the ditch, neither did he step on to the grass verge. It would appear that he walked no further than the area where he left the bicycle, a trampled area of a mere six feet across."

"So that flattened area is nothing to do with it?"

"I did not say that. I suspect that it is a vital clue. As may be that stubby stake, driven into the ground, at the edge of the trampled area."

"But the fellow must have gone somewhere," I protested. "He cannot have vanished into thin air."

"Of course not. We are not dealing with a phantom. Our man is not here now, so obviously he went elsewhere."

"Then I was right, he retraced his footsteps back to the house. I've got it! One of the servants, perhaps Bellingham himself, took the bust, let himself out of the house, carried it to an accomplice, retraced his steps exactly and then locked the door again!"

"Brilliant, Watson. So where is the bust? Where is the accomplice? Did I miss them both sitting in the middle of the carriageway by the bicycle?" Holmes banged on the roof: "Drive on!"

Several days later Holmes handed me a package.

"Would you do me a great favour, old chap?" he said. "These are the lists of guests present at several social gatherings. I would like you to sort through them and find the names of anybody who was at all five functions."

"Of course I will do that for you, Holmes. Perhaps you would explain the purpose of the exercise?" I replied.

"You may recall that, when we visited Lord Mersham's house and took lunch with him and his good lady, she mentioned that Lord & Lady Washington had held a ball a few days prior to their theft. The Mershams had a *soirée* prior to the theft of the Canova. It seemed obvious to me that it would be sensible to check on the remaining robbed houses. My esteemed friend Inspector Lestrade has his uses and was able to tell me that, as I surmised, in all cases there had been a gathering with a multiplicity of guests a few days prior to each robbery."

"So you think that one of them is responsible?"

"I have obtained a complete list of the guests at each function, again through the good offices of Lestrade, and it would be reasonable to assume that any person present at every function would come under suspicion, don't you think?"

"Surely there will be many guests in common? London society being composed as it is, the same people are bound to be at all these gatherings."

"To some extent yes. I think you will find that most names occur at two functions, many at three, several at four and a few at all five. It is those few on which I will turn my gaze."

"I cannot think that a person drawn from the highest strata of society is likely to be a common house-breaker, Holmes," I protested with some warmth.

"Exactly, Watson. But we are not dealing with a common house-breaker. In four of the five cases there was no break-in at all. We are looking for someone who is freely admitted, nay welcomed, into the houses of the great."

"I do not follow you, Holmes. Surely the thefts took place long after the gatherings, days afterwards. You are not suggesting our quarry hid himself away for days in the house, after all the guests had left?"

"Of course not. Look here, Watson, imagine you had entered this room for the very first time. You see something you covet – say a picture. Imagine your picture of General Gordon there was an old master worth thousands of pounds. You want to steal it. What would you do?"

"And you are here, sitting as you are now?"

"Yes."

"Well, I'd look around to see the arrangement of everything and then consider the possibilities of removing it from the wall, unseen by you."

"Unlikely. I, of all people, would see everything. But you might consider coming back when I am not here."

"Yes, I could do that. But how would I gain entrance? Presumably you would have locked the door?"

"Of course."

"I could have spied out the possibility of entering by the window –"

"Yes?"

"And other possibilities."

"Such as?"

"Well I can't think exactly at the moment."

"You could perhaps, whilst I was pouring you a hospitable drink, steal the key of the door?"

"I say, Holmes, I could. But you would notice that. Not at the time perhaps, if I were deft about it, but later, when you wanted to lock the door. Then you would be suspicious and, at the very least, change the lock."

"But what if you replaced the key before I noticed it had gone?"

"When you poured me another of your hospitable drinks?"

"Perhaps."

"What would be the point, Holmes?"

"The point being that, at some time during the evening, you would find an opportunity to make an impression of the key in a pad of wax."

"Holmes!"

"Be a good chap and sift through those names. I have to go out."

It did not take as long as I had thought, sorting the names, as there was only one really large ball having an excess of 200 guests. When I had struck through the names, one by one as I found them absent at other functions, the list narrowed rapidly. At last I was able to hand Holmes the following list when he returned:

Lord and Lady Melchett

Sir Algernon Fitzwilliam

The Dowager Lady Huntingdon

The Hon Harold Coningsby

Baroness Burdett-Coutts

"Thank you, Watson. You have done well." He glanced at my other lists. "But not well enough, I think. You have omitted Lord & Lady Mersham. They were present at all five events."

"Of course. They were the hosts at their own function thus are not named upon the guest list. Perhaps the other hosts should be added? Their names are not given here."

"No, that is in order; of the hosts, only Lord & Lady Mersham were at all the evenings, I have checked that already. Perhaps you would be so good as to pass *Burke's Peerage* and *Who's Who?*"

Holmes poured over these tomes until he suddenly said "Ah, I have him, Watson."

"Who, Holmes?"

"Listen – The Hon Harold Coningsby. Youngest son of the 7th Baron Trent. Born 1865. Educated at Eton and Cambridge. Blues for rowing and boxing. Captain in the Household Cavalry, resigned his commission. Renowned sportsman, etc etc. Addresses: Trent Hall, Nottinghamshire; Albany, London. Clubs: White's, Sporting, etc etc."

"But that does not signify anything to me," I protested.

"Surely this person is a more likely suspect than the Dowager Lady

Huntingdon who is over 80 years of age; Baroness Burdett-Coutts, one of country's richest ladies and Sir Algernon Fitzwilliam who is a delicate aesthete renowned for his rather precious sensibilities? I must see Lestrade. We will have our man by the end of the week, Watson."

"Surely you cannot suspect a pillar of the aristocracy like the Hon Harold Coningsby?" I protested.

"Everybody is suspect until I have caught the right man. But I am a little fatigued with London, I think a day in the country would do me good."

I was astonished by this statement as Holmes had no love of the countryside at all and rarely left London either for pleasure or for his health's sake.

Two days later Holmes asked me to accompany him to Albany where the Hon Harold Coningsby resided when in Town. On the way we met Lestrade who was as baffled as I with these proceedings.

"What is all this, Mr Holmes? You can't go invading the gentry for no good reason."

"Have you your handcuffs with you, Lestrade?"

"Yes, but –"

"Now listen. This is going to be a delicate affair. Please do as I say. If I am wrong about this you can place me in jail."

"Mr Holmes, if you are wrong I would think it very likely Mr Coningsby will see to that."

"Now, Lestrade, I shall introduce you as my designer. You, Watson, shall be my works foreman."

"Designer of what?"

"Baskets, Lestrade, baskets."

"Has he gone mad, Doctor? What is he on about?"

"Here we are. Now I have arranged an appointment. We are expected. We must play it by ear. Please both be alert. If there seems to be any chance of him getting away, jump him and clap the bracelets on him." The door was opened by a manservant. "Good evening, may we see your master? We have an appointment. I am Josiah Crabtree, these are my colleagues."

Holmes handed over a card. It was not unfamiliar as I had seen it used before. It was from his collection of visiting cards. If I remembered correctly, Mr Crabtree proclaimed himself as a supplier of sporting equipment.

The Hon Harold Coningsby greeted us warmly.

"Come in, gentlemen. I was very intrigued to get your message, Mr Crabtree. I am always interested in the latest technicalities."

"I know that, sir, your reputation is well-known and when my designer here, Mr Graham, showed me his innovations I thought of you straight away."

"And what exactly are these innovations, Mr Graham?"

Lestrade was taken aback at being addressed directly and started to bluster, but Holmes smoothly intervened by producing some drawings and laying them before us.

"I think this will explain better than any words, sir."

I stared with surprise as Holmes laid out some finely detailed drawings of balloons with baskets. Coningsby, however, was quite unperturbed.

"Very fine, Mr Crabtree, but I see no difference in these diagrams to the baskets I already use."

"Quite," said Holmes smoothly. "This is the standard basket. But what if it were made somewhat shallower?"

"I should probably fall out. What is this, Crabtree?" replied Coningsby.

"Do you prefer a round basket or a square one?" asked Holmes.

"I should prefer to know what is the purpose of intruding yourself and your companions into my apartment under the guise of a manufacturer of balloon baskets. I suspect you are newspaper reporters."

"I was merely testing to see if you knew about the sport of ballooning, sir."

"Of course I know about the sport. Anybody connected with the art of ballooning – it is an art, sir, not a mere sport – would tell you I am probably the country's leading practitioner. I do not boast when I say my reputation is world-wide."

"That is what I had heard. I understand you can place your balloon down, accurately, on the head of a pin."

"Anyone who claims that is a fool and knows nothing of the sport. The balloon is at the whim of the thermals and wind direction, although by increasing and decreasing the amount of hydrogen and casting ballast judiciously, one can carry out a certain amount of guidance."

"I understand you are able to fly your balloon in the dark."

"That is so – so foolhardy. No navigator would do that unless unavoidable. I am not stupid."

"Oh I do not for a minute suggest that you are stupid. Far from it. Rather clever, diabolically clever."

"I think you had better leave. Gregory!"

As he called for his manservant, Holmes leapt on him calling "Now, Lestrade!" There was a *mêlée* as Holmes and Lestrade struggled to put the handcuffs on Coningsby. At the same time the manservant entered.

"Stand back, don't interfere!" I cried. Fortunately the fellow, deciding that his master could manage without his help, or realising all was useless, fled.

"I arrest you for the robbing of five noble houses. I am Sherlock Holmes, the detective, and this is my colleague Dr Watson The other gentleman is Inspector Lestrade of Scotland Yard so I suggest you cease to struggle."

"I don't know what you are talking about, release me at once!" blustered our victim. Holmes produced a length of rope and eventually Coningsby, realising further struggling was no avail against our combined forces, gave in and allowed himself to be tied to the chair.

"Now, Coningsby, I will tell you exactly how you committed your crimes. You will then tell me where you placed the various stolen items," said Holmes.

"I must warn you that anything you have to say may be used in evidence," said Lestrade."

"You attended these functions as an honoured guest. You are a man from one of the first families of the land. But you decided that you would behave like a common criminal and steal from your friends. At each of these houses you seized an opportunity to obtain a key to a back door of the premises. During the course of the evening you made an impression of the key in a pad of soft wax. You then returned the key to its proper place. You spent the evening deciding which item you wished to steal and noted where it was kept. You then went home. You made, or had made, a key using the wax impression. At a date a few days later, presumably chosen for the ideal flying conditions, you sailed in your balloon during the hours of the night and silently landed on a lawn, or some other level part, near the house. You tethered your equipment to a stake, or perhaps a handy tree, calmly went to the door and unlocked it, entered, found the object of your intentions and left again locking the door behind you. You then climbed into your balloon, cast off and sailed away silently into the night."

"You are talking about fairy land!" snarled Coningsby. "One is entirely at the mercy of the wind direction, day or night. At night there are no thermals to assist your rise. Nobody could direct a balloon as accurately as that in the dead of night."

"Not many people could, but you can, because you are a world-renowned expert. I do not suggest you sailed far each time. You positioned your balloon according to the wind direction so that you could sail over the boundary wall. Afterwards, you need only soar away as fast as you could. I have seen the signs of your basket in the snow on the drive of Mersham Hall."

"So that is what made the flattened square!" I exclaimed.

"Yes, the basket often bounces on the ground before coming finally to rest. At Mersham Hall there was a stake in the ground to which Mr Coningsby tethered the balloon. After his theft he would simply climb into his basket, cast off and sail away."

"Diabolical," I breathed.

"The balloon he used is quite a small one but powerful enough to raise a single person over the roof tops. The basket too is quite small but sufficient for one man and his loot. If you would examine Mr Coningsby's evening wear, Watson, I think we may find evidence of the key ploy."

I went into the bedroom and ferreted amongst Coningsby's cuff-links and studs. I searched the evening clothes which his manservant had laid out as though he were to don them shortly. I examined the pockets but could only find a silver cigarette case, a watch and the usual gentlemen's equipment. I returned to Holmes and reported my lack of success.

"Did you look in the cigarette case?" asked Holmes and I had to confess that I had not. I immediately returned to the bedroom and abstracted the case. On opening it I revealed the contents to be not cigarettes but soft wax.

"Amazing, Holmes. You were right in every particular," I cried enthusiastically.

"Now where's the loot?" snarled Lestrade.

"Find out from Mr Clever-clogs Holmes," replied Coningsby.

"Well, Lestrade, as we are here, perhaps a search of the premises may prove fruitful, then I think at Trent Hall, where Mr Coningsby bases his ballooning activities. He has a rather splendid barn and stables there, in which he keeps the very latest in ballooning equipment. Oh, and if you climb the rather steep ladder in the corner by the door you will come to a loft. In that loft is a wooden packing case, about the size of a common tea chest. Inside you will find a rather splendid marble bust executed by the Italian master Canova."

"How do you know all this, Mr Holmes?"

"Because I saw it there yesterday when I went for a breath of country air."

All the stolen property was found either in Coningsby's bachelor apartment in Albany or at his ancestral home Trent Hall. His intention had been to take them with him to Paris where he was to participate in an International Ballooning Event.

The Hon Harold Coningsby was subsequently arrested, tried and imprisoned. His family lineage availed him naught. His father the 7th Baron Trent never recovered from the shock and humiliation and died a broken man, long before his son was released from prison. Holmes and I were discussing the case later.

"I was never clear why Coningsby took the bicycle and pushed it along."

"I think you might have done the same, Watson, when you found out the weight of the Canova bust. He carried it outside, but realised he would never reach his balloon without assistance. He was fortunate to find the outhouse open with a bicycle inside. So he rested the bust on the saddle and walked with it to his tethered balloon."

"So the bicycle, together with the fortuitous fall of snow, gave you the necessary clues. But how the devil you realised the footsteps ceased because the fellow ascended in a balloon is a stroke of pure genius. How on earth did you get on to that?"

"You told me, Watson."

"I told you?" I expostulated.

"You may lack intuition, Watson, but you have the happy knack of hitting the truth directly by stating the obvious. You said the man could not have disappeared into thin air. That made me suspect it was exactly what he did do. You may not be a luminary in yourself, Watson, but you are an excellent conductor of light to others."

"You know, Holmes, you never explained to me why Coningsby found it necessary to break in at Mosscote Manor. Did he not obtain a wax impression of a key there?"

"That was his error, Watson. He did have a key made but it would not turn the tumblers. Probably a poor impression or a faulty lock. If he had been sensible he would have gone silently away and nobody would have been any the wiser. But his specialised mode of transport meant that he might have to wait a long time for favourable weather conditions to repeat themselves. Having got there, he was determined not to be thwarted, so resorted to the tactics of a common burglar. It was that break-in which convinced me someone was entering from outside and that all the servants under suspicion were entirely innocent."

"It is a relief to know that the households had loyal servants."

"It is unpleasant to contemplate that their employers immediately suspected them. A man's nobility comes not from his social position, but from his innate goodness. As we have now seen – an aristocrat can be as dishonest as a thief and a beggar can be as honest as a bishop."

The Singular Adventure
of
THE HAUNTED HOUSE

THE man who consulted Sherlock Holmes was quite venerable in appearance but even I could observe his frayed cuffs and well-worn hat. I put him down as a retired clergyman of modest means. He told us his name was Joshua Pettigrew.

"I am the owner of a medieval house called Twelve Trees in the county of Kent. I must tell you that I am something of an antiquarian and it gives me much pleasure to live in such an ancient dwelling. I was, in fact, born there and it has been in my family for six generations."

"And why do you seek my assistance, Mr Pettigrew?" asked Holmes in his urbane manner.

"Because, Mr Holmes, I am haunted, or I should say, my beloved home is haunted. I have tried to be a reasonable man but I confess that I have been driven almost out of mind with one shock after another."

"Pray tell me more of this haunted house," said Holmes drily.

"Oh I know nowadays it is not fashionable to believe in haunted houses. People say these things can all be explained by scientific principles. I am sure you gentlemen do not believe in ghosts."

"Truly I do not. But, if I had actually seen a ghost, then my opinion might be different," said Holmes. "Have you seen a ghost in your house?"

"I have suffered torment these last six weeks, Mr Holmes, but no, I have not actually seen a ghost. Let me relate what has happened. Pictures have fallen off walls several times; solid objects have floated in the air; ornaments and crockery have mysteriously and inexplicably crashed to the ground; items have moved; things have appeared and disappeared."

"It sounds very much like what our German friends call a poltergeist," I stated.

"Poltergeist? What is that?" asked Pettigrew.

"A noisy restless spirit that causes damage and destruction."

"Then it is exactly that spirit I have in my house."

"Usually these manifestations occur when there is a young person in the house. Often a female approaching puberty," I went on to explain. "Is there such a female in your household?"

"Why no, sir. My household comprises myself, my daughter, who is a grown woman, and my son-in-law, whom my daughter married about a year ago."

"What about your staff?" asked Holmes.

"I keep very few servants as my wants are simple. Only a housekeeper, who also does the cooking, and a girl who acts as general maid. She is the youngest in the house but past the age you suggest. Perhaps seventeen or eighteen. I have never asked her age."

"There may be another explanation for your poltergeist. I merely mentioned the most common. I am not, by any means, an expert in this field, but I understand it has all to do with electrical impulses from within the body. A kind of animal magnetism that becomes out of control," I offered.

"Poppycock, Watson," said Holmes rudely. "I don't believe a word of your poltergeist theory."

"Oh dear," said Pettigrew, "I was hoping you had hit on the explanation, Doctor, as the events in my house sound very much like your poltergeist."

"Then what suggestion have you to offer, Holmes?" I asked tartly.

"I have said, many times, it is a mistake to theorise without facts. Facts are what we need first. Now Mr Pettigrew, when was the first of these odd happenings?"

"I'm not perfectly clear but it must have been six or seven weeks ago. I did not remark it at the time, it was only after other things happened that I thought back to this first manifestation."

"And what happened?"

"A silly little thing really. I was reading a book in bed, as is my wont, and left it by my bedside. In the morning it was no longer there. I found it back on the shelf in my library."

"And that's it?" cried Holmes.

"Yes, that was the first thing."

"Pshaw man, probably your maid doing a bit of tidying up."

"No, no. I did, in fact, question her. She disclaimed all knowledge of it. But that was a trifle compared with what followed. I have lost track of all the alarming things that have happened to me, but there is no question that my house is haunted. When a picture falls off the wall you can blame a rusty picture hook, or a worn string, but not when pictures have fallen a dozen times."

"Pictures have fallen a dozen times?" asked Holmes in disbelief. "The same picture or different pictures?"

"All different pictures, but some more than once, after I have re-hung them."

"And crockery falling to the ground, you said?"

"Falling and flying. I have had so many breakages that I do not have a full set of china in the place. We are now obliged to dine off a motley collection of pottery."

"Hum. Do these things happen during the day or at night?" asked Holmes.

"Usually in the evening. I have taken to going to bed after dinner to escape the persecution."

"Persecution you call it?"

"Undoubtedly. I am sure that I have been singled out for some purpose, as these things do not seem to happen when I am not present. My daughter and son-in-law say they have only suffered when in my company."

"Perhaps you, yourself, are emanating malevolent vibrations?" I suggested.

"Do please spare us your mesmeric mumbo-jumbo, Watson." Holmes can be very hurtful at times. "If, Mr Pettigrew, all this has been going on for some weeks, why have you not consulted me before?"

"Well, Mr Holmes, I did not at first realise these things would go on and on. And now, frankly, it is getting me down. My son-in-law makes light of it, but it is undermining my health. Last night was the last straw. We were at dinner when I was violently thrown to the ground."

"What do you mean? Somebody seized you?" queried Holmes.

"No, it was much stranger than that. My chair, the one I was actually sitting on, rose up and threw me on to the floor. That was the breaking point. I was so shaken I thought I must seek help. I did not know where to go, so I enquired at Scotland Yard. The inspector there was most unsympathetic and said they only dealt with criminals in the living world, not the spirit world. In fact I thought he was rather rude, but he did suggest that you may be the man to help me."

"Well, Mr Pettigrew, I can only say that I, too, cannot deal with ghostly villains, but I am prepared to come to your house and examine it. If these things happen in the evening, perhaps you would be so kind as to invite Dr Watson and myself to dinner and to stay the night. I suggest we arrive late in the afternoon so we can look around your house and grounds. We can spend the evening in the bosom of your family, then should any of these odd things happen, I will be present to deal with it."

"I shall be forever in your debt, Mr Holmes. Even if you cannot stop these manifestations, I will feel relieved to be able to share my troubles. When will you come?"

"One moment. There is a very particular condition that I must impress upon you, if I am to come." Holmes got up and went to the box wherein he kept an assortment of visiting cards. He rifled through them, finally selecting one, and handed it to Pettigrew. "Does anyone know you have come to consult me?"

"Why no, Mr Holmes, until the inspector gave me your name I confess I had never heard of you."

"Such is fame, Watson. I thought everyone knew my name as a result of your sensational essays. So much the better. Now sir, what I am about to say is of the utmost importance. If you do not obey me to the letter I cannot help you."

"I will do, exactly, whatever you say, Mr Holmes."

"Take this card. As you see, it says Robert Hubbard & Company, Architects. That is the guise in which I shall come to your house. Do not, on any account, forget that. You must address me only by that name. Watson will be my assistant. Also, you must not be surprised in any way at my questions, appearance or demeanour. Now is that clear? Inform your household you have instructed a firm of architects to look over the house, as you are thinking of having some renovations and alterations carried out. Would that appear feasible to your children?"

"Oh, most certainly. My daughter and her husband are always pestering me to have repairs done. I should warn you that my house is in rather a decrepit state."

"Indeed? May I ask why? Presumably a want of money?" asked Holmes.

"No, Mr Holmes, have no fear of your fee. I am now, in fact, quite a rich man, though I was very poor until recently. The frugal habits of a lifetime are hard to shake off overnight. My daughter has a fervent desire to move. She would like a modern house with gas, or even the new electricity. You know what women are like."

"I can understand anybody who prefers not to live in a gasless ruin. Surely, as she has a husband, she would prefer to live in her own establishment?"

"Ah well, I'm afraid her husband is penniless; he relies on my bounty. It is this way: as I say, I am an antiquarian and I employed this youth – he is only 25 or so now – to assist me in my work. He came to me with good references. He has been to university and is quite a scholar. But, really, he remains a penniless student. It was while working for me that he fell in love with my daughter and she with him. I approved the match, and the wedding took place just over a year ago. They are both dependent on me for money."

"But surely your son-in-law could better himself elsewhere, with his qualifications?" I protested.

"I am sure he could, but my daughter does not wish to leave me alone, all on my own. She is a good and dutiful girl."

"But surely, if you are as wealthy as you intimate, you could set them up in a home of their own?" said Holmes.

"I could not bear to lose my daughter, she is all I have, and I only consented to the marriage on the condition that they both remained in my house. Now I have come into some money I fully intend to undertake some comprehensive restoration works."

"I think you have made the position clear. We will come down by train tomorrow. What is your nearest station?"

"Sevenoaks. I will have a trap meet you."

"Do not forget: no matter how bizarre our behaviour, there is a purpose to all I do. Take this card. Do not fail to address me as Hubbard."

"I will remember. Until tomorrow then – Mr Hubbard."

The next day we were on the train, rushing through the beautiful Kentish countryside. I thought it was a pleasant change for Holmes to get away from the filth of the city and breathe some honest country air and ventured to say so.

"The air may be purer, Watson, but there is more evil lurking in the green countryside than ever raised its head in the black city."

"Why are we masquerading as architects, Holmes? I hope I am not expected to know about joists and flying buttresses," I quipped.

"Do you not think ghosts and poltergeists may be reluctant to manifest themselves if they are aware that a consulting detective is present?"

"You think the manifestations are not genuine?"

Holmes snorted. "Watson, I am a rational being. I thought you were too. Of course there is some jiggery-pokery going on. As yet I do not know how or why, or who is responsible, but I have no doubt that I will know everything by this time tomorrow."

"There are more things in heaven and earth, Horatio, than are dreamed of in your philosophy. Hamlet."

"Poppycock, Watson. Holmes." With that Holmes turned to the window and gazed at the countryside, saying not another word until we alighted at Sevenoaks. A trap was waiting and we were taken to Twelve Trees. The reason for the house's appellation was clear. There were no fewer than a dozen mighty oaks surrounding the house. Some were almost touching the house wall and all were of a great age, judging by the girth of their massive trunks.

"You can point out that the proximity of the trees is bound to cause disturbance under the house with their roots, can't you, Watson?" whispered Holmes as our host came out to greet us.

We were shown round the house, which was not enormous, but, even so, it was clear that only about a quarter of it was in use. Our host had intimated that it was in a bad state of repair. It was more accurate to say that it was virtually a ruin. It would be an extremely wealthy man who had the funds to restore it to its former grandeur. Of great age, the place had obviously been neglected for centuries. Constructed of mighty timbers in the old fashioned way, age had caused them to twist, bend and sag. The walls, infilled with willow wands embedded in a mixture of clay and straw plastered over, were crumbling, and it needed no architectural training to see that the place was in danger of imminent collapse.

To my great astonishment, on arrival Holmes adopted a rather effeminate manner and whereas Mr Pettigrew was obviously quite taken aback at this, he remembered Holmes' caution and made no comment. We had a good look round the house with our host constantly warning us that this part of the floor was unsafe, that wall was dangerous, and so on. Finally, we returned to the main living room, which was the most habitable part of the house. There we met Pettigrew's daughter and her husband.

"This is my daughter Laura and her husband Mr Timothy Wallis."

"I am very pleased to meet you, my dears," said Holmes in his newly adopted voice. "This is my assistant Mr Jonquil Watson."

I had a great struggle to keep in command of myself. If Holmes wished to adopt an effeminate persona, then I am sure he had good reason, but I cringed inwardly to think that this most masculine of men should choose to appear to the world as a gilded butterfly. I certainly did not wish to be tainted with a name like Jonquil, but Holmes has an odd sense of humour at times.

"What an extraordinary house you have, Mr Pettigrew, I really must make some sketches. The spandrels are most unusual; Jonquil drew my attention to them."

I sincerely hoped I would not be called upon to expound on spandrels, whatever they were. I could only presume that Holmes knew what he was talking about.

"I hope you don't mind my saying so, Mr Pettigrew, but I do confess to finding your house a little eerie," lisped Holmes.

"Eerie? It's downright absurd!" burst out young Mr Wallis. "It is ridiculous that Laura should have to live in a ruin like this, when her father has enough money to build a palace!"

"I have said that repairs will shortly take place, Tim, that is why Mr Hubbard is here; to advise me on the most appropriate steps," said Pettigrew mildly.

"Oh, Mr Wallis, it does you great credit to support your delightful lady. You look so handsome when your face is flushed – don't you think so, Jonquil? I do wish I had brought my camera to take a likeness."

I was amazed by this new version of Holmes. I hoped it was an example of his superb acting powers and not an indication that he had been mixing with aesthetes.

"I understand that my father has asked you to make recommendations about repairs, Mr Hubbard?" said Laura Wallis.

"Indeed. Mrs Wallis. I must say, I do admire your costume, Mrs Wallis. Very fetching don't you think, Jonquil?" simpered Holmes.

"Most becoming," I managed to agree gruffly.

"Yes, we have been on a tour of inspection," said Holmes.

"The place is falling down, man! It's way beyond repair!" cried Timothy Wallis. "I hope you are not going to cozen the old man into paying for expensive repairs, to line your pockets."

"Ooh, what an accusation! You shock me, Mr Wallis. I am sure you are not usually so disrespectful to your father-in-law and his friends," said Holmes petulantly.

By this time Pettigrew had given up trying to follow the conversation or understand why Holmes was acting like an effeminate poet and was whispering to a matronly woman who had sidled into the room. I presumed this was the housekeeper.

"Mrs Pledge tells me that dinner is ready if you will take your places in the dining room," announced Pettigrew.

We were led into the adjoining room. It was now quite dark outside and the table was lit by candles, which flickered as we disturbed the air seating ourselves. We had been advised that the Pettigrews did not dress for dinner so it was quite an informal meal, although Mrs Wallis had written out place cards indicating where we were to sit.

"Perhaps you would take this chair, Mr Hubbard," said Wallis, "and your colleague the one over there?"

The meal proceeded quite normally with somewhat desultory conversation about harmless topics, during which Holmes skilfully and subtly elicited information about the family and house. I began to relax a little and my feeling that I had come to either a madhouse, or was part of a chapter out of one of Mr Dickens' more bizarre plots, began to subside. Also I admired the fact that my friend Sherlock Holmes was a consummate actor and regretted that the legitimate stage had lost a very great talent. For what purpose he had adopted this posturing pose I could not begin to guess though at times seriously thought he was taking leave of his senses.

It transpired that our host was, indeed, a rich man, although his wealth did not seem prodigious enough to restore his dwelling to its former glory. He had such an affection for his old home that he did not want a thing altered. He had been born there and wished his grandson to be born there too. As he had been poor all his life, he could not afford to do anything at all in the way of repairs. But very recently, through the death of an uncle, he had come into a great deal of money. His son-in-law wanted him to raze the whole place to the ground and build a brand new modern house. This was totally at odds with Pettigrew's antiquarian instincts and he would not contemplate that idea. Belatedly he had realised the true state of the old building and thought to restore it to its original state, which would be without lights or other modern conveniences. It was clear that Pettigrew had eccentric ideas, but I think even he must have realised the gulf between his wealth and his ambitions.

Gradually the conversation turned to the subject of ghosts, at which Holmes shuddered delicately and said "Oh that would clinch it for me, Mr Pettigrew. I am so afraid of ghosts. If I thought there was a vestige of a ghost I would pull the whole place down."

"Excuse me while I see what Ruby is doing," said Mrs Wallis, and left the room.

"But that's just my point, Hubbard! Why carry out expensive repairs and still have to live with a ghost? Better to demolish it and start afresh, I say," said Timothy Wallis. "It would cost a fraction of the money and we would all have a bright modern house."

"But the ghost may move to the new building," I could not help but point out.

"Oh Jonquil, what a pessimist you are!" said Holmes pettishly.

"I do not think it is usual for ghosts to inhabit new buildings, Mr Watson," replied Wallis.

Further discussion on the topic was abruptly halted when a picture on the wall suddenly crashed to the floor.

"There you are, gentlemen!" cried Pettigrew. "That is what I have had to live with these past weeks!"

"Oh, how awful," said Holmes. "I could not live in a house like this. I hope you have put Jonquil and I near each other. I may become frightened in the night."

Holmes was so convincing in his role that he made me feel physically sick. When Mrs Wallis returned with news of the pudding, she was told about the picture. We were all somewhat shaken so Wallis suggested to Pettigrew that it would be a good idea for him to get a bottle of brandy from the cellar.

During Wallis' absence the pudding was served and we were all enjoying the food, which was in truth excellent, when Laura Wallis gave a cry as she was hurled to the ground by some monstrous physical force. I was immediately round the table to render assistance, when to my utter astonishment, just as I was helping her to her feet, Holmes, too, was thrown to the ground in a similar manner. We were all ready for the brandy when Wallis returned with it.

The rest of the meal proceeded uneventfully but we were all very subdued. Holmes was obviously in a state of severe shock and, though he kept up his aesthetic pose, he had ceased to prattle in the inane fashion he had adopted earlier.

Eventually the meal ended and Mr Pettigrew bade us good night, retiring to his bed. Mrs Wallis went to supervise her staff of two, and Wallis led Holmes and myself into the library. The floor of this room comprised flagstones of great size, as opposed to the dining-room floor, which was of wood. Wallis proposed a nightcap and poured whisky from a cut glass decanter which he placed on a side table. We three huddled round the fire.

"I don't know what you think, gentlemen, but I make no secret of the fact that my wife and I would be very pleased to leave this accursed house. We have no means ourselves but, if this haunting business gets any worse, we will leave anyway, penniless though we be," said Wallis.

"Oh I quite agree, Timmy, my dear boy," said Holmes. "I do not know how you can bear it a moment longer. I have only been here five hours and my nerves are in shreds. You must all leave immediately. I do not know if Mr Pettigrew will listen to me, a mere hired artisan, but I will definitely recommend that he has the house pulled down and builds a beautiful new one. But do not think I am angling for the contract for my firm. Of course it would be lovely to create a wonderful new home for you and Mrs Wallis, she's such a dear, but, totally regardless of whom you employ, I think you are completely right about it. Don't you, Jonquil?"

"Oh, indubitably," I managed to gasp.

Our further conversation was interrupted by the sound of shattering glass as the half-empty whisky decanter crashed to the ground, breaking into a myriad of pieces.

"My God!" said Holmes, leaping to his feet. "My nerves can stand no more!"

"I'm sorry, Mr Hubbard, the manifestations have been particularly bad tonight, possibly the spirits are annoyed at the presence of strangers in the house.

We rarely have visitors. I will show you to your rooms."

With that Wallis lit three candles and, each of us clutching one, led us upstairs where we were allotted two adjacent rooms.

"I'm sorry they are not very comfortable, gentlemen, but nowhere is, in this house. They are the best we have. Sleep well." Wallis disappeared into the darkness and Holmes, with a cheery "Good night, Jonquil, I hope you didn't find sand in your whisky," went into his room and closed the door.

I looked around my room, illuminated by only the single candle and the moonlight pouring in through the uncurtained window. Even in that meagre light I could see that the ceiling had sagged so much it was only prevented from falling by resting on top of the mighty four-poster bed, which clearly had never been moved since placed there in ancient times. Although all the small glass panes were present in the leaded window, cold air was blowing in all round the rotten wooden frame, where old newspapers had been stuffed in an attempt to stop the draught.

I examined the bed and, although the maid had put a hot water jar between the sheets, decided to sleep fully clothed. I lay there, my head in turmoil. What a bizarre place we had come to. The combined effect of wine, brandy and whisky contrived to keep me awake, and the thought of the poltergeist did not help matters. Every time I heard a creak in the old timbers my ears pricked up. Holmes is a good chap, but there are things he knows nothing about – the solar system, for instance – and I fancy my knowledge of the human body is superior to his. I am, after all, a trained doctor. But why he chose to act like Bunthorne, the fleshly poet in Gilbert & Sullivan's latest piece of nonsense, I could not fathom. And what was that about sand in the whisky? I lay awake with all these thoughts churning round my head and still had not slept when I checked my watch and saw it was four in the morning.

But I must have drifted off eventually, in spite of everything, as I was forcibly shaken awake. I opened my eyes to see Holmes standing over me and bright sunlight streaming in through the window.

"Wake up, Watson, I have breakfasted some hours ago, but, if you descend now, you will have the company of Mr and Mrs Wallis. Pettigrew has gone out."

"What time is it?" I asked blearily.

"Time to confront our ghost," replied Holmes. I was instantly alert.

"You have found an explanation for the manifestations?"

"Did you find sand in your whisky, last night? Come on, man, stir yourself." And with that he was gone.

Nonplussed as to why Holmes should keep harping on about sand in the whisky, I quickly straightened my crumpled attire and five minutes later joined the Wallises in the dining room. I must confess the place looked rather more wholesome in the morning light.

"Good morning, Mr Watson. I hope you slept well?" asked Mrs Wallis.

"Yes, excellently," I lied.

"Your colleague does not seem to have arisen as yet. Do you wish to call him?" asked Wallis.

"Oh, I think he is up and about," I said diffidently.

"Indeed I am," said Holmes, entering the room as he heard my reply. I was relieved to note that he had dropped his effete pose.

"Coffee, Mr Hubbard?" asked Mrs Wallis.

"Thank you, no. I have already breakfasted in the servants' quarters," said Holmes. "I owe you an apology Mrs Wallis, Mr Wallis, but I fear you owe me and Watson a greater one. I have come to you in disguise. I am not called Hubbard, neither am I an architect. My name is Sherlock Holmes and I am a private detective. This is my colleague Dr Watson, the eminent medical man and author. I fear that my adopted character alarmed him, as much as it misled you."

"What is the meaning of all this?" blustered Wallis, leaping to his feet. "Are you in Mr Pettigrew's confidence?"

"Pray seat yourself, sir. I understand that your father-in-law is out walking, and that is to the good, as we can discuss this affair quite amicably. Firstly, I know all about your ghostly pranks. I know that you are both responsible for these so called manifestations."

"That is an insulting statement to make, Mr Holmes," said Mrs Wallis.

"I do not speak lightly, madam. I also know how each one was perpetrated. Firstly, the falling picture, which was obviously a favourite ploy, as you repeated it on several occasions. Last night that picture fell down from that wall whilst you, Mrs Wallis, were out of the room. It fell because you made it do so. The internal walls of this house are made in the ancient way of laths with a plaster of clay mixed with straw and horse-hair, known, I believe, as pugging. The walls are not very thick and I think you thrust a long needle, perhaps something like a hat-pin, through the wall from the other side and hung the picture on the protruding point. When you required the picture to fall, you merely had to withdraw the pin from the other side of the wall."

"Ingenious," I breathed. "But how did you deduce that, Holmes?"

"It was very obvious to me that none of the ghostly happenings occurred when we were all present. Even Lestrade would have made examining the picture hook his first priority. There was no hook or nail anywhere to be seen on the floor by the fallen picture. The hole in the wall clearly went right through to the other side. This could have been by chance in these old walls, but I examined the places where other pictures had fallen, and the same tiny holes were present."

"Amazing!" I said in admiration.

"You cannot prove that, Mr Holmes," said Wallis urbanely. "And even if you are right, there is nothing to point to Laura and me as being in any way concerned."

"I am right, and I can prove it, as the small reproduction print of the Landseer over there is still hanging on such a contrivance. Perhaps you had forgotten you had set up more than one picture. But no matter, let us consider other things that happened last night. For instance, why Mrs Wallis was violently hurled from her chair by an unseen malevolent hand. In fact, you merely threw yourself sideways off your chair and pretended you had been propelled by a spirit force."

"But, Holmes, you, yourself, were thrown off your chair and Mr Pettigrew told us he had suffered a similar fate," I protested.

"I was indeed, and I agree that the innocent Mr Pettigrew had previously suffered from being toppled from his chair. The same chair. A very clever idea, Wallis, I must congratulate you – a pity you had to be absent to work the trick. It became clear to me why, when apportioning the places at dinner, you insisted I took that particular chair. Watson, being a much more heavily built man, may have thwarted the trick. My spare frame and your father's frailty meant you had less weight to shift."

"Of course, that happened when he had gone to fetch the brandy," I cried.

"From the cellar. Observe this floor is made of wood, ancient oak I fancy, whereas the other ground floor rooms are mainly stone flags. The cellar is under this floor. Now which was my chair last night? This one you are sitting on, Mrs Wallis – may I?"

Mrs Wallis rose to allow Holmes to take the chair which he promptly turned upside down. I could clearly see a hole bored in the base of one of the back legs.

"There is a metal tube inserted the entire length of the back leg. If you look at the floor – there, see it, Watson? – a hole bored in the floor boards. My chair was placed with the fake leg over that hole."

"I follow you, Holmes, but how did that enable you to be thrown off the chair?"

"A hefty metal rod was pushed up through the ceiling of the cellar, hence through the floor of this room, via the hole and right up into the chair. All that was necessary was for Wallis to apply his full weight to the pole in the cellar thus moving it sideways, which had the result of tipping the chair above. With two feet of rod in the chair above, and five feet down below, there was ample leverage to tip a none too solid man from his chair. Afterwards the pole could be pulled out and there was nothing to find."

"Diabolical!" I breathed.

"All rather fanciful I think, Mr Holmes," said Wallis.

"The chair leg and hole are there for all to see. I found a seven foot metal pole in the cellar. It is still there."

"We have been discovered, Tim!" cried Laura Wallis.

"You have indeed," said Holmes sternly. "Why do you wish to terrify your father? Perhaps you wish to give him a heart attack, so that he will die and leave his large fortune to you!" Mrs Wallis looked appalled.

"Oh no, no, Mr Holmes. I wish no harm to my father, he is very dear to me."

"Then you have a strange way of showing your love," replied Holmes.

"You are not as clever as you think, Mr Holmes," said Wallis. "We do not wish our father's death. That would not benefit us at all. Laura is a dutiful and loving daughter. You will not be aware that under the terms of Mr Pettigrew's will all his wealth, except for this house, passes to the Antiquarian Society of London. All Laura would inherit is this accursed house that would be a millstone not a blessing."

"Then be so good as to explain the purpose of your foolish pranks," demanded Holmes sternly.

"All we sought to do, Mr Holmes, was to frighten my father-in- law into wishing to leave this house. I mean – look around you – the place is about to fall down. It is no place to bring up a baby. It is cold, damp, insanitary and dangerous. We want him to build a new house. We can't bring up a baby here. Surely you can understand that?"

"I have no wish to leave my father, Mr Holmes, I love him dearly, but there is the next generation to think about. I am sure you will agree that a mother's duty is to her new-born child, rather than her father."

My heart went out to the young couple as Wallis explained their predicament.

"I cannot, under any circumstances, condone your extraordinary behaviour," said Holmes, "but, as far as I am concerned, this is entirely a domestic matter in which I am not qualified to interfere. I urge you to confess all before your father and trust to his benevolence. I agree he seems to be an eccentric man who cannot come to terms with his sudden riches, but he is your father and it is your duty to be either guided by him, or leave his house."

"Perhaps, as a medical man, I could point out the dangers to a pregnant woman, and subsequently, a new baby," I volunteered. But at that moment Pettigrew entered crying "What have I done to you, my children? I have been here some time and have overheard much of your conversation. Why did you not tell me I was to be a grandfather? Why did you not tell me that I am a foolish old man who thinks a decrepit old house takes precedence over my own flesh and blood? I am not angry that you played those terrifying tricks on me. No – I am sad that I drove you to such a desperate expedient with my blinkered outlook. I have been out walking and thinking very deeply. I had come to the conclusion that it was unfair of me to make you suffer for my antiquarian foibles. But now I realise the true position, I am doubly ashamed. Oh, my children, embrace me!"

Holmes caught my eye and with a slight gesture of his head indicated that we would be wise to slip away.

On the way back to London in the train, I could not forbear to praise Holmes for his masterly acting as the effete architect. He was embarrassed.

"I decided that ghosts were unlikely to appear to a strong-willed man so I took it upon myself to portray a spineless ninny. I beg you will not mention it again."

"I think you had your suspicions about the poltergeist before we ever left town," I ventured.

"Of course. A rational man seeks a natural explanation for the extraordinary."

"I am still unclear how Wallis got the whisky decanter to fall. Nobody was near it. Did Mrs Wallis pull a thread or something?"

"That was the most ingenious trick of all. In fact it was solving that problem first that led me to the solutions for the other tricks. Although I leaped away as in fright from the smashed decanter, it did not prevent my observation of a quantity of sand, spilt on the floor, where the broken glass lay shattered. This morning I was up at first light and caught the maid before she could dispose of the broken glass pieces. I did a little examination and tried to piece back together the broken decanter. An impossible task, but I found some pieces of thin glass. Curved and clear as though they had formed part of a dome. As you know, the decanter was straight sided, no curves anywhere and of faceted glass. I also found traces of wet sand."

"Wet sand? But what could that mean?"

"I realised that an hour glass had been placed in the decanter. I examined the place where the decanter had fallen and found traces of sand there too. On questioning the maid, she said that, when she had swept up the broken glass, there had been a quantity of sand amongst it. I deduced that Wallis had placed an hour glass in the decanter, in such a position, and at such an angle, that the sand in the upper bulb gradually running into the lower would disturb the balance of the decanter. By placing the decanter at the extreme edge of the table – something that I had already noted at the time with great interest – the shift in balance was enough to cause the thing to topple."

"The cunning devil!" I exclaimed in astonishment.

"I pray that that young man's ingenuity does not run to further criminal acts. A man as clever as he deserves to succeed in some honourable profession."

The Singular Adventure
of
THE ABSENT PROFESSOR

THE lady who graced our humble bachelor dwelling was striking, in both her looks and forceful personality. She was of middle height and appeared to be in her early thirties.

"My name may be not unknown to you, Mr Holmes," she said. "I am Amanda Burling."

"You are the wife of the missing Professor Burling?" asked Holmes.

"That is correct."

"Then I must inform you I think it very unlikely that I can help you. If you had come to me when the professor first went missing, some two months ago, then I would have been pleased to place my services at your disposal. But I fear that after this length of time any clues which may have given an indication of where he has gone will have been completely obliterated."

"My husband has been absent six weeks and four days, Mr Holmes, but it is not his mysterious disappearance about which I wish to consult you. The police are still thoroughly investigating the situation, and the government, too, is making every effort to trace him, so I am confident to leave the matter in their hands," replied Mrs Burling.

"Then, madam, I apologise. What is this further matter that requires my humble investigation rather than the police or government?" asked Holmes.

"Mr Holmes, I am being watched. I have noticed of late that at least two men are watching the house."

"Watching the house, or you personally, Mrs Burling?"

"I do not know for sure. Myself, I think, as I have seen one of the men in the park when I have been taking my little ones for recreation. One man is very big with a bushy red beard. The other is much less significant. A rather weasely-looking man with a moustache. I have seen both of them several times watching the house, and, as I say, on one occasion the red-bearded man was lurking in the park."

"Have you attempted to address these men?" asked Holmes.

"No. I intended to approach the man in the park but he hurried off."

"And what, precisely, do you desire me to do, Mrs Burling?"

"I thought you may be able to find out who these men are and why they are observing me. I do not want to bother the police, on what may be a trivial matter, when they are busy seeking my husband."

"Yes, I think it is within my capabilities to accost a pair of strangers and ask their business. Please to give me your address and I will do as you require."

"Thank you, Mr Holmes. Here is my card."

"Thank you, Mrs Burling. Oh, just one more thing. Why would the government be seeking your husband – would they, too, not be content to leave the search to the police?" asked Holmes.

"My husband was doing some secret research work for the government, so naturally they are concerned at his disappearance."

"Ah, naturally. Thank you for coming to see me. I shall bend my best endeavours to your behalf. Good day," said Holmes, bowing out the professor's wife.

"Well, Watson, what do you make of that?"

"A handsome woman, Holmes," said I.

Holmes sighed. "I meant what did you think about what she had to say?"

"Oh, ah, well, it occurs to me that these men are probably plain clothes police officers who are detailed to watch the house in case the professor returns."

"That won't do, Watson. Why waste a couple of men on that, when surely Mrs Burling will immediately inform the police should her husband show up?"

"Then, perhaps, they are watching for the professor, but are not from the police?"

"Better, Watson, that seems a more likely hypothesis, but the lady thinks they are watching her. Hence her comments about the man in the park."

"Hum, then I am at a loss."

"I must have more information before I can decide anything. It is always a mistake to try and construct a theory from insufficient data." With that Holmes picked up his violin whereupon I decided it was still light and mild enough to take a walk.

For the next few days I saw little of Holmes, apart from his comings and goings in a variety of artisans' guises. I assumed he was keeping watch on the watchers. However, one morning at breakfast, I was surprised to read in the newspaper that the body of Professor Burling had been pulled out of the Thames the day before, and was now reposing in the mortuary, pending police inspection. Holmes was not in so I marked the paragraph and left the paper where he could not fail to see it.

That night Holmes returned exhausted and threw himself into the chair. "This is a rum business, Watson."

"You saw the paper?"

"Yes. Thank you for calling my attention to it. I immediately went down to see Lestrade, who happens to be in charge of the search for the professor. He was pleased he could call his men home but, of course, a dead professor is as inexplicable as a missing one."

"So that's it then, Holmes?"

"Not quite. I had a look at the body, Watson; not a pretty sight. It had been in the water for weeks."

"And only now come to the surface? I would have thought it would have risen before now, or been washed out to sea."

"Yes, it would appear to have got caught somewhere under the water. A group of children playing on a mud-bank were throwing stones at it before they realised it was a body and called a policeman. There seemed to be no signs of wounding and the police surgeon concluded it was death by drowning. The authorities appear to think it was either an accident or suicide. The body was identified by the professor's brother and one of the professor's colleagues at Cambridge. However, the clothing was more interesting than the body."

"In what way Holmes?"

"Have a look at that, Watson." Holmes produced a paper parcel, from which he took a shoe.

"Is this the professor's?"

"It is from the body. I have borrowed it with Inspector Lestrade's kind permission. He thinks that his case is closed so he was quite accommodating over the matter."

"Is the shoe significant?"

"What size would you estimate it to be, Watson?"

"It is large. Very large." I held it against my own. "Size 10 or 11 perhaps?"

"It is a size 12, Watson, and especially made for the professor by Lobb, the well-known shoe maker. See, here is his trade mark. Perhaps you would like to come with me tomorrow to Mrs Burling's?"

"You wish to enquire about the shoe?"

"I wish to enquire about the professor's feet."

The next day we went along to the late professor's house. The curtains were drawn and the door was opened by a snivelling maid who told us that Mrs Burling was not receiving. At Holmes' insistence she carried off a message to her mistress. She returned to say that we would be seen and we were shown into what was obviously the professor's library.

"Well, Mr Holmes, I think the task I set you seems rather trivial now my husband has been found in such tragic circumstances," said Mrs Burling, after greeting us.

"I am very sorry to intrude upon you at such a moment, madam, but I have found some curiosities in my investigation. Do you recognise this shoe?"

"It is my husband's, I was with him when he ordered them."

"From Lobb?"

"Yes, the professor always went to Lobb. He was rather careful about his feet. I used to tease him about them as they were exceptionally large. Lobb used to say my husband had the largest feet of any of his regular customers."

Mrs Burling did her best to keep her voice level and her speech bright, but it was too much for her and she broke down into inconsolable weeping.

"Please accept my heartfelt condolences, I am sorry to intrude at this time of grief. Come, Watson." So we left the sorrowing widow and went on to visit Lobb the shoemaker.

"Mr Lobb?" enquired Holmes of the ancient stooping figure that appeared to answer our request.

"Our founder left us several years ago, sir. The younger Mr Lobb is, I regret, absent. I am Hargreaves, the manager of this establishment, how can I help you?"

"Do you recognise this shoe?" asked Holmes, offering it up.

"Where did you get this? And may I ask who you gentlemen are?"

"I am Sherlock Holmes and this is my colleague Dr Watson. The shoe was given to me by Inspector Lestrade of Scotland Yard."

"Ah, I see. This is in connection with the tragic death of Professor Burling?"

"I have reason to believe this is his shoe."

"Indeed, Mr Holmes. There is no doubt. The professor has – had, very large feet. In the region of size 12 by the standard measurement. This is certainly his shoe. I can easily tell you the date he collected the pair if you wish."

"That will not be necessary, thank you, Mr Hargreaves. I really wished to be reassured that there was no doubt that this was the professor's shoe."

"Oh, none whatever, Mr Holmes. We have his last here and full details of the style and records of every pair. But I can tell you just by looking."

"I presume the professor had feet of equal size?"

"It is funny you should ask that, Mr Holmes, because he did have feet that were excellently matched. In fact, many of our clients have feet of slightly differing proportions which is one reason they prefer to have their shoes made to measure, but the professor had feet of exactly the same size."

"How much would a pair of feet differ? By a full size?"

"It could be. Usually up to half a standard size is common, sometimes more, but that is rather unusual."

"But not by, say, one foot a size 9 and the other size 12?"

"Oh no, that would be ludicrous, Mr Holmes, freakish in fact."

"What would be the difference in measurement between a size 9 and a size 12, Mr Hargreaves?"

"Originally shoes were sized by three ears of corn to the inch, and each increment was one ear of corn, so a size 12 would be fully an inch larger than a size 9."

"So a size 12 shoe would be very slack on my friend Watson, here, who takes a size 9. Not very comfortable."

"It would be impossible to wear them at all, Mr Holmes. You might wear two pairs of thick socks to enable you to wear the next size up, but you could not even attempt to walk in shoes that were three full sizes too big."

"Thank you for your assistance, Mr Hargreaves, you have proved most helpful."

As we walked along Holmes was very silent. I ventured to ask "Well what's all this about, Holmes?"

"The corpse of the professor was wearing one shoe only, when it was fished out from the Thames."

"Presumably the other had come off in the water."

"Yes, or before that, if there had been a struggle to push the body into the water."

"You do not think it is suicide?"

"Why would a shoe come off, if it was securely fastened?"

"Perhaps it was not securely fastened. Perhaps the laces were not done up properly. Perhaps the shoe was slack on the foot."

"It *was* slack on the foot, Watson."

"Well there you are then."

As we walked along, a further thought struck me. "Holmes, if the shoe has disappeared, how could you possibly know that it was slack on the foot?"

"Because the foot was no larger than a size 7, Watson."

Back in our rooms Holmes explained to me how he had examined the corpse and had seen immediately that the feet on the body were considerably smaller than the size of the remaining shoe.

"Whoever was responsible for examining the body obviously stripped it of clothing without a thought. It would probably have been apparent that the suit of clothes was a poor fit also. I reasoned that the shoes were not the shoes habitually worn by that man. As the shoemaker told us, it was inconceivable that a man could walk in shoes that were so over large. Thus if the shoes did not belong to the body, the body did not belong to the shoes. We have now conclusive proof from Mrs Burling and Mr Hargreaves that they were, in truth, the shoes of the professor. Therefore, the obvious conclusion is that it is not his body."

"Holmes, what does this mean?" I cried.

"I cannot tell as yet, Watson. But there is some very nasty skullduggery going on, I'll be bound."

"But surely, Mrs Burling is not involved in anything underhand?"

"No, I do not think so. I rather think that poor lady innocently believes that her missing husband has been found dead."

"What will you do now?"

"Pursue my enquiries, as the police say."

It was a couple of days later when Holmes asked me if I was prepared to accompany him to Professor Burling's funeral.

"Of course, Holmes, if my presence can add any comfort to the grieving widow. But were you mistaken in your prognosis? Was the corpse the professor after all?"

"Of course I was not mistaken, Watson. I rarely make mistakes. The man they are to bury is certainly not the professor."

"But surely you cannot allow the burial to proceed without notifying the authorities? What about poor Mrs Burling, mourning a man who is not her husband?" I protested.

"She won't know, will she?"

"Holmes, you are heartless."

"I have to uncover a great wrong, Watson. I know what I am doing. Will you come with me, or not?"

"Of course I will."

"Stout fellow. We may have to grapple with a powerful felon."

"I will take my hefty stick."

So we made our preparations. Holmes placed into his pocket a cord about a yard long; for what purpose I could not guess.

When we arrived at the churchyard there were many mourners making their way into the church, for the professor had been an eminent man. There were also many onlookers, for his recent notoriety had made the name Burling familiar to a public who would not previously have heard of him. Holmes drew my attention to Inspector Lestrade of Scotland Yard who was just going through the church porch.

"The complacency of that man astounds me, Watson. He thinks his case is closed. I hope within the next half hour to open his eyes to his dullness."

To my surprise Holmes made no effort to enter the church but stood among the onlookers like a common loafer. The funeral procession arrived and the coffin was borne inside on the shoulders of the pall bearers. The family mourners followed, Mrs Burling, veiled and clad in sombre black accompanied by her children, then the professor's friends and colleagues. Holmes gripped my arm and hissed in my ear.

"See the fellow there – the small man with the moustache? There – just passing the tree?"

"What about him?"

"He is the weasely man who has been spying on Mrs Burling."

"Who is he?"

"He is a government agent of some sort."

"What's all this about Holmes? It seems very fishy."

"Espionage, Watson. And, by God, there's our man." Holmes nodded over to a secluded part of the church yard where I now saw a big man with a bushy red beard. Some of the crowd had drifted away now all had entered the church for the service and there was nothing more to see but there was still a knot of people around the man and we both silently slid over to join the group, unobserved by our quarry. We were able to get right up to him, one on each side, and he was still not aware of our presence as he seemed to be straining to hear what was happening inside the church.

"What the devil?" the red-bearded man cried as he was suddenly aware of something brushing against his leg.

"Now, Watson!" called Holmes and, with all the weight that had been such an asset to my college rugger team, I hurled him to the ground. Holmes had surreptitiously wrapped a loop of cord around the man's legs, so that he was quite unbalanced and went down like a ninepin. I promptly sat astride him and tried to grab his flailing arms while Holmes tied his legs firmly together. The gawping bunch of idlers stared at the three of us but fortunately did not interfere. Holmes turned to the least vacant-looking.

"I am a police officer. This man is a criminal. Go into the church and ask for Inspector Lestrade. Quick man, away with you; there's a shilling for you when you bring him back. Tell him you come from Sherlock Holmes."

The idler sped away to do as he was bid. The bearded man had stopped struggling, but at the name Sherlock Holmes he made a mighty effort to throw us off, which would have succeeded, had not his legs been firmly bound, as he was a powerful man. After more struggling Holmes managed to get a pair of handcuffs on him before Lestrade came puffing up.

"What's the matter, Mr Holmes? This fellow ruined the service, rushing in shouting for me."

"Here, my good man," said Holmes, giving his messenger the promised shilling. "Lestrade, I believe you have been looking for this villain for some time."

"Have I? Who is he? I've never seen him before," spluttered Lestrade.

"I rather think this chap has led you a merry dance for seven weeks." Thus saying, Holmes pulled at the bushy beard which came away as the face behind it cursed. Lestrade gaped in amazement.

"Professor Burling!" he cried.

Back in our familiar quarters we refreshed ourselves. There were four of us: Holmes, Lestrade and myself, plus the weasely little man who had been introduced to us as Brinsley Cunliffe of Her Majesty's secret service.

"Well, Mr Holmes, I think you had better tell us exactly what you've been up to," said Lestrade.

"I had been asked by Mrs Burling to investigate people watching her house. By dint of some careful watching of my own I soon discovered that there were two separate watchers. A small man with a moustache – our colleague Mr Cunliffe, here – and a large man with a red beard. I do not think each was aware of the other."

"No, Mr Holmes, I had never observed the red-bearded man. A flaw on my part, I must confess, but I was watching out for very different birds. You see, the professor was engaged on secret work for the government – I cannot tell you more, because I do not know myself, but you will realise this information is of the utmost importance and it is essential that not a whisper should reach an enemy government. When the professor disappeared we immediately suspected that he had been kidnapped by a foreign power. My particular task was to keep the house under observation, in case there was any contact with the professor's wife from the – er, representatives of this foreign power who are, I may say, quite well known to us."

"So that explains your purpose in lurking outside the house. But there was still the enigma of the bearded man. I kept him under long observation and came to the conclusion that it was certainly not the house itself he was watching, nor was it strictly Mrs Burling. The man was watching for the children. When the children were taken out by the governess they were followed, even though Mrs Burling clearly remained at home. Why should he do that unless he had a particular interest in the children or the governess? I was able to discount the governess so it became obvious the man was watching the children – his own children."

"I am not surprised at that. To put pressure on the professor our enemies threatened they would kidnap his children if he did not fall in with their wishes," said Cunliffe.

"But what about the man we fished out of the river?" asked Lestrade.

"That made things clear at last," said Holmes.

"It seems to confuse things more, as far as I can see," grumbled Lestrade.

"Obviously the corpse was dressed up to look as though it were the professor. I was immediately suspicious when I saw that the corpse had feet far too small to go with the foot-wear it had been dressed in. So slack were the shoes that one had floated off to disappear for ever. After checking up on the shoe you kindly loaned to me, I then examined the footprints left by the bearded man. There was no question that he was wearing shoes of a similar size and type. I knew the red-bearded man was Professor Burling in disguise."

"But, Holmes," I cried, "why did you not have him arrested in the street? Why did you permit the funeral to proceed?"

"Because, my dear Watson, the red-bearded man disappeared as the professor himself had done. I could not find him. My only hope was that he would not be able to keep away from his own funeral. In that I was right. He dare not enter the church but he could not resist standing guard over his family while they were grieving for him."

"The villain!" I cried.

"We must not be too hard on the professor, Doctor. Much pressure had been put upon him and, truth to tell, I think his mind was somewhat turned. You see, he had come under the influence of our enemies and was being persuaded to betray his country. All his work was to be handed over to the very people we oppose. His mind was in torment because he had great sympathy with the ideals of our opponents. He had been recruited to their cause when an undergraduate at Cambridge and, though his sympathies had lapsed, this recent work made him very important to both sides," said Cunliffe.

"I cannot sympathise with a man who would betray his country," I said.

"I wish we could all have our ideals so clearly defined, Doctor," said Brinsley Cunliffe. "In fact, the professor decided the only thing to do was to wash his hands of the whole affair, especially as his children were being threatened. But it is impossible, once one is embroiled, to get out of it, except by death. So he faked his own demise. It was a desperate measure and nearly worked. My superiors believed it when the corpse was found, so did our opposition, that is why they have gone away. It was only your astuteness, Mr Holmes, that revealed the truth."

"But I cannot believe that any man could do that to his wife – of all people," I protested.

"I think perhaps the professor's intention was to secretly make himself known to his wife and children when all the fuss had died down, then take them away to a new place and start a new life," suggested Cunliffe.

"Where did the corpse come from? Did he commit murder as well?" asked Lestrade.

"I think not," said Holmes. "I fancy he would have found a suitable body from a colleague in the anatomy schools. As you know, the bodies of derelicts usually end up there."

"I think it inexcusable that a man should pretend to be dead to those who are closest to him. I thought it so before, when a certain person I know appeared to be drowned, but was in fact gallivanting around Europe," I felt compelled to state.

"Another whisky, gentlemen?" asked Holmes, reaching out to the tantalus.

The Singular Adventure
of
THE RED-NOSED ARTIST

OF ALL the remarkable cases that my friend Sherlock Holmes solved during his long career, the affair I am about to relate is one of the most bizarre. Several times I have taken up my pen to narrate the circumstances of this singular case but, as I have many readers of the fairer sex, my natural reticence has precluded a satisfactory description of the events. However, a world-wide conflagration has brought many atrocities into the harsh light of day and our womenfolk are made of sterner stuff than in the days of the good old Queen. Therefore, I feel I can now tell my tale without incurring the taint of prurience and with a frankness impossible at the time.

One sunny morning in the early summer of 1895 we were just finishing our breakfast when it was interrupted by Mrs Hudson who said that a gentleman was at the door demanding to speak most urgently to my friend Mr Sherlock Holmes.

"Did he give a name, Mrs Hudson?"

"No, Mr Holmes, but he seems a most respectable gentleman."

"Very well, warn him we are still at breakfast but show him in and bring another cup and saucer."

As Mrs Hudson bustled out Holmes reached for the coffee pot and I attacked another sausage. She returned with the extra china, followed by a man of about forty who looked very respectable indeed.

"You have caught us at a disadvantage. Pray excuse us continuing our meal and do join us in a cup of coffee," said Holmes.

"I am very sorry to interrupt you so early in the morning but a lady's life is at stake and her affairs will brook no delay," said our visitor in great agitation.

"Mr Morrison, as a solicitor you will know that the law grinds exceedingly slowly, nothing is precipitate," replied Holmes smoothly.

"How do you know I am a solicitor? And how can you know my name? I neglected to send in my card." The bewildered man handed over his card which read *Edward Morrison; Morrison, Morrison & Dodd,* with an address in the City.

"If you wish to conceal your identity it would be wise not to write your name on the lining of your hat, or at least make sure you hold it in a manner which does not expose it. As for being a solicitor, I confess I made an assumption that you may be the Edward Morrison who is a partner in the lawyers' firm that retained me in the matter of the *Matilda Briggs* affair."

"It is so. My name is Edward Morrison and I am the junior partner in that well established firm. It is because a colleague has always spoken highly of you that it seemed to me you were the very man to assist me. I am exceedingly concerned about a client of mine. Mrs Alicia Massoni. Perhaps her name is known to you? She is the wife of the eminent artist Gerald Fordun Massoni. Or, rather, I should more correctly say she is his widow. Massoni was found dead early this morning with a knife in his chest."

"How very interesting," purred Holmes, "pray continue."

"I beg you to finish your meal as quickly as possible, Mr Holmes, and return with me to Garrick House. Mrs Massoni has been arrested by the police."

"I will certainly come with you as soon as we have breakfasted. Are the police still at the house?"

"Yes, an Inspector Lestrade is in charge of proceedings."

Holmes leapt to his feet, knocking his chair over. "Then I must come at once; Lestrade's flatfoots will trample over any shred of evidence there may be. Are you game, Watson?"

"Of course," said I, gulping down my coffee.

"I have a cab waiting," said Morrison.

We grabbed our coats and hats, pausing only for Holmes to pick up a few items of equipment that he thrust into his pockets, and followed our visitor to the cab waiting outside.

On the way Morrison explained the situation. "Gerald Fordun Massoni is, or rather was, a well regarded artist. His work is highly sought after by a certain type of collector and, as he was not very prolific, his works command a high price. I am surprised you do not know his name, Mr Holmes."

"Although I am descended from an eminent French artist on my mother's side, it would seem my own artistic proclivities have expressed themselves in music rather than the visual arts. But please continue."

"This morning one of Massoni's models called at his studio and found the artist sprawled on his back on the floor with a dagger in his chest. The woman immediately went round to the front of the house and roused Mrs Massoni who despatched a servant for the police."

"What time was this?"

"About six o'clock."

"Six o'clock? Surely Massoni was not up and about to start work at that time?"

"No, well, Massoni was not a man who lived as other men. It is no use concealing these things, they are bound to come out; Mr and Mrs Massoni lived separate lives. Massoni was a totally unknown artist when they first met and Alicia was won over by his charm and talents but as soon as they were married she realised that she had married a fiend and libertine. He was penniless, she was an heiress and lived in a fine Georgian House. It is called Garrick House because the eminent actor is thought to have lodged there. To encourage Massoni she allowed him to take all kinds of liberties both with her wealth and her emotions. Eventually she found that he was entertaining many women in his studio. Some were models who fell for his dubious charms, others were simply loose women. And not just poor wretches; he also seemed to attract some of the foremost ladies in society. It is a sad fact that some otherwise respectable women are attracted by the grossest of men. Alicia wanted to be free from him but that was impossible; so, while they still both lived at Garrick House for the sake of appearances, they went their separate ways."

"How do you know all this, Mr Morrison? Is it common knowledge?"

"By no means, Mr Holmes. To the world they appear, if not a devoted couple, at least a respectable one. But I am Mrs Massoni's solicitor; dealing with her legal affairs has brought me very close and I have been privileged to have many intimate conversations with the lady."

We soon reached the house. It was a finely proportioned brick house with stone quoins and possessed a symmetrical façade typical of that elegant age. However, one of the ground floor windows had been crudely enlarged and filled with extra panes of sheet glass so that the entire architecture had been brutally vandalised.

"Good God," I exclaimed, "what wretch has done that work!"

"That is Massoni's studio. He needed extra light," said Morrison.

"But surely he could have used a room round the back, somewhere where it would have mattered less?" I protested.

"An artist requires northern light, Watson, and as you can see from the position of the sun this is the north facing side of the house."

"Oh the wretch could have had his studio anywhere in London, but it delighted him to torture Alicia with his stupid demands. The door to the studio is via a private entrance round at the back – it is totally separate from the rest of the house, there is no connection and is quite self-contained."

"What a cad he must be to ruin such a beautiful house!" I cried. "I cannot believe an artist could be so unfeeling."

"Come, we must alight here and go round the side to the studio entrance."

So saying, Mr Morrison led the way to a small unobtrusive door partly masked by shrubbery. A constable stood outside.

"Sorry, sirs, you can't go in there," he said, placing his arm out.

"Of course I can, I am Mrs Massoni's solicitor. I demand to see Inspector Lestrade," blustered Morrison.

"I'm sorry, but I have my orders."

"Quite right, constable," said Holmes smoothly, "I will see your superior hears of your doing your duty. However, be so kind as to tell Inspector Lestrade that Sherlock Holmes has arrived and would appreciate a word. We will wait here for your return."

"All right. But you stay there."

The constable went inside and within seconds reappeared with Lestrade.

"Why, Mr Holmes, this is a surprise. I am amazed that the news of this crime has reached you so swiftly. Ah!" said Lestrade suddenly seeing Morrison, "I see. Well you had better come in; but you, sir," he said sternly to the solicitor, "I have already warned to stay away. You can do nothing here."

"But my client must be represented," protested Morrison.

"Your client is at the moment at Bow Street police station. When I have finished my investigations here I will be interviewing her. I suggest we meet up there early this afternoon, say two o'clock?"

"Has she been charged?" asked Morrison.

" No, nothing like that. Mrs Massoni is merely complying with my request to assist me with my enquiries. So be a good fellow and take yourself off."

Morrison started to protest at this unwarranted rudeness so I took him by the arm and gently escorted him away from the door. I managed to calm him down and assured him all would be well and that he could place every confidence in Holmes. He would positively find out the truth. Eventually, after a little more persuading, Morrison went off, a worried but calmer man. I returned inside to find Holmes and Lestrade chatting quite genially about the tiresomeness of lawyers.

The sight that met me was similar to that we had been led to expect from Morrison's description. The body was still there spread-eagled in the middle of the floor with the hilt of a dagger still protruding from his chest. However, most bizarrely, the dead artist's nose in the midst of his pallid face was a bright red.

"What's this, Lestrade?" said Holmes, pointing to the nose.

"Paint. Red paint. It would seem that the murderer having slaughtered the man decided to mock him by painting his nose red like a clown."

"How singular," murmured Holmes.

"That's not all that's painted red, either."

"What do you mean?"

Lestrade glanced around; "This must not get out, you understand. Not a word." He gently raised the artist's smock and to our surprise the body underneath was completely naked and the masculine organ too was painted with red paint.

"Great heavens!" I cried.

Holmes's eyes gleamed. "At first I resented being dragged from my breakfast but this may be a very interesting crime."

"But why is the man naked?" I asked. "I thought the whole point of an artist's smock was to protect his clothing."

"I think I can answer that," said Lestrade. "The woman who found the body has been very forthcoming about the dead man. She was one of his regular models and knows a lot about him. I do not wish to disgust you gentlemen but it seems it was Massoni's way to habitually dress like that for work. To put it crudely, he was a randy old goat and was always ready to slip in Dainty Davie by simply raising the hem of his smock."

"How disgusting!" I cried.

"These artist-chaps don't live like the rest of us, do they?" said Lestrade. "It seems as if no female was safe within a mile of him. Well he's got his come-uppance now," he growled with sour humour. "But for God's sake, keep this to yourselves, we can't do with the Grub Street lads catching on to it."

"Have you examined everything, Lestrade?" asked Holmes.

"Just about, I've been here nearly two hours."

"What time do you estimate the murder took place?"

"The police surgeon reckoned somewhere between nine and ten o'clock last night."

"What do you make of this tobacco ash?"

Lestrade shrugged. "It's all over the place. The man smoked like a chimney I suppose."

"Just so," said Holmes, scooping up some of the ash and placing it in an envelope. "Havana cigars at a guess."

"That's right," answered Lestrade, "there's a box in his desk."

Holmes then repeated the procedure. "Any sign of Turkish cigarettes?"

"No, not that I've found. Why?"

"I have identified two distinct types of ash. Until I have analysed them I cannot be certain. I have written a monograph on the different types of tobacco ash, which might prove an interesting study for the detectives at Scotland Yard."

"That's as may be, but it doesn't help us here, does it?"

"Perhaps not. But surely it indicates the presence of a second person in this room? That person could be your murderer."

"I think I have my murderer, Mr Holmes," said Lestrade smugly.

"Mrs Massoni, I presume?"

"Well, Mr Holmes, I'm sure you don't need me to tell you that often the murderer is someone very close to the victim."

"That is true, but hardly sufficient for an accusation."

"I haven't accused her, Mr Holmes. She has been placed in police custody pending investigations."

"So what are your suspicions?"

"Well, Dolly – " Lestrade paused and looked at his notes, "that's Dorothea Leng the artists' model who found him, told us the sort of man he was; I don't think many wives would care for a husband like that. I've interviewed the servants and I know the couple was estranged although they shared the same house."

"That's not a crime," I protested.

"No, Doctor, it isn't but carrying a knife in case your husband attacks you may lead to one."

"Carrying a knife, you say?" asked Holmes.

"The cook told me that Mrs Massoni never went anywhere about the house without a knife in her sleeve," said Lestrade.

"That is certainly unusual," mused Holmes. "And is this her knife, Lestrade?"

"I suppose so."

"You suppose so! Have you asked the lady? Have you asked the cook?"

"Of course, Mrs Massoni denies it is, but she would."

"Is it possible for me to have a word with Mrs Massoni?"

"I don't see why not."

"You can't keep her locked up just because she carried a knife and this man was killed with a knife," I protested hotly, thinking what a calamitous effect this might have on the poor woman's nerves.

"There's more to it than that," replied Lestrade. "Look at this." He opened his hand and showed an ornamental button.

"A button. From whence?" asked Holmes.

"It was loose on the floor. I reckon that it was pulled off in a struggle as she tried to stab the chap."

"You say 'she'."

"Surely it's from the frock of a lady, an ornamental affair like that."

"It would seem so, but Mrs Massoni is not the only lady who wears dresses," said Holmes mildly.

"True. That's why I placed her in custody. I want to examine all her clothing to find a match for this button. I will do that as soon as I have finished here."

"But she may have dropped it at any time. Look at the state of the place, it hasn't been cleaned for months. That button may have been dropped at any time. Massoni had women coming in to pose for his paintings on a daily basis. It may simply have come adrift when one of them disrobed."

"I agree, Mr Holmes, but I have to consider all things."

"Well you can't charge Mrs Massoni on any of that."

"Perhaps not; but I think I can get a confession out of her."

"And what if she is totally innocent?"

"Then she won't confess, will she?"

"I think you're barking up the wrong tree, Lestrade."

"You have your methods, Mr Holmes, I have mine. I know if there's no proof I can't take her to court, but I'm convinced she did it. She is estranged from her husband, she carries a knife in case he forces his attentions on her, he lives a sort of Bohemian life, she is a respectable woman, he is a curse to her. It all adds up. Last night he probably got drunk and tried to insist on his marital rights and she stabbed him with the knife she habitually carries in her sleeve."

"What do you make of the red paint?" asked Holmes.

"A bit rum that. The fact that she painted his wotsit would seem to be a sort of defiance or mockery, don't you think? And painted his nose like a clown to show he was a buffoon?"

"Excellent, Lestrade. I think you have it. The only flaw in your reasoning, it seems to me, is that any one of dozens of women could have done it. You have learned that Massoni was a man of prodigious promiscuous propensities."

"Well I suppose so," grumbled Lestrade. "In that case we'll never find her."

"Have you seen this, Lestrade?"

"Yes, it's an account book."

"How very interesting. It looks as though your Bohemian was very methodical where his income was concerned. See, Watson, this lists the titles of all his paintings and how much he sold them for and to whom."

"Pretty tidy sums too," said I amazed.

"Yes, they start off quite modestly at a hundred guineas then gradually increase in price. You see by the dates how his popularity increased over the years. Look, here he is now getting a thousand guineas a picture," said Holmes as he turned the pages.

"Good Lord!" I cried. "Look at that – two thousand guineas!"

"Ah, yes, but that's a one-off. The price drops again to a thousand for the next few entries. Ah, he is now getting twelve hundred, no, a thousand again. How interesting; the last few, which are of this year's date, are priced at a thousand or twelve hundred."

"He probably tries to sell at twelve hundred but is prepared to drop his price rather than lose the sale," I suggested.

"You are probably right, Watson. But why, three years ago, was one sold for a sum twice as much as his going rate?"

"Perhaps it was a bigger picture – twice as big, double the work."

Lestrade was becoming irritable; "This is all very interesting, gentlemen, but somewhat irrelevant."

"Sorry, Lestrade," said Holmes. "One cannot afford to neglect anything in an investigation."

"You would be better occupied turning your attention to the remaining pictures." Lestrade indicated several frames scattered haphazardly on the floor. The picture in each frame had been slashed to ribbons. "No doubt the murderer did that as part of her vengeance."

"How curious," muttered Holmes.

"What's curious about it? It seems to me a more natural revenge than painting his nose and wotsit with red paint," said Lestrade.

"There should be six pictures but there are only five."

"Why should there be six? How do you know how many there should be?"

"There are six listed in his book without a buyer or a price and if you look along the wall you will see quite distinctly in the dirt and dust on the floor the marks of six frames. Where is the sixth picture?"

Lestrade made a note. "I'll ask Mrs Massoni about that."

"I wonder which is the missing picture? See they all have titles – *The Martyrdom of St Sebastian, The Roman Baths at Philippi, David, Odalisques at Leisure -* "

"Have you finished, Mr Holmes? I want to go round to the house now and examine Mrs Massoni's wardrobe. I fully expect to find a match to this button."

"Sorry, Lestrade, but this case is quite fascinating. May I see Mrs Massoni?"

"Come down to Bow Street at four o'clock; I'll be there."

"Thank you. Come Watson."

"Remember - not a word to anyone about what you saw under the smock," urged Lestrade.

We were having dinner that evening.

"Did you see Mrs Massoni?" I asked.

"Yes. A very strong forthright lady. Very calm. She is perfectly capable of stabbing her husband although he was gross and she quite *petite*."

"Good Lord, you don't mean she actually did it?"

"I think not, Watson. She quietly and calmly insisted over and over that she did not do it. Furthermore, she said she had never, never, since the studio was contrived, been into it. I believe her. She admitted carrying a knife just as we had been told but denied that the knife sticking in her husband's body could be hers. She said the knife she carried in her sleeve would be found in the drawer of her dressing table. Lestrade admitted he had found one there."

"What about the button?"

"Mrs Massoni had no garment with a button remotely like the one Lestrade had found."

"So Lestrade has nothing to go on at all," said I, relieved that the poor lady appeared innocent.

"Nothing. But he is hoping to keep on at her until she confesses. It is an easier way than deducing the facts from clues."

"It is inhuman!" I protested.

"Your concern does you credit, Watson, you are always gallant where the fair sex is involved. But he may be right, we may have to look no further for our murderer."

"But you said you believed her!"

"Indeed. But in spite of the impression you convey to your loyal readers, I am not infallible."

At that moment there was a tap on the door and Mrs Hudson entered.

"A telegram just come for you, Mr Holmes."

"Thank you, Mrs Hudson, and the rabbit pie was excellent."

"It certainly was!" I agreed heartily. The good woman thanked us and discreetly withdrew. Holmes read the telegram and passed it to me saying "That should soothe your mind, Watson."

The wire was from Morrison the solicitor informing us that his client had been released and was now back at home. No accusations had been made.

"I certainly am relieved, Holmes. I did not like to think of that poor woman's sufferings; Lestrade can be a callous fellow. I'm glad she is well looked after by Morrison, he seems exceptionally caring of his client."

"Yes, I wonder why her affairs are looked after by a firm that specialises in mercantile machinery?" mused Holmes.

In the days that followed it became clear that Lestrade had no leads to follow and Holmes, having satisfied himself that his client was now no longer involved, took no further interest in the case. The public prints made a lot of huffing and puffing about the morals of the artist as several people came forward to declare various unpleasant things about Massoni's character. He appeared to have been a notorious libertine and was labelled corrupt and depraved. There was much discussion as to whether a man's morals should be condoned if he were an artistic genius. Some commentators said that the famous composer Mozart was an example of one who was a womaniser of dubious morals but whose music seemed to be inspired from above and the man could not be separated from his music. Others talked of Christopher Marlowe who, it seems, was a poet to rival Shakespeare but was a pederast and an atheist and was killed in one of a succession of drunken brawls. As opposed to these opinions, a faction claimed that Massoni was no genius at all but merely a fashionable painter who emulated Alma-Tadema in providing pictures of flimsily clad females under the pretence of painting classical themes. Nobody could cast any further light on the corpse having to suffer a painted red nose and the general opinion was that the purpose was to ridicule him.

After a couple of weeks other news displaced the artist's death and this bizarre affair slipped to the back of the public's memory.

*   *   *

Some two years later I was reading my morning paper when I chanced on a paragraph saying that two pictures by the late Gerald Fordun Massoni were to be sold at Bonhams Auction Rooms.

"I say, Holmes, remember the affair of the red-nosed artist?"

"Of course."

"Two of his pictures are coming up for auction. It says they are the first to come on the market since the death of the late lamented artist."

"As I recall, the artist's death was very far from being lamented at the time," said Holmes sardonically. "Good riddance to bad rubbish seemed to be the prevailing opinion. Does it say which pictures they are?"

"*Saturnalia at Caligula's Baths* and *Lonely Shepherd Boy.*"

"Really?" Holmes perked up and held out his hand. "May I read it?"

"There's little more than that," I said, handing over the paper.

"Very interesting," he mused. "Do you fancy a visit to Bonhams this morning, Watson?"

"Nothing would give me greater pleasure."

Thus later that morning we viewed the afore mentioned paintings at the Auction Rooms. The *Saturnalia* was a typical Roman scene of bodies decorously cavorting about amongst marble columns and seemed to me to be excellently painted with the figures executed in a very life-like manner. Any possible offence was avoided by the customary method of the naked forms having drapery fluttering around the bodies or posing them to hide any indiscretions. The

Shepherd Boy painting was a full length portrait of a handsome youth seated pensively on a rocky outcrop in a scene that was surely of some Biblical land.

When Holmes enquired of the vendor, we were told only that they were the property of a gentleman. The auctioneer did volunteer the opinion that they were totally unable to gauge the expected price the pictures would fetch as they were the first to come on to the open market.

"At the time of his death Massoni's work was fetching in the region of a thousand to twelve hundred guineas."

"And sometimes more, I fancy," said Holmes. "I have heard of two thousand guineas changing hands for one picture."

"Really? That must have been a private sale. I have not heard of those sort of figures ever for a Massoni. But now his *oeuvre* is limited there is no knowing to what heights the prices may go."

On leaving Bonhams Holmes decreed that we must now go and visit Mrs Massoni, for what purpose I could not guess and he would not say. All the way in the cab he was silently mulling over some deep thought.

When we reached Garrick House it all looked very much the same as two years previously. Mrs Massoni was in and agreed to receive us.

"This is a surprise, Mr Holmes."

"May I present my colleague Doctor Watson," said Holmes.
The lady was a little older than I had imagined but otherwise my vision of her seemed pretty accurate. How Lestrade could treat such a fair creature so wantonly and with so little cause I could not imagine.

After some inconsequential talk Holmes came to the point of our visit.

"I wonder if you still possess the account book in which your late husband kept details of all his pictures?" he asked.

"I really have no idea, Mr Holmes. You may find this hard to believe but I have left the studio just as when you were last here. I turned the key after the police investigations and have not ventured in there. As I told you, I had never entered that room before my husband's death and I have never entered it since. Come, I will take you round and you may seek for the book you mention."

We three went round to the rear of the building, that beautiful proportioned Georgian house ruined by the grotesque window enlargement. Again I wondered how a so-called artist could be so insensitive. The rear door, which two years ago had been somewhat obscure, was now almost covered with assorted greenery.

"Oh dear," said Mrs Massoni, "I did not realise it was all in such a state back here. I must get a gardener to come and deal with all this, especially as I am shortly going to sell up and move."

"You are moving? Too many sad memories here, perhaps?" said I sympathetically.

"I am to be re-married," she said crisply.

"Congratulations," I murmured, wondering who the lucky devil might be. Holmes had already attacked the foliage and with my assistance a way was quickly cleared. Holmes took the key and opened the door to the scene of the crime.

"I shall come in with you," said Mrs Massoni bravely. I took the lady's arm and gently led her in.

"How disappointing!" she cried. "From all the fuss in the newspapers I was expecting something far more sinister than this. It hardly looks like the den of an evil beast."

"I fear much that is gross has taken place here," said Holmes as he immediately went to the drawer where he knew the notebook should be. He gave a grunt of satisfaction as he withdrew the volume.

"As I thought," said he. "The picture on sale, the one called *Saturnalia at Caligula's Baths*, is the one priced here at two thousand guineas. I am gratified that my memory is so trustworthy." He went through the book turning the pages slowly, reading all the titles. "But no *Lonely Shepherd Boy*. May I borrow this book, Mrs Massoni?"

"You may keep it, Mr Holmes, I have no use for it."

"Perhaps it should be deposited at the Royal Academy so that the right authority will have a complete record of Mr Massoni's works. It would help in the case of forgeries and copies and so on," I suggested.

"Excellent idea, Watson," said Holmes. "It shall be done."

We took our farewell of Garrick House and, as Holmes had kept the cab, the driver was now told to take us to Woburn Square.

"Why are we going there, Holmes?" I asked.

"I wish to interview Mr Cedric Sneath who, I suspect, is the vendor of these two pictures."

Mr Sneath's house was a tall narrow one in a fine row set on one side of an elegant square near Regent's Park. This house certainly had not been ruined by crass alterations but remained handsome and well preserved. We were fortunate again in that Mr Sneath was at home and willing to speak to us. He was a mature, thin man with an aquiline nose and long, thin, tapering hands that were rarely at rest. Although smartly and conventionally dressed, he wore a colourful brocade waistcoat and was smoking a cigarette via an over-long cigarette holder. I presumed he was something of a *dilettante*. As a doctor it is an unfortunate ingrained habit of mine to carry out a mental instant diagnosis on first introduction, and Mr Sneath immediately confirmed my suspicions by almost immediately informing us he was a "martyr to his nerves."

"I understand you are selling two Massonis," said Holmes without ceremony after he had introduced himself as Henry Wheeler and me as Quentin Pyecrust. I am sure he chooses to bestow upon me these ludicrous pseudonyms through some warped sense of humour.

"That is correct. They are to be auctioned at Bonhams in two days time."

"I wonder if you would be prepared to accept an offer prior to the auction?" asked Holmes.

"I would certainly consider such an offer and if it exceeds the amount I am hoping to raise by auction then I would be strongly biased in favour of selling to you privately. What figures are you proposing?"

"I suggest two thousand guineas for the *Saturnalia* and one thousand for the other," said Holmes smoothly.

Mr Sneath laughed out loud. "My dear, Mr Wheeler, you can only be a dealer if you think I would accept such trifling amounts. I expect to raise ten times those sums at auction."

"No, I am not a dealer but a humble connoisseur. However, my resources are not infinite and those are highest sums I could pay," answered Holmes.

"Then you must lower your sights, sir. These are masterworks of the first order. They will command high prices and be much sought after."

"Then why are you selling them?" asked Holmes.

"That has nothing to do with you, sir!" snapped Sneath.

"I am sorry. You are quite right. That was an unwarranted question which I withdraw. I do apologise."

"Yes, well –" Sneath lamely tailed off, trembling with agitation.

"If it is not indelicate, might I ask if you bought the pictures from the artist himself or via a dealer?" continued Holmes.

"What? Oh – from the artist. Several years ago."

"Was he a personal friend of yours?"

"How dare you, sir!" Sneath almost exploded. "He was not! The man was a libertine, a philanderer of the basest kind. Did you not read the papers at the time of his death? The man was little better than a beast!"

I was shocked by this sudden outburst, obviously the man had something seriously amiss with his nervous system, perhaps a brain tumour. I sought to placate him.

"But surely the morals of a genius may be regarded in a different light from those of we common folk?" I suggested, remembering the comments in the newspapers at the time. Unfortunately this inflamed the poor fellow even more.

"Genius? Pshaw! Lewdness and debauchery! He was nothing but a foul coarse animal. He was worse – he was a satyr – a human goat. No wonder his murderer anointed his phallus with paint. No female of any class was safe anywhere near the man. God knows what his wife made of such a vile, corrupt, malign creature! Oh you must go! My nerves!"

I felt terrible at having roused the poor man and wondered what I should do to calm him. Out of the corner of my eye I glimpsed Holmes doing something with a piece of paper, he seemed to be ignoring the outburst altogether.

"Could I suggest sitting yourself down and taking some deep breaths? And perhaps you have some brandy in the house?" said I.

"It's all right," gasped Sneath, "I'm sorry. I get these bouts of anger. It's my nerves. You incensed me. You were not to know that I hated the man. I'm sorry. There. I'm calmer now."

"We will take our leave now, Mr Sneath. I do apologise for any distress. Perhaps we will meet at the auction? Will you be there?" asked Holmes.

"Most certainly I will be there. I cannot wait to learn how much the pictures will bring."

We made a few further commonplace remarks then left.

"What an alarming fellow," I remarked when we were back in the comfort of 221B Baker Street. "Very highly strung."

Holmes had found the notes he had made on the Massoni death two years previously and gave a chuckle.

"Yes, and he smokes exactly the same type of cigarette as the man who visited Massoni's studio."

"How do you know that?" I asked.

"While you were baiting the man with your theories of morals and genius, I took a small sample of ash from his ashtray and wrapped it up in a twist of paper. Now I have had opportunity to analyse it I see from my notes the ash I found two years ago on the floor of the studio is exactly the same."

"That only proves he visited the studio, it may not have been on the day the artist died," I pointed out.

"That is quite correct, Watson. But that is not the only clue gained from our visit. Did you remark the rather ornate waistcoat that Sneath affected?"

"Of course. But a dandified waistcoat is nothing rare."

"Not rare – but not commonplace I think. I have been perusing this account book of Massoni's. I can find no painting titled *The Lonely Shepherd Boy*. However, you will no doubt recall that five pictures were ruined beyond recognition at the time of the murder."

"That is so, but you said there should be six, one was missing. Are you saying that *The Lonely Shepherd Boy* is the missing one?"

"I find among the last six titles, *David*. Correct me if I am wrong, Watson, but I recall from my youthful bible studies that David was a shepherd boy."

"That's right, he was the one who slew Goliath with a shot from a sling."

"I think Sneath's picture is the one stolen from Massoni's studio on the day of his death. Obviously the thief was unaware of the picture's official title and named it as a description of the subject. If we were to look carefully, we should probably find evidence of the subject being David."

"I am sure you are right," I breathed.

"Will you be able to go to the auction?"

"Thursday afternoon at 3? Yes I am free. I would love to go."

"Then I would be infinitely obliged if you would do so. I have another engagement just at that time which will prevent me."

When Thursday arrived I set out for the auction with great excitement. I had never previously attended an auction except when I was in the army when it was commonplace to auction off the effects of some poor soul who had been slain.

But the purpose of those auctions was not to obtain the lots as cheaply as possible but to provide for the poor chap's dependents. This was a far different thing, for myself, not being one who could afford or desired expensive works of art, it would be a new experience. Holmes left the house at the same time looking very smart but, as is his way, he did not confide whither he was bound.

The Auction Room was well filled and looking at the catalogue I saw some 134 lots were on offer, Sneath's pictures being the final two, obviously the stars of the collection. Sneath himself was there, in a waistcoat even more gaudy than the one he had worn when we called on him. He appeared in a jovial mood and was obviously known to several persons as he chatted amiably to a small group.

The auction started and I was amazed at the rapidity with which each lot was knocked down. Most of the time I could barely see who was bidding and was never clear which man had won the lot. The prices raised did not seem very high, ranging from about thirty pounds up to, at the most, £500. Certainly not in the range that Sneath was talking about. Very swiftly the sale reached the climax. The *Shepherd Boy* picture was held up. I could now see that among the various accoutrements slung about the boy's body, a horn, an oriental flask and so on, was something I realised was the sling used by David to slay Goliath. Holmes had undoubtedly hit on the whereabouts of the stolen painting.

"Lot 133. This is a major work by the late Gerald Fordun Massoni *Lonely Shepherd Boy*. I am going to start the bidding at five hundred guineas. Who will start?" asked the auctioneer. There was a silence. "Come gentlemen, do I hear five hundred?" A long pause. "Very well, four hundred?" Apparently he had a bid. "Thank you. Now who will raise me to four-fifty. I have four-fifty, can I say five? We are at four-fifty. Will nobody offer five? Is that final? Four hundred and fifty guineas? Any advance on four hundred and fifty guineas?"

I looked over to where Sneath was seated, his face ashen and his eyes bulging. The auctioneer continued. "Going at four hundred and fifty guineas – sold." He banged down his gavel. "We come now to the final lot in this sale. A masterpiece by the late Gerald Fordun Massoni *Saturnalia at Caligula's Baths*. Please take a good look at this wonderful painting which is probably the finest example of this artist's work to have been offered to the public in open sale. I must warn you that there is a reserve on this picture. Who will start the bidding at a thousand guineas?" An audible wince went round the hall. "Come gentlemen, this is a work of art of much higher calibre than anything previously offered in this sale. Who will start me off? Very well, who will make any offer? I have two hundred down here, thank you, I will take increases of a hundred guineas. Do I hear three hundred? Three. I have three. Who will give me four? I call for a bid of four hundred?"

And there the bidding seemed to stick; nobody was prepared to go higher, until somebody offered four-fifty which the auctioneer deemed an insult and warned again that there was a reserve which was obviously much higher than anything bid so far. People were now drifting away and the auctioneer announced that as the reserve had not been reached the lot was withdrawn. He thanked everybody and announced the next sale which was to be of ceramics and glassware and it was all over. I looked at Sneath, then leapt to my feet as he appeared to have collapsed with a small group gathered round. I pushed my way through.

"Give way, I am a doctor," I asserted.

I did the usual checks and his pulse was strong. I surmised it was a simple faint or swoon brought on by the shock of not selling his picture. The only thing I had with me was my hip-flask of brandy and I tried to force a little into his mouth and then loosened his clothing.

"Give air, please, stand aside," I ordered and the group broke up and dispersed. The hall swiftly became quite empty except for the officials of the auction and a small knot of people who were collecting and paying for their purchases. Sneath eventually came round and started a peculiar moaning.

"What shall I do? What shall I do?"

"Calm yourself, sir. I am a doctor. You have had a faint. You will recover. Take your time."

He did not appear to recognise me as the man with the ludicrous appellation who had visited him two days previously. In fact he seemed oblivious of his surroundings altogether, simply moaning the same words over and over.

"What shall I do? What shall I do?"

Suddenly there was a flurry of activity at the entrance and who should stride in but Sherlock Holmes closely followed by Inspector Lestrade and two police constables.

"There he is, Lestrade," pointed Holmes.

"Cedric Sneath, I arrest you for the murder of Gerald Fordun Massoni. You need not say anything but if you do it can be used in evidence," said Lestrade.

All Sneath said was "What shall I do? What shall I do?" and he was led away still mumbling.

It was some days later that Holmes asked me to accompany him to the prison where Lestrade had invited him.

"Welcome, Mr Holmes, Doctor," Lestrade greeted us. "Sneath has asked to see you. It's all right. He is well recovered. I think he had some sort of brainstorm but he has had every care from the prison doctor and he seems to be on an even keel now. I told him that his arrest was due to clever sleuthing on your part and he said he wanted you here when he made his confession. This he now wants to do and I have a short-hand reporter ready to take it down. Come this way, please."

We were taken to an interview room where we sat with the short-hand writer. Sneath was brought in by two warders. I was relieved to see that he appeared restored to health. He smiled weakly when he saw us both.

"Ah, I understand now. You visited me pretending to be buyers."

"A necessary ploy. I am Sherlock Holmes and this is my colleague Dr Watson."

"It becomes clearer to me now," said Sneath with a shrug.

"You are not here to converse. Will you tell us what happened at Massoni's studio two years ago?" asked Lestrade.

"I will, but first I must go back to 1892. I am a collector of artistic erotica. You understand what I mean?"

"You mean you peddle filthy pictures," sneered Lestrade.

"I will not debate that matter with you. I admired the paintings of Massoni, I thought he was a great talent. Like others he specialised in depicting historical scenes but with a faithfulness previously unknown. He was becoming very popular as respectable people could hang his pictures with a clear conscience. However, as a collector of erotica I recognised that there was an element of titillation in his work. I was sure this was a deliberate intention and went to see him. I wanted him to paint me a picture on his usual lines but make it more accurate. These ancient Romans were not refined like in his paintings – his figures were really respectable modern people in tasteful fancy-dress. I wanted him to show a real Roman orgy – a saturnalia."

"In other words, Massoni's pictures were not hot enough for you," snarled Lestrade.

"Massoni agreed to paint such a picture but said it would ruin his reputation and that I must keep it hidden in my home. He also demanded twice his normal fee which was a thousand guineas and insisted on it in advance. So I paid him two thousand guineas and awaited the picture."

"More money than sense," Lestrade threw in gratuitously.

"Three months later I received a message to say my picture was ready and I went to collect it. Well you have seen the painting. It was one of his usual style. A bit of titillation but no orgy as I had ordered. When I complained he just laughed and said 'Take it or leave it'. I was beside myself with anger. I could have bought that sort of picture for far less money – I could have got an Alma-Tadema or an Edwin Longsden Long for two thousand guineas. So we had a row and in the middle of this argument he did something strange and appalling. He lifted up the hem of his smock and exposed his private parts. As no doubt you now know, it was his custom to wear no clothes under his painting habit, he was quite naked under there. He wiggled himself and laughed, taunting me, saying 'Did you expect me to paint these?'

"It seems to me you were all a bunch of perverts," commented Lestrade. "Are you getting all this down?" He turned to the short-hand writer who nodded. "We might have to clean it up a bit for the court. And you two can stop smirking as well." He glared at the warders. "Go on."

"Well I left, taking the picture. What else could I do? The years went by and I saw that Massoni's fame was increasing. I knew that my picture was also appreciating but it was still worth nowhere near the price I had paid. Then I had a brainwave. Massoni was a lazy man and only painted a few pictures per year, hence his increasing value. I worked out that his complete *oeuvre* was probably under fifty or sixty pictures and, if there were no more to come, these existing pictures, including mine, would leap in value. So I determined to kill him."

"Let me be clear, please," Holmes spoke for the first time. "Your motive for killing Massoni was simply so that the value of your painting would increase?"

"Not only increase – soar."

"Go on," commanded Lestrade.

"So three years had gone by; I did not even know if Massoni still lived at the same address. I just bought a knife and went there. It was in the evening, about eight o'clock but still sunny and bright, the sun had not yet fallen. I did not knock, I simply tried the door, which was unlocked, and walked in. The knife I held behind my back. I never considered that Massoni may be absent or other people may be there, a model, friends visiting. I suppose if there had been I would have made an excuse and left, I don't know. But there was nobody. Just Massoni relaxing with a cigar in his chair. I think he had been working on a canvas as he was wearing his smock and he had his palette to hand. I assume the fading light had defeated him He turned and regarded me without surprise. He recognised me straight away, leaped to his feet and said 'Have you come to ask me to paint some more of this?' and the blackguard lifted up his smock again. The man was a foul satyr – he exposed himself priapic – I think he was aroused by his own paintings. I don't know. I just knew I had to kill him. And I did. I stabbed him. The look on his face was better than any picture I have ever seen. I laid him out flat on his back and suddenly had this idea to paint his nose – if he acted like a buffoon I would adorn him like one. His palette was there with fresh paint. So I made him into a clown. Then I went further and painted that loathsome tool that he had pointed at me in derision. I felt very satisfied. I was about to leave when I saw the paintings propped against the wall – six new pictures – they would devalue mine so I slashed them beyond recognition or restoration."

"But not all of them," Holmes said gently.

"No, as I was doing it I realised that I was destroying the work of a genius. A loathsome, horrible, vile human being but a major artist. The *Shepherd Boy* painting appealed to me so I decided, not only to save him from the knife, but to take him home. As a parting shot I drove the knife once more into the villain's chest and left it. I deemed it wise to wait a while before trying to sell the paintings but events overtook me. I was plunged into a financial mess that meant I had to sell everything – if I could get £20,000 I would be in the clear. I thought the two pictures would bring in the best part of that so put them to auction. I was completely wrong. Nobody wants Massonis now. They are worth far less than when they were painted. Massoni twisted me when I commissioned the *Saturnalia* and now he's managed to twist me again from the grave."

The poor fellow sat hunched, staring at the floor. My heart went out to him, villain though he was. What strange by-ways our minds can take us when we become possessed on a course of action. Then I recalled how his deed had almost ensnared an innocent woman and my sympathy receded.

"Well that seems to be that. Have you anything to add?" asked Lestrade. Sneath shook his head. "Take him away. And you two – keep all this to yourselves." This was to the two warders guarding Sneath. "I don't want to hear about any sniggering tale-telling in the canteen."

After the room was cleared Lestrade said "Well, Mr Holmes, you were in the right of it again. How did you get on to him?"

"Firstly the two different types of tobacco ash which made me suspect a second man had recently been in the room."

"Oh yes, your famous monograph," replied Lestrade.

"Then the button you offered as a clue. I took a tracing of it and placed it in my notes. When I met Sneath and saw his penchant for fancy waistcoats with elaborate buttons I dug it out. While Watson was watching him at the auction I went to his house and, under the guise of a close friend, told the maid that her master had left an important paper in one of his waistcoats and had prevailed upon me to fetch it. As he could not recall which one of the dozen garments he was wearing at the time would I go to his wardrobe and search through them. This I did while she stood by and soon saw a waistcoat with buttons of the design I sought. Needless-to-say that garment lacked one of its buttons."

"Brilliant, Holmes," I congratulated him.

"Just a minute," said Lestrade. "The ash and the button may prove he was in the room but it doesn't prove he stabbed the artist."

"No, that's true," I agreed.

"When we visited Sneath he was in a highly agitated state and he said that Massoni had got his just deserts, was a figure of fun and deserved to have his phallus bedaubed."

"His phallus?"

"Artists and historians prefer the term to describe a gentleman's private parts."

"Oh, his wotsit."

"As you so astutely kept that information from everybody, Lestrade, only the detail of the red nose becoming common knowledge, I knew that only a handful of men knew about it, we three, and the murderer."

"He gave himself away!" I cried.

"Well he's confessed all now," said Lestrade with satisfaction. "To be honest, the whole lot of them seem like a pack of loonies to me."

"There is one point on which you may be able to satisfy my curiosity, Lestrade."

"What's that, Mr Holmes?"

"Massoni's wife. When I interviewed her she was under suspicion of murder but she was not at all concerned or agitated."

"But she was innocent, Holmes!" I protested.

"Of course, Watson, but you tell me of an innocent woman who admits to hating her husband, carrying a knife and wishing him dead yet can calmly sit protesting her innocence without some trace of a fear that she may be falsely found guilty."

"That's easily explained, Mr Holmes. She had a cast iron alibi. She spent the entire twelve hours, from 6pm to 6am the next morning when the body was found, in the company of a man – her lawyer Morrison who was her lover, or as arty folk and historians would say, her paramour."

"So that's why he was involved so early in the morning," I exclaimed. "Well at least that good lady will find happiness; she told us she was shortly to re-marry."

"That's right, Doctor, I have heard that."

"Judging by the little I saw of him, Morrison seemed a sound chap, he will make her a good husband."

"Oh," said Lestrade, "she's not to marry him. She's marrying an Italian count she met on a pleasure cruise."

The Singular Adventure
of
THE INTERMITTENT JIGSAW PUZZLE

IT was a cloudy spring day in the year 1890. Holmes was crouched over his microscope indulging in one of his interminable scientific experiments. I was idly flicking through a newspaper.

"You know, Holmes, we are very fortunate to live in such interesting and progressive times." These thoughts were prompted by an article I was reading in the paper. "The progress in scientific matters, manufacturing innovations and so on is increasing at a phenomenally rapid rate. It says here how much electricity is contributing to new inventions and talks about something called carbon arc welding where by means of an electric spark you can actually fuse two separate pieces of metal into one."

"Indeed. I hear the Americans have invented a death chair worked by electricity to execute criminals," said Holmes as he peered into his microscope.

"It says here that a man called Fink has invented a lens that fits on the eyeball and corrects deficiencies of vision. Amazing! The person can see clearly yet does not appear to wear spectacles or other artificial aids as the lenses are totally unobtrusive."

"I fear we must defer further discussion on the nation's progression as it seems we have a visitor," said Holmes as Mrs Hudson entered.

"A lady to see you, Mr Holmes," she announced as she proffered a visiting card. Holmes glanced at it as he asked Mrs Hudson to show in his client.

The lady who entered was a fine specimen of womanhood of about thirty years of age. She was dressed very tastefully in the latest fashion and, unlike many of Holmes' female clients, was very much self assured and self composed.

"Do take that chair, Miss Dysart. I am Sherlock Holmes and this is my colleague Dr Watson. How may I help you?"

"Please take a look at this." The lady handed a small flat piece of wood to Holmes which he promptly examined with his lens.

"It appears to be the corner of a dissection. Obviously a photograph has been mounted on to a sheet of plywood and then divided up by means of a saw. See on the back there are pencil markings to guide the track of the blade. What is remarkable about it?"

"It was put through my door several weeks ago. Since then, at intervals of one a week, I have received further pieces." Out of a paper bag she tipped several more pieces.

Holmes spread out the pieces and eagerly scanned them. I immediately recognised that these were parts of one of the jigsaw puzzles that had gained in popularity in recent years. Another aspect of the progress in inventions. When I was a boy I learned my geography of the British Isles from a wooden map dissected into the counties. It was great fun to assemble the parts to form the complete country thus being a way of teaching that was an unobtrusive pleasure. Since those days mechanisation has brought many kinds of automatic saws into use and I understand that these puzzles are now being cut with a treadle saw and as a result can be made much cheaper than hitherto fore. Today it is possible to make wooden puzzles from all kinds of pictures and photographs.

"Ten pieces. Do you recall in what order they were sent?" asked Holmes.

"The four corners were the first ones although I cannot say precisely the sequence. There is no doubt as to the most recent. That is what has caused me to come to you. At first when these pieces started coming in I thought it was probably some kind of tease from my friend Penny – Penelope Boughton – as we often exchange trinkets and amusing trifles."

"But you are sure these pieces are not from your friend?"

"I am positive. I have challenged her about them. She denies all knowledge of them."

"I say," I interrupted, "perhaps it's one of those advertising stunts. You get one of these each week and when you finally put them all together it reads 'Buy Wilson's Pork Sausages' or something of that sort."

"Do you think so?" asked Miss Dysart eagerly.

"Ingenious suggestion, Watson. Perhaps you could have a career in persuasion. Judging by the way London is desecrated with advertising posters there must be a good living to be made out of it. However, I do not think you are right about this picture. See, although it is far from complete, if such a message were inscribed we would surely have small parts of letters visible on at least some of the pieces."

"Well we do not know the size of the complete picture, Holmes. We only have a handful of pieces. Some of these puzzles can have a hundred pieces or more."

"True, Watson, but as we are obviously looking at a photograph I think the likelihood is that we should expect the complete size to be one of the conventional photographic sizes such as plate or half-plate. Let us assume that we are looking at a half-plate which is 6½" by 4¼". So far we have ten pieces. There are the corners; if I place them apart at roughly those dimensions we can see that our ten pieces cover approximately half the area. I think, perhaps, we have roughly half the picture here and the perpetrator has deliberately sent alternate pieces so that none can be linked together."

"Mr Holmes, this week this piece arrived. You will find that you can attach it to that one there." Miss Dysart handed him the piece and indicated one on the table.

"Thank you, madam. Indeed you are right."

"If you look closely you will see why I am sure this is not a tease from a friend. I am positive no friend could be so cruel!" cried Miss Dysart.

Holmes examined the pair of linked pieces. "It is now clearly a tombstone and I can just make out the name on the stone. Why – it is Rebecca Dysart. A relative perhaps?"

"Rebecca Dysart is my name, Mr Holmes."

"But your card proclaims you as Victoria Dysart."

"I was named Rebecca Victoria Dysart. My mother and grandmother were both called Rebecca and it was important to my mother that I was named so too. I don't know why, but my father hated the name vehemently and insisted that I was called Victoria after Her Majesty. As my mother was called Rebecca while she was alive, it was natural to refer to me by my second name Victoria, to avoid confusion."

"I see. So your mother is dead."

"Yes, she died when I was twenty years old, eight years ago. You may have heard of Dulwich cream slipware? It is quite popular in some households. The pottery was founded by my maternal grandfather and as he had no sons to pass it on to he was very pleased when Mama met and married William Dysart. He took his son-in-law into the business and it proved a very wise thing to do because my father built up the business to a level my grandfather could only have dreamed about. By the time my father died some six months ago the firm employed a hundred men and exported to over two dozen different countries throughout the Empire."

"So are you now the owner of that enterprise?" asked Holmes.

"I have one brother, Bertram, who manages the business. I have nothing to do with the running of the factory but I have shares in the company providing me with a very respectable income."

"You are not married. Do you have your own establishment?"

"Yes. My father owned a house in Dulwich and I preferred to go on living there after his death. Although a little too big for a single lady, it is well placed in College Road with very pleasant neighbours. But, to be frank, gentlemen, I do not expect to remain a spinster all my life. The fact I have not married is not through a lack of suitors but a desire to remain with my father who missed my mother terribly."

"Tell me, Miss Dysart, you say these pieces have come singly each week. Do they come through the post?"

"No. Each one has been wrapped in a twist of newspaper and pushed through the letter box at night."

"At night, you say?"

"I presume so as they have been found on the mat in the morning and were certainly not there when the last of the staff went to bed."

"Perhaps one of your staff is responsible," I suggested.

"Of course I have thought of that but, whilst I cannot of course be certain, I do not think so. My lady's maid Sophie and I are very close and there is little that goes on in my household of which she is unaware."

"Hum," mused Holmes, "are they always pushed through on the same night of the week?"

"No, the nights vary."

"But always only one per week?"

"Yes."

"We now have eleven pieces. If my assumption is correct, we are but half way through building up this complete picture. From now on I think we will find that the pieces all begin to interlink. That means we have some ten weeks or thereabouts before the full picture is revealed. At present I do not think I can do anything until we have more of the picture which I expect will reveal the purpose of subjecting you to this tortuous procedure. Take heart, Miss Dysart, the whole thing may be totally harmless, there may be no sinister purpose in it at all."

"But the tombstone with my name on it? I am sure that is some sort of warning to me," protested the lady, near to tears.

"It does appear to bode ill," agreed Holmes, "but it is too early, as yet, to establish any facts in the case. As my friend, Watson, will tell you, it is not possible to formulate theories until one has the facts of the matter in place. I beg you not to distress yourself, Miss Dysart. You have done the correct thing in coming to me; there is no better man in all London. Please accept my assurance that nothing will happen to harm you before the photograph is complete. Before then I expect to have solved your mystery. I need to keep the pieces here so as each piece arrives would you pass on to me?"

"Certainly, Mr Holmes. My mind is much relieved. I feared you would not take my problem seriously." The lady left us with a much lighter heart than on her arrival.

"Can you make anything of it, Holmes?" I asked.

"No, Watson. But I hope a little patience will reveal a little light."

As forecast, over the following weeks the collection of jigsaw pieces increased at weekly intervals and Holmes devoted much study to the photograph as it was gradually assembled. Meanwhile, of course, he had other cases to occupy him but the jigsaw was left permanently on display on a side table and from time to time I often caught him staring at it. Eventually, when there was little of the picture left missing, we were brought the expected weekly piece by Mr Bertram Dysart the brother of our client.

"My sister has great faith in you, Mr Holmes," said our visitor. "For my part I think it is a lot of fuss about nothing."

"What do you suppose is the purpose, Mr Dysart? Why should a person or persons unknown take this extraordinary procedure of delivering a dissected photograph piece by piece?"

"I've no idea, Mr Holmes. I agree it is most peculiar but I cannot see that there is much harm in it. Victoria seems to think it indicates that she is in great danger in some way."

"I fear she may be right, Mr Dysart. I would not seek to alarm her unnecessarily though. I hope to get to the bottom of all this before any such danger manifests itself."

"You alarm me, Mr Holmes. I had dismissed the whole affair as a harmless prank."

"Perhaps it may turn out to be so, but to send a picture of a gravestone with a person's name on it that bears the same name as oneself is a little unsettling, would you not say?"

"I have brought the latest piece myself because I was apprehensive that Victoria was being encouraged by irresponsible persons but, having met you, I realise that you are in earnest."

"I am in deadly earnest, Mr Dysart. May I have the piece you have brought?"

Holmes slotted the new piece into place in the puzzle. "Ah, I think we are wanting but two more pieces and the picture will be complete. Have a look, Mr Dysart."

"Good heavens, it is quite a pleasant scene. A country churchyard. I had the idea from Victoria that the picture would appear malevolent in some way."

"Oh, no, not at all. It is, as you say, a pleasant vista; the sort of picture a visitor might take home as a reminder of a stay in the country. But look more closely at the area surrounding the missing pieces. You see, above the gravestone?"

"I see. There are some hands resting on top of the stone and what appears to be part of a coat."

"There will be a man standing behind the stone. Not only are the hands resting on the stone, the position of the arms suggests he is almost embracing it. When we have the two remaining pieces the man will be displayed in his entirety."

"But who is this man?" asked Dysart.

"There you have me, sir. I presume the whole process is to delay revealing who the sender is until the final moment."

"You mean the sender of the pieces will be the man depicted in the picture?"

"That is possible. But the obvious conclusion is that the revelation of the man's face will be of the utmost significance to Miss Dysart. If it be not he himself then obviously there is some close connection. There is also a close connection with your sister as her name is so clearly delineated on the stone."

Dysart was visibly shaken. "I am glad I came to see you in person, Mr Holmes. No wonder my sister is so upset over this affair. It is most sinister. What do you propose to do?"

"Well, Mr Dysart, now you have brought the latest piece thus completing the picture but for the centre perhaps you would describe it to us?"

"What? Well – it is a photograph taken on a summer's day. The scene shows a country churchyard with a portion of the church on the left. On the right is a thatched cottage. There are some trees, then a vista of open country. The churchyard has tombstones dotted about, many of them ancient judging from their inclinations. There is a scythe leaning against the church wall and it looks as if the photograph were taken during mowing as most of the grass is still long but that around the stone in the centre – the focus of the picture – there it has been cleared. I think that is about all I could say about it."

"Excellent, you have picked up all the points of importance. My intention is to find the churchyard shown here and pay it a visit."

Both Dysart and myself gaped at Holmes.

"Holmes," I protested, "there are tens of thousands of churches in the country, how can you possibly find the right one?"

"We have a few useful clues in the picture. It is, as you, Mr Dysart, rightly point out, situated in the countryside, therefore it is not in a town or city. Thus we can immediately eliminate half the churches in the country. Take a look at the section of building showing on the left of the picture."

"I see it," said Dysart eagerly, as we three poured over the photograph.

"Do you observe that there is no corner? The building is obviously round."

"A round tower, you mean?" cried I.

"Just so. And note the construction of it."

"It looks as though it is made from large pebbles. Certainly not stones or bricks."

"Very observant of you, Mr Dysart. It is indeed a round tower constructed from flint stones. A type of building unique to one particular area of this country."

"Norfolk!" I cried. "I remember when we took our holiday there. You were very interested in the church architecture."

"Correct, Watson. These towers appear on churches all over East Anglia, the majority in Norfolk and a lesser number in Suffolk."

"Excellent, Holmes!" I cried.

"But there will be hundreds of churches in East Anglia," protested Dysart.

"Yes, sir, there are approximately a thousand churches in Norfolk alone, but only one in ten of those have round flint towers. So you see, from the tens of thousands of churches in the country we have, by looking at this picture alone, narrowed our field down to one hundred."

"Amazing!" said Dysart.

"Even so, Holmes," I pointed out, "one would still have to visit each parish to look at its church before finding this particular one. Although possible it would take months whereas we have only two more weeks before the picture is completed."

"Correct, Watson, but I think we can squeeze a little more juice from this scene. Pray take my lens and examine the thatched cottage on the right." I did as I was bid. "Well?"

"A thatched cottage, Holmes," was all I could say, returning the lens.

"Thatched with reed, Watson. Most cottages are thatched with straw. Sometimes with heather, sometimes with reeds. It usually depends on the readily available material close at hand. Reed is very common in Norfolk, especially in fenland and estuary areas, as you should know from our foray there some years ago."

"But as you say, it is commonplace, there will be many such areas spread about the county. It hardly narrows the field."

"No, in itself it is not very useful but it confirms my other deductions and will assist in my further ones."

"I am dazzled," said Dysart in wonder.

"Permit me to dazzle you a little more, Mr Dysart. You have pointed out to us the vista of open country. Do you not observe an area of higher ground in the distance?"

"Yes I see that, but is that important?"

"The county of Norfolk is notoriously flat. I believe the highest point in the county is no more than 300 feet above sea level. Therefore such elevations as we see here are particularly prominent on contour maps. As you may know, towers are invariably built on the west end of a church, therefore we can tell that this hill or hillock is situated to the west of our location. Unfortunately, as camera lenses vary in their focal lengths, it is not possible to estimate the distance between hill and church in any way but tracing the general direction should be sufficient. With the aid of a detailed map I hope to pinpoint all the possibilities and visit each in turn. I shall be departing tomorrow and I have permitted myself a week to carry out the task. The situation will not become critical for a further week as we have two more pieces to arrive before the photograph is entire."

Our visitor left reeling with wonder. I doubt if his everyday business of manufacturing and exporting cream slipware pottery often brought him into the compass of an analytical mind such as Holmes'.

"You will come with me, Watson?"

"Of course, Holmes, if you desire it."

"We will cover the ground twice as fast if we divide our resources."

Holmes had marked some six areas of high ground that he deduced conformed to the topography of the area we sought and methodically set out a system we were to follow. Taking the first area he made a sweep on the map eastwards of the high ground and noted the positions of the churches as depicted on the map. We then established our headquarters at the largest settlement within the sweep and divided the area in two sections from that base. Taking one section each we hired a boy with a pony and trap to take us from village to village, church to church, systematically covering our own area. We had lists of village names which we struck off when we had viewed the church. Essential to our campaign was to show, at every available opportunity, the copies of the photograph that Holmes had had made to locals in the areas we visited in the hope that somebody may recognise it. Each evening we returned to our base and exchanged our information which was marked off on the master plan.

Thus in that way we combed through the countryside. It was a succession of long, arduous, tiresome and frustrating days. Most often, on approaching the location of a church and immediately seeing from a distance that it had a square tower, I could cross it off my list at once. At others my heart would leap up as I discovered a round tower but on close inspection it was not the one we sought. It was a frustrating business as most of the churches were far from each other and the connections were via small winding country lanes. Most days I managed no more than six or seven churches. I presume Holmes found much the same conditions on his inspections.

Once we had exhausted the entire neighbourhood of one base we moved to the next designated area and started the whole process again. Had we the time available to us, I am certain we could have viewed every single church in Norfolk by these means. However, time was of the essence and even by stretching our allotted week to ten days, a rate of twelve churches a day crossed off the list meant we would only cover some 120 churches out of the thousand or so available to us. I could only hope that Holmes' deductions were correct and that we would sooner, rather than later, find the one we sought.

It was on the fourth day when I had a stroke of luck. I had found a round-towered flint church which again, alas, had proved not to be the one we sought, but in the churchyard a man was digging a grave. He was the sexton, a man of well over fifty years of age. I showed him the photograph to enquire if he recognised the locale. He pondered a good while then said "No, I do not recognise the place but that is a Swaffham scythe." He explained that agricultural tools varied depending on the place where they were made, and what may appear to be two identical rakes will, on close inspection, reveal various differences unique to the maker. Apparently over the years these differences become part of the essential style of the tool and can be recognised on a regional basis.

"Now that scythe," said he, "is definitely from the Swaffham area. Take a look at the snaith. Snaiths always have a double curve but the Swaffham one is straighter than most and the beard on the chine is less cut away. Oh aye, that's definitely a Swaffham scythe."

"So this church is in or near Swaffham?" I excitedly sought confirmation.

"Now, sir, that I did not say. I said the scythe was made in that vicinity."

"But there is a very good chance that a scythe will be employed in the area where it was made?"

"Aye, sir, in the olden days you could be sure that a man bought all his tools locally. Why, see these spades? I've had them nigh on forty years and they was made by the village blacksmith that we had in those days. Him and the wood turner used to make spades between them. But now, with the railways come, you can buy spades from a catalogue and have them sent from Lord knows where. But you don't know what you're getting. I reckon a man needs to try the tools first. With a scythe especially. It should be made specially for your height. You would be a foolish man to buy a scythe without seeing if it fit you."

I thought this information about the scythe pictured leaning against the church wall was a good omen and was eager to dash back to our headquarters to inform Holmes. But, of course, he would be still out in the field until much later so I decided to carry on with my planned day but secretly sure that I was looking in the wrong area entirely.

When we met up for our meal that night I could tell Holmes was flagging in spite of his efforts to conceal it.

"Well, Watson, the good thing about not finding our church is that our field of search is now much narrower," he said with assumed cheerfulness.

"I think we should try Swaffham, Holmes," I said.

"Swaffham, why? That is the last on the list. I did not draw up this list in an arbitrary manner, Watson, it is carefully selected with the order based on probability."

I then explained about my encounter with the sexton.

"Excellent, Watson, it is the only clue we have gained. Do you think the man knew his business? He was not some country dotard?"

"I am sure he is right about the tool, Holmes. But whether it has remained in the same area that it was made is something nobody knows until we find it. But I think we should switch operations to Swaffham. Time is running out on us."

"Very good, Watson. Swaffham it is. We move off in the morning."

On the second day in the Swaffham area at the village of Thorpe St Napier I found the church and its graveyard with the elusive grave. The headstone read in its entirety *Rebecca Dysart, born 1835 died 1863*. There was no other writing. I sought out the vicar and made arrangements for Holmes to interview him the following day.

The Rev Artemis Johnstone immediately informed us that although he had not been the incumbent back in 1863, having arrived some years later, he had the parish record book to hand and hoped that he could be of some small assistance in whatever matter we sought his co-operation.

"Firstly, may we find the entry for the burial of Rebecca Dysart?" asked Holmes.

"I have already done so, Mr Holmes." He opened the book at the necessary page. The entry told no more than the bald statement on the gravestone: *14th November 1863 Rebecca Dysart aged 28 years buried.*

"Are there any more entries with the name Dysart?" asked Holmes.

"I do not know, Mr Holmes. It is certainly not a name known in this area. Please feel free to examine the book for yourself."

Holmes ran his fingers backwards up the entries and eventually found what he sought.

"Here we are *14th June 1856 William Dysart bachelor aged 25 married Rebecca Howard spinster aged 21.*"

"Ah, now that is very interesting, Mr Holmes. As no doubt you will have noticed, the name Howard is prominent in the records. The Howards are a long established local family. They claim to be related to the Dukes of Norfolk though I cannot say as to the truth of that. But there have been Howards in this parish for centuries."

"Are there any elderly Howards living in the parish now?"

"Indeed. In the cottage next to the church is old Mrs Carr. She is the widow of Jabez Carr. The Carrs are another old Thorpe St Napier family. Before marriage Mrs Carr was a Howard, she may well have the information you require."

We all made our way to the cottage and found Mrs Carr, a very ancient lady, but not too ancient to be highly suspicious of Holmes and his questions. It soon became clear, however, that it was not Holmes who was under suspicion but the vicar. She did not wish to reveal any family secrets before the vicar. The vicar who, no doubt, was accustomed to his parishioner's hostility made an excuse and left. From then on, after getting Holmes' assurance that he would not say anything to the vicar, Mrs Carr was very free with her answers. As with many old people she kept straying from the point and we had to endure quite a lot of side ramblings before Holmes could elicit the information that he sought. I will spare the reader the many diversions and paraphrase the gist of the story she had to tell.

Mrs Carr's mother and Rebecca Dysart's mother were cousins. Rebecca was a daughter in the more well to do branch of the Howard family. The future Mrs Carr was in the peasant branch. Rebecca Howard, renowned as a local beauty, had many admirers and was considered an excellent marriage prospect by the families of the district. One day from nowhere into the village rode William Dysart, a young man of stunning good looks and considerable charm. The hearts of local young ladies were thus set a flutter, and, as he appeared to have wealth to go with his attributes so the heads of their parents were also quite turned. Many a young lady set her cap at William Dysart but he chose Rebecca Howard. She was madly in love with him but her parents did not consider him a suitable match and Mr Howard refused permission to wed. The young couple defied him and were married in the village church. But they were shunned by the villagers because Mr Howard was a powerful man and nobody wanted to cross him.

Shortly after the marriage it transpired that Dysart owed money all over the place. But by then the young couple had left the village and no one knew where they had gone. Nothing more was heard from them until seven years later when Rebecca returned with a child. A son aged six. She was ill and destitute. The child was weak and sickly. Dysart had abandoned them both shortly after the child was born. He had married Rebecca on the assumption that he would be welcomed into the Howard family and that he would have a place of comfort and wealth and could not believe that all his roguish charm had failed. When the son was born he was sure the hearts of its grandparents would be melted but when the Dysarts visited in stealth they were turned away. Shortly after that Dysart finally realised that he had backed a loser and fled, leaving his wife and baby to fend for themselves. This they did for several years, though nobody knows where or in what manner. Obviously at the end of her tether, eventually Rebecca returned home hoping for some compassion but her parents were as obdurate as ever and she was again turned away. Scraping along on charity for a few months, she had eventually succumbed to death in the very room in which we were sitting.

Although the parish church had a special area where the Howards were buried, Mr Howard refused to have her buried there. In fact he tried to stop her being interred anywhere in the parish but the then vicar stood firm and she was buried as we had seen. An uncle, ashamed of his brother's behaviour, had provided the stone. The inscription was a compromise between the brothers' wishes.

"What happened to the boy?" asked Holmes.

"He was sent away to an orphanage somewhere. I don't know where. He was a thin puny sickly thing so probably died in there," replied old Mrs Carr.

Back in our rooms Holmes took stock of the situation. "When you write up this case, Watson, no doubt you will have me on my first sight of the photograph arrogantly proclaiming 'it is obviously the church of St such and such situated in the village of such and such' without mentioning all the hours I have spent pouring over maps in the library of the British Museum and the many tiresome hours we spent trotting all over East Anglia."

"Fortunately we found the place in time. What would you have done if we had failed?" I queried.

"I should have had to rely entirely upon the plan we are now about to carry out. We must capture the man as he delivers the last piece. The last week starts tonight, so we must go over to Dulwich and make our preparations with Miss Dysart."

That good lady was very relieved to see us. "I am so pleased you have come, Mr Holmes. When I enquired, I was told that you had gone away."

"Have there been any developments?"

"No. No. It is just that I am so afraid and feel so much more at ease when I know you are near to assist me."

"Dr Watson and I will be here every night from now on until the last piece arrives which will be within the next seven days."

"I am so relieved to hear you say that, Mr Holmes."

"However, I think you may be in some personal danger. Is there somewhere away from here where you can stay?"

"I could go to my brother Bertram."

"I think not. I am not certain of the malevolence of the man we seek. It could be your brother too is in danger."

"Heaven forbid!" cried the distressed woman. "What creature is this? Why are we so persecuted?"

"All will become clear soon, Miss Dysart. But can you arrange to stay away?"

"Park Lane. My friend Miss Boughton resides in Park Lane."

"Excellent. Pray make arrangements to move there at once and remain there until you hear from me."

"But what will you do, Mr Holmes?"

"Dr Watson and I will stay here during the hours of darkness. These packages arrive during the night after the household has retired. When that hour approaches Dr Watson will be on watch, concealed outside the house. I shall be in your hall immediately behind the door."

This was the first I had heard of this plan but of course I was willing to go along with the arrangements. However, a place of concealment was not easy to find. Miss Dysart's house stood without a front garden of any sort. There were a mere three steps from the pavement up to her front door. Fortunately, almost opposite, the house on the other side had a small hedge of laurel bushes and Holmes decreed that I should crouch there. An unexpected hitch, however, arose when he explained his part on the procedure.

"The door will be left unlocked. I shall be immediately behind it. When the package drops through the letter box I shall swiftly open the door and apprehend the man as Dr Watson approaches him from behind."

"I'm afraid you will not be able to leave the door unlocked."

"Why not pray?"

"Well, the policeman who does the night patrol checks all the doors in the street to ensure they are locked. If one were to be found unlocked he would rouse the household to ensure that they were safe and then have it locked."

"Hum, I see. Is there a particular reason for this policeman's zeal?"

"It is since the burglary a year ago."

"Burglary?"

"Yes. We were at dinner, entertaining friends, when there was a knock at the door. The servant who dealt with it came and told my father that there was a rough looking man insisting on coming in although told that we were not at home. My father heard shouting as our staff grappled with the man in the hall and went out in person. It was awful, Mr Holmes. This tramp was trying to force his way in and my father was striking him. He knocked the man to the ground and was kicking him. I had to drag him off with the help of our guests. He was like a mad man shouting and swearing, I had never seen him so angry. The police were sent for and the tramp taken away. My father calmed down but he was never the same after. At the court hearing he accused the man of stealing a silver clock and an antique vase that were in the hall-way. But the poor man had never touched them at all. As far as I could tell nothing had been disturbed, the man had tried to come in and had been prevented and that was the extent of it. In the circumstances I think my father's brutal attack was most unwarranted. Two of our manservants were successful in controlling the intruder."

"Most interesting, Miss Dysart. You say your father made accusations at the trial? Were you there?"

"Yes, I felt sorry for the poor man. My father behaved in a totally outrageous manner. He tried to get the man transported. When it was clear that such a punishment was far too extreme for the crime for which he was committed, my father put up every thing he could to blacken the man's case."

"We have not transported criminals for many years, Miss Dysart," said Holmes.

"I do not know about that sort of thing but Father accused him again of stealing. He is a powerful man in our community, Mr Holmes, and his word carries a lot of weight, but the magistrate trying the case probed through the welter of accusations and, with my testimony, the charge was reduced to trespass by force. The man was only a poor tramp. No doubt he was merely knocking on doors begging but was simply too persistent in his importuning. Certainly, in the circumstances, my father's behaviour was totally extreme. Alas, from that time on his character seemed to alter. He was always a forceful man but now he seemed to have periods of great anger whenever some trivial thing annoyed him; then he would be plunged into gloomy morose periods. I think it likely that in the scuffle he received a blow to the head and this caused some disorder in his brain. Six months later he was dead."

"A very strange affair. And what sentence did this tramp receive?"

"Twelve months in prison."

"I see. Well, as regards the door, the matter is simply solved. I shall turn the key but leave it in the lock. The bolts will not be used. It will take but a second to turn the key – which is of little moment – as I shall be fully alert. I do not wish to complicate matters by confiding in your policeman."

From 11 o'clock that night I was concealed behind the laurel bush. It was a dark night but fortunately there was a gas lamp situated not far from the house and a pale weak glimmer illuminated the doorway sufficiently. As house lights were dimmed and my eyes became accustomed to the dark, the patch of light seemed quite vivid enough to see when anyone approached the door. A few carriages passed by and an occasional pedestrian but once midnight had passed a complete absence of movement fell upon the street. It was rather cold and the position I was in was very cramping. My time in Afghanistan has taught me to withstand heat rather than cold and as the hours wore on I began to fervently wish for my comfortable bed.

At three in the morning I heard footsteps. Immediately I was alert, all my senses roused to their full abilities. A figure appeared out of the gloom and approached the door. I made ready to spring out as arranged but relaxed as I recognised the familiar shape of a London bobby. He tried the door quietly and satisfied went on his way. I heard him stop as he tried the next door then his footsteps resumed fading as he passed further down the road.

As the household arose Holmes opened the door and beckoned me in. "Have some breakfast, Watson, the cook has kindly laid a table for us." So, at an unaccustomed early hour, we partook of breakfast then returned to Baker Street.

The following two nights passed in an identical manner and I was becoming used to going to bed after having my breakfast! When Holmes caught up on his sleep I do not know.

On the fourth night I felt bound to remonstrate with Holmes. "I say, Holmes, I think we should do this guarding turn and turn about. It's all very well for you sitting here in the warmth but I am outside perishing cold night after night."

"My dear fellow, I am so sorry, how thoughtless of me. You are quite right. Tonight I shall condemn myself to the laurel bush and you must be in the hall. But please be alert as I am not, as yet, convinced that the packets are not being placed by someone who works inside the house."

"You astonish me, Holmes!"

"We can rule out nothing, Watson, and this could well be our one and only chance of catching the villain."

It was a much more comfortable billet sitting on a chair in the hall. I had a light, I had a book to read and my hand was within reach of the key. The hall being so comfortably warm, as the night wore on I found I was becoming a little drowsy. The book was not capturing my full attention and I am ashamed to confess that I slid into a doze. I woke with a jerk as the book made a noise falling to the floor. I noted with shamed alarm that by the hall clock I had probably been asleep for some forty minutes. But I would surely have been roused by Holmes shouting had the felon appeared and all was quiet and serene. I determined not to fall asleep again. I abandoned the book and thought to keep awake by trying to recall complete verses of poems and mathematical formulae. Then I saw it. On the floor in front of the very chair where I was sitting. A twist of newspaper. The thing had arrived whilst I was asleep!

But Holmes had not acted. He would have seen the man and pounced. Obviously the packet had been planted by somebody within the house. Possibly each night they had tried but Holmes, being constantly alert, had thwarted them. As soon as dozy old Dr Watson took over then the coast was clear for them to silently put the packet in place. I opened the door and called softly. Holmes came raging across.

"What is it Watson?" I showed him the paper.

"But that is impossible!" he exclaimed. I had to confess that I had fallen asleep.

"I'm sorry, Holmes, I have let you down and failed miserably." I burbled on trying to allay his anger at my folly. "But it proves that the papers are left by somebody in the house. That has narrowed the search down considerably."

Holmes stalked into the sitting room and flung himself into a chair. He lit his pipe and closed his eyes. I thought it prudent not to say anything further and I took another chair some distance away and sat burning with embarrassment.

We remained thus until the cook arose and, as was her wont, made us breakfast. This we ate in silence. Then Holmes leaped up and said "Our cab is here." We had arranged for the same man to collect us each morning and return us to Baker Street.

"Baker Street as usual, sir?" asked the cabby.

"No, cabby, the police station," said Holmes.

As we walked into the police station the sergeant on duty recognised Holmes immediately.

"Why, it's Mr Sherlock Holmes! This is a surprise and an honour. What brings you to our humble station so early in the day?"

"Good morning to you, sergeant," said Holmes pleasantly. "I think we have met before?"

"Indeed we have, sir. I was present at all that nastiness in Limehouse a couple or three years ago. Foster's the name."

"I remember you well, Foster. I am pleased to see you thriving. I am conducting an enquiry in the neighbourhood and I wonder if you could tell me which constable was on patrol down College Road last night?"

"That was Constable Stead. He has gone off duty now."

"Where can I find him?"

"I should think at this very moment he will be tending his vegetables, very proud of his garden is Arthur. I could send for him if you wish?"

"Pray do not trouble to do that. I would like to talk to him though; have you his address?"

"I'll write it down for you. It is not far away." The sergeant pushed a slip of paper towards Holmes. "I hope he is not in any sort of trouble?"

"Not at all, sergeant, just a query about a happening some time ago."

We did, indeed, find the policeman in his little garden amongst a fine selection of vegetables.

"Good morning, Constable Stead," said Holmes cheerily. "I can see you truly have green fingers."

"'Tis good soil here, sir," replied the bobby.

"Your sergeant gave me your address. I am Sherlock Holmes."

"The famous detective?"

"This is my colleague Dr Watson."

"Well, I don't know what to say. I'm really flattered having such well known gentlemen in my little garden. I hope there is nothing wrong?"

"I have one or two questions if you could spare me the time from your magnificent tomato plants."

"Certainly, sir. Anything I can do to help the law is my duty."

"Last night you posted a tiny packet through the letterbox of a house in College Street. Is that correct?"

"Yes, sir, I did. I hope there was no harm in that?"

"It is not the first time you have done it; you have posted similar packets on numerous previous occasions."

"I have, sir, I would think almost two dozen."

"Are you aware of the contents of these packets?"

"Well, I presume they all contain a piece of jigsaw puzzle."

"You presume? You do not know?"

"Perhaps I should explain, sir?"

"I think an explanation would be welcome, constable, as it is a rather singular thing for a policeman to do."

"My brother asked me to do it."

"Your brother?"

"Yes. Some month's ago he asked if Mr Dysart's house was on my beat; when I said it was, he asked if I could pop a little twist of paper through his door when next I was on the night shift. So I did."

"Did you not ask what the twist of paper contained?"

"I did, sir, but George – my brother – said the least I knew about it the better. George is a decent chap and if he thought it was all right for me to deliver it then there would be no harm in it. That was good enough for me."

"But then there were many more."

"Yes, he kept them coming and, as I'd obliged him the first time, it seemed a bit churlish to start refusing such a simple request. After all, I have to try the door every night so it is hardly a chore to carry and post such a tiny thing."

"Were you not curious about the contents?"

"I was, sir, yes. After I had delivered two or three I thought there may be something illegal in these packets so I opened one. When I saw it was a harmless piece of jigsaw my mind was set at rest."

"I see."

"Is there some harm in it sir?"

"No, no. It is just that this curious procedure has alarmed the lady of the house."

"Oh, I did not intend any alarm, sir. Were the pieces not expected then?"

"Tell me: does your brother make these ingenious puzzles?"

"Oh no, sir, George couldn't do anything like that. No, my brother is a warder at Wormwood Scrubs prison."

"Ah!" smiled Holmes in satisfaction. "All now becomes clear. Thank you my good man, you have provided the final piece in my own personal jigsaw puzzle."

"I have, sir?" asked the baffled bobby.

"Many thanks, Stead, and best wishes for a bumper crop of tomatoes."

We had retained the cab and now Holmes instructed the cabby to take us to the offices of the local newspaper. I could not imagine the purpose of this and was getting quite dizzy with all this dashing from place to place. There he requested to look at the back issues of the Dulwich weekly newspaper.

"Here we are, Watson," he whispered as he turned up a front page with the lurid headline *Eminent Dulwich Man Defeats Burglar.* Our case is complete. See the name of the so-called burglar?"

"Norfolk Howard," I read in wonder.

"Come, Watson."

Once again we leapt into the cab and this time we were whisked over to Wormwood Scrubs Jail. Holmes changed manner entirely as he rapped on the forbidding door. A trapdoor behind a grill opened and a bewhiskered face appeared.

"I'm so sorry to trouble you. I am from the Prisoners' Aid Society. We have been informed that Norfolk Howard is to be released today. Can you confirm that, please?"

The trapdoor snapped shut.

Holmes and I exchanged looks and wondered if that was a sign that the interview had been abruptly terminated. But after several minutes the little door opened again.

"No, not today. Tomorrow. Norfolk Howard is on the list to be released tomorrow."

"Thank you, thank you, you are too kind," said Holmes unctuously; and the cabby was at last instructed to return us to Baker Street. Finally we had a respite and I spent the day comatose before going to bed early.

The next day on coming down to breakfast I found Holmes had already finished.

"Good morning, Watson," said he pleasantly. "If you would like to be in at the *denouément* of this tragic case pray make yourself ready to leave immediately."

So after snatching a bite of bread and a gulp of coffee we once more took ourselves to Dulwich. I was beginning to wish I had never heard of the place.

"What now, Holmes?" I asked.

"Yet again we are to wait patiently, Watson. But this time we will be in comfort and at leisure in Miss Dysart's sitting room. I visited her at her friend's house yesterday whilst you were catching up on your lost sleep. All arrangements have been made with her staff to treat us as if we were residents."

And thus we spent the morning sitting at ease waiting, with Holmes never taking his eyes from the street outside. After some hours he hissed "He's here, Watson, don't let him see you."

Concealed by the window curtains I peered out and saw, loitering over the road, a thin badly dressed man. He wandered up and down the far pavement, glancing at the house at frequent intervals.

"What do you think he will do, Holmes? Is he waiting for darkness?"

"I doubt if he will attempt to enter the house after the treatment he received the last time he tried it. No, I rather think he is waiting for someone to enter or leave the house."

"Miss Dysart, you mean?"

"No, Watson, Mr Dysart."

"But he's dead!" I protested.

"Indeed he is," said Holmes. "Perhaps it would be a kindness to inform his son of that fact. Come, Watson."

We left the house together putting into operation a plan that Holmes had pre-conceived. He turned left and walked one way – I turned right and walked the other. We both ignored the waiting man. Having gone some distance we both crossed the road and returned towards our quarry, timing it so that we arrived simultaneously at either side of him.

"Mr Norfolk Howard? Otherwise known as William Dysart I believe?" said Holmes. "Grab him, Watson!" The man tried to escape and run but being enfeebled by a year of prison diet and a naturally weak constitution was easily overpowered as we marched him across the road and into the house.

"Now, Mr Dysart, I am Sherlock Holmes a consulting detective retained by Miss Victoria Dysart. This is my colleague Dr Watson. I have to tell you that I know a great deal of your story. I also think you were loitering outside with the intent of killing, or seriously maiming, your father Mr William Dysart Senior."

"Blast you, whoever you are! I have suffered enough through that accursed man! Now the minute I regain my freedom he sets his bully boys on to me!"

"Listen to me, Dysart. You cannot be avenged by killing your father. He is already dead."

"Dead?" The poor man stared.

"He died some six months ago. You cannot now wreak your revenge."

Dysart laughed a bitter laugh and drew out from his sleeve a vicious looking knife which he tossed on the floor in front of us.

"That's it then. It has all come to an end at last."

"I know your father deserted you and your mother many years ago. I know your mother died in poverty and destitution and is buried in the churchyard at Thorpe St Napier. I have visited the grave."

"I don't know who you are to be so conversant with my history. Why should you know about me? I who know nobody and have only just returned to this country," said Dysart in bewilderment.

"You were placed in an orphanage. What happened then?"

"I was only six years old when I was put in the orphanage. It was not a bad place, it was not a cruel existence like you read about in *Oliver Twist* – but miserable enough. When I was fourteen I was sent, with other boys, out to Canada. Indentured labourers they called us but it was nothing but official slavery. We were all split up and dispersed over the prairies of Canada. Those poor pioneers were trying to make a living from taming the wild land and we lads were allocated to them. I suppose some boys were kindly treated but most were like me – cruelly abused, beaten and half-starved. If you ran away you were caught and sent back to the farm. It was a wretched existence – even our masters were in a desperate plight. Seven long years of that destroys a young man's spirit. But, by law, it all ended when you reached twenty-one years of age and you became a free man.

"Many lads never reached adulthood and many spent the rest of their lives in that same wretched existence of abject poverty. But I had a bit of luck, the only luck I've ever had in my entire life, and got a job with a carpenter who taught me the trade. I had an aptitude for the craft and soon became very good, receiving decent wages for my work. I saved every penny I could as my sole desire was to return to England to find the villain who had killed my mother and destroyed me. I bought my passage back, sought out my mother's grave and had myself photographed mourning over it. Then I started searching for my father.

"Eventually I tracked him down to this house. I watched and waited outside. I watched him come and go. Although I had had it in my soul to kill him instantly on the spot, when I saw the respectable house, the honest area and decent normality of it all, I faltered in my purpose. Here was a man with children and a prosperous business – a pillar of the community. Perhaps he repented of his evil past, perhaps he had spent years in remorse? Perhaps he had even made extensive attempts to find his first born son? I decided to approach him and make myself known to him. Then I would decide what to do.

"He had not changed one iota. As soon as he realised who I was he tried to kill me. He would have succeeded too if some people in the house had not dragged him off me. The best he could do was to have me banged up in jail under the pretence of attempting to rob him by force. In jail! In all the hard times of poverty and trial in my life I have never done anything to warrant being put in jail, and here was my own long lost father doing it to me knowing that I was his own son who he had not seen since I was a little boy. And he got me put in jail simply because he was not able to kill me."

The poor soul wept bitter tears.

I thought I knew my friend Sherlock Holmes very well after all those years together but his behaviour sometimes surprised me by differing markedly from what I had deduced to be his character. He was not a man who tolerated displays of emotion and I had often seen him exasperated by the tears of a woman, much less those of a man. He rang the bell and very soon our friend the cook appeared bearing a large tray with tea, hot buttered toast, scones and the like which Holmes had pre-arranged. She set this down and left. Holmes, taking up the tea kettle, poured tea and offered food.

"Come, my friend, do have a toasted tea cake. I always think it a mistake to confine tea to teatime," he remarked while passing a plate.

Gradually Dysart came round and silently took tea with us.

"I am not clear who you gentlemen really are, but thank you for treating me with such kindness."

"We represent your late father's daughter Miss Victoria Rebecca Dysart."

"Rebecca was my mother's name."

"Indeed. And of course, that lady is your half-sister," I pointed out.

"She was the lady who spoke up for me at the trial. She is a very nice lady."

"Because of the death of your father, she received your pieces of jigsaw puzzle. As she did not understand the import she was distressed when a gravestone with her own name on it was revealed," explained Holmes.

"Oh poor lady!" cried Dysart. "I had no idea. How upset she must have been. What worry I have given an innocent creature!"

"How were you able to make the puzzle and send it out of the prison?" asked Holmes.

"The system of the jail is that groups of prisoners are permitted to manufacture items in workshops. They give training in certain skills such as basket weaving, tin ware manufacture and so on. By nature of my trade I was assigned to the carpentry workshop. In that workshop we made wooden toys and novelties. The best of them are sold in the shops. They are made in a top class fashion. In fact I hear that there are complaints from manufacturers about unfair competition from prison made goods. Of course I was under the eyes of strict warders but it was a joy to me to be doing something useful other than picking oakum and other mindless tasks as in the old days. Fortunately my sentence did not include hard labour like some of the poor wretches. One day the warden overseeing me asked if I could make him a dissected picture puzzle. I had never made one before but I had seen one and it is only a matter of careful cutting with a fret saw. I don't know why they have started calling them jigsaw puzzles as it is a fret you need, not a jig. Anyway I made one for the man and he was very pleased and it turned out he was the brother of the policeman who had arrested me. I then got the idea to turn my photograph into a similar puzzle and asked the warder if he could get his brother to deliver the pieces. He was an obliging chap and between us we worked out the way of doing it a week at a time so that, if he should be caught, one little piece of jigsaw would be a harmless trifle. You know, sir, we poor folk like to help each other. So it was done. Neither the warder or his brother had any love for William Dysart after the way he had tried to murder me and then shift the blame.

I knew that my father would be fearful of what would happen when I emerged from my prison, so I taunted him with the picture. I knew he had never seen the gravestone of my mother and I wanted to put the fear of God into him. I had no idea the man had died. I did not foresee the prospect of somebody else receiving the pieces. Oh my poor sister! Does she know who I am?"

"No. She knows nothing. All she knows is that some unknown person is sending her a photograph with a gravestone bearing her name. She knows that the last piece will bear the perpetrator's face. I have intercepted it. I have it here."

"She must not know, sir!" burst out Dysart. "She will recognise me as the man her father sent to jail. She must not know who I really am!"

"Calm yourself, my dear sir, calm yourself. The matter is entirely in your hands. You must be aware that your father married again and had a son and a daughter. His second wife died some years ago. He built up the business inherited by his wife and that business is now being run very prosperously by his son Bertram who is, of course, your half brother. If they knew you were their kinsman they may be prepared to share some of their wealth. I would think, after the vicissitudes of your life, that would be welcome."

"No! I cannot appear from nowhere and thrust myself into these good people's ordered lives! A convict and ne'er do well. They would turn me away. I will ask for nothing."

"You may call them good people, and so they are. But you must be aware that your father married while your mother was still alive. It was a bigamous marriage and was, therefore, illegal and not binding. You are your father's legitimate son, your half-brother and sister are, unknowingly, illegitimate."

"I realise that. It makes no difference to me. I do not belong here. Now Dysart is dead my business is finished. I will return to Canada."

"Have you the means?" asked Holmes.

"I can earn the fare. I'm a good carpenter. I can make a living."

"It would be no hardship for your kinsmen to supply you with a thousand pounds to take you back to Canada and set yourself up there."

"Don't insult me, sir! I do not need paying off! I am an independent man. I need help from nobody!"

"I understand your feelings, sir, and find them commendable," said Holmes. "But you are not being 'paid off', as you call it. Unless you, yourself, reveal the connection, your brother and sister will not even know who you are. Permit me to make a suggestion. I will ask them for a contribution to the Prisoners Aid Society – a charity which assists ex-prisoners. The Society will fund your passage to Canada. How will that suit?"

"Well," said Dysart grudgingly, "I can see no harm in that if that is what this Society does."

"Very well, it shall be so!"

Holmes arranged for Dysart to return to Canada and he sailed from Liverpool in better style than he had arrived. He had been persuaded to accept money for clothing and other means to respectability. An account in the name of Norfolk Howard had been opened at the Bank of Ottawa and £500 had been deposited therein for emergency use. As far as I know, to this day it has never been touched.

The Singular Adventure
of
THE SPURIOUS AMBASSADOR

IT was some time since I had seen my old friend Sherlock Holmes. At this period of my life I had settled into a routine of domestic bliss with my wife Mary and, after spending the day ministering to my somewhat sporadic roster of patients, I liked nothing better than to sit by the fire in contemplative company with my dear wife.

Late one rather blustery and rainy autumn night I was alone by my fireside having a whisky and soda nightcap and a not too earnest read of the latest edition of a medical journal, containing an article devoted to something the author described as 'defects of character', when there was a knock at the door. Glancing up at the clock to see it was 11.30, I groaned inwardly assuming it was an urgent summons for me to sally forth into the night to attend some ailing patient, but to my surprise it was a figure with which I was acquainted, if not familiar.

"Good Lord, Mycroft Holmes, come in, come in. You look drenched."

"Thank you, Dr Watson. I hope the late hour is not an inconvenience to Mrs Watson."

"Mary is not here at present, she has gone to visit her sister until Saturday. I am living a bachelor's life this week. The maid does not live in and leaves the house after dinner so I am quite alone. But what on earth brings you to visit me at this time of night in such wretched weather? Here, let me take your coat."

"Thank you, Doctor."

Suddenly the thought struck me: the only connection between us was his brother, my friend Sherlock Holmes. Mycroft moved in a very limited sphere, alternating between his office at Whitehall and the Diogenes Club when not at home. I had no idea where his home was, or if he were married. "Has something happened to Sherlock?" I gasped.

"My visit does not concern my brother at all, Doctor. As far as I know he is in excellent health. Pray do not alarm yourself."

Although my dread was assuaged I realised even a person of such eccentric habits as Mycroft Holmes would not choose to visit at 11.30 on such a vile night, without an ulterior motive.

"So what brings you here, Mr Holmes?" I asked. "It is most opportune that Mary is away, as I fear if she had been here we would have both been abed at this hour."

"How is Mrs Watson, still as charming as ever, I trust?"

"She is very well and I consider I am the most fortunate man alive."

"I'm sure you are, Doctor, I'm sure you are." There was a long pause, then Mycroft Holmes said "How would you and Mrs Watson like to meet the Queen?"

"What an odd question. Of course we would both be extremely honoured to be presented to Her Majesty. Is there any likelihood of that?"

"Possibly, quite possibly. And you, now, how would you like to attend a gala performance of the Italian Opera, as the guest of Lord Daviot?"

"Well, I would not wish to slight the noble lord, but I would prefer it if he took me to see something by Gilbert and Sullivan. I am not too partial to the opera, especially in foreign languages I don't understand."

"I wonder if you would contemplate attending the performance if you knew your presence would be of inestimable service to your country and may even prevent an outbreak of hostilities in the Balkans."

"Really, Mr Holmes, have you been drinking prior to calling on me! What balderdash! As if my presence anywhere could affect anything, other than a very slight increase in the box office takings," said I, chuckling at my little sally.

"Tomorrow night, at Covent Garden, there is a gala performance to be given in the presence of, and in honour of, Count Slovamky who is the new ambassador to the Court of St James's. He represents Leskovakia which, as you may know, is a tiny state in the Balkans."

"Actually, Mr Holmes, I do know, as I have not long finished reading the evening paper in which all those things were announced."

"Have you seen a photograph of Count Slovamky?" Mycroft Holmes held out a picture for me to take. It depicted a hearty looking man of about forty years, with a large moustache and side whiskers. He was dressed in military uniform, with a vast collection of medals and ribbons adorning it.

"A fine figure of a man," said I, passing the picture back.

"Does he not remind you of anybody?" asked Mycroft Holmes.

I took the picture again and examined it. "Nobody in particular – perhaps the Tsar of Russia?"

"You, Doctor Watson."

"Pardon?"

"He has a strong resemblance to you. Or if you prefer, you, my dear Doctor, could pass for the noble Count."

"Preposterous!"

"I mean it, Doctor."

"At fifty paces, on a dark night, with the light behind me," I joked. "Really Mr Holmes, I am in serious doubts about your sanity."

"I was never more serious in my life."

"What is all this? First you ask me if I want to meet the Queen, then if I want to go to the opera, now you insist I have a passing resemblance to some foreign Count. Do you wonder that I question your sanity?"

Although I reacted in this fashion, in my heart of hearts I knew that Mycroft Holmes never did anything without a reason. Mycroft was an important man in the government of the country. He was the only man who knew everything that was happening. He was the centre of an organisational web which enabled the various disparate departments of government to come together. As far as I was aware he had no other interests apart from his governmental work. If he chose to visit me in the dead of night there was certain to be a very serious purpose behind it.

"Very well, Dr Watson, I will come clean. This is the story: During the last few months a person, highly placed in the British government, has been passing information to Slovamky in Leskovakia. We do not know who that person is but it is essential that we find him. Now that Slovamky has come to this country, there is the likelihood that this person will make contact with him."

"You speak of spies?"

"I prefer the word traitor. This traitor is either selling, or giving, state secrets to the Count Slovamky."

"For what purpose, Mr Holmes? Surely Leskovakia is a tiny state with no political power in the world?"

"It is tiny, yes. But, on the contrary, it holds the balance of power in the Balkans. That area is a powder keg; Leskovakia is the fuse. All the Balkan states are wooing Leskovakia, but there is a disaffected faction trying to undermine the stability, such as it is, of the region. Anarchists are trying to destroy the current rulers and the slightest thing could cause war."

"But surely the affairs of a few unstable states in a far off area do not concern the British Government?"

"Believe me, Doctor, if the trouble in the Balkans is not contained, the whole of Europe will be at war within the year."

"You astonish me, Mr Holmes!" I cried.

"Tomorrow, the new Ambassador will be at a reception at Lord Daviot's residence, followed by a visit to the Italian Opera. We have reason to believe that during the evening the traitor will make some form of approach. Therefore we have plans to detain the Ambassador under a false pretext. In his place will be a substitute. Nobody has yet met Count Slovamky in person so, providing the resemblance to known photographs is satisfactory, the substitution is quite safe and will not be discovered."

"But surely there will be some kind of official entourage?"

"The Count will be present with two attendants only. His wife has yet to join him, the purpose of the gala really being to show him off in public at the first possible moment. His official duties will not commence until next month."

"Are you seriously proposing that I counterfeit a foreign nobleman? Are you mad? What language does he speak? German? Slovene? Russian? Apart from a few words picked up during the Afghan campaign, I speak nothing but English. The scheme is far-fetched and preposterous!"

"The Count speaks impeccable English. Lord Daviot will be in attendance throughout and, of course, is fully conversant with the plan. You need have no fear of detection. All you are called upon to do is to go along and enjoy yourself. If, as is suspected, the traitorous spy makes an approach, you merely have to note who the man is and report it to Lord Daviot confidentially."

"But, Mycroft, you need an actor! I cannot dissemble. You must get Henry Irving to do it!"

"Do you seriously think an ancient and frail stage actor could pass himself off as that man?" Mycroft Holmes dramatically held out the portrait to me. I could see that a resemblance to me was not too far-fetched, but I baulked at all the implications of the scheme.

For ages I argued as Mycroft Holmes countered all my objections. Until, wearily, as it was now 2 o'clock in the morning, I capitulated.

"Excellent, dear fellow!" cried Mycroft Holmes. "I knew I could rely on you. I will be here tomorrow at 6 in the evening. Be dressed in your finest formal wear and I'll bring decorations that must be worn. An expert in the art of disguise will accompany me in order to adjust your moustache and attach side whiskers etc. It will be quite a simple job. A carriage will then take you to Lord Daviot's, where the reception will merely be a few *canapés* and a glass of wine. You will stand alongside Lord Daviot and various people will come up to be introduced. You merely bow courteously and shake hands. That's all there is to it. The reception will last an hour, then you will go with Lord Daviot to the opera. You will be in the box normally reserved for Her Majesty and have the use of the private royal ante-chamber in the intervals. Do not worry, Dr Watson, you stick to Lord Daviot and all will be well."

Having agreed to his fatuous plan, I bade Mycroft Holmes a good night and retired to bed. I slept very poorly. I realised what a foolish thing I had committed myself to, resolving to send word in the morning that I had changed my mind. Mycroft Holmes must find another, more willing, participant. But when morning came, I realised that, even in dire necessity, I had no idea how to reach Mycroft Holmes. No doubt I could find him by way of Holmes but how pathetically feeble I should seem to my good friend. Moreover I had given my solemn word to go through with it and could not back out. It had been made very clear to me that the task I was to undertake was my duty as a loyal subject of Her Majesty. I was relieved to think Mary was away and that, when she returned, it would be no more than a bad dream. And of course, as there would be some kind of official recognition, it would be nice to take Mary to meet the Queen and be able to say that I had rendered the country some service that sets me apart from other men.

During my rounds that day I could think of nothing else but my forthcoming impersonation. I had a new patient to visit about midday and I made the experiment of speaking to him in an accent that I imagined to be vaguely Slavic. I was almost too successful, as the patient complained that he had presumed that I would be an English doctor with a name like John Watson and he had a strong prejudice against foreign physicians.

Eventually six o'clock arrived and I togged myself up as grandly as my humble circumstances would allow. I ventured to suggest that my formal wear was, perhaps, not the height of fashion, but Mycroft Holmes assured me that nobody was likely to know what the height of fashion might be in Leskovakia and that the various orders and decorations worn would be ample to convince. He had also brought a man called Douglas with him who seemed to be some sort of expert on the Count and Leskovakia. He kept giving me tit-bits of information that I could use if necessary. Apparently I had three children, a boy and two girls, all under the age of ten.

The disguise man quickly transformed my own moustache into a semblance of Count Slovamky's and added some luxuriant side whiskers. Looking into the mirror I could fancy myself sufficiently transformed to be taken for a genuine Count.

When all was ready Mycroft Holmes said "Well, Doctor, best of luck."

"Are you not to be present?" I demanded.

"I'm afraid not. I am not privileged. Douglas, here, will be with you all the time, purporting to be a member of your staff. Should anything tricky come up he will intercede for you. At Lord Daviot's there will be another man who will join you. He is in the nature of a body guard. Daviot himself will ease things too. The only purpose of all this is to entrap a traitor."

"But how will I know? I've read that these spy chaps sidle up and say something fanciful like 'At full moon the donkey brays' and expect an equally bizarre reply as a password."

"Should that happen we are certain to pinpoint our man."

After a few last minute instructions I left home in a carriage, accompanied by Douglas. He was an agreeable enough companion on the ride and he certainly made me feel quite at ease, almost making me forget the ludicrousness of my position. At Lord Daviot's residence Douglas introduced me to the noble lord and his lady, and the charming couple chatted quite easily and readily to me as if I were the real Count. There was no hint that Lord Daviot knew that I was an imposter but I had been assured, by both Mycroft Holmes and Douglas, that he knew all about the plot and was, in fact, central to it.

Various people were led up to greet me and I bowed and shook hands and said I was delighted to meet them. I adopted a slight guttural tone to my voice, rather than an accent, chiefly to reassure myself that I was supposed to be somebody else. It was accepted by everybody without question. Each person I met uttered a few platitudes then made way for the next. There were a couple of awkward moments. Once, when a matronly lady enquired about my wife and I was not really sure what my expected reply should be, Douglas smoothly stepped in and said my wife and family would be joining me next month and that the Countess would be delighted to attend *soirées* at the noblest houses. I immediately agreed and that seemed to get me out of that satisfactorily.

The other incident was more serious and could have ruined the entire plot.

I heard a voice at my elbow say 'Wood mould like a glossy campaign alters natives'. I turned to see an obsequious waiter holding out his tray of glasses. With my head reeling to grasp what had been said, and its sinister meaning, I took another glass of champagne and the fellow retreated. I was thus left in the rather foolish position of holding a glass in each hand. Fortunately it was merely for a second or two as Douglas skilfully took my half empty one and slipped it on to a side table without losing the thread of the current introduction that Lord Daviot was making.

After a few minutes converse there was a pause before the next person came up to be introduced and I was able to say in an aside to Douglas that the waiter was our man, as he had said an unintelligible password to me. Daviot was able to forestall the next introductions while Douglas and I went into a huddle. Douglas excused himself and I was left to greet the next set of people unaided. There were no further problems and soon it was time to leave for the Opera House. I was feeling rather smug for carrying it all off so well. I had succeeded in locating the traitor, although I had expected a person of more importance. Perhaps the waiter had been sent as an emissary to test me out before the traitor revealed himself?

When Douglas returned he asked me again what had been said and I replied that, as far as I could remember, it was something about altering natives and a glossy campaign.

"The waiter remembers precisely what he said to you, Count. His actual words were 'Would my lord like a glass of champagne or an alternative?'"

"Oh, I'm sorry. I did not quite catch the words exactly. He – er, did not speak very clear English. Not as other people."

"No, Count, he is an Italian waiter."

"Ah."

"Shall we go, Count? We must not keep the singers waiting," said Lord Daviot.

On getting into the noble lord's private coach I was surprised to see a man already seated within. Douglas said this was my personal bodyguard Samuel. He did not look as though he would be much use in a fight, being quite slim, but I presumed the organisers of this whole farrago knew what they were doing. So we jolted along to Covent Garden, the four of us – Douglas, Samuel, Lord Daviot and myself. I was rather surprised that Lady Daviot was not to accompany us to the opera. In fact, we four comprised the whole party.

We entered the building by the private entrance used by Her Majesty and were shown into a small but elegant chamber where more refreshments were laid out on a table. The manager of the Italian Opera, with much bowing and scraping, indicated that we should go through a small door that he held ajar. As we did so a great sound of applause greeted us and I realised that we had stepped into the Royal Box of the magnificent auditorium. As I stood there peering around, with Lord Daviot at my side, I could indeed visualise myself as a visiting dignitary. Lord Daviot raised his hand in a gentle wave of greeting so I emulated him and bowed to the house at large. I was a little peeved when Samuel, rather rudely I thought, pushed himself forward and stood at the edge of the box nearest the stage and glared at the audience below.

Eventually we seated ourselves, but Samuel remained standing where he was. He seemed a curmudgeonly fellow and had barely said a word, but I suppose he was only there as my protector and would not normally associate with the nobility. As honoured guest I was given the most favoured chair but I have to say that the view of the entertainment from this extremely sideways box was far inferior to the pit, where I normally sit on my infrequent visits to the theatre.

Never, in all my life, have I been so bored in a public place. I appreciate that the singing was wonderful, but it was all in Italian, the tunes few and far between and not very memorable. Personally, I like catchy tunes that you can join in with, or at least sing on the way home. This was all rather solemn, and I could not follow the plot. Samuel seemed not to be enjoying it either, as he never once looked at the stage, but kept his gaze relentlessly roving about the auditorium.

Lord Daviot, who seemed to understand everything that was taking place on stage, applauded heartily when *arias* came to an end, while Douglas sat totally unperturbed, as he had been ever since I was introduced to him, no more than three hours previously. It was incredible to realise it was only a few hours ago that I had been an anonymous London doctor and now, here I was, a Leskovakian Count at the opera.

I found my eyes drooping with the tedium of the evening, but fortunately during the first interval we repaired to partake of refreshments in our ante-chamber, although all too soon we had to return to endure the next act of the piece. My glance kept wavering from the stage and I noticed a fine-looking woman in the opposite box. I must have been staring rather hard as she suddenly looked up from the stage, straight at me, giving me a charming smile. I gave a slight inclination. She was quite a stunner and I wondered what my dear wife Mary would say if she knew I was at the opera, in the royal box, flirting with an obviously titled lady!

I dropped my gaze to the stalls and noticed, without any particular curiosity, that there seemed to be a rather excessive number of male attendants standing against the walls in the side aisles. The principal tenor was holding forth centre-stage with a large male chorus grouped behind him further towards the back of the stage. It was a *brindisi*, or drinking song, and, as is the way of these things, the chorus of about thirty stout men had half a dozen empty flagons that they pretended to quaff with relish and pass around. I was only half aware that one of the men's chorus had detached himself from the group and had come downstage until he was almost alongside the tenor. Suddenly he produced a pistol from under his cloak and, to my horror, pointed it directly at me!

Before I could think or blink, two things happened simultaneously: I heard a gun shot and I was knocked off my chair to the ground with someone on top of me.

A voice in my ear hissed "Lie still, Watson." It was the voice of my friend Sherlock Holmes. As I lay underneath Holmes I could hear the orchestra petering to a halt. The singing ceased, women were screaming and men shouting, then I passed out.

I came to in the ante-chamber and found myself lying on the floor. A strange man was forcing brandy between my lips. Holmes, Lord Daviot and the manager of the Opera House were standing anxiously looking at me.

"It's all right, Count. I am a doctor," said the man who was supporting my shoulders.

"So am I," I spluttered, trying to scramble to my feet.

"Are you all right, Watson?" asked Holmes.

I looked at him. He was different somehow. Then I realised that he was half in and half out of his bodyguard disguise. My old friend had been with me all the time, in the guise of Samuel. I was then aware of Lord Daviot speaking. "It has worked splendidly, Dr Watson. The would-be assassin was caught by a stage hand and disarmed before he could leave the stage. Douglas is round there now, dealing with things. I am not surprised you fainted. It was a very brave thing you did. Not many men would knowingly sit in a public place, aware that they were going to be the target of an assassin's bullet."

My mind was clearing rapidly. I began to understand the words being spoken and thankfully my blurred vision was also clearing. I started to jabber at Holmes but the doctor restrained me and urged me to calmness. I felt so weak. The door opened and Douglas entered.

"You all right, Dr Watson?" he enquired cheerily. "I must say, he caught us on the hop a bit there, didn't he, Mr Holmes? We had all the stalls covered, and all the different tiers. Over sixty trained men were out there, Dr Watson, all ready to pounce when the assassin showed himself. But we forgot the stage. We never thought that the shot would come from there. We were all so busy scouring every member of that audience with our eyes, we took little notice of what was happening on the stage."

"You knew that someone was going to take a pot-shot at me?" I asked feebly.

"Not at you, Doctor, but at Count Slovamky. It was very noble of you to volunteer to take his place. I should imagine you will be awarded Leskovakia's highest honour for your bravery tonight," said Douglas.

"Rest assured that the British Government is truly grateful for your self-sacrificing action. It is not overstating the case to say that war, itself, has been avoided tonight," said Lord Daviot.

"War?" gasped the manager of the Opera House.

Suddenly everyone was aware that things were being spoken openly that should remain forever buried. Lord Daviot urgently took the manager by the elbow and ushered him out of the room, speaking quietly in his ear. Douglas asked if I would be all right and the doctor, assuring him I would, closed his bag and left.

"We had better get you home, Watson," said Holmes.

"I would prefer Mr Douglas to see me home," I said icily.

"Come, Watson, permit me to take you home. You have been most outrageously duped. You are entitled to some explanation. It is the least I can do," said Holmes.

I did not want Holmes to take me. I was too distressed to find that my old friend had obviously connived with his brother in tricking me into this dangerous enterprise. But I was too shaken to resist the arrangements that Douglas was busily making so, in the end, there were just the two of us jogging homewards in Lord Daviot's private carriage. I could not speak. I was so perturbed that Holmes of all people, my dearest friend, should expose me to the likelihood of sudden death.

"Speak, Watson, I cannot bear this intolerable silence."

"How could you, Holmes?"

"Let me explain the matter to you. I assure you I knew nothing of Mycroft's plot until four o'clock this afternoon. It was unforgivable. For the last few weeks I have been on the trail of a villain with foreign connections and finally I was closing in on him. I was down by the docks this afternoon when two fellows took exception to the enquiries I was making. Of course, as you saw this evening, I was heavily disguised and so, it turned out, were the other two and I ended up at Whitehall where brother Mycroft appeared and told me that I had come very near to ruining his plans. It seems my villain was a known assassin and was in this country for the express purpose of killing Count Slovamky. The spycatchers in the pay of the British government were convinced he would strike this very night. It was at that point Mycroft revealed his plan and was forced to confess his ploy to enrol you as the substitute Count. Watson, I was appalled! I pleaded with him to abandon the scheme but he would not. He said he could not. You see, Watson, Mycroft has no friends or family but myself. He is nothing more than a vast thinking machine. His only loyalty is to his country. As you know from previous acquaintance he does not value men's lives very highly. He assured me there was little danger. He said he had the entire audience thoroughly covered.

I then insisted that I should be of the party. If this dangerous scheme was to go ahead then I must be there to protect my dearest friend. He argued against it but, when he saw that I was earnest in my desire to ruin his scheme unless I were included, he capitulated. It helped that I had the advantage of knowing what the assassin looked like – the others had never seen him. As they described the plot to me, Watson, I thought it was sound. I must be slipping. I forgot to account for the possibility of the shot coming from the stage."

"But Mycroft lied to me. All that cock-and-bull story about rooting out a spy was just a ruse to get me to impersonate the Count."

"I am afraid it was, Watson, Mycroft didn't think you would have agreed to do it if he had told you the truth."

"No, I rather think I would have turned down the chance to be the victim of an assassin's bullet."

"He was desperate, Watson. You see, he had laid these plans weeks in advance, he had a trained man lined up to impersonate the Count but at the last minute that man was unavailable."

"Unavailable? Why?"

"I believe he was unavoidably detained at the bottom of the Danube. Mycroft's friends play a very dirty game. So he had to resort to other means. It was fortunate for him, and very unfortunate for you, that there is a passing resemblance between you and Count Slovamky."

"That Mycroft deceived me is bad enough but I count that for naught. But I cannot accept that he has caused me to lie. All these fine people: Lord Daviot, Mr Douglas, the British Government and, I assume, Count Slovamky, all think I accepted this chore willingly. They think I am a brave man who chose to do this foolhardy deed out of patriotism. All Mycroft could think of was a cunning plan to catch an anarchist. And it seems your only concern now is a dent to your professional pride because you did not spot the organisers' neglect to cover the stage in their preparations."

The carriage had stopped outside my humble little dwelling. Holmes made to open the door and get out but I stayed him with my hand.

"Have you no feelings, man? Can you not realise what a position Mary would have been in if her husband had been slaughtered in this foolish masquerade?"

Holmes had the grace to look discomforted "That was an aspect I did not consider but, believe me, Watson, I would have ensured the assassin's bullet struck me before it should harm you."

"Do not get out. I do not want you in my house again." Pushing past him, I jumped down from the carriage and hurried into the security of my little home.

My mind was in turmoil. I could not take in the half of what Holmes had told me. But after sitting calmly, my mind ordered itself and one thing became abundantly clear. Although powerless to prevent the plot going ahead, my friend, my very dear friend Sherlock Holmes, was prepared to lay down his own life to save mine. I was extremely proud to know such a man.

Several weeks later I received an impressive document from the Leskovakian Government. It said that a grateful people wished to award me the Cross of St Simeon, the highest civilian honour their country could bestow. I refused it. My dear wife and I were graciously invited to take tea with Her Majesty, after which she offered me a jewelled tie-pin. I accepted it. It is one of my most treasured possessions to this day.

On the way home Mary kept pestering me as to the nature of the service that I had rendered unto Her Majesty to warrant this handsome gift. I merely said that it was a medical matter, that I had comprised one of a team of doctors and that, naturally, it was confidential.

"Then why did Her Majesty talk about Mr Sherlock Holmes?"

"I presume she knows of my work in writing up his cases," I said dismissively. "I think you will find that Mr Sherlock Holmes has done many a deed on the Crown's behalf."

"It is a long time since we have seen your friend. Do you not think you should invite him to dinner some time?"

"He would not come. Holmes is not as other men. He does not indulge in social activities."

"I know he is a very strange fellow. You have always said he has no emotions and is simply an intellectual machine."

"The Holmes family is unique, thank God. If you find Sherlock strange, you should meet his brother Mycroft," I answered fervently.

"I find it hard to accept what you say – that Sherlock Holmes has no feelings, just a highly developed brain."

"Oh, I wouldn't say he has <u>no</u> feelings, Mary. The last time I parted from him he had a distinct tear in his eye."

If you enjoyed this book you may like a "whodunit" by
the same author

SHERLOCK HOLMES
and the Singular Adventure of
THE GLOVED PIANIST

ISBN: 978-0-9565013-1-8

www.mrsherlockholmes.co.uk

www.vesperhawk.com

Lightning Source UK Ltd.
Milton Keynes UK
UKOW042010071112

201851UK00002B/103/P